THE FIRST
CONQUISTADOR

THE
FIRST
CONQUISTADOR

A Novel

ROBERT L. FOSTER

SUNSTONE
PRESS

SANTA FE

The events in this book of fiction take place in Spain, Cuba and Mexico. Names of characters, places and incidents are either the products of the author's imagination or are used fictitiously, and any resemblance to actual persons, living or dead, countries, cities, events or locales, political structure or culture is entirely coincidental.

Sunstone books may be purchased for educational, business, or sales promotional use. For information please write: Special Markets Department, Sunstone Press, P.O. Box 2321, Santa Fe, New Mexico 87504-2321.

Book and cover design › Vicki Ahl
Body typeface › Book Antiqua
Printed on acid-free paper
∞
eBook 978-1-61139-401-6

Library of Congress Cataloging-in-Publication Data

Foster, Robert L. (Robert Lee), 1933-
  The first conquistador : a novel / by Robert Foster.
      pages ; cm
  ISBN 978-1-63293-081-1 (softcover : acid-free paper)
  1. Explorers--Mexico--Fiction. 2. Conquerors--Mexico--Fiction. 3. Aztecs--History--16th century--Fiction. 4. Aztecs--First contact with Europeans--Fiction. 5. Mexico--Discovery and exploration--Spanish--Fiction. I. Title.
  PS3606.O766F57 2015
  813'.6--dc23

                                        2015026204

Sunstone Press is committed to minimizing our environmental impact on the planet. The paper used in this book is from responsibly managed forests. Our printer has received Chain of Custody (CoC) certification from: The Forest Stewardship Council™ (FSC®), Programme for the Endorsement of Forest Certification™ (PEFC™), and The Sustainable Forestry Initiative® (SFI®).

The FSC® Council is a non-profit organization, promoting the environmentally appropriate, socially beneficial and economically viable management of the world's forests. FSC® certification is recognized internationally as a rigorous environmental and social standard for responsible forest management.

WWW.SUNSTONEPRESS.COM
SUNSTONE PRESS / POST OFFICE BOX 2321 / SANTA FE, NM 87504-2321 /USA
(505) 988-4418 / ORDERS ONLY (800) 243-5644 / FAX (505) 988-1025

THE FIRST CONQUISTADOR

1

Off the Northwest Tip of Yucatan, 1516

The Catalan's heaving deck made it impossible for the crew, hunkered below, to move about the ship. Twenty-four hours of screaming hurricane winds slowly faded to gale force, and the battered Spanish caravel plowed steadily through the swells of the weakening storm.

"Get your lazy asses up there!" shouted Master's Mate Juan Narvaez. "We've got to get that mess cleaned up." Sailors scrambled up on deck and scurried about picking up debris scattered about the ship by the unexpected hurricane which ripped into the Catalan yesterday, nearly capsizing her twice.

Captain Julio Alvarez slowly climbed the companionway from his cabin to the deck where he and Narvaez scanned the spars and braces for any signs of damage, then hurried forward to inspect the temporary mast wedges, convinced the hurricane's force must have pulled the masts clean out of their seatings. Alvarez sighed with relief to find them undamaged.

Narvaez shouted above the wind, "The pumps are taking care of water in the hold and only one man is slightly injured. The Virgin has smiled down on us once again."

Alvarez nodded with half a smile as they walked along starboard rail, gazing down into the surging wake swirling along the ship's side, stretching out behind in a pike-straight line. The helmsman waved, letting them know the Catalan was now easier to handle.

The officers descended the companionway to Alvarez's cabin. He motioned Narvaez to the chart table and poured them each a cup of rum. Together they studied the only known map of the western Caribbean area. Alvarez growled, "That hurricane blew us a hell of a long ways off course."

Narvaez nodded agreement. "I figure we're almost thirty five leagues west of the northeastern tip of Yucatan." He traced his finger along a position line and pointed, "about here."

"Still a mighty long ways from Cuba," Alvarez grimaced. "What do you figure. Maybe two-hundred leagues?"

"At least." Narvaez sipped his rum. "If I've calculated correctly it'll take us three days to get back on our original course, traveling a little over a league an hour. If I can get that ripped foresail mended it'll give us half a league more speed."

"My God! Three whole days?" Alvarez's face showed disappointment. "Are you sure?"

"I'm afraid so." Narvaez pressed his lips together, wishing he could have provided better news.

"Damn," snapped Alvarez. "That'll throw us a week late getting home. Cortez will have my ass and probably bust me down to seaman."

"You really think so?" Narvaez frowned. "Good hell, Captain, what more could we have done?" Seems to me he'd want to congratulate you for saving his ship."

"You don't know Cortez! When he gives an order he wants it carried out without excuses, even if our excuse is the worst hurricane I've ever experienced."

"Let's wait and see," Narvaez said. He dipped a quill pen in ink and drew a long dark line from their current position northeast to Cuba. "This is the shortest route. All right with you, Captain?"

Alvarez waved a hand. "You're the navigator. I trust you."

Alvarez wasn't thinking clearly. Twice Narvaez's age, he only wanted to lay his tired body down and sleep. He was dead on his feet. With no sleep for the past forty eight hours, his eyes burned, and every bone in his body ached.

"God, Juan, I'm so tired of the sea," Alvarez yawned. "I'm too damned old for hurricanes, wild Indians and pirates!" He twisted his head back and forth trying to relieve his stiff neck. "Well, I have one consolation. This is my last voyage, so Cortez told me when I left Cuba. Did I tell you about that?"

Narvaez's head jerked up, his eyebrows raised in concern. "No sir, you didn't. You mean he's giving you the boot after your many years of loyal service to him?"

"Oh no! It's nothing like that!" Alvarez quickly countered. "He's letting me retire to my little farm in Punta del Piedras. Giving me a pension too. 'You've been at sea way too long,' he told me. It's about time for a younger man to take over command of the Catalan.'"

"Did he mention any names?" Narvaez asked with subdued excitement. Alvarez nodded. "Two or three." He took a long swallow of rum.

He stared into Narvaez's weather-beaten face, scarcely able to believe he'd been lucky enough to find such a knowledgeable man for his second in command. He liked Narvaez the first time he laid eyes on him, and immediately started grooming him for command of the Catalan. A strange thought suddenly flitted across Alvarez's mind. The Catalan, though somewhat shabby, with a disreputable air, seemed to be a reflection of Narvaez himself. He'd run away to sea when he was ten, and crowded many hair-raising experiences into his thirty-two years. Indistinguishable from an ordinary sailor in his white canvas trousers, pull over shirt and run down seaman's boots, he was equally at ease with gentlemen such as Cortez and Alvarez or Cuba's bordello women.

"Well," Narvaez asked impatiently, "who are they?"

"Your name's at the top of the list," Alvarez answered casually. "My name? Really?" Narvaez's surprise was genuine.

Alvarez laughed. "Keep this to yourself, Juan, but Cortez told me he's chosen you as the Catalan's next captain."

Narvaez stared at him, eyes wide with disbelief.

"Yes, m'boy, it's true. Cortez thinks highly of you! You know how to command men and you're a fighter. He admires that in his ship's captains."

Narvaez flashed a grin. "Captain Alvarez, that's the best news I've heard since I got to the new world! I'd say it calls for another drink!" A delighted Narvaez refilled their cups and handed one to Alvarez. "Damn!" Narvaez shook his head in wonder. "Captain Juan Narvaez! That has a mighty nice ring to it, don't you think?"

"I do indeed!" Alvarez replied and raised his cup. "To the future Captain Narvaez!"

Outside, one of the great swells of the Caribbean rolled slowly toward the ship—an acre of brilliantly blue water trembling like a shaken bowl of porridge. The crippled old vessel jogged her way through it, like the veteran sea pacer she was. Every now and then a shoal of flying fish, scared from under the bows leaped into the air, and fell the next moment like a shower of silver into the sea.

The lookout, high above in the crow's nest, scanned the rough sea ahead with his long glass, in case the storm should reverse itself and bear down on them again. As the ridge sucked up water to add to its height, bits of flotsam appeared on its smooth side; wreaths of seaweed, pieces of wood, broken tree branches and a log-like canoe. The lookout watched the ponderous swell carry the canoe steadily toward the Catalan, as though offering a gift.

A loud pounding on Alvarez's door brought him out of his chair as a breathless sailor tumbled in. "For the love of Christ, what now?" Alvarez growled irritably.

"Captain, off the larboard bow. The lookout spotted something you should see."

"Well? What the hell is it?" Alvarez spat out.

"We're not sure, sir. It could be a canoe or a just a log," answered the seaman.

Captain Alvarez and Narvaez walked to the cabin's streaked rear window; but couldn't see anything through the haze and mist. Alvarez, long glass in hand, followed by Narvaez and the sailor hurried up on deck.

"Deck ahoy there," came a sudden shout from the lookout whose outstretched arm pointed to the left. "There. In the water, a point off the larboard bow."

"Well what is it, man?" Alvarez shouted back. "A small boat!" came the lookout's reply.

Crewmen jostled each other, running to the railing to find out what the commotion was about, welcoming anything to break the long voyage's dull monotony. In three steps Alvarez reached the rail, his head leaning out as he tried to locate the small boat. He and Narvaez searched the running seas ahead of the ship but saw nothing.

"Masthead, can you still see it?" shouted Alvarez, sounding annoyed.

"It's gone now, sir!" A long pause. "There Captain," shouted the lookout. "There it is again, on the side of that incoming swell."

A thin line of the purest white foam flashed along the swell's crest. Then with a slow, dignified motion the great mound of water broke. For an instant the sea was covered with foam as remnants of the swell swept past the ship. Then came a score of eager cries from the sailors, and a dozen fingers pointed toward the log canoe about a hundred meters of the port bow.

Alvarez braced himself against the rail and raised his long glass.

The round aperture swept rapidly over dissolving bits of foam and focused on the small boat.

"It looks empty, Juan," he said to Narvaez. "No sign of life." Alvarez kept his glass trained on the boat. "Looks to me like a log canoe. Can you make it out?"

Narvaez startled Alvarez with, "It's a pirogue, sir. Some kind of Indian craft." Narvaez could see better with his naked eyes than his old captain could see with his glass.

Narvaez craned his neck forward and squinted for a closer look. "There's someone lying in the bottom of the boat. Shall I launch the longboat and find out who it is? The sea's still pretty rough, but I think we can get close enough for a look see."

"Do it, Juan, but be careful," Alvarez warned.

Narvaez shouted to the Bosun, "Bring some men and help me launch the longboat." Narvaez swung himself into the boat, which the crew quickly lowered as the Catalan sunk into a trough. The top swells lapped against the longboat's bottom. The stern and aft hooks simultaneously jerked free and the boat struck the water with scarcely a jolt.

"Out oars," Narvaez shouted. Seamen dipped oars in unison and the longboat sliced through the rough sea toward the pirogue.

"Put your backs into it, men," Narvaez ordered, standing in the boat's stern, its tiller under his firm, steady hand. As they drew near, Narvaez studied the pirogue with professional interest. He'd never seen anything like it. Her bow was razor-sharp, with several strange symbols carved into the wood. As the men brought the longboat alongside, Narvaez carefully jumped across into the pirogue.

He stared down at the biggest African he'd ever seen. Lying face up in the sloshing seawater, the man was totally naked, except for a small gold necklace of curious workmanship about his muscular neck. The seven-foot black man's head was white with crusted salt. His right hand clutched a strange looking knife made of sharp, white stone.

Narvaez pried the fingers open, took the knife and tucked it in the waistband of his trousers, under his shirt. He felt the man's pulse to see if he was alive. A faint heartbeat and a muffled groan stirred Narvaez to action. "Throw me a rope and tow us back to the ship. You, Ortaz, take the tiller."

As the longboat towed the pirogue alongside the Catalan, Narvaez helped the seamen transfer the African from the pirogue to the ship's longboat. Narvaez gave the pirogue's interior one quick glance before shoving it away. His eye caught movement of something afloat in its stern. He grabbed a small, scroll-like parchment and shoved it in his waistband next to the knife and jumped across to the longboat. Sailors on the ship hoisted it aboard the Catalan.

Even before Captain Alvarez got a good look at his new passenger, he shouted, "Bosun, get us underway!"

Crewmen jostled and shoved each other, trying to get in close to see who the castaway might be. "Make way there," growled Narvaez. "Give us some room."

Two muscular seamen carried the limp, unconscious black man below to the captain's cabin. "Is he alive, Juan?" Alvarez asked.

"Yes sir," Narvaez answered.

"Does he have anything that might help us identify him?"

"Yes sir. He had two…"

Alvarez interrupted. "Hold on a minute, Juan." Alvarez grabbed a seaman by the shoulder. "Fetch me Old Barba. Quickly now."

Alvarez nodded for Narvaez to follow him below to his cabin, where they found the African lying on Alvarez's bunk. Someone had covered his naked body with a blanket.

Old Barba hurried, but all it really amounted was an awkward shuffle, not much faster than his normal gait. No one aboard knew where the old Basque came from. Rumor had it he'd been with Master Admiral Columbus when he discovered the new world twenty four years ago; but he'd neither confirm nor deny the rumor. The crew trusted Old Barba. He could set broken bones, remove bad teeth, and even help relieve the pain of scurvy. He was the nearest thing to a ship's doctor aboard.

A slight tapping on Alvarez's door announced the ship's cook. "Come," shouted Alvarez. The rheumy, bent old man limped into the cabin, cap in hand. "You summoned me, Captain?"

"Yes. We have a patient for you," Alvarez pointed to the black man. Old Barba shuffled to the couch and pulled the blanket down to the African's waist, bent down and put his ear on the black man's chest, over his heart.

Unnoticed by Old Barba, intent on his examination, a fly crawled across the black man's broad forehead, along his nose and over his closed eyelid. The exhausted African tried to raise his right hand to swat it, but he couldn't summon enough strength to draw his hand from what felt like mud.

Panicky, he wondered where he was. The only thing he remembered was jumping into the small boat and the painted, war whooping savages racing to kill him. In a mighty effort he battered and crushed five strong Aztec warriors to death with his bare hands before he finally broke free and floated out to sea.

He was alarmed by his weightlessness, feeling as though he was suspended in the air. His face was scorched and his lips were cracked, but saltwater had stopped their bleeding. His teeth chattered with the cold and he shivered uncontrollably. He heard raspy breathing and felt someone's's head on his left breast. Oh my God! The Aztecs have me again; and he imagined himself stretched back down over a sacrificial stone, and an Aztec holy man was feeling for his heart. He forced open a crusted eyelid, just a slit, and saw a gray bearded white man.

"Who are you? Where am I?" the African grunted hoarsely, in Spanish! Momentarily startled, Old Barba jerked back. "Christ Jesus!" he exclaimed.

Captain Alvarez and Narvaez stepped quickly to the bunk to interrogate this unusual castaway. But the black man lapsed back into unconsciousness. He appeared to be about thirty, superbly built, with a slender waist, and a chest and shoulders so heavy and muscular Alvarez and Narvaez assumed he must be a slave. His skin was so dark it had a blue cast.

Old Barba straightened up and announced his diagnosis. "Captain, he's been without food and water for many days, but he's a very strong man. With rest and my special potions I'm sure I can bring him round."

"Thank you, Barba," Alvarez smiled. "We'll question him as soon as you feel he's ready."

"Give me a couple of days, Captain, and I'll have him on his feet."

"You've got it," Alvarez replied. "Can you care for him below deck in the store room?"

"Aye, Captain. We've used up most of the supplies. There's plenty of room."

"Excellent! I'll have some men carry him down. Be sure you keep an eye on him."

When Barba walked out and closed the door, Narvaez pulled the strange looking knife from under his shirt, and handed it to Alvarez. "Take a look at this, Captain. Have you ever seen a weapon like this before?"

Hefting the knife, Alvarez felt for its balance. He turned it over and ran his forefinger over the smooth stones in the handle and along the razor sharp obsidian blade. "Hmm. As strong and as sharp as steel."

Hewn, flintlike, out of white chalcedony, the blade was a hand's span in length. The handle, cunningly carved to represent an eagle-masked warrior, was encrusted with a mosaic of turquoise and shell, inlaid with small emeralds and amethysts, in a most curious design. Stains along the knife's serrated edges appeared to be dried blood.

"Well, what do you think, Captain? Narvaez asked. "I doubt it's a tool of war. It's too heavy for a knife and too light for a sword. Perhaps it's used for dress or display."

"It is most peculiar," admitted Alvarez. "What else did the black man have with him?"

"See that gold necklace around his neck? It's pure hammered gold. Where did it come from? I've never seen one like it in all my travels."

"It's exquisite all right," Alvarez said, "but it doesn't tell us anything about the man. Did he have anything else?"

"This." Narvaez held up a scroll of bark parchment. He carefully unrolled it on the chart table and saw it was a crude map. Alvarez stepped in close and stared at the map. Seawater stains had blurred and faded the blackened lines, but it was still readable. Jagged charcoal lines indicated some type of long, curving coastline.

Narvaez held the map up to the light of the cabin window and said, "The original charcoal has all but disappeared. But look here." He pointed. "A few words are barely legible, but they are in Spanish. I can only make out one word, Papantla."

Alvarez scratched his head. "I've never heard of such a place."

"Nor I," admitted Narvaez. He leaned over and studied the map more intently. "Look, here in the corner! I can make out a name. H. Ortega." Narvaez mouthed each letter as his finger moved along the corner of the parchment.

Alvarez's mouth dropped open. "Good God, Juan. That's got to be Hector Ortega!"

Narvaez stared at Alvarez and asked, "Would that be the same Ortega I heard about back in Cuba? Rumor had it he led some kind of secret expedition to Indian country."

"That's him," Alvarez nodded. "Last year Cuba's Governor, Don Diego Velazquez, launched a secret expedition, led by Ortega, to see if there was any gold to be had among the Aztecs."

"What did Captain Cortez think of that?" Narvaez asked.

"He was mighty damned pissed," Alvarez smiled. "Cortez hates and despises that sonofabitch Velasquez. Captain Cortez has been planning the same kind of expedition himself, with King Carlos' backing. It's all kind of a hush hush deal. No one knows much about it."

Narvaez leaned toward Alvarez, his eyes tight on his face, and asked, "So what happened to Ortega? Did he make it back to Cuba with ship loads of gold."

Alvarez laughed gently and shook his head. "No, thank God. No one knows what happened to him. If the Aztecs have any gold it's still there in the Aztec empire. So Captain Cortez still has a fair chance to beat Velasquez to the treasure—if it exists."

A barrage of questions attacked Narvaez's mind, all leading to one thought, which he put to Alvarez. "Do you think the black man lying there in your bunk is a survivor of Ortega's expedition?"

Alvarez pursed his lips, and remained silent for a moment. "It's very possible. Whether he is or isn't, we'd better get a move on and get him back to Captain Cortez and find out what he wants to do. Can you get any more canvas on this old girl?"

"I'm afraid not, Captain. We're carrying every rag of sail we can."

"Damn that storm," Alvarez growled. "Well, do the best you can."

🐜 🐜 🐜

Two days passed and the Catalan scudded along under full sail toward Punta del Piedras. During the day the sky presented a clear expanse of the most delicate blue, except along the far horizon, where you might see a thin drapery of pale clouds which never varied their form or color.

At eight o'clock the second morning after the black man came aboard Old Barba limped up to Captain Alvarez standing at the rail searching the horizon through his long glass.

Hat in hand, the old man coughed once. "Yes, Barba?"

"The big black man is on his feet this morning, if you'd like to talk to him."

"Thank you, Barba. You're indeed a man of your word."

A toothless smile lighted Old Barba's face. "Gracias, Capitan." He ambled happily back to his pots and pans.

Alvarez spotted Narvaez coming up from below deck, after completing a final inspection of the ship. "Juan!" Alvarez hailed, "A word with you. It's time to question our mysterious passenger."

2

ZARAGOSA, SPAIN, NOVEMBER, 1517

Captain Luis Escudero finished his dinner at an inn on the outskirts of Zaragosa, Spain, as dusk settled over the broad valley. He paid the inn keeper, walked out and turned down a long alley leading to the stable.

He moved easily for one so tall and broad shouldered. He took about a dozen steps into the alley when he sensed swift movement behind him. Reacting with bristling readiness which was second nature to him, he spun around and dropped into a wide-stanced posture, poised on the balls of his feet, facing the dark forms coming at him. His assailants immediately knew whatever they'd been paid to kill this man wasn't near enough. One look at his coiled attitude and killing eye and they knew it would be a fight to the death.

Luis was trapped, his back to the wall. He caught the glint of lamplight on a sword, but waited and warily watched the two men crouching forward.

"You're a dead man, Escudero!" shouted the first man, thrusting at Luis with his sword.

He was too slow. Luis' dagger slid easily into his hand. He hurled it in an arc and it thudded into the man's throat; and he sprawled headlong to the cobblestones, dead before he hit the ground. The second man lunged at Luis with his sword. In the alley's gloom, Luis felt more than saw the sword slashing toward his neck and leaped out of the way. He pulled his sword, parried the blow and sidestepped quickly. The frightened assailant took his eyes off Luis for a split second, looking for a way to escape. Luis ran his sword into the man's stomach. He screamed pain, and dropped his sword on the cobblestones. He clutched his belly with both hands then dropped to his knees, his face contorted with hate.

In a dying effort, the man pulled his dagger to stab Luis, but Luis' hand caught the man's knife arm and forced him to drop the knife. He grabbed the man by the shirt "Who are you?" he growled. "Why did you ambush me?"

"Go to hell," the man grunted. "You and your Flemish king, you…" There was a choking gurgle and the man fell dead at Luis' feet.

Luis retrieved his dagger, cleaned his weapons and searched the corpses for clues which might identify them. He pulled a small silver coin from the pocket of the man lying dead at his feet. Holding the coin up against light from a nearby window, he squinted to make out four small letters, Cuba. But why, he wondered, would someone from Cuba, if that is where these assassins were from, want to kill me? Cuba is thousands of miles from here in the new world.

Nothing more could be done here. He left the bodies where they fell, hurried to the stable, saddled Pedrito, jammed his heels into the horse's side and galloped out of Zaragosa.

Luis was exhausted, but he spurred Pedrito toward Madrid, a few more leagues southwest. Tired as he was he kept an eye open for a fork in the road peasants a ways back told him about. It was impossible see anything on this black road flanked by stunted trees and thick underbrush. Pedrito fought to keep his footing on the rock-studded road. The long journey through rain and unseasonably cold weather from Vienna across Lombardy, the southeast corner of France, through the high pass in the Pyrenees and finally onto the flat lands of Spain had taken its toll on the huge warhorse.

A week ago, despite Luis' best efforts to keep Pedrito on firm, dry footing whenever possible, he discovered tell-tale signs of greased heel. Pedrito's front hooves had suffered too much mud. They were rotting. Still the magnificent animal was game, trotting steadily along the road.

Not far ahead was a small inn where Luis could get hot food, a bed for the night and a good rubdown for Pedrito. They needed food and rest.

🐾 🐾 🐾

Captain Juan Navarro played a hunch Luis Escudero would follow the Zaragosa route and stop at this inn, the only one for fifty miles in any direction, though he wasn't sure when. Navarro's cavalry troop was impatient and tired of waiting. There was no action, no women—nothing to do but play cards and shoot dice.

Sergeant Odano sat at the bar and chugged down his wine. The mug left a wet ring on the bar. He set it down carefully on the ring.

"How much longer do we have to lay around here, Captain?" Odano asked Navarro. "Until Captain Escudero arrives," Navarro answered sharply.

"When the hell will that be?"

"Soon," Navarro said. "He's got to be in Madrid for his appointment with the king on December first—six days from now."

"How about me and some of my men go out and look for him?" Odano said.

"No, Sergeant, " Navarro glared at him. "What I want you to do is take a couple of bottles of wine to your men bivouacked out back and tell them to settle their asses down. Find something for them to do—curry their horses, polish their saddles—anything, just keep them busy. When Captain Escudero gets here we'll move out. Understand?"

Odano blinked at him. "But sir..."

"Sergeant, for Christ's sake, just do what you're told!"

Count Guy de Vey, Flemish nobleman and King Carlos' closest advisor, sat relaxed in front of the fireplace sipping brandy, smiling as he listened to Navarro and Sergeant Odano. Sergeants were no different now than years ago when he was a soldier.

"Come, Navarro," de Vey motioned. "Sit and have some brandy. You've earned it. You and your men made record time getting me up here from Madrid." He poured Navarro a brandy.

"Tell me, Captain," de Vey said. "Do you know this Luis Escudero very well?"

"We've campaigned together from time to time."

"The King seems quite taken with him. He told me Escudero is one of the best soldiers in the Spanish army." de Vey paused and sipped his brandy. "I'm new to Spain so I know very little about your army. Yet everywhere I go I hear the most fabulous rumors about Escudero—he's some kind of legend, almost god-like. I'd like to separate fact from legend. Please tell me about him."

Navarro was silent, and smoothed his glass with his fingertips. The silence stretched on and de Vey was tempted to prompt him; but he waited for Navarro to gather his thoughts.

Finally, Navarro said, "Luis joined the army when he was seventeen. He fought in the African campaign, also against the Lombards, and in many other battles. He's never lost a fight that I know of."

De Vey smiled. "He's evidently a mighty fine warrior."

"He certainly is that, sir," Navarro agreed. "That being said, I've wondered why one of Spain's finest cavalry officers, who's been serving as military attaché at our embassy in Vienna, is being recalled to Madrid. Is he in some sort of trouble?"

De Vey shook his head. "Certainly not. However, I'm not at liberty to say why King Carlos has called him home from Vienna. This I can tell you, the King's business with Escudero is most urgent." de Vey swirled the brandy in his glass. "Please continue, Captain."

"He's twenty four, very popular and extremely well known in our army. He's sometimes criticized by other officers for his treatment of men under his command."

De Vey's eyebrows shot up. Puzzled he asked, "How so? Is he not a good commander?"

"Oh no, that's not it," Navarro said. "Just the opposite. He treats his men as equals! He's not an aristocrat with their philosophy that commoners are only good for cannon fodder. Men under his command would follow him to hell if he gave the order. He'll not order any man to do anything he wouldn't do himself. That strategy rankles hell out of Spain's high ranking officers."

De Vey grinned. "It sounds like Escudero is a very good friend?"

"He is, sir. I wish I could be more like him."

De Vey's eyes were now full on Navarro, his voice was low and grim, when he asked, "Do you think the king is wise in considering Escudero for a very special and dangerous assignment?"

Navarro said quietly, "Not knowing what the assignment is, it's hard for me to say; but this I can tell you, based on my experience serving with Luis on several battlefields, I don't think there's any assignment he couldn't handle and handle extremely well."

"I'll take your word for it, Captain!" de Vey grinned, and unwound his six foot three inch frame from the comfortable chair by the fireplace, stood and stretched. "Let's get to the table, my boy. I'm hungry enough to eat a horse."

🐾 🐾 🐾

Luis pulled his collar tighter about his neck and buttoned his cloak against the cold north wind. His head sagged as Pedrito limped slowly through the pitch blackness. Luis' mind wandered. Had he been wise to join the army after his parents died? He didn't know what else to do. Maybe he should have settled for something less dangerous, found a good woman, settled down and started a family. He smiled inwardly.

Settle down? That had never been an option! He'd dreamed of being in the army since he was a child—and the army had been good to him, even though it had been extremely dangerous, and he'd been wounded many times.

He was still puzzled and a bit worried by his sudden recall from Viennal in mid-assignment. King Carlos' note on his personal stationary, carried by Luis' replacement, was short and straight to the point: Report to the royal palace in Madrid for an audience with King Carlos on or before December 1, 1517.

Luis had never met the boy king newly arrived from Flanders, though he'd heard all sorts of rumors at the Spanish embassy in Vienna. Six months ago, when Luis left Madrid for Vienna, Queen Joanna, the retarded daughter of Ferdinand and Isabella, sat the throne of Spain. A marriage of convenience was arranged between Joanna and Phillip, Archduke of Austria and together they produced a son whom they named Carlos. As a baby, Carlos was whisked off to Flanders for safekeeping against the capriciousness of his retarded mother.

While Luis was away in Vienna, Joanna went completely insane from the strains placed on her already weak mind by the monarchy's strenuous duties. She was confined behind brick walls, and gossip had it she'd remain there for the rest of her life.

Luis wondered if King Carlos was anything like his mother. Luis heard King Carlos was a bit odd and acted strangely at times. Well, no need to stress over it. Whatever lay in store for him was only a few days away. He wished to God there was a faster means of transport. The distance was so great and the method of travel so slow. He'd make it to Madrid at the appointed time, but it required every ounce of strength he possessed to stay in the saddle day and night over such a great distance.

Groggily awake again, he strained his eyes, hoping to see the small inn where he could spend the night. He urged Pedrito on with a gentle boot nudge to his flank. Finally he caught a whiff of drifting wood smoke, and could see the inn's light in the distance. Pedrito's head jerked up, and too tired to neigh, he just bubbled air through his lips; and the spittle coming from his mouth was flecked with blood. The gallant stallion's lungs had finally given out. Luis reached over and patted Pedrito's great muscled neck, acknowledging the horse's mighty efforts to get him to Madrid.

Luis pulled Pedrito up in front of the inn, climbed down, gave the stable boy a coin to take care of the horse and stepped inside.

Navarro jumped up from the table and shouted, "Luis? My God, Is it really you? "You look like hell, boy!" In a few quick steps Navarro grabbed Luis in a bear hug. "It's good to see you! Here, let me take your hat and cloak."

Luis eyes went wide, surprised to see Navarro in this remote part of Spain. "What are you doing here?"

"Me and my cavalry troop were ordered to find you and escort you to see the King. Seems you're moving up in the world, old friend. The king even sent his chief counselor to make sure we get you to Madrid safe and sound—and on time."

"The king's counselor?" Luis asked incredulously.

Navarro nodded toward the tall, middle-aged knight, walking toward them. "Luis, meet Count Guy de Vey, King Carlos' chief counselor."

Luis snapped to attention, while de Vey looked him over. What impressed de Vey first were Escudero's clothes. His cloak was light blue. He wore tight white trousers with cavalry boots and a polished sword. Then de Vey forgot the clothes in the impact of the man himself. Taller than the average Spaniard, nearly as tall as de Vey himself, Luis was solidly built. The Count read endurance in Luis' face. He was especially taken with Luis' light blue eyes. Unusual in a Spaniard. His clean shaven face was lean and hard and burned from the high forehead to his firm tapering chin. As the Count walked closer he saw this was because the brows were drawn in a frown of fixed habitual alertness. Beneath them, those pale blue eyes missed nothing. de Vey liked him!

He grabbed Luis' hand. "Glad to meet you at last, m'boy. Navarro, get him a glass of brandy. His hands are like ice. Then we'll get some food into him."

Navarro went to the kitchen to order food and drink for Luis. "Sit yourself down, lad. Sit yourself down," de Vey said.

Luis sat in the chair de Vey indicated, which was directly opposite his own. Food was brought and de Vey watched Luis eat.

Luis couldn't tell how old Count Guy de Vey was. He was showing the marks left on him by many years of soldiering. His hair was grizzled, and there were two deep furrowed lines running from his nose down to his chin; his face looked weathered, but his body had the hard thickness of a hardened warrior. Luis silently decided he'd not like to cross swords with him.

Luis ate. The conversation was purposely general until Luis, bursting with curiosity, asked de Vey, "I don't suppose you can tell me why the king ordered me to Madrid?"

He was surprised to see de Vey's head go back and his mouth open wide as he laughed a deep hearty laugh. "I wouldn't want to spoil they king's surprise, now would I? For now, let's just say your reputation precedes you. King Carlos has heard of your exploits and wishes to meet you."

Boldly Luis responded, "Oh come now, there's got to be more to it than that."

De Vey now looked Luis steadily in the eyes. His voice was low when he said, "Perhaps."

"Well sir,..." Luis hunched his shoulders apologetically. "If that's all you can tell me right now, I guess it'll have to do."

De Vey got to his feet. "If you'll excuse me, gentlemen, I'm going to turn in. We'll leave for Madrid first thing in the morning."

🐾 🐾 🐾

Sitting by the fire, sipping brandy, Luis quietly asked Navarro. "What the hell's going on?"

Navarro shrugged. "Damned if I know! The only thing Count de Vey would tell me was the king has an assignment for you."

"Why all the secrecy? Why a troop of cavalry and a king's counselor to escort me? de Vey didn't tell you any more than that?"

"I was damn lucky to get that much from the man!" Navarro replied. "Don't worry. The king probably has a routine boring shit detail all lined up for you."

Luis grinned. "You're probably right. That's the only kind I've been getting lately!"

3

MADRID, SPAIN, DECEMBER 1, 1517

Luis climbed out of bed early, stretched, then pulled back the curtain and stared out the window at the lowering sky. Heavy dark rain clouds billowed toward Madrid.

Luis slipped into his best uniform. He stopped by Navarro's room on his way to the royal palace and found him still in bed, yawning and stretching luxuriously.

"You're up early, my friend," Navarro said pleasantly. "Got a busy day?" Luis grinned. "You know damn well I do."

"Are you apprehensive about meeting the king?"

"Wouldn't you be?" Luis asked.

"I doubt I'll ever have that opportunity," Navarro said quietly. Then he smiled. "Put your fears to rest. The king is just a boy; he doesn't even speak Spanish. Count de Vey will be there to introduce you to the king and he'll translate for you. That'll give you an in with King Carlos to start off with."

They looked at each other for a moment, in uncomfortable silence.

Luis said, "Perhaps you're right." Then asked, "Do you think I'm in for a reprimand or a court martial?"

"Neither," Navarro grinned. "If it was a court martial the king wouldn't be involved. No, my friend, it's something very important. Damn! I wish I could be there to find out what it is! But whatever you're in for, good luck, Luis." Navarro stretched out his hand and Luis grabbed it.

Luis felt refreshed and walked briskly toward the royal palace, called the Alcazar. It felt so good to be walking after endless days in the saddle. He was butt-sprung! Along the broad cobblestone avenue he noticed carriages with aristocratic crests on the doors, their passengers descending and walking into grand buildings—women in splendid gowns and men in the latest foppish fashions, often laughing together.

The magnificent white stone alcazar loomed at the end of the street. Luis' heart beat faster with apprehension. He couldn't grasp the notion he'd soon be standing before King Carlos. What the hell would the king want with a common man like me, a working soldier with no aristocratic connections or political ambitions? Well whatever it is, let's get on with it!

🐾 🐾 🐾

King Carlos' male secretary greeted Luis by name, with respect, and ushered him into the king's large, well-apportioned high ceilinged waiting room.

"The king will be with your shortly, Captain," said the secretary. Pointing at two large, framed paintings on the wall, he said, "We received those portraits of King Ferdinand and Queen Isabella last week, if you'd like to look them over."

Luis paced nervously, his stomach tied in knots. He stopped for a quick look at King Ferdinand's portrait and assumed it must have been painted by a Flemish artist because of the bright colors and life-like facial features. Ferdinand died last year, and Luis wondered if Carlos would measure up to his famous grandfather. Luis doubted it very much, judging from all the negative rumors he'd heard about Carlos, especially that he'd led Spain into a downward spiraling economic disaster.

Suddenly the door to the waiting room swung open and Count Guy de Vey walked in followed by a swarthy, well dressed man with a big face and heavy black brows and a beard, and black eyes that looked enormous. The man wore a sword, had no hat on his head and his scraggly looking black hair hung down over his ears.

"You're not going to let me see the king after I've traveled all the way from Cuba with a message from Governor Don Diego Velasquez? I am his emissary, you know."

De Vey stood blocking the doorway, his feet apart, staring at the angry, frustrated man. "No, Don Ruiz, no I am not going to let you see the king," de Vey said flatly.

The two men stared at each other for a matter of seconds before Ruiz hissed, "You'll be sorry, de Vey. Governor Velasquez has many friends in high places, here and in the Caribbean. You'd better let me in to see the king!"

To this de Vey answered, "Don't you threaten me, or King Carlos for that matter. If you're not out of here in thirty seconds I'll call the guards and have you locked up!"

"To hell with you, de Vey, and to hell with Carlos too," Ruiz spat out. "We'll launch our expedition to Mexico with or without his permission."

De Vey scowled. "You tell Governor Velasquez if tries it, there'll be hell to pay, and Cuba will have a new governor."

Ruiz shook his head disgustedly and growled, "We'll see."

Luis watched Ruiz stomp away, pushing his way roughly past people in the long spacious hallway.

De Vey saw Luis and walked over. "Welcome to the Alcazar, Captain Escudero," he said cordially and grabbed Luis' hand. "It's good to see you again."

"What was that all about, sir?" Luis asked with a slight grin. "Maybe I came at a bad time?"

De Vey dismissed the incident with a wave of his hand. "It was nothing you need be concerned about. Just another day of intrigue here at Court. Come, my boy, follow me. The king is most anxious to meet you."

Carlos stood staring out a window when de Vey walked in followed by Luis. de Vey cleared his throat and Carlos turned.

When Luis saw the king's face he knew the flamboyantly dressed young man was Carlos. The long pale face, with its hanging jaw and gaping look, revealed his Hapsburg blood. His face, framed by ringlets of black hair gave him a girlish look.

"Your Majesty," said de Vey, "This man is Captain Luis Escudero, the soldier you sent for." Luis bowed respectfully.

Carlos' eyes went wide as he studied Luis. "So this is our legendary Captain Escudero, eh, de Vey? What a fine specimen of a man!"

There was nothing the least effeminate about Carlos' greeting as he stepped quickly forward and grabbed Luis' hand. "I'm very happy to meet you, Captain," he said, and steered him to a chair in front of his desk.

"Please be at ease, Captain. I'm so happy you are here safe and sound. Thank you for coming on such short notice. It must have been a very difficult journey for you."

Luis didn't understand some of the king's Flemish words, but was overwhelmed Carlos treated him like a long lost friend.

De Vey jumped in. "Well, Captain, you're probably bursting at the seams wondering why in the world you're here today."

Luis nodded.

"It's quite simple. We need you for a special assignment. But before we get into that, the king wants me to explain our current situation here in Spain."

Luis could tell de Vey was the power behind the throne. Authority radiated from him like heat from the sun. The penetrating eyes, the aggressive thrust of the beard, even the way the tall, thickset body now sat, not lolling, not relaxed, but alert, assertive, seemingly ready to spring from his chair. without warning.

De Vey said, "As you rode through Zaragosa and south you probably noticed thousands of Spaniards are out of work. Over half our small businesses have been forced to close. People are literally starving. Spain's agricultural production is the worst it's been in two centuries and severe droughts plague our northern provinces."

As de Vey reviewed Spain's economic, political and military problems, Carlos silently scrutinized the legendary soldier sitting before him—a man who'd fought in battles and seen sights Carlos only read about. The twenty-four-old soldier was not a great deal older than the seventeen-year-old monarch himself. Luis' pale blue eyes were the eyes of an honest man and a dreamer too. It was difficult for Carlos to imagine Luis hacking his way through hordes of desert bedouins in Africa.

Tall for a Spaniard, and the way he carried himself, left no doubt he thoroughly enjoyed dangerous adventures. And there was something instantly noticeable about Luis' manner too. Most men Carlos met every day were fawning courtesans. Luis was courteous but not fawning. Carlos like that in a man—he liked it a lot!

Luis listened to de Vey, and occasionally glanced at Carlos absently twirling his quill pen. Not handsome by any means, the king was the butt of many cruel jokes among Spanish courtiers and army officers. They despised him because they didn't consider him a true Spaniard. He didn't even speak the language!

De Vey finally concluded his remarks. "Any questions so far, Captain?"

"No sir," Luis answered.

"Good. King Carlos and I have been working on a plan to break us out of the economic depression which now holds us captive. We'll get to that in a minute."

De Vey grabbed some papers on Carlos' desk. "This is your military dossier. We find your military accomplishments extraordinary, more so than those of any other officer. That's why you're here today."

De Vey held up the papers. "These don't really tell us much about the man under the armor. We need to know something about your family, where you come from, something about your boyhood years. Can you provide a little background for us?"

Luis' mind raced, wondering where to start! What would impress Spain's two most powerful men? What would they want to hear? He began slowly.

"My mother died of smallpox when I was eight. I remember she was a beautiful, kind woman, part English, with a stubborn, fierce pride. Father was a soldier, a cavalryman, always drunk, but richly dressed, who visited occasionally between campaigns. He struck terror into the servants and me too! He was killed in battle when I was sixteen. He didn't leave me any money or property. My grandfather took care of me for a year until I joined the army. I didn't know what else to do. I'd wanted to be a soldier ever since I was a little boy."

Luis paused while de Vey interpreted his remarks into Flemish for Carlos, who leaned forward and smiled, very interested in hearing more.

De Vey nodded. "Please continue, Captain."

"Master Admiral Columbus found the new world when I was only eight. All over Spain many of us little boys made up our minds to emulate the great mariner. I wanted to be like Columbus and travel to strange, exotic places, especially to the new world he discovered."

Carlos chuckled and interrupted. "Me too! Did you know that?"

"No sire."

"Yes. I hoped to travel to exotic places, but duties of the monarchy impose too many restrictions. But we're not here to talk about me." He waved a hand. "Please continue."

"One day I snuck away from home. I saw a poor old farmer working in his field, behind a skinny, spavined old horse pulling a crude plow. I was utterly fascinated. I thought it would be fun to walk behind the horse and plow the land. I walked up to the old man, bold as brass, and said, I want to guide the horse! I figured the old fellow would hand me the reins. He just stared at me—then laughed! I got angry, but it didn't impress him a bit! These damned Spanish peasants have great spirit!

'Here, let me show you how,' the old man said. 'For one so small, you must be very careful.' He walked with me and showed me how to guide the plow. I was in a child's heaven. At that very moment I fell in love with horses. To me that spavined old horse was as beautiful as my father's warhorse was to him. The freedom of the open land, the uncomplicated cheerfulness of my new friend and his horse made me as happy as the gulls which screamed and soared above us, hoping for a fat worm to be turned up by the plow.

Afterwards he invited me to his home to sup with him and his wife. How proud I felt when he said, 'you did a mans' work today.' He lived in an old stone house with a sod roof. Today I know it was a miserable, cold, dirty hovel and the old man and woman were wretchedly poor. But, gentlemen, back then it was an enchanted world—smoke blackened walls, chairs made of old barrels, a plank stretched across, from wall to wall, served as a table. The old woman cooked over an open fire. I never enjoyed a meal as much as I did that one! As we dined, the old man told me stories of his warrior days, of soldiers and glory and places he'd been. I listened. I ate. I absorbed the atmosphere. That was one of the happiest days of my life, if not the happiest! I was with a real family; there was a quiet, unspoken love between the old man and woman. What a feeling of accomplishment it was to work and earn my supper! I'd never done that before. I can't describe it any better than that. Right then and there I secretly made up my mind I'd work and make my own way in the world, and soldering would be the way."

Luis was embarrassed by this bit of youthful reminiscing which he hadn't thought about for a long time. Evidently it had an impact on King Carlos and Count de Vey for they both smiled, nodding their heads in approval.

De Vey smiled warmly. "How very appropriate, Captain, because we have a soldier's assignment for you—one which may change the world as we know it!"

4

Luis stared at de Vey and Carlos and didn't say anything for a moment, for he was looking at the expressions on the faces, both with curious smiles. Luis inclined his head toward de Vey as a barrage of questions attacked his mind. "A soldier's assignment you say? You don't know how wonderful that sounds to me. I wasn't overly fond of that political assignment in Vienna. I'm not cut out for politics."

De Vey grinned at Luis, now in relief. "Glad to hear it, m'boy. But enough of this chit chat. I assume you've heard of Hernando Cortez, our senior captain in the new world?"

"Certainly, sir," Luis responded. "Everyone in Spain has heard of him."

"Good." de Vey handed Luis a rolled up parchment. "I want you to read this dispatch from Captain Cortez, then we'll talk."

Luis unrolled the parchment and read:

Majesty,

On April 7, in the year of our Lord 1516, our merchant vessel Catalan picked up a black man adrift in the Caribbean Sea approximately two hundred leagues south and west of Punta del Piedras, Cuba. He was in poor condition, having been at sea many days without food or water. His name is Kano. He's now recovered from his ordeal and is in good health.

Captain Julio Alvarez, master of the Catalan, interrogated Kano and learned he was a member of Hector Ortega's expedition secretly dispatched to the Aztec Empire last year by Governor Velasquez. Kano is the sole survivor of the expedition. Recovered with him were three items: a strange stone knife with a small amount of gems inlaid in the handle, a water-damaged map on some type of bark paper, and a small gold necklace. These items, however, do not provide sufficient proof there's gold and silver to be had among the Aztecs.

Kano speaks the Aztec language! Such skill will give us an edge when our exploratory expedition is ready to sail. Kano has changed allegiance to our cause and we're keeping him out of sight aboard the Catalan so Velasquez doesn't find him.

I trust Luis Escudero has accepted command of the first scouting expedition into Mexico... Luis' eyebrows shot up! He gawked at Carlos and de Vey in open-mouthed astonishment! "Continue, Captain." de Vey instructed. "There's more!"

We're recruiting some good men for him. Of the ones who've signed on there's not a coward in the lot. There's not a man among them who is not a law unto himself. They're as rough a lot of ruffians as we've ever assembled under Spain's banner. There isn't one who thinks he's an ordinary man!

Every one is a veteran of several campaigns. With addition of four or five more men, we'll have a full compliment as discussed. Escudero will find them equal to any challenge that lies before them.

One last thought in closing, Majesty, so I can get this aboard the packet sailing for Barcelona this afternoon. I respectfully urge we move with utmost speed. Not only is Governor Velasquez in the process of mounting another expedition, but French and English warships have been sighted in the Gulf of Mexico. Even at this moment our hated enemies are sniffing about like hounds, trying to pick up the scent of gold and silver. I'll keep you advised as our plan develops. With nothing further at the moment and wishing you continued health and success I remain, Your most obedient servant,

    H. Cortez

The two men studied Luis' stunned look. They couldn't tell what was going on in his mind. Even Luis himself would have difficulty defining his thoughts and emotions. The first thing he wanted to know was how Cortez's information would affect his future!

"Well, Captain, what do you think?" de Vey asked. "Extraordinary, is it not?"

"God's eyes, Count! I don't know what to make of it. I hope you'll enlighten me!"

"Certainly," de Vey nodded, with a smile. "I've explained our grave financial crisis. The only way to solve it is with an immediate infusion of gold and silver into our treasury or Spain will be totally bankrupt. To put it quite simply, we need the gold, silver and precious gems rumored to be in the Aztec Empire."

"That should be very simple, sir. Send Cortez in to take it, if it's there."

"That's our dilemma! We don't know for certain there is any gold or silver," de Vey answered. "No white man has ever entered Mexico and survived. Sending Cortez with a large army, ships, men and munitions requires a huge outlay of money, with no guarantee he'll find enough gold to fill a tooth. No Captain Escudero, the cortes, our parliament, would never authorize such a wild adventure. They're still boiling mad over the Columbus affair. As you know, he discovered a totally new and unexplored world, but after several voyages he completely failed in his objective of finding a shorter route to India or anything of value at all. Carlos' grandparents spent millions financing his expedition and he didn't find anything of value."

"I wouldn't say Columbus failed, de Vey!" Carlos interjected defensively. "After all it did open up new areas, did it not?"

"True Majesty, but not one thing of any value has come from that area to date. That's all I'm saying. The cortes will not authorize any funds for a grand expedition to Mexico without some guarantee they can recoup those funds and put money in the treasury."

"Perhaps you're right." Carlos admitted petulantly.

"Well, let's get down to business!" de Vey motioned Carlos and Luis to follow him to a map table in the corner of the room. The two tall soldiers dwarfed the small, pale-faced boy with the physique of a sparrow, as they stood with their heads over the table staring at a map.

"This, gentlemen, is a composite chart of Mexico's coastline." de Vey tapped the map with his forefinger. "We've researched every known source of information, from that furnished by Master Admiral Columbus and Hernando Cortez to rumors picked up from rude savages."

Luis leaned in and studied Cuba's location in proximity to the long, jagged black line to the west, which indicated an immensely long seacoast running north and south. Mexico must be enormous!

Sensing Luis' thoughts de Vey said, "It looks big, eh? But we have no idea how big it really is. With the scanty information we've gathered we don't have a clue as to what we'll find in the fabled land of the Aztecs. It might as well be on the moon. Exactly where Mexico is, its size, its history, whether it's an island or a continent we have some mighty confused notions. Our cartographers who make the charts by which our ships navigate believe the Caribbean Sea is part of the Indian Ocean, and the Bahamas are the spice islands of Asia. My God, Captain, with such outmoded thinking I seriously doubt Spaniards could find their asses in the dark with both hands!"

Luis laughed out loud, taking no offense at de Vey's sarcasm, knowing he spoke the truth. Columbus was not a Spaniard, though he sailed for Spain; and were it not for him the new world would still be shrouded in the mists of rumor.

Returning to their chairs, Carlos said, "Captain, let me impress upon you the extreme political pressures I face. Our parliament hates me. The Spanish people are against me because I come from Flanders. My overseas governors are disloyal. Our treasury is bankrupt. And I'm extremely worried about Don Diego Velasquez, mentioned in Cortez's dispatch."

"He's your governor in Cuba?" Luis asked.

"He is!" Suddenly Carlos' voice was scathing. "He acts like he's God Almighty and takes no orders from me. Damn it, I'm the King and

Velasquez treats me like some lowly peasant. Without proper authorization, or any authorization at all, he's spent several years and thousands of ducats exploring Mexico's coast searching for gold, which rightfully belongs to the crown. The blackguard's even had the gall to write and ask me for money, men, horses and equipment to mount a great expedition. It'll be a cold day in hell before I grant Velasquez favors of any kind."

"This mention of Cuba, sire," Luis interjected, "is most interesting. In Zaragosa I had a run in with two assassins who tried to kill me." He explained the fight, then pulled the Cuban coin from his pocket and handed it to Carlos, who scrutinized it carefully, turning it over a couple of times.

"Velasquez men, no doubt," Carlos said. "He wants you stopped!"

Luis let it go, unsure what Carlos was talking about. "This Velasquez you speak of, maybe he's mistaken. Maybe there is no gold."

"Oh there's gold there alright, I'm convinced of it!" Carlos responded positively, "and Velasquez will try to steal it right out from under us. I know he will. I don't trust him! Even as we speak he's trying to form an alliance of governors in our Caribbean Territories. He's won over the Hieronymite Commission in Santo Domingo. Can you believe that? They're fathers of our holy church! Even our church turns against me!" The frustrated young monarch, on the verge of tears, tried with difficulty to control his temper.

De Vey jumped in. "That bastard Velasquez has been busy all right. His emissary, Don Ruiz, was here this very morning, demanding an audience with you, sire. I kicked him out."

A pause followed. de Vey tapped his hand on the desk. "We'll have to be very careful gentlemen. Velasquez has spies everywhere. They've already learned of our plans for you, Captain, and they want you stopped."

"Exactly what are those plans?" Luis asked.

De Vey smiled broadly. "As you read in Cortez's dispatch, you sir, are going to lead a highly secret Spanish exploratory expedition to the Aztec empire."

"Me?" Luis gasped, utterly taken aback—at a loss for anything else to say.

"Yes. You!" de Vey confirmed. "King Carlos, Captain Cortez and I have confidence in your abilities to lead the first group of white men ever to penetrate the Aztec empire."

Luis lower jaw worked from side to side before he said, "I'm flattered and delighted to accept, of course."

"Whoa," de Vey held up a hand. "Hear us out before you thank us. The stakes are so high in this wild scheme Carlos and I stay awake nights wondering if we're doing the right thing. We think we are.

Cortez came all the way from Cuba and we worked out a tentative plan with him, which he approved. He's in overall command of the entire operation. He's recruiting and training your men at Punta del Piedras, Cuba, as we speak. You're going to lead those men to the Aztec Empire, map a feasible route to its capitol city and determine if there's enough gold and silver to warrant organizing a full-scale expedition."

"What?" Luis' eyes sprang wide. "That's a mighty large order, sir. Do you think I can handle such an assignment?"

"Oh that's not all, m'boy!" de Vey said, trying to sound amiable. "You must be accomplish it within sixty days. That'll allow Cortez time to assemble men, provisions and horses for the conquest if you're successful."

Luis silently calculated the distance horsemen could cover in sixty days. He ran his hand through his hair and said, "This Kano mentioned in Cortez's dispatch will accompany us as interpreter?"

"He will!" de Vey said exuberantly. "Fortunately, or by the grace of God, you'll have a man with you who's actually set foot in that strange Indian empire, one who speaks their language."

"This adventure gets more interesting by the hour," Luis voice was low as he mulled over in his mind the myriad of details thus far discussed. "It's going to require an extremely strong hand and a wise head." He raised a big brown, long-fingered right hand, watching it close to a hard fist then open. "I may have to rely a bit on providence, though I'm not a religious man. But I'll take help where I can find it!"

"As we all must," de Vey agreed. "We've drafted a letter guaranteeing lands and percentages of any treasure you find to men in your expedition. Five hundred acres of land to each, in addition to whatever you and Cortez feel is an adequate share of the treasure. We'll leave the details to you, since all men do not perform equally well."

"I appreciate that, sir," Luis smiled, knowing such an incentive would go a long way in building loyalty in the men he'd soon command.

Carlos twirled his quill pen absently, then fixed Luis with a penetrating stare and issued an ominous warning, "Be very careful Captain

Escudero! Velasquez is an extremely dangerous man—to you and to me! And don't forget the blood-thirsty Aztecs who probably butchered Ortega and all his men. We don't want that to happen to you!"

⁂

Conversation continued for another hour and specific details were worked out. de Vey concluded the meeting with a repeat of Luis' orders. "Present yourself to Captain Cortez on or before March 1, 1518, in St. Jago, Cuba, for further instructions. Here's your orders." de Vey handed Luis a small packet sealed with wax, bearing the king's seal.

De Vey continued, "We've placed our fastest vessel, the Santa Marta, at your disposal. She's small and is commanded by our best navigator. She's ready to sail, so you won't have time for any unfinished business."

"I have none, sir."

De Vey and Carlos escorted Luis to the door. de Vey grabbed his hand. "By the Virgin, sir," he breathed with emotion, "I'd go with you if I could. God speed and good luck."

King Carlos managed to say, in heavily accented Castilian, "Via con dios, mi capitan." Then in a rare gesture, he pulled Luis into a Spanish embrazo embrace, cheek to cheek, and patted him on the back. As they looked into each other's eyes, Luis felt Spain's future had just been transferred to him!

⁂

Luis waved away the waiting carriage. He was simply too charged with energy and anxiety to sit in a conveyance, even though it was raining lightly. The empty carriage rattled away over the cobblestones.

He began walking toward the inn, walking faster and faster, his boot soles and heels rasping and clicking on the street. The tension built in him faster than he could walk it off, a kind of savage bright eagerness which held off around the dark edges of his subconscious, a throng of nameless and unadmitted fears, as a campfire in the wilderness holds off the wild things. He knew what those fears represented, but wouldn't let his consciousness use their names, which are disappointment and death, and worst of all, failure.

He shook his head as if to dispel the deep thoughts running through his mind. One thing at a time. And he knew his next stop in this strange mission was to get himself and his gear to the Santa Marta in Barcelona and make a quick passage to the new world!

5

Punta del Piedras, Cuba, December, 1517

Sergeant Martin Lopez, out of work and down on his luck, didn't cut a very impressive figure, sitting there drinking rum in the Shark's Lair, a waterfront cantina. A portly man in his forties, he looked more like a grocer than a cavalry sergeant. But men who knew Lopez weren't deceived by his appearance—no one pushed him around! He could be jovial and friendly—to a point. But if men under his command fouled up, he'd snap at them, "I was born a few minutes before the rest of you fools. So do what I say and stay alive—just remember that." Lopez had never met a man he couldn't whip in a fair fight—or in a knock down drag out fight for that matter.

Lieutenant Jorge Sandoval was looking for a good top sergeant. Everyone in Cuba told him Lopez was the man he needed. He found Lopez at the Shark's Lair, sitting by himself at a table, nursing a half empty bottle of rum.

Sandoval walked up. "Are you Sergeant Martin Lopez?"

"Who's asking?" Lopez responded casually and took a gulp of rum, while he studied Sandoval, dressed in civilian clothes.

"I'm Lieutenant Jorge Sandoval. I hear you've had some military experience making ordinary men into first rate fighting soldiers."

Lopez motioned Sandoval to a chair and took another pull on his rum. "I've taught a few men how to stay alive and how to kill, if that's what you mean."

"Would you be interested in doing it again?"

Lopez was cautious before answering, unsure what to make of Sandoval, who scared hell out of him, and probably everyone else. Lopez had served under many officers, but none the likes of Lieutenant Sandoval! Tall and slim, about thirty five, steel hard with a patch over his right eye socket, where his eye used to be, he commanded respect mingled with fear.

Looking into that stern unsmiling face, Lopez wondered why a man that old was still a lieutenant.

"Well? What about it, Sergeant? It doesn't look too exciting sitting here in a cantina. A little action might be just the thing you need." Sandoval smiled for the first time.

"I'm listening," Lopez said.

"I need an experienced top sergeant to help me recruit some men and whip them into shape for a very special, and highly secret military mission."

"Who's in command, sir?" Lopez wiped his face on his shirt sleeve.

"Does it matter?" Sandoval's one eye was flinty, glittering, unfathomable.

"To me it does!" Lopez answered firmly. "I won't serve under any chicken shit officer who's afraid to lead, especially if I'm going to be putting my life on the line. I've had some experience with officers like that a time or two. I don't want any more."

"A captain is coming from Spain to take command."

"Do you know him, sir?"

"No," Sandoval answered. "I've been told he's young and battle hardened, a leader of men."

Lopez's gaze came to rest on Sandoval and he looked steadily into his one good eye. "Where do you fit in, sir?"

"I'm the executive officer," Sandoval answered.

For a moment there hung over the empty cantina a silence in which the only sound was the soft strumming of a guitar somewhere in the background.

"From the scars you carry, sir, I assume you've had some combat experience?" Lopez asked. "You assume right, Sergeant. So how about it? Do you want in?"

Lopez replied with enough of a grunt to let Sandoval know he was interested. He took a pull on his rum and asked, "May I buy you a drink?"

"Thank you, no. I never touch the damned stuff."

"As you wish, sir. I'll have one for you." Lopez took another drink, and asked, "Where is your little expedition headed?"

"I don't know," Sandoval answered truthfully. "Probably west of here into Indian country."

`"That's all you can tell me? Just west?" Lopez questioned.

"You'll be told just like I will be when the time is right," Sandoval said sternly. "This much I can tell you now. It'll be dangerous as hell. We may not get back alive. It's a chance we'll have to take."

That didn't worry Lopez at all. He nodded and cocked a brow. "What about the pay, sir?"

"You'll receive a top sergeant's regular pay plus a hefty share of any treasure we happen to find."

That was it then. Lopez, half drunk, couldn't think of anything he'd forgotten to ask. This might turn into a pretty good deal—or it could get me killed. Ah, what the hell? We all have to die sometime.

Lopez grinned and stuck out his hand. "You just hired yourself a sergeant!"

🐾 🐾 🐾

Lopez had serious reservations while he interviewed Alfredo the blacksmith. The man's scarred, battered face gave him a vicious evil look! Reason told Lopez to reject the scoundrel, but there was something totally intriguing about him. He was without a doubt the toughest, wildest man either Lopez or Sandoval had ever seen. His huge bulging biceps and massive chest gave him the strength of several ordinary men. In a fight where odds against survival might be a hundred to one, this blacksmith would be an indispensable asset! His blacksmithing skills would be critical in caring for the horses and mules.

"Can you follow orders?" Lopez asked, and watched Alfredo's eyebrows contract.

"Hell yes—if your offer is half decent. I'll not sweat my balls off working my guts out on some stinking expedition when I don't even know where we're going or who we're fighting."

"We'll probably be fighting Indians," Lopez said, "and you'll be paid in gold when the job's done, if you live that long!"

"Indians? What the hell? I've never done that! I've fought nearly everything else, but I'd go through a whole horde of filthy, stupid low life Indians for a handful of gold!"

Against his better judgment Lopez growled, "Make your mark and report to me Monday morning." Alfredo made a cross on the paper and walked out without a backward glance.

Lieutenant Sandoval leaned back in his chair, amused and intrigued as he watched the savage animal of a man swagger out the door.

"Sergeant, I'll bet that stinking bastard hasn't had a bath for a least a year. Whew, the reek of the man! Tell him to get a bath, will you? The heathens will smell us before they see us if he doesn't!"

Lopez grinned. "Yes sir."

Sandoval left to attend to other duties and ordered Lopez to conduct the remaining interviews. Lopez drew another sheet of parchment paper onto the table, dipped quill into ink, and wrote the next candidates name, Corporal Eduardo Martinez, who Lopez knew personally. Garrulous and affable but an iron-hard ruffian, Martinez was afraid of no one. They'd fought side by side at the Battle of Cordoba Pass. Lopez knew men would follow Martinez, not out of respect, but because he'd make their lives a miserable hell if they didn't! Nearly as big as Alfredo the blacksmith, Martinez was a bit more flabby, but he could fight like a demon when necessary. With his two-handed broadsword he was a one-man army. He showed no mercy when it came to killing enemies!

"So you want to go adventuring, do you?" Lopez grinned. "Do you think you can handle another mission? Looks to me like you're getting a bit soft."

"I can put your big fat ass in the dirt any day of the week, Sergeant!" Martinez scowled. Name the time and place!"

Lopez smiled slightly. "You sign on with me Eduardo, you'll take my orders. Do you think you can do that?"

Martinez rubbed a hand abrasively over his huge ugly face. "It depends on the orders. Where the hell are we going anyway? Why all this secrecy bullshit?

"You'll be told when the time is right." Martinez took his time thinking it over.

"Well?" Lopez growled. "Do you want to sign on? I don't have all day." He held out the writing quill to the big corporal.

Martinez grinned, put his hands down as if lifting a gown off the floor, and curtsied gracefully. "Sergeant Lopez, sir, your most humble servant."

Lopez shook his head and laughed. "You big dumb asshole!" He grabbed Martinez's huge, hairy hand. "Welcome aboard, my friend. I'll sleep better knowing that broadsword of yours is backing me up wherever we're headed! On your way out send in those four young men standing outside."

The four Spanish soldiers who strutted into the room seemed mere boys, in their late teens or early twenties.

Jorge Ribera was distantly related to Lopez, a third cousin on his mother's side, if Lopez had calculated correctly. They knew each other, but Lopez had never formally met the others: Roberto Esperanza, Pedro Taragona and Leon San Estevan.

A feeling of fatherliness swept over Lopez as he studied his new charges. Raising his cup to his lips, Lopez took a long draught of fiery Cuban rum. "So you want to enlist in our little expedition? Well, let's start you lads off on the right foot. There'll be no more bloody rides like that last escapade." Lopez was referring to a controversial battle against the Lombards a few months ago, which caused Captain Sandoval to be busted to lieutenant.

"Kinsman," said Ribera seriously, "We were in a war. We only followed our orders. We parleyed with the Lombards until we were blue in the face. Tell him, Esperanza, about those backstabbing Lombard sonsabitches. You got there before any of the rest of us. You were the scout."

Esperanza nodded. "Jorge speaks the truth, Sergeant. The Duke of Lombardy offered Captain Sandoval a truce and said he would fight no more. That lying bastard of a duke guaranteed us protection under his banner. Captain Sandoval believed him. We hadn't gone a league before we ran into the Lombards' cunningly planned ambush. Captain Sandoval's younger brother was the first one killed—by a bolt from a Lombard crossbow."

Lopez stared doubtfully at Esperanza. Lopez had heard conflicting reports about Sandoval's reprisal against the Lombards for the ambush and for the murder of his brother. The depth of the depravities committed on the Lombards by Sandoval and his men shocked the entire Spanish court.

"I see you don't believe me, Sergeant," Esperanza said. "But him it was, Captain Sandoval himself, I swear to God, who commanded us to neither give nor ask for quarter."

"Really?" scoffed Lopez, shaking his head. "Why man, that whole Lombard valley lies more than half depopulated. Whole villages were burned to the ground. There were no women who were not well- raped widows, damned few trees that didn't dangle with the rotting carcasses of Lombard men. Seems like senseless savagery to me."

Esperanza shook his head and smiled humorlessly. "You weren't there, Sergeant. We could have done without the killing and butchery. But you didn't see what they did to our men caught in the Lombard's cunning ambush. Me and Ribera here, along with Taragona and San

Estevan, found our comrades' dead bodies naked and horribly mutilated. The Lombards took the head of Captain Sandoval's brother. When the captain saw his brother's decapitated body he lost his mind for a time and turned into a raving madman."

Lopez didn't speak or interrupt Esperanza until he was finished, and sat gazing at him through the hazy light from the window.

"The way I heard it," Lopez said, "a military court martial found Captain Sandoval and his men guilty of an atrocity. Those who didn't resign voluntarily were reduced in rank and shipped to the new world. That right?"

Esperanza proudly nodded affirmatively. "That's right, Sergeant. None of us resigned. We didn't do anything wrong. But they shipped our asses to Cuba anyway."

"Lieutenant Sandoval too?" Lopez asked.

"Him too," Esperanza said. "He's a soldier like us. They busted him in rank, but he's still our captain!"

"Well, boys, that's all in the past," Lopez said. "Lieutenant Sandoval wants me to sign you on, if you're not afraid of a little danger."

"Danger doesn't worry us, Sergeant," said Roberto Esperanza, who was spokesman for the group. Smoothing back a lock of his raven-wing hair with a quick gesture, the twenty year old scout said, "We want to know about the expedition. Where is it going? Will there be gold?"

"Whoa." Lopez held up a hand. "Slow down, Esperanza. "I'm not at liberty to tell you anything about the expedition, except we'll work your asses off. Rations may be short, the hours long. And it'll be dangerous as hell. Discipline will be severe I assure you. Chances of survival are not good. But lads, if we live through this adventure there'll be ample rewards."

Lopez consciously set his face in a smile so the four young men might not think him worried or displeased. He was definitely not displeased. These lads came recommended by Lieutenant Sandoval himself. They were young, yes, but each a professional soldier, with a valuable fighting skill.

Roberto Esperanza grinned and said, "Shit, Sergeant, sign us up. We're ready to go."

"You're sure?" Lopez cocked a brow. "You'd sign up with no more information than I've given you?"

"Why hell yes!" Esperanza said. "What makes this any different from other campaigns we've signed on for? We've been flogged, kicked, maimed, abused and fed swill or nothing at all, under those high and noble officers of the Spanish army."

"And has that taught you anything?" Lopez shifted his gaze from face to face, measuring each of them, sizing them up.

"You're damn right it has!" Esperanza answered forcefully. "I'm the best scout in the Spanish Army. Your kinsman, Ribera, there, is the deadliest ax man in the Caribbean. He can hurl a knife or an ax with pinpoint accuracy—and can split a man from thigh to brisket before he can blink his eyes."

Lopez stared at Ribera with new respect

Esperanza continued. "Taragona's the best crossbowman in the army; and San Estevan can knock a bird out of a tree at thirty yards with his arquebus."

"No!" Lopez hissed in total astonishment. "That cannot be. No man can do that with one of those clumsy weapons. It takes at least two good men to hold one up to fire it."

Esperanza grinned. "Not San Estevan's arquebus, Sergeant. It's quite different from the arquebus you're familiar with."

"How so?" Lopez asked with interest.

"Hey Roberto," San Estevan interrupted. "Am I allowed to speak to the sergeant?"

"Be my guest," Esperanza grinned.

San Estevan said, "My father's a gunsmith, and a damn good one too. But everyone laughs at him because of his novel ideas about firearms."

"Like what?" Lopez leaned forward with anticipation.

"He's developed a new design quite different from the standard arquebus, which is long and very heavy, with a block of wood for a stock. The shooter must have someone hold the barrel up or place it on a support. He must then pull the block of wood against his chest, point the barrel in the direction of the target and shoot. The shooter is mighty damned lucky to hit anything unless it's right on top of him."

"I certainly agree with that," Lopez said. "That's why I've always put my trust in the sword and the crossbow."

"Most military men do, Sergeant," San Estevan said. "But my father wondered why the arquebus has to be so big and heavy. Why couldn't it have a shorter barrel and a lighter wooden stock which would fit against a man's shoulder instead of against his chest? That way the shooter could hold the weapon by himself, pressed it tight against his shoulder, aim straight along the barrel with his eye, and hit the target dead center."

"Oh, come now, Esperanza! You're pulling my leg!" Lopez scoffed. "It would never work!"

Esperanza, Ribera and Taragona laughed. They'd seen San Estevan shoot his arquebus many times; and he never missed the target.

"Oh but it does work, Sergeant!" San Estevan countered. "My arquebus has an engraved stock and is much smaller than a regular arquebus. My father made it special just for me. He even fitted it to my shoulder."

"It really works?" Lopez was skeptical. "Is it a matchlock?"

"I'm afraid so. My father hasn't yet figured out a better way to put fire in the priming pan than the one being used—a piece of rope burning at both ends, so if one end goes out the other end can be used. It makes the gun useless when it rains. My father keeps coming up with ideas for a better firing mechanism, but nothing's worked so far."

"Has he sold any of the new guns?" Lopez asked with interest.

Esperanza shook his head. "Only ten. When my friends saw mine they paid my father to make one for them. Those ten men are coming in to sign up for this expedition."

"Hm," said Lopez softly, giving the matter some thought. "Such a weapon could have potential for the Spanish Army as well as the armies of Europe, if it's as good as you say it is."

"My father certainly hopes so! But it probably won't be in his life-time. Change comes slowly. European armies are too set in their ways. Father does a few custom jobs, now and then, and earns enough to put food on the table."

Lopez nodded thoughtfully. "Having eleven of the new arque-buses could give us a decided advantage against any enemy we come up against." He grabbed a jug of rum. "Get yourselves a cup over there boys." He pointed to a table.

He poured a liberal measure into each cup, and a larger amount into his own! "Bottoms up!" shouted Lopez. They banged cups together and gulped the rum.

Lopez would have preferred older, more experienced soldiers; but these young men were fearless and tough, with battle experience under their belts. They'd do!

"You're all hired. Here's a few reales. Buy yourselves another drink at the cantina, then go straight to camp. But you'd better be sober when you get there or Lieutenant Sandoval will have your asses!"

Roberto Esperanza laughed. "We know all about that, Sergeant. The captain hates alcohol like poison!

6

St. Jago, Cuba, February, 1518

Cuba's Governor, Don Diego Velasquez, stared from his office window at St. Jago's peaceful bay, where several ships lay at anchor, their naked masts swaying gently with the rolling tide. Where the hell is Ortega? Velasquez wondered. Not one damn word from him since he sailed for the Aztec empire over two years ago! Velasquez had stared out that window almost every day since Ortega sailed, hoping his ship might soon slip into port.

Captain Pedro Armand sat silently in a large chair, sipping a glass of sherry, waiting patiently to find out why Velasquez summoned him to the governor's mansion. In preparation for the meeting Armand did some cursory research on the governor so he'd be prepared for any eventuality or opportunity.

What Armand discovered about Velasquez surprised him.

Although fifty years old, Velasquez had been a good fighter in his day, and still had lots of fight left in him. He founded Cuba's cities and was a man of vision. Now comfortable in his office, he had until recently been content to rest on past triumphs. But no longer. That hated Flemish boy king Carlos, who recently ascended the throne in Madrid, was planning to replace Velasquez with a Fleming, or so local rumors had it.

Big, handsome and jovial, Velasquez enjoyed being governor and reveled in the popularity men of his stamp could command at the center of a community that vied in chivalry, luxury and dissipation with the Castilian court in Madrid. He was older, but no less visionary than before. Now, however, he could pay other men to do the adventuring. He wasn't about to take a backseat to some boy aristocrat in Madrid who didn't even speak Spanish!

Velasquez turned abruptly and said, "Captain Armand, my agent tells me you were kicked out of the army in Spain and made your way to Cuba. May I ask how that came about?"

"Is it important, sir?"

"It is to me," Velasquez answered sharply.

"I took some money from our regimental fund. I figured I earned it, putting my life on the line time after time and not getting paid."

"In other words you stole it?"

"They owed it to me," Armand answered firmly.

"And now you're an out-of-work soldier seeking a new opportunity?" A crafty gleam came into Velasquez's eyes.

"Yes sir, I am."

"What can you do?"

"Anything. I had two hundred men in my last command and we served for ten years together."

"Cavalry or infantry?"

"Both. We were never beaten in battle, if that's what you're getting at."

"So I've been told." Velasquez didn't press it further. "That's why you're here today. I need a strong, reliable commander like you to lead an expedition I'm forming. If you're successful you'll end up a very wealthy man. If you fail you'll wind up dead."

Armand flicked a smile at Velasquez. "I'd prefer ending up wealthy, if you don't mind "

"We'll see about that," the governor responded.

Armand's expression changed. "Maybe you better spell out exactly what you want me to do."

"I want you to take an expedition to Mexico, right into the heart of the Aztec empire. Find out if there is gold to be had, and if so bring samples back to me."

Armand chuckled. "Is that all? That's a mighty tall order considering no white man has ever gone there and come back alive."

"It'll be dangerous as hell, there's no getting around that." Velasquez's voice remained level, under full control. "But people I talked to said you weren't afraid of a little danger!"

Suddenly the room seemed to get larger and quieter, and Armand felt uneasy. "I've heard rumors you already sent one expedition on that errand. What happened to it?"

Velasquez answered reluctantly, "I dispatched Captain Hector

Ortega to Mexico over two years ago. I figured he was a man I could trust, convinced he'd bring back some gold or at least some useful information about the Aztecs. That was a mistake! Ortega disappeared to only God knows where."

"You've had no word from him at all?" Armand asked.

"Not one damned word," Velasquez growled. "He was such a hot-headed impetuous bastard he probably got himself and all of his men killed."

Armand nodded thoughtfully. "Wouldn't it save a lot of time and aggravation if I went out and looked for him, rather than launch a new expedition?"

"Good hell no! I've written him off as lost. There's no time to reminisce about that now."

Sensing he'd made Velasquez angry, Armand asked quietly, "What makes you think there's gold in Mexico?"

"My slave Kano, who's been in my household for many years, told me the Aztecs have gold. He speaks their language. From communicating with Aztec traders who come to these islands he learned there's so much gold in Mexico it would take a huge fleet of ships to haul it all back to Cuba."

"Humpf," Armand snorted in disbelief. "I've been in this part of the world for a year now and I've not seen enough gold to fill a tooth, except that your Indian workers take from those hills." He pointed north to the Sierra Alto Range jutting up from the sea.

Velasquez's lower jaw worked from side to side and his dark eyes had a hard glitter as he searched Armand's face to determine if any insult was intended. Everyone in Cuba knew the governor reaped rich profits from his mines. When the mines on Santo Domingo dried up in 1511, Velasquez led an armed expedition to Cuba and conquered the entire island, though the natives fought fiercely against the Spanish invaders. Velasquez captured their chief; and after torturing him for several days forced him to give up his heathen ways, as well as his resistance. Even so, Velasquez burned him at the stake as an example of what would happen to anyone who resisted the Spaniards. The Indians quickly submitted and worked as slaves until they died in Velasquez's hot humid mines. Half of Cuba's Indian population had already perished in those dark, dangerous tunnels.

Velasquez shrugged, convinced Armand was stating a plain fact and nothing more. No insult was intended.

He stared at Armand. "I'm convinced the Aztecs have gold and I plan to get it before King Carlos does."

Armand's eyes went wide. "Won't the king have some objection to such a plan?"

"To hell with the king," Velasquez bellowed. "He won't dare meddle in Caribbean affairs at the moment. Every decent Spaniard hates him. The smell of revolt is in the air. Believe me, Armand, if Carlos makes one false move the throne will collapse and bury him. Now's the very time to launch our expedition. By the time you get back from Mexico, Carlos will be banished from Spain and back in Flanders licking his wounds."

Armand's face lighted with a sardonic smile. "I believe you're actually serious. Where will you get your authority to launch this expedition you're talking about?"

Velasquez smiled at him, but it was a strange smile, a smile that made Armand uneasy. "From the Hieronymite Commission." Velasquez's words were quiet, his tone pleasant. "I'm related to Juan Rodriguez de Fonseca by marriage. He's the powerful Bishop of Burgos, who rules the Council of the West Indies through Hieronymite Commission. He's given me all the authority I need."

Armand wasn't totally convinced. He studied his hands, turning them over. "I don't know," Armand's voice trailed off. "going up against a king..."

"I trust you, Captain," Velasquez said soothingly. "We can talk in confidence. Carlos is a boy and a Fleming at that. It won't be easy to unseat him because he has the full support of the Spanish army, and can bring in his Flemish knights at a moment's notice if he needs them. We will have to be careful. But you needn't worry about such matters. Leave the politics to me. What I need to know is, will you command my expedition and swear complete loyalty to me?"

Armand stroked his chin and stared at Velasquez. "Where do I get the men for this expedition?"

"You can select some of my garrison soldiers."

"Have they had any combat experience?"

"Not really," Velasquez answered, but I'm sure they're up to the task."

"What about supplies?"

"I'll give you two ships, horses, mules, munitions and food."

Armand pursed his lips thinking it over. His forehead creased. "I could use a drink."

"What can I get for you?"

"Brandy would do."

Velasquez poured Armand a drink and handed it to him. Armand took it all down in one gulp. "Well?" Velasquez said.

Armand came to the edge of his chair. His voice was tentative when he asked, "What's in it for me, governor?"

"You want to know what's in it for you? I'll tell you. One third of the treasures of the Aztec empire—if it's there. You think about that for a moment. Are you willing to take the gamble?"

Armand drew in a sharp breath. "A third? Governor, I'd climb down to the pit of hell and kick the devil's ass for that much gold." Armand grinned. "From what you've told me, the Aztec empire is just like a big-uddered cow waiting to be milked. Let's make sure were holding the bucket. I'll consider it an honor to command your expedition, sir."

Velasquez's worry lines softened and he smiled. "That's the spirit! Now this is how I see it. When you return from Mexico with Aztec gold we'll organize an expedition of conquest. I'll finance it as a military stock company made up of influential men here in the islands, as well as the banking cartels in Barcelona and Madrid. The gold samples you bring back will be the collateral I need. Each member of the stock company will profit according to his investment. I do believe we can both become very wealthy men—but we must play our cards wisely. I'll have the Hieronymite Commission notify Carlos if and when you find any treasure, so everything is on the up and up. Until then there's no need to advertise our activities. We'll keep this venture to ourselves. The Hieronymite Commission is very adept at politics and will guarantee that the crown receives a percentage of the treasure."

"What kind of percentage?" Armand asked with evident interest.

"A small percentage to be sure," Velasquez smiled deviously. "If we take the risks and fund the expedition it wouldn't be right for the crown to receive equal shares, don't you agree?"

Armand rubbed his chin thoughtfully. "Are you suggesting we... ah... control the accounting of the treasure?"

"That's exactly what I'm suggesting!" Velasquez paced back and forth, his mind racing with the possibilities of his grandiose plan. He could finally put that swaggering whoreson of a Cortez in his place! Ever since Cortez returned from Spain after meeting with King Carlos, he acted like God Almighty: He blazed with energy and spoke fearlessly, even curtly with Velasquez, as if the governor was no more than some tiresome port official who had to be humored until Cortez could get his own expedition underway. Velasquez's friends warned him time and time again, "You mess with Cortez and he'll run his sword through your liver!"

Velasquez poured himself and Armand a drink, then said, "Through my contacts in Madrid I've learned King Carlos has authorized Hernando Cortez to organize a secret exploratory expedition. Even as we speak Cortez's underling, Captain Luis Escudero, is on a fast ship from Spain due here in a few days, to take command of that expedition."

Armand whistled under his breath. "I know Escudero personally!"

"Tell me about him," Velasquez said.

"He's one hell of a soldier—one of the most admired soldiers in the Spanish army."

"Where do you know him from?"

"We were in recruit training together some years back in Barcelona."

Velasquez pursed his lips."What are the chances we could twist his arm to switch his loyalty to our cause, maybe offer him..."

"Not a chance," Armand interrupted. "He's a king's man through and through. No amount of gold would ever entice him to turn traitor."

"Honest, eh?"

"Too damned honest," Armand agreed. "That's why he's risen through the ranks so rapidly."

Velasquez nodded. "Ah well, we can deal with him later. You needn't worry. You'll have more men, more horses and guns."

Armand chewed at his upper lip. "I don't know how to say this without sounding impertinent, sir, but why don't you do away with Escudero right here in Cuba, and destroy his expedition? It seems the simplest way to solve the entire problem and eliminate the competition."

Velasquez exploded. "Because Hernando Cortez is one clever bastard, that's why! He and King Carlos are in bed together and have it all plotted out to steal all the Aztec gold in Mexico. I can't risk any kind of confrontation here in Cuba with Cortez, Escudero or anyone working for them. King Carlos would have my head. No, my friend, you must destroy Escudero somewhere in Mexico and make it look like the work of Aztecs."

Velasquez watched Armand's eyebrows contract. "You want me to kill Escudero?" Velasquez's cold stare flicked across Armand. "Him and all his men. Can you handle that?"

"Yes sir, if that's part of my assignment."

"Good," smiled Velasquez. "We understand each other."

"Do you have any other orders for me, Governor?"

"Get yourself to Punta del Piedras as soon as possible. Find out everything you can about Escudero's expedition. Disguise yourself and avoid even the appearance of inquisitiveness. If you're told things well and good. If you are shown things, better still. Find out what Escudero is doing, how soon he plans to sail and report back to me as quickly as possible. Any questions?"

"Yes sir. "What about your slave Kano? I'd like to meet him. Perhaps he could accompany me as my interpreter."

"I'm afraid not." Velasquez's expression changed, becoming serious. "He went with Hector Ortega's expedition which never made it back to Cuba, so I assume Kano is dead. He would have been a Godsend to you. You'll have to communicate with the Aztecs through sign language and do the best you can."

Armand's face mirrored disappointed. "There's no one else in these islands here who speaks the Aztec tongue?"

"No," Velasquez answered. "Kano told me it's a very complicated language, very difficult to learn."

"All right," Armand said, "I'll deal with that when the time comes. I'll leave for Punta del Piedras first thing in the morning and see what Escudero is up to. As soon as I have some information, I'll bring it to you."

"You do that," Velasquez said, then hissed a deadly warning. "Don't cross me, Captain, or you will regret it."

"Why, sir, such a thought never entered my mind," Armand responded.

"Keep it that way." At this Velasquez sat back in his chair and closed his eyes and Armand left the room quickly.

✿ ✿ ✿

Can he do the job? Velasquez wondered. He's intelligent and has good instincts to be sure, but he seems a bit neurotic. Armand's sneering speech inflections hinted of some immaturity. Yet Armand was all Velasquez had. He'd have to do. Time was too critical to find a replacement.

7

St. Jago, Cuba, March, 1518

Luis Escudero stood alone at the Santa Marta's starboard rail as the ship glided slowly around the harbor's rocky point, and he got his first glimpse of the new world—a green jungle paradise so totally different from Spain's barren Aragon hills where he'd been born and raised.

Sailors aloft reefed the sails as large gannets and smaller terns skimmed across the blue waters and thousands of seagulls filled the air with raucous, screeching cries. St. Jago possessed a quaint charm, a relaxed, peaceful feeling. Cuba was exactly as Luis dreamed it would be—so enchanting it seemed impossible this island could have risen from the sea by chance, wild and impetuous along its shores, yet serene in its interior.

The captain put the ship on its final tack as hands went to their stations. Two small sails flapping in the breeze were the only sounds as the ship bumped alongside the dock.

Over a month at sea, out of the sight of land, tossed about on the stormy Atlantic, Luis was happy to walk down the gangplank into a new world and a new adventure.

Standing on the pier waiting to greet him was Captain Hernando Cortez. "Captain Luis Escudero?" he asked.

"Yes sir."

"I'm Captain Cortez. Welcome to Cuba," he said enthusiastically and grabbed Luis' hand. "I didn't think your damn ship would ever get here."

"Me either," Luis grinned.

"Are you hungry?"

"Yes sir."

"Come along. There's a good cantina, which I happen to own, just a short ways." As they walked along together Luis was surprised at the attention they created, himself especially. Dressed in civilian clothing he looked like an affluent banker. News of his arrival had preceded him. Heads turned and stared at him. Women in open doorways and in gardens watched him. Men nodded and waved. Indians and black slaves stopped and watched him go by.

Rumor had it this tall handsome soldier was Captain Cortez's pick to lead a secret expedition into the heart of the Aztec empire. But nothing that happened in Cuba could be kept secret.

Long before Luis arrived, out of work soldiers toiling at routine labor flocked to Cortez's banner—tough, illiterate mercenaries from various backgrounds. Ten came from Velasquez's prisons, serving sentences ranging from highway robbery to rape and murder. Cortez, through skillful negotiation, diplomacy and bribery, obtained their releases. No one asked any questions. If Cortez was involved that's all they needed to know.

At the cantina Cortez ushered Luis to a table and ordered food and wine. The wine was from Spain and Luis was grateful for it, saying, "Oh, this tastes good. After being at sea so long it's good to be ashore at last, though I feel like the ground is rolling beneath my feet. I'm glad I'm a soldier and not a sailor."

"Me too," Cortez agreed with a smile. The bartender brought food and Luis ate. He liked Cortez already. The thirty-four-year old warrior dressed in simple garb of a working soldier. He was immaculate. No speck of mud soiled his boots. The half unlaced jerkin of white buckskin gleamed. His ruff was crisp and newly pressed.

His countenance was open and manly, and his hair, the color of chestnuts, was curled close to his head; and he was strong and sinewy. A lisp in his voice caused Luis to think Cortez wouldn't be a good public speaker. He was energetic in his movements, open and honest, a proud man who someday planned to outshine Columbus in Spain's fascinating history.

Cortez ordered rum, took a quick drink then said, "May I see your orders?"

Luis reached inside his jacket and handed him the sealed document which Cortez deftly sliced open with his dagger and glanced at it.

"Ah, good," Cortez nodded. "Our expedition is confirmed by the king. I assume he and de Vey briefed you before you left Madrid?"

"They did, sir."

"Well then, let me bring you up to date what's been happening in this part of the world. "I've secured some good men for your expedition. They're a lusty, whoring lot, fornicators all, with a couple of exceptions. But in a fight they're the kind of men you want beside you. Lieutenant Sandoval has them whipped into shape physically, but they're a damned sloppy bunch. His biggest challenge is getting them to follow orders and work together as a team. You two will have correct that!"

"Who is Sandoval?" Luis asked.

"Lieutenant Jorge Sandoval. Your second in command. A good man, Jorge, although he does have his shortcomings. Nothing for you to worry about though. You'll find his skills most valuable. He's the best cartographer, map maker, in this part of the world. He has an uncanny flair for recording historical events. Makes 'em come alive. He's studied everything that's ever been written about the Americas, which is scant little. I might warn you, however, he can be an insubordinate bastard on occasion. If he gets angry his lips seal as tight as a virgin's ass, and you can get nothing from him. A mighty strange man, Jorge! I've never seen the man drunk, and he leaves women strictly alone. Something to do with a promise he made to his wife."

Cortez took a pull on his rum. "Men who don't drink and fornicate make me nervous! Too deep and moody, most of 'em. I told Jorge once he should have been a priest. But enough of Sandoval. He's your problem now."

Anxiously, Luis asked, "How soon before I can get the expedition under way?"

"That's up to you and Sandoval," Cortez responded, "but it better be damned soon. One of my ships, the Catalan, is being prepared as we speak."

"When can I meet the African, Kano?" Luis asked.

"Later today when you get to Punta del Piedras. He will be the most important man in your expedition, remember that. Without him you wouldn't stand a chance among the Aztecs. Not only does Kano speak the Aztec tongue, he's familiar with Mexico. I'm sorry I can't go along and introduce the two of you."

That took Luis completely by surprise. "But sir..."

"I know! I know!" Cortez held up a hand. "Things are moving much too fast. Too many loose ends. You'll just have to live with that, Luis. I'm leaving for Santo Domingo within the hour. Just yesterday I learned of a plot to assassinate me, and I've got to find out who's behind it."

Luis' eyes went wide. "Who would dare plot against your life, sir?"

Cortez laughed. "The list gets longer every day! But I have no doubts it's Governor Velasquez. Did King Carlos tell you about him?"

"He told me the governor is a very dangerous man and to be very careful."

"He is that! But more than dangerous, he's treacherous! He has spies everywhere. He knows about your expedition and he'll try to stop you, but how I haven't the foggiest notion." Cortez finished off the rest of his rum, stood and pushed his chair back and pulled on his gloves. "Well, I must be off, Luis. There's just one cautionary thought I want to leave with you, so please, remember it. Many expeditions have come to grief because of divided objectives, when leaders and those they lead cannot agree on whether they are pursuing loot or some higher goal. Remember, your main objective is exploring and mapping. You must impress that upon your men, do you understand?"

"I understand perfectly, sir."

"Good. Then get back here alive—and bring me a detailed map of the Aztec empire. If you find any gold, silver or precious stones bring samples back with you. It"ll help me secure funding for my expedition of conquest."

Luis grinned. "I'd like to get back alive!"

"We understand each other then." Cortez paused for a moment as he adjusted his cap. "I won't beat around the bush, Luis. Where you're going, no white man has ever gone before. Kano will explain in vivid detail what you'll be up against. So I warn you now, keep your wits about you! Death will stalk you at every turn. Even so, you're on your way to an audacious adventure which will try your every resource. I pray God to be with you. However much you trust in yourself, never be too proud to get down on your knees to Him."

"I'll do that, sir."

"You'll succeed, Luis. I know you will. God has ordained it!"

"I have no doubts about that whatsoever!" Luis agreed.

"Oh, I almost forgot," Cortez said. "Your expedition scout, Roberto Esperanza, is waiting outside to show you the way to camp at Punta del Piedras. I found a good horse for you to ride."

Cortez grinned at Luis with tight bitten lips, wishing he were in Luis' place. But he knew he must remain behind and fight political battles until Luis returned from Mexico with samples of gold. He gripped Luis' broad shoulders with both hands and made as if to shake him.

"You're as solid as oak, Luis, my friend. I'm so pleased with you. May God go with you and protect you." Then as if embarrassed by this bit of emotion, Captain Hernando Cortez turned and walked swiftly out of the cantina.

Outside, Luis found a magnificent stallion tied to the hitching rail. The horse tossed his head and neighed when he saw Luis.

"Diablo likes you already, Captain!" said a young man, mounted on a horse next to the stallion. "I'm Scout Roberto Esperanza here to escort you to Punta del Piedras."

Sliding from the saddle, Esperanza walked over to Luis, who stretched out his hand. "I'm happy to meet you, Esperanza," Luis said, and grabbed his hand. "Who owns this beautiful animal?"

"You do, sir. "His name is Diablo. He's a gift from Captain Cortez. He told me you'll need a good horse where you are going."

"He gave it to me?" Luis asked incredulously.

Esperanza's head went back and he laughed outright, saying, "Captain Cortez is like that, sir. He gives gifts to friends, even to people he doesn't know sometimes. The other day he was riding into town and saw a little girl standing by the roadside staring at his huge warhorse. She seemed frightened but fascinated too, by such a huge beast. The captain was busy talking with his mounted lieutenants, but he noticed the little girl's awed interest. You know what he did?"

"No," Luis said.

"He dismounted and picked the little girl up in his arms. He said to her, 'you like my horse, eh, Nina? Well then, how about a ride?' He lifted the girl up and put her in the saddle. Then he walked along, leading his horse by the reins, while his mounted lieutenants rode alongside discussing business."

"He must be a kind man, then," Luis said.

Again Esperanza's head went back and he laughed. "Sometimes, sir! But don't get on the wrong side of him. Be loyal to Captain Cortez and he'll be loyal to you. That's the kind of man he is."

Luis rode at an easy canter along the coach road north from St. Jago toward Punta del Piedras. He exchanged friendly waves with farmers whom he passed, working in their fields of sugar cane. None would have guessed Roberto Esperanza following behind was hard pressed to maintain the pace.

Luis slowed Diablo while Esperanza pulled alongside. Indistinguishable in appearance from an ordinary field hand, and dressed in civilian clothes, he seemed no more than a boy. But he was very muscular and smiled easily. Looking at the sword hanging from his side Luis had little doubt Esperanza knew how to use it.

Suddenly Luis pulled Diablo to a stop and glanced around apprehensively, back down the road, then from side to side and into the jungle, but saw nothing unusual.

"Esperanza, are we being followed?"

"Yes sir," Esperanza grinned. "But it's nothing for you to worry about. A couple of Don Diego's men have been trailing us, keeping out of sight."

"Don Diego?" Luis questioned.

"Governor Don Diego Velasquez," Esperanza answered. "That old bastard, begging the captain's pardon, keeps an eye on every new comer to the island."

"Do you know him?"

"Not personally, sir. Never cared to either. He hates Captain Cortez, and any enemy of the captain's is no friend of mine."

"Sounds like a personal feud between Cortez and Velasquez," Luis said. "Why are they enemies?"

"Well sir," Esperanza said, "there are several reasons. To start with, Captain Cortez stole one of Velasquez's women, the one the governor planned to marry. But there are other things too. Captain Cortez always has the upper hand, no matter what the circumstances are here in Cuba. Like the town we're riding to. Punta del Piedras is Cortez's town. It rankles the living hell out of Velasquez that he doesn't control every town on the island. He's even tried to take our town by force. But it'll take more than his stupid, ill trained garrison soldiers to take our town!"

Luis stared at Esperanza. "How can they both live on the island here without killing each other?"

Esperanza smiled. "It's not very easy for either one of them. It's kind of humorous to see them together in the same room. You know they hate each others' guts, yet there's nothing either of them can do about it. Velasquez, being governor, is Cortez's superior. So they are forced to act like gentlemen in public. A very interesting situation, huh?"

"Indeed!" Luis replied.

The young scout wiped sweat for his forehead. "Tell me Captain, is this your first visit to the new world?"

"It is, and it's more beautiful than I ever imagined."

"You'll find many beautiful things here," Esperanza said, "but it's a hard, dangerous land, make no mistake, sir!" There was nothing ominous in Esperanza's voice. He was calmly stating a fact.

🐾 🐾 🐾

The afternoon sun descended lower in the western sky as the two soldiers galloped on toward Punta del Piedras, trailing swirls of dust behind them.

Within the hour their horses topped the last hill to a flat plateau where the small village of Punta del Piedras overlooked a circular cove sheltering the bay and its white sandy beaches. A battered, but seaworthy caravel was tied to the wharf, alongside a long wooden warehouse. Sailors scurried about shoving cargo from the warehouse to ship's side, where crewmen hoisted it aboard.

"Is that ship the Catalan?" Luis asked

"Yes sir, Captain. She's almost ready for sea."

8

Luis and Roberto Esperanza galloped into Punta del Piedras, shaded with delicious groves of fruit trees, the entire area elevated about five hundred feet above the sea. The bold, rock-bound coast, with the surf beating high against its lofty cliffs, was broken here and there into deep inlets. The white ensign of Spain, whipping in the breeze atop a tall flag pole, sent a chill through Luis. Although not a religious man, he couldn't shake off the feeling God had predestined him to be in this exact place at this precise moment in time.

"Roberto, I'm going to the Catalan. Meet me there in a couple of hours and we'll ride on to camp. Find yourself a tavern and have a drink and something to eat." He handed the scout some coins.

Luis rode down the road to the pier, dismounted and tied Diablo to a post. He studied the Catalan for a few moments. She looked seaworthy, almost identical to Columbus' caravels the Nina and Pinta.

She was equipped with a combination of square sails and lateen sails, with triangular for-and-aft sails set on a long, sloping yardarm.

Luis knew the lateen sail enabled a ship to take advantage of a wind from the side of the vessel. She had three masts, a foremast, mainmast and mizzenmast, and a high poop deck at the rear of the vessel.

Sailors lined the rail and stared at the stranger taking measure of their vessel. Luis climbed the gangplank to the deck.

"Permission to come aboard?" he asked a burly sailor. "Are you Captain Escudero?"

"I am."

"I'm Juan Narvaez, ship's mate. Please follow me, Captain Alvarez is expecting you." Luis followed him to Alvarez's cabin, where Narvaez introduced them.

"Captain Escudero, how wonderful to meet you!" Alvarez grabbed Luis in a Spanish embrazo embrace, cheek to cheek. "Have a seat and make yourself at home! Juan, pour us a drink, then fetch Kano."

Alvarez was about fifty, bearded, a bit rotund. The intelligent eyes in a tanned brown face, his energetic cheerfulness and hospitable warmth immediately put Luis at ease. The ship's cabin was very warm, the air still like a vacuum. It was dry and a bit hard to breathe, as if all the moisture had evaporated in the heat of the day.

Narvaez poured rum, then went to find Kano. Luis coughed slightly as the fiery Cuban liquor burned his throat and made his eyes water.

Alvarez laughed and put a hand on Luis' arm. "Damn stuff takes some getting used to, my friend, but it washes down the dust."

"I assume Captain Cortez told you why I'm here?"

"He explained your mission to me and Narvaez and Kano, but no one else." Alvarez talked in a low voice, so as not to be overheard by curious crewmen. "Kano has agreed to be your interpreter." Luis nodded approval.

"That'll give us a slight edge. It looks like you've got the Catalan almost ready for sea."

"Aye, Captain, she's in top notch shape. But she'll be mighty crowded with the four horses and three mules Cortez ordered aboard. We've built special stalls for them. That means we'll have to put the men and much of the cargo on deck." He swirled the amber colored rum in his glass.

"How long will it take to get to Mexico?" Luis asked.

"I estimate we can land you near Papantla in eight to ten days, give or take a day or two."

"Excellent!" Luis responded. "May I take a look at the things Kano had with him when you picked him up?"

"Certainly." Alvarez pulled the strange obsidian knife from a drawer and handed it to Luis.

He grasped the weapon's handle and ran his forefinger along its sharp, serrated stone edge. "Almost as sharp as steel. I've never seen stone like this before."

"Nor I," Alvarez replied and handed Luis Ortega's parchment map.

Luis studied the water stained map, trying to decipher some meaning from the smeared, blurry lines.

Narvaez found Kano leaning against the ship's rail idly watching dozens of circling gulls. His touch on Kano's shoulder brought the black giant wheeling around in a fluid movement, pulling his knife, ready to strike, before sight of Narvaez halted him in mid reflex.

Narvaez stared at him in wide eyed surprise and threw up his hands. "I'm sorry Kano, I thought you heard me coming."

Kano said nothing and sheathed his blade. Then his face softened. "Next time make a little noise. My mind was on other things."

"One day that knife of yours is going to get you into big trouble!"

"Or out of it!" Kano replied.

"Captain Escudero just arrived. Captain Alvarez wants you to meet him!"

Kano was the tallest man Luis had ever seen! He lowered his head and bent his neck to clear the overhead beams. He was blacker than midnight, wearing loose fitting white canvas trousers which hit him at mid calf, and a pullover shirt, too small, exposing his bare stomach.

"You wish to see me, Captain?" Kano asked in a deep bass voice, without bowing.

Luis' first thought was, what an arrogant man! Well, not arrogant perhaps—but equal. But that's nonsense. Blacks possess neither arrogance nor equality! All Spaniards knew blacks were far too lazy and irresponsible to take pride in themselves. The only things blacks could be relied upon to do with any consistency were eating and mating. Still, there was something remarkable about this man which didn't fit the stereotype Luis had been taught from childhood, that blacks were not human beings, but a lower order of primate. Yet here stood a perfectly formed man, handsome in his own fashion, who smiled easily.

Luis forced his preconceived notions to the back of his mind, silently vowing to evaluate the man on his own merits, as he'd always done with any man under his command.

"Kano," Alvarez said, "meet Captain Luis Escudero, recently arrived from Spain."

Kano's dark eyes quickly took in the young Spaniard. Raising his hand in greeting, he bowed slightly and smiled. In that instant was formed a bond of friendship. Perhaps it was the black man's warm eyes and his flashing smile; or perhaps the interpreter sensed a feeling of trust in the white man's honest, pale blue eyes.

Alvarez handed Kano a glass of rum, refilled the other glasses and motioned Kano to a chair. "Please tell Captain Escudero about yourself."

With a sigh of relief Kano sat down, relieved to straighten his neck from its bent position.

"My name is Kano, which in my native tongue means The Wind. I was born in Africa, and was initiated into the lion clan of warriors when I was a teen ager. I was the fastest runner in my village. When I was fifteen the hated Portuguese and their Arab allies invaded my village, killing, raping and pillaging, taking anyone left alive as slaves. The men of the village were forced to build the Portuguese a fortress while they used our women for sport. I was taken captive and ended up on the slave block in St. Jago and purchased by Governor Velasquez. I was taught to speak and read Spanish."

"How did you learn the Aztec language?" Luis asked

"I sailed many times on Governor Velasquez's slave ships to the Las Islas de Perlas, the Pearl Islands, to help capture slaves for his mines. Those same natives supply the Aztec nobles with pearls. The governor made me learn the natives' language, which is almost identical to the Aztec language, so I could talk them in to gathering pearls for the governor."

"Your translating skills will be extremely valuable where we're going!" Luis said. "Now I'd like you to tell us about Ortega's expedition and the Aztec empire."

Pleased at being the center of attention, Kano presented an almost unbelievable tale!

"We sailed in two ships from St. Jago, and encountered a heavy gale which blew us off course and we were lost! Three weeks later we found ourselves along an unmapped coast we assumed to be

Mexico. Wherever we landed the natives wanted our blood; they met us with the most deadly hostility. Captain Ortega was wounded several times. Only I escaped without a wound."

"Why was that?" Luis asked.

"They thought me some kind of black god. They were afraid of me. But back to my story. Captain Ortega had one hundred ten men with him. Only I survived. The captain died of his wounds fifteen days after we landed on the Mexican coast."

"Were you able to gather any information about the area, the people, whether there was any gold or silver?" Luis asked.

"Yes." Kano rose and stepped to the large wall map of known Spanish territory, and traced the dotted lines highlighting Mexico's unexplored coast line. "Our two ships ran into a fierce night storm. Come daybreak we were alone in the Caribbean. We went about, Captain Escudero. As heaven is my witness, we went about to look for our companions, though half of the crew was wounded or sick with fever. We patrolled back and forth for several days. There was no sign of them, not so much as a floating board."

"You never found any of them?" Luis asked.

"No." Kano moved his finger along the map. "We landed here, at a place called Papantla. Our ship was battered and needed repairs and provisions."

"Did Ortega give you any information about Papantla after he went ashore?"

"No sir. It wasn't necessary. I went into Papantla with Captain Ortega. I was amazed at the type of civilization we found there. I believe that city is the northeast fortress of the Aztecs."

"Why do you believe that?"

"The Aztec high priest told me so. It's evidently an empire of immense size and power. The holy man told me told me a great and mighty emperor rules from a magnificent city called Tenochtitlan."

"Did he tell you where it's located?"

"Not exactly," Kano answered. "Only that it's about one hundred leagues inland to the west."

Luis said, "You mentioned an advanced civilization. What was it like?" He, Alvarez and Narvaez came to the edge of their chairs.

"The entire area was covered with buildings constructed of stone and lime. There were temples and pyramids like those in Egypt, which I saw in a picture book when I worked for Governor Velasquez. Captain

Ortega said the cultivation of the soil was as advanced as any he'd seen in Europe. The Aztecs dressed in garments of delicately textured cotton, and wore many types of gold and silver ornaments about their bodies."

"Gold and silver?" Luis' blue eyes sparkled.

"Yes sir! More gold and silver and precious gems than I ever saw anywhere in my life."

"Incredible!" Luis interjected. "Go on, man, go on!"

"There were stone roads leading from Papantla to other major cities within the empire. Because I could speak their language I learned many things. The Aztecs are very intelligent, but very fierce and warlike. They have an organized army that fights well. We were heavily armed but were unable to stop Aztec warriors armed with only bows and arrows and clubs."

"Yes, yes," Luis growled impatiently. "But what of the gold and silver? Were you able to take any of it?"

"Yes. We took as much gold and silver as we could carry. We barely escaped with our lives. We set sail south along the coast, hoping to find a friendlier reception. But news we were in the area traveled fast, by Aztec runners. Every city knew of our presence."

"Did Ortega find a safer place to land?" Luis asked.

"We landed at a place called Tlactaplan, about fifty leagues south of Papantla. The Aztecs were waiting for us, and drove us away. We patrolled for fifteen days and were still in the Aztec empire! We saw huge cities from the deck of the ship. Aztec warriors came out in huge war rafts to battle us. Some of their high ranking chiefs wore solid gold body armor and silver helmets inlaid with emeralds."

"Holy Mary, Mother of God!" Alvarez blurted. "To have been there! Can you imagine what it would have been like?"

Luis rubbed his chin. "I'm trying! It's like a wild dream! Go on, Kano."

"We landed at a small, peaceful looking beach. Captain Ortega was wary of ambush so he had the ship's guns run out. I went ashore with him and his landing party. When we got about half a league inland, screaming Aztecs hit us from every side. They were on us before we could retreat and every man of them was killed, except me. I outran them back to the ship. The ship's guns slaughtered hundreds of them, but they just kept coming! They swarmed over the ship before we could get it underway. Again I managed to escape. That's all I remember until I was picked up by the Catalan."

"You're very lucky, my friend!" Luis said. "It's providential you were spared and the information you've shared with us will be most valuable. Do you think we could get into Mexico with a small force of men?"

"Not if you use Captain Ortega's tactics. He used force to get what he wanted and it got him and all his men killed. I urged him to use a little diplomacy, offer to trade some of our goods for gold and silver. He was arrogant and felt the Aztecs were unworthy adversaries. I knew he was wrong!

Papantla's holy man told me the emperor's personal bodyguard consists of fifty thousand professional warriors. He has over two hundred thousand men guarding the empire's borders. When I translated that for Ortega he wouldn't believe a word or it!"

"What the hell was the matter with the man?" Luis muttered under his breath. Alvarez sank back in his chair, his face mirroring disappointment.

Narvaez leaned forward. "I see Kano's information disturbs you, sir. But we've come too far to turn back now."

Alvarez looked grim. "What do you think, Captain Escudero? It seems to me it would be sheer suicide to take your expedition to Mexico! Do you understand the odds against you?"

Luis smiled. "Despite what Kano's told us, gentlemen, there's nothing supernatural about the Aztecs. They're highly dangerous, but Kano's information is invaluable in helping us plan a strategy. We'll be cautious where Ortega was impetuous. We'll take some trade goods. The sooner we get started the better! Captain Cortez said if we don't get off our asses, and right soon, the French and English will walk in and take the Aztec treasure right out from under us."

He paused for a moment and drank the rest of his rum. "Captain Alvarez, how soon can we sail?"

"Five days!"

"Good. I'll have my men here, ready to board."

🐾 🐾 🐾

It was late. Peering around the corner of the darkened warehouse, Pedro Armand, dressed as a beggar, kept watch on the Catalan until the meeting ended. Although the curtains were drawn, light from the cabin silhouetted four men, one of them so tall his head touched the ceiling.

By ship's lantern a shadowy figure descended the gangplank and walked to a horse tied to a post.

Escudero! No mistake about that. Our intelligence from Madrid was accurate. Armand mounted his Arabian stallion and whipped him into a run toward St. Jago, where he'd report to Don Diego Velasquez.

9

Punta del Piedras, Cuba, February 1518

Luis dozed in the saddle. Esperanza rode ahead, leading the way. It was pitch black midnight when the sentry waved them into camp. Esperanza loosened the cinches on the horses, dumped the saddles and blankets and turned them loose.

"There's a tent set up for you over there," Esperanza pointed. "Shall I wake Lieutenant Sandoval?"

"No." Luis removed his hat and slicked back his hair. "I'll see him in the morning. Thank you for your help today, Roberto." Luis walked to the tent, undressed and fell sound asleep moments after his head hit the pillow.

Before dawn Luis awakened to a variety of itchings, predominant among them being clusters of mosquito-bite swellings in the skin of his wrists and around his collar bones. The soft ocean breeze sighing through the palms was pleasing to his ear. Jungle birds twittered from the trees. The tent was still dark, but a gray-pearly softening of the night was beginning. His nostrils picked up the commixture of wood smoke from the smoldering fires, and the soft perfume of the Cuban jungle.

In that soft daze between sleep and awakening Luis heard someone shouting. He opened the tent flap and watched a very stout sergeant walk among the sleeping men prodding them with his booted foot. "Up! Up on your feet you lazy scum, we've work to do!"

Luis slipped into his uniform and walked from the tent, listening to soldiers grumbling and cursing as they scratched and yawned. Gazing over the camp now bathed in daylight, he heard whooping and laughter as an air-launched boot caught the sergeant on his broad backside.

"Who threw that? Godamn it, who threw that?" he shouted, turning in a complete circle, glowering at each man. When his fierce gaze reached them they looked down, busily engaged getting dressed.

Lieutenant Jorge Sandoval, a stern, sinister looking officer, with a black patch over his eye walked up to Luis. "You must be Escudero!"

Luis nodded. "Captain Luis Escudero, Lieutenant!" Luis spoke softly, but with the authority of one used to command.

Sandoval grimaced as if he'd been struck. "As you wish, sir."

Corporal Eduardo Martinez, a few yards from the officers, whistled tunelessly through his teeth, taking a little time to damn the fate that had sent them a pretty-boy aristocrat who probably didn't know his ass from a hole in the ground. Probably didn't know the first thing about soldiering, especially about fighting Indians. Martinez picked his teeth where a chunk of meat had lodged the night before, spitting it out on the sand near his boots. "Shit," he whispered to Taragona, "I'll never figure the army!"

Luis said, "Line them up, Lieutenant, and I'll take command."

"Sergeant Lopez," Sandoval growled. "Line them up."

Lopez shouted, "Stand at attention for Captain Luis Escudero."

The men fell in, in a single line, amid disarrayed blankets and other gear scattered over the ground. They stood puffy eyed and rumpled under Escudero's blistering stare. He was angry and the men could see it in his face.

"I'll make this short! I'm Captain Luis Escudero!" His voice cracked open the morning silence "The next time you line up you'll do it as a military unit, not like a bunch washerwomen. Any man who doesn't believe that is free to leave. Where we're going our survival will depend on absolute discipline!" Luis was so charged with power and fury at the men's slovenliness he could hardly contain himself.

"Now, who wants out? I won't have any soldier in this unit who will not follow orders."

"Begging the captain's pardon, we were hired by Captain Cortez. He didn't tell us anything about the mission except it was dangerous and there might be treasure. And now by God, we find he's tricked us."

Luis whirled to his right and confronted a huge, burly soldier without a shirt. "We expected him to lead it."

Sandoval whispered, "That's Alfredo, the blacksmith."

"You feel you've been tricked?" Luis asked. Up and down the line men nodded agreement. Sensing his companions' support Alfredo became bolder. "He didn't tell us some aristocrat from Madrid would be in command. If he had none of us would have signed on!" Again the men nodded agreement.

Luis couldn't let the blacksmith's insubordination pass, or he'd lose command before the muster was over. He came at the blacksmith like a hungry cat. That took Alfredo by complete surprise. His brows knotted with hatred, but he wasn't sure what to do.

"I guess you're a tough one?" Luis said sarcastically. "Why hell man, you've probably been drinking and whoring so much you're as soft in the head as you are in the belly!"

Alfredo eyed Luis warily, uncertain what the consequences of doing battle with his captain might be. The situation unfolded on him faster than he could think it through. He'd been on the brink of his very life more times than he could count, and wasn't one to shrink from a fight. He held up a hand. "I'm warning you, Captain, I'm the toughest sonofabitch in this man's army."

"Really? Let's find out!" Luis took a deep breath and moved harder and faster than he'd ever done before.

"Tear his balls off, Fredo," shouted Ribera, the ax man, who loved a good fight. Others were making bets on the outcome.

Alfredo was the fiercest human Luis had ever encountered! He came fast, crouching like an ape, his huge long arms dangling loosely, waiting for the right moment to catch his prey and crush it. He lowered his head and charged like a mad bull.

Luis dodged to one side and brought up both fists, one clenched inside the other, in a mighty blow which thudded into Alfredo's hurtling torso. It was like hitting a falling tree, but it knocked a loud grunt from him.

Soldiers jostled about, shoving each other for a better position, shouting encouragement, urging their friend on; Ribera's hand stole stealthily toward his shiny war ax. He looked up when Sandoval's sword tip tickled the back of his neck.

"Don't even think about it!" Sandoval growled.

Alfredo recovered quickly and the next instant Luis was entwined in those merciless arms tightening like the coils of a huge python. Luis saw red and yellow blazes behind his eyes and couldn't breathe. He brought his knee up into Alfredo's groin as hard as he could; the death-like grip loosened for a split second. It was all Luis needed; he slipped free. With a flurry of heavy blows to Alfredo's face, the big man retreated, searching for a weapon. He grabbed a piece of firewood. Holding it in both hands, he stomped forward swooshing the wood back and forth to deal a death blow.

"Here, Captain!" Sandoval threw him a short tent pole. Luis side-stepped the wildly swinging blacksmith and smashed the pole into his stomach. When he doubled over, Luis smashed him across the back of the skull. He dropped like a pole-axed cow, face down in the dirt, a pathetic rasping sound gurgling from his throat as he gasped for breath.

Luis stood over him for a moment, breathing hard. He threw the tent pole down, aware the men were staring at him, awe-struck by his prowess. His eyes sparkled, and a faint smile played across his face. "Sergeant, line them up. I want each man to state his name and rank!"

Sergeant Lopez shouted, "Fall in and stand at attention!" The men didn't move for a moment, then formed up, and their faces melted into friendly grins. Lopez walked over and helped Alfredo to his feet. The blacksmith rubbed his head and staggered into place in line. He glared hatefully at Luis, silently vowing one dark night he'd kill that aristocratic bastard!

🐾 🐾 🐾

"Do you think we're ready, Lieutenant?" Luis asked as they re-viewed names on the roster.

"They're a bit rough around the edges, misfits to a man, but there's not a coward in the lot. Each man has a special skill. In a fight they have no equals anywhere in the Spanish empire."

"You included?"

"Even me!" Sandoval admitted, not the least embarrassed to explain the unfortunate details of the Lombardy action which got him busted to Lieutenant. "Had it been five years earlier the king himself would have given me a medal for that day's work. But politics being what they are, we now have an alliance with the Lombards."

"I assume you'd like to regain your captaincy?"

Sandoval's head jerked upward and he gave Luis a surprised look. "Certainly!"

"This expedition will open the door for you! Captain Cortez picked you for this assignment. That means he has great respect for your abili-ties. That, added to the fact that I know the king personally, could work to your advantage—if we come back alive!"

"The king doesn't even know me," Sandoval replied skeptically. "He will if you help me succeed with this expedition."

Sandoval gaped at Luis in complete amazement, at a loss for words.

Luis added, "You work with me, give me your total loyalty and I'll forget your past. Your future begins today. What do you say?"

Sandoval's one good eye brightened. "What can I say? I'll never get a better offer than that!"

"Good!" Luis poured Sandoval a drink and one for himself. "Tell me a little about yourself."

Sandoval took a sip from his cup. "I don't have to sing my praises, Captain, what few there are. I stay sober and work hard. I know my job. My motives are about the same as yours. I'm a soldier of Spain with a thirst for adventure and gold. I have some small skill in the art of cartography, making maps and charts, which I learned in school. I've mapped most of the islands in this area for Captain Cortez."

"Yes, he told me. Now you'll have an opportunity to map new, unexplored areas! I understand you're also a fair hand at recording details. Your journal entries will be absolutely essential to Captain Cortez, when he starts out for Mexico next year. I assume you have an adequate supply of paper and ink?"

Sandoval nodded. "Everything we need. I even have a waterproof container so we won't lose valuable information to the weather."

During the next half hour they discovered many things about each other. Though there was a difference in their ages, Sandoval being thirty seven, they were much alike. The invisible barrier between them vanished.

Luis fascinated Sandoval, using a natural charm that made men eager to serve him, and above all made them feel important. In those few minutes Luis added a devotee to his personal service.

Before Sandoval left the tent he asked, "When will we find out about the mission?"

"In a couple of days," Luis replied. "Please tell the men. Just for your information, by this time next week we'll be at sea, on our way!"

Sandoval grinned. "Where too?"

"Everything will be explained in a couple of days!" Please send in Sergeant Lopez." Within moments, stout jovial Lopez presented himself and stood at full attention.

"Sergeant, from now on I want you to take a firm hand with the men. Lieutenant Sandoval will be working closely with me. We'll make the plans, you'll see that they are carried out. Do you understand?"

"Yes sir!"

"Stand at ease. I'm very impressed with what Lieutenant Sandoval told me about you. You know how to handle men and you've done a great job getting these misfits ready for our mission. I'm grateful to you."

A wide grin lighted Lopez's face, revealing a gap in his mouth where two teeth had been knocked out in a fist fight earlier in his career.

"Tell me, how long has it been since the men have been to town?" Lopez hooked his thumbs in his broad uniform belt. "Six weeks, sir."

"Why so long?"

"Captain Cortez ordered us to keep them confined to camp so no one would suspect what we're doing here."

"Are there any women in Punta del Piedras?"

"Si, Captain. Lots of women! Some are pretty wild, hardly house-broken! Captain Cortez has never been one to deprive his townsmen of women and drink." He grinned lasciviously.

"Could you handle a highly confidential mission for me? I want you to round up twenty or thirty women to come to our camp tomorrow night to entertain the men. Perhaps some musicians and dancers. Food and wine too. Could you handle such an important assignment?"

"Why hell yes! I mean yes sir!" A deep laugh rumbled up within Lopez. He knew he was going to like this new captain! "There's also some excellent wine jut arrived from Barcelona, and a shipment of rum from St. Jago is being unloaded as we speak."

"Very well, Sergeant. I'll leave the details in your capable hands!"

Lopez jerked to attention, hitting his head on the top of the tent, knocking his helmet off. Luis caught it before it hit the ground.

"A thousand pardons, Excellency." Lopez reddened and apologized when Luis handed him the helmet. He extended his right hand to Lopez who hesitatingly clasped it in his big, beefy hand.

"It's going to be good serving with you, Sergeant!"

Lopez swaggered slightly as he left Luis' tent, his rolling gait akin to that of a sailor.

Luis returned to his paperwork, taking a closer look at the written profiles of men under his command:

Eduardo Martinez, Corporal. Age 23. Convicted by court martial of brutality to civilians, two counts of rape and one count of striking a superior officer. Sentenced to ten years in St. Jago military prison. Veteran of five campaigns.

Alfredo Orlando, Trooper. Blacksmith. Age 27. Convicted of murder by court martial...did show grave disregard for human life and contempt for military authority by resisting arrest, severely injuring five soldiers taking him prisoner. Sentenced to life imprisonment. Veteran of two campaigns. Excellent blacksmith. Expert in the use of all weapons.

Jorge Ribera, Trooper. Age 22. Discharged twice for continuous drunk and disorderly conduct. Awarded the Kings Cross at the Battle of Avila. Expert in the use of the war ax...

Pedro Taragona, Trooper. Expert crossbowman. Age 21. Veteran of three campaigns. Independent...convicted of insubordination. fined six months pay...

Roberto Esperanza. Trooper. Scout. Age 20. Veteran of four campaigns...exemplary service...could be considered for promotion...leadership abilities...expert swordsman...needs to develop mature judgment and control temper.

Luis read and committed to memory the strengths and weaknesses of his men.

10

"**W**here are you off to, Sergeant?" Sandoval asked as Lopez saddled his horse.

"On an errand for the Captain, sir. I've ordered Corporal Martinez to drill the men."

"Very well, but don't be gone too long!"

"Yes sir." Lopez saluted and galloped off toward Punta del Piedras.

Lieutenant Sandoval found Corporal Martinez and growled, "Keep your boot up their asses today, Corporal! A fast trot along the beach won't hurt them at all."

Martinez scuffed his feet and scowled. "But sir, it's hotter than hell and they'll be carrying twenty kilo packs on their backs. They'll drop dead with sunstroke!"

With a tongue dipped in vitriol, Sandoval snapped at him. "Bullshit! When we go into battle the enemy won't let up on them! Do at least five miles today. Do you understand me?"

"Yes sir." Martinez stomped away. Goddamn sonofabitching slave driving officers!

🐾 🐾 🐾

Lopez pulled his lathered horse up at Pedro Contraras' cantina, where he gulped down a tall glass of rum and bargained with Pedro for thirty women, a couple of guitar players, a cask of Barcelona wine and a cask of Cuban rum!

"How much time do I have to do this favor for you?" Pedro asked.

"This afternoon would work just fine," Lopez grinned and poured himself more rum. Pedro cocked an eyebrow. "I might be able to work it out, but it will cost extra!" Lopez nodded. "Fine. Put it on Captain Cortez's bill."

🐾 🐾 🐾

After supper, exhausted troopers clustered around the cook fire, discussing their new captain and bitching about Lieutenant Sandoval pushing them beyond their limits.

"Piss on him!" snarled Alfredo. "Piss on them all! Who's for dice?" He fumbled in his pouch for dice as several men gathered round. Ribera handed him a pewter pot. Alfredo threw the dice in, shook and rattled them in the pot, and rolled them out on the hard ground. Men cheered when they won, others moaned when they lost, all intent on the game.

All heard the sentry's loud challenge, "Quien es?"

They all grabbed for the nearest weapon.

Sergeant Lopez rode in, leading a strange retinue of women, laughing and giggling, followed by a couple of musicians strumming guitars.

"Where in the hell have you been and what in God's name do you think you're doing?" shouted Lieutenant Sandoval. "We're not running a goddamned whorehouse here! Turn those whores around and boot their asses back where you found them!"

Lopez ignored the order and saluted Luis, leaning against a palm tree. "Mission completed, sir." Sandoval glared at Luis. "You authorized this?"

"I did."

Sandoval's eyes blazed with anger. "Why?"

"Come with me and find out." Sandoval followed Luis to the cook fire.

Luis smiled at the puzzled men. "You've trained hard for the past six weeks. But your training is coming to an end. It's time for a little relaxation. Enjoy yourselves tonight because we're leaving in a couple of days, and it'll be a long time before you see a white woman again. Tomorrow I'll explain our mission."

Not all of the women were beautiful. Some were middle aged, some were young and some were of mixed Indian and Spanish blood. But they were all willing, and they were female, a fact not lost on the lusty soldiers.

Under a bright Caribbean moon and sparkling stars, with lilting guitar music in the background troopers paired off with the woman of their choice. Wine and rum flowed freely as Sergeant Lopez dipped directly from the casks and poured into their cups, liberally helping himself!

A bull like shout split the night air when Corporal Martinez called to Esperanza, "A song, Roberto! Let's hear a ballad!"

Esperanza stepped into the firelight and spoke softly to the guitarists. They strummed softly and Roberto sang La Mujer de Barcelona, a popular Castilian ballad, the soldiers' favorite.

Roberto's smooth tenor singing style, along with the song's simple lyrics touched their hearts. Their thoughts flashed back to loved ones and homes in far off Spain—warm, sunny hills, vineyards, people mingling, family!

Not a sound came from the hushed assembly while Esperanza sang from his heart. Loud cheers and shouts of well done and bravo erupted when his song ended. He bowed gracefully.

🐾 🐾 🐾

Luis knew Sandoval wouldn't stoop to cavorting with whores. So he said, "You're duty officer tonight. Stay alert! When the men have had their fun round up the whores and get them out of here."

"Yes sir!" Sandoval replied sarcastically, gritting his teeth.

A tension racked Luis' muscles. It always happened before a battle or a crisis. It wasn't fear, but a terrible storing up of energy. It became a force that drove at times like this, like a spring unbearably compressed. Tomorrow he would tell his men he was taking them to a land peopled by savages, more ruthless than any they'd ever faced before. At times like this he needed a woman to wipe out this strain, to pour out his energy in a wild, slithering panting flurry of limbs. That's the way he preferred his women. He wanted no relationships. He needed a woman for an hour or two and a berserk release of himself from this self control.

He looked up from the table where he studied a map, surprised to see a lovely young native woman at the tent flaps, holding a cup.

"Capitan," she smiled, "I'm Tacuba. Sergeant Lopez asked me to bring you this special Barcelona wine."

"Please come in." Luis took the wine, sniffed its bouquet and slowly sipped, all the while eyeing the swell of Tacuba's breasts beneath the scoop of her peasant blouse.

"Do you find me pleasing?" she asked.

"Very pleasing!" He walked around and closed the tent flaps.

He took off his sword and handed it to her. She knelt and helped him off with his boots. He sat on the edge of his bed and watched Tacuba slowly and sensually remove her skirt and blouse and stand naked before him.

He pulled her to him and gently kissed her on the lips, suddenly washed over by a powerful wave of sexual desire. A succession of faces, hands, and arms flickered through his memory—young women and girls from his village in Aragon, the perfumed women of the Austrian court, naked Indian girls he'd observed on his way here from St. Jago, bathing in cool streams along the road.

He embraced Tacuba's warm responding body. She trembled as he caressed her and stroked her long black hair. That hand continued to stroke her supple body while her hands undressed him. He cupped her face in his hands and kissed her gently as they fell to the bed. She turned him on his stomach and rubbed her soft hands on his back where his flesh was smooth and rock hard. Her fingers wandered over his body. His powerful neck and shoulders were as hard as those of her riding horse. When he turned over on his back, his long curving manhood throbbed wildly. She climbed up, threw her leg over and straddled him, impaling herself on his fully erect member. Slowly she slid down its entire length until it was buried shaft deep in her warm tight depths. She undulated up and down, slowly at first then faster and faster until he groaned, tensed and released himself deep inside her. She shuddered and groaned, then bent down and kissed him passionately.

It was over much too quickly, but Luis was totally relaxed. With a light spat on Tacuba's rear, he sent her on her way and fell into an exhausted sleep.

Lieutenant Sandoval walked slowly around the camp's perimeter, concentrating on security rather than wine and whores. His mind slowly turned to the past. No matter how hard he tried he couldn't blot out troubling memories of that horrible battle in Lombardy where he should have died. Though he led a cavalry charge up the hillside and drove through the enemy position like an armor-tipped arrow, slashing and stabbing, his brother Hector was captured and beheaded. Esperanza found his body in a wooded ravine. When he led Sandoval to the spot he screamed like a madman. His men held him and finally bound him so he couldn't harm himself. To this day he'd sometimes wake up screaming from that terrible nightmare which never went away.

He stood under a bright Caribbean moon, idly staring at the high Cuban mountains silhouetted in the distance. They reminded him of mountains near his home in Valencia, Spain. At that moment he was disconnected from the whoring revelry of the camp. He could hardly control a subdued excitement about tomorrow! He'd finally learn where they were going! This expedition was an opportunity to regain his captaincy and put enough gold in his pocket to bring his beautiful wife, Rosa, to the new world.

Beneath the leather patch covering his left eye he felt an annoying itch. He fought the impulse to lift the patch and scratch the empty socket. Instead he smoothed his soft graying beard, bringing memories of Rosa's soft fingers running through it, which always aroused him. He'd not seen her for three years; but he could close his eyes and see her as clearly in his mind as if she just been with him yesterday.

He pleaded with her to come to Cuba, but her family absolutely forbid her to consider such a preposterous request! They'd never permit her to go to a land peopled only by savages and outcasts, away from the comforts of civilization. Sandoval knew her family despised him because of his reduction in rank. His father-in-law, a hard-headed aristocrat, respected nothing but money and power. Maybe one day soon, if he lived that long, he'd have both!

🐾 🐾 🐾

The hour was late when Sandoval found Roberto Esperanza curled up in the arms of a pretty young woman. "Roberto, lad," Sandoval said in a fatherly tone. "Let's round up the women and get them on their way."

Amid grumbling and drunken grunts from men and women sprawled on blankets on the ground, they helped the women to their feet, softly patted their behinds and sent them staggering back to Punta del Piedras.

Luis awakened the following morning to a narrow shaft of light coming through the tent flap. He stretched luxuriously in memory of lovemaking with Tacuba, which banished all tensions and worries from his body and plunged him into a deep, dreamless sleep.

Rolling over, he fumbled for his clothes. He dressed and headed for the creek to freshen up.

"Buenos dias, Captain," Sergeant Lopez called out. "Did you sleep well?"

"You ought to know, Sergeant," Luis grinned and winked.

"I thought you'd like Tacuba!" Lopez beamed, as Luis leaned down and washed his face in the cool clear water.

He wiped his face on a towel, then said, "Sergeant, have the men fall in. It's time for me to tell them where we're headed with this little expedition."

11

Luis was amazed at what a night's drinking and whoring had done to lift the mens' sagging spirits! Smiling, they quickly seated themselves on the ground, in a semi circle, eager to learn where the expedition was going.

"I know you're anxious to learn about our mission," Luis began, "so listen carefully and I'll lay it out for you. King Carlos has ordered us to sail to the Aztec empire and scout and map its cities and towns and learn all we can about the Aztecs."

A sudden chill ran down Sergeant Lopez's spine, though he continued to perspire under the blazing morning sun. "Begging your pardon, sir, we're going to the Aztec empire? With this handful of men? It can't be done!"

"Why not?" Luis asked pleasantly enough, knowing Lopez's concerns were also those of the men.

"The Aztec empire is a place of death!" Every man nodded agreement. "No white man has ever gone there and come back alive. It's nothing but jungle, wild beasts and fierce war-like Indians, who may be cannibals!"

Esperanza raised his hand. "Sergeant Lopez speaks the truth! I've talked to sailors who've been near that place."

Martinez, who hadn't ever spoken ten words in Luis' presence, spoke up. "The Aztecs will butcher us as soon as we land! What kind of guarantee do we have of getting in and out of there alive?"

"There are no guarantees in this business!" Luis answered firmly. "You've all been in enough tight places to know that or you wouldn't be here. But please, hear me out before you jump to wild conclusions. Captain Cortez and I met with King Carlos. Together we developed a plan we feel will give us a fair chance of succeeding. We're gambling on the fact most Aztecs have never seen horses, cannons, arquebuses or other weapons such as swords and crossbows. That alone gives us an advantage."

"How will we communicate with the heathens when we get there?" Lopez asked. "None of us speak their language."

"We've found a man who does!" Luis replied matter of factly, which created a stir among the men. "Who is he?" Sandoval asked with surprise.

"You'll all meet him very soon," Luis answered. "He went to the Aztec empire and came back alive—with valuable information about the Aztecs."

Heads nodded affirmatively. However, there was still a very puzzling question on everyone's mind—and Sandoval asked it! "Captain, you said we'll map the Aztec empire, do some geography, find out more about the Aztecs. There's something missing. Maybe you'd better spell it out for us! The king wouldn't authorize this mission unless something bigger was at stake. What's in it for us? We need something more than the paltry wages we're being paid."

Heads nodded. Right on, Lieutenant!

"Let's talk about that," Luis responded. "But first, how about a drink? Sergeant will you do the honors?"

When the drinks were poured, Luis raised his cup. "To Spain and us!"

"To Spain and us," came the answering shout. Then an attentive silence settled over the soldiers.

"So, what's in it for you?" Luis began in a confiding sort of tone, passing an intense stare around, making each man feel he was being addressed personally. "How about gold, silver and precious gems? Would that interest any of you? We believe there's more gold and silver in the

Aztec empire than all the rest of the world put together. We're going to find out if it's there. If so, a larger expedition of conquest will be organized next year." Luis paused.

Every eye was focused on him. "We're listening, Captain. Go on," Sandoval said.

"Any gold or silver we find will be equally divided among us. I believe we'll come back with enough gold to live like gentlemen the rest of our lives."

"What if there is no gold, Captain?" Sergeant Lopez asked.

"I'm almost positive there is, Sergeant. But whether there is or isn't, each man will receive five hundred acres of land anyplace within the Spanish empire. I know, gentlemen, it's a big gamble to be sure, but where in this world will you find a better game of chance?"

There wasn't a sound! They stared at him with ruddy faces, masked with complete disbelief! On other expeditions officers and financiers kept anything of value and the soldiers received little or none of it.

They began to stir with excitement and eagerness, and to a man, except for one among them, agreed the Captain's plan was well worth the gamble.

"How about it men?" Luis shouted. "Who wants to go?"

"All of us!" shouted Sergeant Lopez.

Luis smiled. "Good! We'll break camp day after tomorrow and take our gear to the Catalan, load the horses, mules and provisions and be ready to sail with the tide!"

🐾 🐾 🐾

Alfredo the blacksmith didn't like it, not one bit! And it was easy enough for Sergeant Lopez to read it in Alfredo's sullen face. He'd rather shoe horses and mules than take orders from some aristocrat from Madrid!

Lopez took him aside. "What the hell's the matter with you, man? Here's a chance to make your fortune and you're going to piss it all away because Captain Escudero kicked your ass? You deserved it! Forget about it. It's over and done with."

Alfredo spat out the corner of his mouth. "I don't trust him! I'll make him pay for what he did to me in front of the men!"

"Forget it, I tell you! You make any move to harm the captain and I'll see you hanged for mutiny!" Lopez paused momentarily, then glared at Alfredo. "If that's the way you feel toward the captain, why don't you high tail your ass on out of here? Why don't you do it right now?"

"Oh, you'd like that, wouldn't you?"

"Damn right. Maybe I could find another blacksmith to take your place. You've been nothing but a pain in the ass ever since I've known you."

"Humph," snorted Alfredo. "Well then, you'd really miss me, huh? I think I'll stick around just to make your life interesting!"

Lopez gritted his teeth. "If we didn't need you...never mind." He didn't press it further. "Get your tools together and boxed up so we can get them to the ship."

Alfredo pitched in with the others. He gathered his tools, all the while planning to sneak over to Punta del Piedras to find out what was on cousin Pedro Armand's mind. He'd sent word with one of the whores he wanted to see Alfredo. He probably had some dirty deed that needed doing. Ah, what the hell! Armand pays well and I can certainly use the money!

Everyone was so busy, no one noticed him slip away from camp.

"Good God, Alfredo! What the hell happened to you?" Armand grinned. "You look like a Barcelona bull stomped the shit out of you!"

"Never mind," Alfredo growled. "What the hell do you want this time?"

Armand laughed "Just as diplomatic as ever, I see. Well, dear cousin, I have a simple job for you. I need Escudero's expedition stopped, and it can't done here. Too many questions would be asked. I want you to sabotage his expedition as soon as it lands."

"And how am I supposed to do that?" Alfredo asked skeptically. "I'm only one man—and what makes you think I'd want to anyway?"

Armand chuckled. "I've heard how much you love and admire your captain! That's why I thought you might like a little revenge for the beating you took—if the price is right."

"How much?" Alfred's brows shot up. "One thousand golden ducats."

"A thousand? When?"

"Half now and the other half when the job's done."

"How do I do it?" Alfred asked, his dull-witted brain was incapable of coming up with a simple solution.

"You'll destroy their gunpowder and run off the horses and mules. The Aztecs will take care of the rest."

"But what about me, cousin? Won't the Aztecs take care of me also?"

Armand studied his hulking relative. Perhaps he wasn't as stupid as he let on. "Certainly not! The plan is all worked out—but you must keep what I now tell you under your belt—not a word to anyone.

Understand? I'll be leading an expedition just south of Escudero's. He doesn't know this. I'll have my scout meet you at a specified time, after you've wrecked Escudero's expedition. The scout will bring you to my camp and we'll proceed from there. Very simple, eh?" Armand smirked.

"Sounds good, Pedro," Alfredo smiled for the first time. "I hate Escudero! It'll give me a chance for a little payback for what he did to me in front of all the men!"

They discussed specific details of Armand's plan to ensure Alfredo knew exactly what he was supposed to do. "Remember Fredo, I'll have Escudero's expedition under surveillance at all times, so have no fear for your safety."

Armand, however, had no intention of paralleling Escudero's expedition. He'd be in a critical race for the world's richest treasure, and timing would be crucial. Cousin Alfredo was expendable! Once he sabotaged Escudero's expedition, either Escudero or the Aztecs would kill him! Either way he'd be dead!

🐾🐾🐾

Captain Julio Alverez was the only one aboard the Catalan who noticed a ragged, rum-pot of a man staring at his ship, from around the warehouse corner. The beggar's darting eyes missed nothing; four horses, three mules, thirty men, two officers, one huge black slave, one small cannon called a falconet and various supplies.

Loading the expedition's gear proceeded on schedule. One balky mule didn't go aboard ship without a fight—but with Sergeant Lopez's 300-pound bulk pushing and Alfredo pulling, the mule lost the battle. With ear-shattering braying he was lowered into a stall.

Alvarez descended the gangplank stealthily, crept around the warehouse and came up behind Armand, his full attention riveted on the ship.

"Turn very slowly, senior, and you might live through this night," Alvarez growled, his sword ready. Armand turned slowly, pulled his dagger and threw it so swiftly Alvarez never saw it until it thudded into his chest. His sword clattered to the wharf. His knees buckled. He gasped then sprawled dead on the dock.

Armand jammed his foot on the corpse, pulled his dagger from the dead man's chest, wiped the blade on the captain's jacket, and rolled his body behind a crate. He scurried with a fake limp back to town, jumped on his horse and whipped it into a fast run toward St. Jago.

🐾 🐾 🐾

The tide was rolling out and the Catalan was ready for sea. "Where the hell is Captain Alvarez?" Luis asked Narvaez. "I don't know. No one's seen him!"

"We can't wait. Get us underway or we'll lose the tide."

"But Captain Escudero, we can't sail without him!" Narvaez protested.

"That's an order! Get us underway!"

Juan Narvaez suddenly shivered with a cold chill of pure, savage anticipation as he shouted his first command as a ship's captain. "Cast off Bosun! Men aloft to loosen sails!"

The ship bustled with activity. Sailors aloft unfurled the square and lateen sails, which looked like three canvas triangles in descending size order from the main mast to the mizzen mast. The breeze and the tide took the small ship swiftly toward the harbor entrance. Dawn was breaking in the east; and the sun, a huge red ball, was rising from the sea. The Catalan scudded along under full sail, keeled over, racing toward the unexplored Aztec empire!

🐾 🐾 🐾

Armand cast off the ill smelling rags he'd worn in Punta del Piedras and looked resplendent in his Florentine suit of the latest cut, its fashionable, enormous leg of mutton sleeves slashed with gold. His wide velvet hat with a circle of plumes around the crown rested on the table. Relaxing in an easy chair in Velasquez's study, after a long ride, his face was drawn and tired.

"What did you find out, Captain?" Velasquez asked as Armand sipped sherry.

Twenty or thirty seconds elapsed before the exhausted soldier spoke. "I obtained all the information we need."

"Really? You found out how many men Escudero has and what provisions they are taking with them?" Armand explained what he'd seen.

"This slave you speak of," Velasquez said. "You say he's very tall? Hector Ortega had a tall black man with him. It couldn't be the same man could it?"

"Not if Ortega perished, Excellency. Probably just a coincidence. There are many tall black men here in the islands."

Velasquez let it pass and asked, "And you encountered no problems?"

"Only one. I had to kill Captain Alvarez."

"You what? Good God, man, did anyone see you?" Velasquez shouted, livid with rage. Armand stuttered, "I had no choice. It was dark. I'm sure no one saw me."

"Can the Catalan sail without her captain?" Velasquez growled. "Certainly. The first mate, Narvaez is a very capable officer."

"Yes he is. I know him. This means you'll have to sail within the week or Escudero will beat you to the gold."

"What about my ships? Armand asked. "You told me you were having them provisioned and my men standing by."

Velasquez said, "Captain Alonzo Duero has two ships provisioned and ready to go. The horses and weapons are already on board. He'll land you and your men into the Aztec empire. Any questions?"

"He knows where it is?" Armand's eyes sprang wide.

Velasquez nodded affirmatively. "Together Duero and I did some investigating and learned from the local Caribe Indians that Aztec lands are covered with mountains and many beautiful cities."

"Did they tell you how to get there?"

Velasquez nodded. "If you go west for a ways and turn due south you'll find the Aztecs. Their capitol city is called Tenochtitlan. Captain Duero feels confident he can get you to the shores of the Aztec empire."

Armand's face registered doubt. "There's a lot water in the Caribbean and it's easy to get lost. Seems to me like looking for a needle in a haystack."

Velasquez chuckled. "You worry too much, Armand. Captain Duero has been sailing these waters for many years. He'll get you to the right place."

Armand still wasn't convinced. "Do you trust the Caribes?" he asked

"I have no reason not to. However, if that damned Hector Ortega had made it back here alive we'd have much more reliable information." Velasquez sipped his sherry. "In any case, while Escudero is floundering around trying to find the Aztecs, you'll already be in their empire, on your way to the gold!"

"I think you underestimate Escudero, Excellency," Armand said. "He has the advantage of a head start and he's a brilliant leader."

Velasquez glowered at Armand. "Don't you think you can handle this assignment."

"Yes sir," Armand answered. "But I don't plan to underestimate Escudero. While I was in Punta del Piedras I paid my cousin, who's in Escudero's expedition, to slow him down a bit!" He went on to explain the deal he'd made with Alfredo.

Velasquez smiled broadly. "You're a devious bastard, Armand. I'll give you that."

"I've got a good teacher!" Armand responded. "If there's nothing else, I'll be on my way."

Velasquez screwed up his face, trying to remember something important. "Oh, did you finally find someone as your second in command?'

"I interviewed several people, and chose a former Portuguese soldier by the name of Magellan. He's a sergeant now, but was once a captain in our army. He's an excellent scout."

"Good Lord Jesus Christ! The one they call the butcher?" Velasquez's stared at him through narrowed eyes. "He's a raving madman! The crazy lunatic bastard killed his last two captains! I would have hanged him, but he escaped to Santo Domingo and we couldn't find him."

"I'll admit he's a bit unruly," Armand said, "but I'll keep him under tight rein!"

"You'd better. He's not a man to be trifled with. I've put him in prison three times. Sleep with one eye open if you don't want your throat cut!"

"Anything else?" Armand asked.

"Remember, you'll have no way to communicate with the Aztecs, but neither will Escudero. Even so, your chances for success are quite good. We've supplied you with a huge supply of trade goods with which you can buy your way to the Aztec capitol."

"Thank you for that, sir. It will be most helpful."

"Be careful, Armand," Velasquez advised. "And get back here as quickly as you can with gold samples."

"I will, sir." Armand stepped forward and clasped Velasquez's outstretched hand. As the governor held that limp hand, a gnawing feeling distrust was again kindled in the back of his mind!

12

Aboard the Catalan, Gulf of Mexico, March, 1518

The second day out, Luis stood at the Catalan's bow as the first light of dawn streaked across the Caribbean. He studied the western horizon carefully, hoping to see mountains hiding the Aztec empire from view. He let the sun and salt spray play against his face. No matter how hard he wished or prayed, the old ship could only go so fast. He turned and weaved his way to the stern, through men scattered and sleeping on deck, and down to the captain's cabin, to look at the charts again.

The Catalan plowed due west, keeled over under full sail. Apart from cleaning and repairs, sword and arquebus drill and whatever other diversions Luis and Sandoval could devise, the men had nothing to do but trail their lines overboard for tunny fish and mackerel, sing bawdy ballads and gossip.

A ship is small, and secrets, personal animosities and discontent find new, secure hiding holes. Grumbles soon become common property, particularly when there's little action to occupy a man's time or mind.

Corporal Martinez, Alfredo and a couple of other men stood off in a little group, all a bit seasick from the ship's rolling motion.

"Damned round-bottomed whore of a boat," growled Martinez, looking a bit green around the mouth. "Probably the rotten food they're serving us. The sailors get all the good food," Ribera complained.

Kano stood alone, near the bow, leaning against the railing. A ship's officer stopped momentarily to chat.

Alfredo pointed. "Look at that! It's enough to make a person puke. Just look at that ass-kissing fornicator," he spat out. "That black bastard gets better treatment than us! Have you noticed how he and the officers are so damned cozy? What the hell makes him so important? How can they cater to him like that? Blacks aren't even human. In Cuba we use them as animals. They breed just like cattle, right out in the open where people can see them."

"Hold that filthy tongue of yours, Fredo!" Martinez shouted. "All you've done since you came aboard is bitch! Good God almighty, isn't seasickness bad enough without your continual whining!" Martinez dry heaved. "Oh, Jesus, not again!" He jumped for the rail and vomited into the sea.

Alfredo laughed. "Don't fall overboard, you damn dumb fool!" He turned back to his companions. "Look. Just look! He's been there for hours. Never moves. Never says anything. Doesn't fart or even pick his nose."

"Leave it be, Alfredo, I'm warning you," Martinez mumbled weakly, wiping the back of his hand across his mouth. "What concern is Kano to you anyway? He's not causing any trouble."

He put a calming hand on Alfredo's arm. But he shook it off. "Get away from me!"

Alfredo walked toward Kano. Ribera and San Estevan grinned at each other, hoping for a damn good fight to relieve the boredom.

The Catalan's mate stuck his head into the captain's cabin where Narvaez, Luis and Sandoval were bent over the map table, and shouted. "We've got trouble forward. You'd better come." He led the way, the officers on his heels.

Crouched low, Kano, with a gleaming dagger in his right hand, moved cautiously toward Alfredo, who was not as tall as Kano, but his huge shoulders and hairy barrel chest made him a very formidable, dangerous opponent.

Warily they circled each other. Kano feinted with his knife, but Alfredo quickly and deftly slipped aside and deflected the knife with a quick blow to Kano's wrist, and knocked the knife from his hand. Alfredo grabbed him and threw him to the deck, and Kano grabbed the knife. Alfredo hung onto Kano's wrist as he tried to free himself. They rolled over and over on the deck, kicking, hitting and punching with their free hands. Neither spoke. Only their deep grunts indicated the intensity of their struggle. Alfredo backhanded Kano across the face and sent him sprawling backwards. Soldiers and sailors shouted encouragement and bet on the outcome.

"Ten reales on Kano!" shouted San Estevan. "He's quicker than Fredo!"

"You're on!" Ribera took the bet. "Kano's faster but Fredo is stronger."

Alfredo was indeed as strong as three ordinary men, forcing Kano to rely on cunning and swiftness. Still, the blacksmith couldn't take the knife away.

Kano came at Alfredo, swooshing the knife back and forth. Moving quickly for one so huge, Alfredo grabbed Kano's knife hand and drove his knee into his groin. Kano gasped and doubled over, but kept the flashing knife poised.

"Enough, goddamnit!" Luis shouted angrily, stomping up to the two men, Lieutenant Sandoval at his side. Kano backed away from the officers.

"Who started this?" Luis snapped. Neither man answered.

"Give me that knife!"

Kano hesitated, staring at the sea of grinning white faces crowded around. Then he flipped the blade around and handed it, hilt first to Luis.

A sardonic smile played across Alfredo's swarthy face.

"Wipe that smile off your face, or I'll have you clapped in irons and thrown in the hold with the other stinking beasts. Any more fighting and I'll have the skin off your back. Do you hear me?"

"Si, Capitan," Alfredo said and walked away. Under his breath he whispered to his comrades, "Piss on them all!"

Kano's groin was sore, but he straightened and flashed a wide grin. "I must be more careful, eh, Captain? Many women would be very sad if I lost my mighty powers!" His hand moved lightly to his crotch. Suddenly his friendly grin disappeared, and out came a warning. "Beware of the blacksmith, sir, he's not to be trusted." With that he walked away, leaving Luis wondering if Alfredo had done anything more serious than start a fight. Even if Kano suspected Alfredo of underhanded dealings, he'd not tell anyone. Spanish soldiers obeyed an unwritten law that a man's business is his own!

Those who meddle in another man's affairs don't live long!

"Martinez!" Luis spoke sharply. "Where the hell is Sergeant Lopez? He's supposed to keep the men under control."

"In his bunk, Captain, with chronic seasickness."

"You're next in command. Why didn't you stop the fight?"

"Are you joking, sir? Stop Alfredo? I'd rather try to stop a mad bull!"

"I'm not joking, Martinez! There's to be no more fighting among the men. If you can't handle your responsibilities I'll appoint someone who can. Is that clear?"

"Yes sir," Martinez groaned and dashed for the rail again.

🐾 🐾 🐾

Most of the men liked Kano and forgot his color when they got to know him. Even Lieutenant Sandoval, who initially had some reservations about the man, because of his race, came to appreciate his many talents. Once Sandoval ripped his jacket and Kano stitched it so neatly it was impossible to tell where it had been torn. An expert in leather work, Kano repaired the soldiers' boots during his spare time. He also had an uncanny mechanical ability. He could repair an arquebus, adjust the tension screw on a crossbow, repair a broken elevation screw on a cannon, or any other mechanical task.

Though a silent man, he was friendly and helpful; and he gained the respect of the men not only for his domestic talents but for his warrior's skills leaned as a young man in the jungles of Africa where survival depended on one's strength and weapons skills.

Once, and only once, because Kano was not a vain or boastful man, he demonstrated his skill with his short, steel-tipped spear. Tacking a small piece of cloth, no larger than a golden ducat, to the mainmast, he stepped of fifteen paces, turned and hurled the spear. It thudded deep into the mast, its razor-sharp point exactly in the center of the cloth.

Astonished soldiers and sailors gasped, finding it difficult to believe what they'd seen. As they discussed the extraordinary feat, Kano unsheathed his knife and hurled it so swiftly it was only a silver blur until it sliced deep into the wood, burying its blade one hand span above the spear.

Casually he walked the mainmast, pulled his weapons, and sauntered away as though nothing unusual had happened!

🐾 🐾 🐾

Luis befriended Kano because the mission's success depended more on him than any other member of the expedition. During idle moments, Kano taught Luis some of the intricacies of the Aztec language.

"It's not called Aztec, but Nahuatl. It differs greatly from Spanish. It's very repetitious, sounding much like incantations. To you it'll sound like someone strangling. I'll recite a short poem in Nahuatl so you can hear the language flow and get an idea of how the words are pronounced. Then you can memorize the poem. It's the very best way to learn a new language.

Luis nodded. "Go ahead. I'm listening."

"I love the green mountains Land of my fathers.

"But I love most our people That is my song."

Luis listened intently to the clipped, pleasant accents and inflections in Kano's deep, resonant voice. Kano took a deep breath. "Every time I recite that poem it reminds me of my own land and people, who are all gone now, lost to cruelty and death. I've wondered many times if there's a place on this earth where a man can find true peace?"

"If there is, my friend, I don't know where it would be."

They stood silent for a moment before Luis said, "When I first met you, you told me about your boyhood, how you came by your name and how you were captured. But what of your family? What happened to them?"

Embarrassed his captain would be interested in his humble background, Kano responded with dignity. "I was born a free man in a beautiful, green country. Our ways were simple. We had love in our family and among our people. We worshipped simple gods like the rain, the sun, the wind and the earth. My father was the village chief and we lived comfortably. My mother and two sisters took care of the cooking and chores. I roamed wherever I chose." Kano smiled wistfully, savoring that precious memory.

"One day, after swimming in the river, I returned to the village. I heard screaming and shouting. Portuguese sailors and Arabs had come to capture slaves, killing any who resisted them. I was ten years old and I felt so helpless. I couldn't fight them, so to my shame I hid and watched. My father barricaded himself, my mother and sisters in the hut, and fought them. But the sailors got a log and battered down the door, dragged my father out into the open and killed him with their swords.

A huge sailor dragged my sweet, gentle mother out of the hut, and flung her naked upon the ground and raped her. I was so close I could her sobs and groans. Then the others took a turn. The man who had her last ran her through with his sword. Then they dragged my sobbing, terrified sisters out. One was thirteen, the other fifteen. They screamed when they saw our parents lying dead upon the ground. The young one broke away and ran, but there was nowhere to hide. The sailors and Arabs caught and ravaged her and the older girl, but didn't kill them. While I watched, trembling with fear, an Arab snuck up behind me and grabbed me before I could run. I still have horrible nightmares about the terrible day."

He paused for a moment, then added, "Why do the gods allow such things to happen? Senseless cruelty serves no purpose."

Moved by Kano's story, Luis said, "I commend you for surviving that awful nightmare. You could have wallowed in self-despair and let it ruin you. Most men could not have survived what you went through. It would have driven them mad."

Kano smiled and nodded at the compliment.

"You wonder why the gods didn't intervene? Think about it. Those experiences were predestined for a purpose, you know."

Kano's head jerked up. He stared at Luis before emitting a mirthless, "Huh? You must be joking! What purpose?"

"You were put through a refiner's fire to prepare you for this critical mission which might save the kingdom of Spain. Our expedition has come together at this exact instant in time and in this particular place for that specific purpose, each of us with a special talent. You were chosen by King Carlos because you have excellent interpretive skills. There's not another man in the entire world who could take your place!"

Kano leaned back, pondering ideas and concepts he never could have imagined; then stared wide- eyed at Luis. "Thank you, Captain. Your words are like a soothing balm to my troubled mind and heart!"

🐾🐾🐾

After twelve days at sea, sailing due west from Punta del Piedras on Cuba's southeast coast, through the Straits of Florida, Captain Narvaez navigated the Catalan south along the Mexican coastline, looking for a suitable landing spot. Soldiers and sailors crowded the rail, catching their first glimpse of the fabled land of the Aztecs. Lofty hills faded into rugged mountains whose jagged backs jutted skyward like the backs of giant brooding dinosaurs.

Narvaez studied the jagged shore line through his long glass. He saw smoke curling skyward from dense trees along the shore and ordered the helmsman to alter course to port, hoping the Aztecs hadn't seen the ship!

Luis and the men worked frantically getting their supplies and animals ready for landing. They put halters on the horses and mules, all suffering terribly in the dark, pitching hold, especially the mules. Their shrill scream braying forced everyone below decks to plug their ears with cotton. The others loaded goods on pallets, ready for the ship's sling to drop them to the long boat as soon as the ship anchored.

Narvaez swore under his breath, wishing he knew more about the country's geography, tides and winds. Though he could plainly see the rocky coast line, he had no idea where the hell he was!

"Bosun, reef the main and mizzenmast sails," he shouted, keeping enough canvas on the ship to maintain steerage way. The sun sank slowly in the west, forcing Narvaez to make a critical decision. Land now or stand out to sea again! He couldn't risk a night landing on Mexico's uncharted eastern coast.

He summoned Old Barba from the galley. "Fix the soldiers a light meal. I'm putting in to shore within the hour, and they won't get to eat again for hours."

Old Barba served food to Luis' men crowded on deck. A strange, brilliantly colored jungle bird with very long delicate tail feathers circled the ship once, then landed gracefully in the rigging. None but old Barba had ever seen such a magnificently plumed bird which appeared tired from a long flight.

Every man on deck stared up curiously at the unusual jungle parrot.

"Hey, Old Barba! Look up there!" Esperanza shouted, pointing to the rigging.

"Holy Mary, Mother of God! It's a quetzal bird!" Old Barba gasped, and a look of horror spread across his wrinkled face! He crossed himself.

"Jesus Christ, old man!" Alfredo sneered. "Surely you're not frightened of a mere bird?"

"It's no bird, my friend. It's an omen sent by God himself to warn us. A quetzal bird is God's messenger.

"Warn us of what?" Esperanza asked.

"Death! Much death mis amigos! We should turn about and sail away from this evil place!" Barba's face was white and drawn.

"Who's going to die, old man?" Esperanza asked mockingly.

Barba didn't answer. He glanced up again at the colorful bird, then shuffled off to the galley.

13

Narvaez leaned over the Catalan's bow and shouted orders back to the helmsman. Skillfully they maneuvered the ship through extremely dangerous shoals. Her shallow draft allowed her precarious passage to within a quarter mile of the white sandy beach, where she dropped anchor.

Sailors lowered the longboat, and soldiers off loaded their supplies and ferried them ashore. The horses and mules were carefully lowered individually over the side by special harness slings, and swam behind the longboat, a muleteer holding the halter rope to make certain the animals made it to shore. Weak and disoriented from their long stay below decks they perked up the moment their hooves touched solid ground.

Within four hours the men, animals and provisions were safely ashore and a temporary camp set up. "Bosun," shouted Narvaez, "Make preparations for getting underway!"

Luis shook Narvaez's outstretched hand, and said, "We'll meet you here in sixty days, God willing. Our lives are in your hands."

"Don't worry, my friend. We'll be here or we'll be dead!"

The longboat dropped Luis on the beach and he watched the ship's three triangular white canvas sails catch the wind. Ghost like, she glided slowly out of sight, and disappeared over the horizon.

🐾🐾🐾

"Sergeant!" barked Luis. "Get the men and supplies inland, off the beach!"

Luis turned in a slow circle on his heels, surveying the low hills guarding the beach, on up to the distant mountains rising above. His eyes narrowed in a thoughtful squint and came to rest on a mountain pass.

"What are your orders?" Sandoval asked.

"We'll camp here for the night and move inland at first light. See that pass? Let's head in that direction. I believe when we get through there we'll get our first look at the Aztecs."

"If they don't get a look at us first!" Sandoval grinned.

"Good point! I want Esperanza scouting ahead at all times, watching for any unfriendly Indians. And Jorge, you and Lopez make sure the men keep the noise down. No shouting or loud talk. From here on we've got to stay on our toes if we want to stay alive!"

🐾 🐾 🐾

Cempoa, Prince Ruminawi's scout, picked his spot with care. At first he thought of climbing a boulder to get a better view of the beach. But if Aztecs were coming from Papantla they might see him. He chose a small hillside gully which gave him cover and a good view of the country far below. He kept thinking about the Prince's warning before he left town. If the Aztecs come again, I don't know what we'll do! They've already taken too many of our young men and women for their bloody sacrifices.

Cempoa knew the old prince had resigned himself to the fact that the Chichemetlan people would always be Aztec subjects. So all he could do was keep watch and if he spotted Aztec General Teoamoxtli and his warriors he'd run and warn the village, so the young people could hide in the nearby forest.

Cempoa got to the pass before sun up. He sat there for an hour, shifting his buttocks on the rocky ground. The sunlight grew brighter. The air was quite still and the smell of the Caribbean floated across the mountains. He threw back his head and sniffed. He loved the smell of the sea. It was a different smell than that of the Chechemetlan valley where he lived.

Suddenly he caught a brief glimpse of something moving! His eyes stared down at the beach, not believing what he was seeing! A man in a metal suit was climbing up onto the back of a huge, four-footed black beast! The animal danced, and reared! The metal man spurred the beast and away it ran with him at a fast gallop, kicking up sand along the beach.

Cempoa sat bolt upright and sucked in his breath. Then, for a brief instant, he glimpsed other metal men walking slowly up the torturous trail leading toward the mountain pass. Got to think! Count them! His head jerked toward the beach—one man on a beast, about twenty five men walking, leading three beasts loaded down with supplies, and three other men riding on beasts. Who were they? Not Aztecs. They were bearded white men—except one, who was completely black!

Cempoa was scared! He wheeled on his feet and started a steady run back the way he had come to warn Prince Ruminawi.

🐾 🐾 🐾

The old prince was in his fifty-fifth year, tall and distinguished looking with gray hair, the last aristocrat of the Chichemetlan race—the Aztecs had seen to that! Yet his secluded farming valley prospered, and the prince lived in a lovely villa and was greatly respected by his people. He ruled as best he could, being subject to the Emperor Montezuma, as were all the other tribes in Mexico.

Ruminawi's face showed great astonishment at Cempoa's report. "White men and a black man? And they'll be here in a matter of hours?" he asked.

"Yes, my Lord."

"These beasts you speak of. They're unlike anything you've ever seen before?"

"Yes, my Lord."

Ruminawi turned to Sayri, his chief counselor. "Do you think it could be Quetzalcoatl, the white God of Aztec legend?"

"I don't know. But whoever the white men are, don't you think we'd better report this to Guatemotzin?"

"That Aztec mad man?" Ruminawi snorted. "It's none of his business."

"But my prince," Sayri protested. "You know how angry he gets when you keep things from him. If we don't report this, it could be extremely dangerous for us."

"What can he do? Nothing by himself! Him and his priests stay at the pyramid and practice their filthy religion. He never comes to the village."

Sayri built a bit of courage. "He can send for Teoamoxtli and his warriors."

The prince smiled. "Teoamoxtili is an Aztec general—but he hates Guatemotzin as much as we do. I don't believe he would leave Papantla just because Guatemotzin sends for him."

"You forget, my prince, that Aztec priests like Guatemotzin rule the empire. Their soldiers must do what they are told."

Ruminawi gave that thought. "Hm. Let's wait a bit. I'm very curious about these white men. Who are they? Where do they come from? What do they want? Perhaps they've come to free us from the Aztec dogs and their evil practices!"

"What if they are not friendly and plan to destroy us?" Sayri asked.

The smile slid from Ruminawi's face and he stared at Sayri and the others for a matter of seconds. When next he spoke there was a serious note in his voice. "These strange men will come through the pass tomorrow morning. I believe we should go out and meet them."

🐾 🐾 🐾

Roberto Esperanza scouted ahead of the column. The rocky trail sloped upward from the foothills covered with gray rock formations, making it hard going for Esperanza's horse.

Finally the horse clattered to a halt on the mountain's rocky summit in the mouth of the pass. Esperanza studied the valley below. Lush green. A beautiful village in the middle, fields of maize on the out-skirts. A huge stone pyramid on the far side, with a spiral of black smoke wafting skyward.

Peaceful. No soldiers or warriors anywhere in sight. No need to expose himself or his horse to the villagers. Esperanza turned the horse and headed back toward the column, still two leagues back.

The foothills wrinkled up toward the mountain's jagged upheaval. Luis and the men climbed slowly upward. The hills made hard going for the horses and mules loaded with supplies.

At noontime Luis called a short halt for the men and animals to get their second wind. The cook broke out provisions and they ate a cold meal, washed down with water from their canteens. They moved out again, climbing ever higher toward the pass until Luis found a level place to camp for the night.

Three hours later Esperanza raced his horse into camp. "Captain, I made it through the pass and there's a town on the other side!" Everyone quickly gathered round, asking a flurry of questions.

Luis raised a hand and restored order. "What sort of town?"

"It looks much like our villages in Spain—nestled in a beautiful valley—lots of white buildings. Cultivated fields on the outskirts."

"Anything else?" Luis tried to conceal his excitement.

"Yes sir. A strange looking pyramid at the far end of town."

"Well done, Roberto! Get yourself some food and rest up. You've earned it." The men followed Esperanza with a babble of questions.

Luis motioned Sandoval and Lopez to his tent. "There's no way we're going to get around that town without being seen, so we might as well experience our first meeting with the Aztecs."

"Good thinking," Sandoval agreed. "But I think we'd better watch out for ambush—maybe leave ten of the men a ways behind—the arquebusiers, along with the falconet, so that if we're attacked we'll have some backup which can move up quickly."

"See to it," Luis said. "But I want Esperanza, Ribera the ax man, San Estevan and Taragona with me when we go through that pass tomorrow!"

Morning came and the Spaniards struggled up the last stretch of the mountain trail, under a clear cloudless blue sky, each man breathing in clean, refreshing mountain air.

Sergeant Lopez rode alongside the infantrymen, the white banner of Spain whipping from his upheld lance. Mules, loaded with supplies, followed single file behind the muleteer bringing up the rear.

Lopez signaled Corporal Martinez—and ten men quickly dropped from the column and took cover in the heavy growth lining the trail.

Luis pulled Diablo's reins to slow him, and raised a hand to shield his eyes from the morning sun, and studied the mountain pass."

"See something?" Sandoval asked.

"Some people. I can't quite make them out."

Esperanza galloped up. "We've got company, Captain."

"Are they hostile?"

"I don't think so."

14

Luis slowed Diablo to a walk, as six Indians, Aztecs he guessed they were, made their way toward him. Their leader, a middle aged man, leaned on a golden walking staff, panting when he reached Luis. His green loincloth reached his knees, and a feathered cloak of brilliant red and green feathers trailed behind. His head was covered with a plumed helmet crested with emeralds, sparkling in the morning sun.

Luis stared down at him, making his face as tight as the Indian's. "Are they Aztecs, Kano?"

"I'm not sure. It would be a wise gesture for you to speak to them."

They gasped when Luis dismounted, took off his helmet and walked toward them. Until that moment they believed horse and rider to be an inseparable unit.

The elegantly dressed Indian chief trembled, and tried to control his fear of the huge black beast and the metal man. His fear turned to terror when Luis bowed slightly and greeted him in Nahuatl. "Greetings from our king. We come in peace."

The old chief fell back a full step as though he'd been slapped, his eyes wide with dread! "Why is he so frightened, Kano?" Luis asked.

Kano spoke to Golden Staff, then smiled." They're not Aztecs, sir, though they speak and understand Nahuatl. They're Chichemetlans. The old man is Prince Ruminawi. You frightened hell out of him when you spoke in Nahuatl—he thought you were from Montezuma's palace."

"Are they Aztec allies?"

"No, Captain. They're Aztec subjects."

"Will they allow us into their town?"

Kano talked with Ruminawi for a few moments. "The Prince offers his hospitality and bids us welcome."

Luis smiled and bowed slightly. Then he turned to Sergeant Lopez. "Go back and bring up the men we left behind.

🐾 🐾 🐾

Throngs of townspeople lined the street between gleaming white buildings. Fascinated, they watched Prince Ruminawi walk majestically into town, leading white men on great, snorting beasts, clattering steel-shod hooves on the cobblestone street. Several uniformed soldiers, in marching formation, brought up the rear. The friendly Chichemetlans waved, shouted and laughed happily.

Adults wore long cotton gowns covered with gaudy, colorful designs. Naked children ran everywhere. Younger men and women wore short, narrow green loincloths of cotton, hanging from cinctures around their waists. The Spaniards had never seen such healthy, delightsome people, especially so many beautiful women. All had jet black hair streaming over their shoulders.

At the far edge of town, a quarter league east, Luis noticed a huge, truncated pyramid. Atop, in the shadows, stood a lonely black-robed figure, curiously watching the procession wind its way through town and stop at the gates of Ruminawi's villa.

🐾 🐾 🐾

The afternoon was sunny, the sky deep blue; whiteness reflected from the buildings. Ruminawi invited Luis, Kano and Sandoval into his home. When they were seated comfortably a young woman brought fruit.

Luis waited for Ruminawi to begin the conversation, but his expression was that of a man accustomed to periods of enormous patience, periods of waiting.

He finally spoke. "I welcome you to our village. Your coming was a complete surprise. Had we known you would visit us, we'd have been better prepared. Where are you from?"

"We come from Spain, a land far across your eastern sea." Luis replied. "Who is your king?"

"King Carlos. He's a very kind and gentle king who wants to be your friend."

Ruminawi stared at Kano as he interpreted. "And you, black man, you are different from the others. Where are you from?"

"From a land very very far away. It is a huge land where all the people are black." The talk continued.

In the courtyard, Chichemetlan men and boys, totally fascinated by everything about the Spaniards, especially the horses and mules, cautiously approached, whispering comments about the strange beasts. One young man, dared by his companions to pet the big black beast, crept up to Diablo.

"Get away from there!" Alfredo shouted angrily and grabbed him by the shoulder. The boy couldn't understand the huge white man's strange words. "You stupid, clumsy brown-skinned idiot! It's time you learned some respect. I'm going to slap your face and kick your bare ass until you tell me you're sorry."

Before he could bring his big palm across the boy's cheek Sergeant Lopez grabbed the huge arm. The boy broke away and ran. Alfredo jerked his arm free. "Damn you, Lopez. Don't ever grab me like that again or I'll..."

"Or you'll what?" Don't threaten me, you insubordinate bastard!" Lopez's hand snaked to his sword. "I've taken enough of your bullshit! Defend yourself!"

Hearing the commotion, Luis rushed from the villa. Alfredo again! The blunt head was anchored on a thick neck and it was easy enough to read the sullen face and crafty eyes.

"One more problem with you and I'll have the skin off your back. Leave these people alone! Do you understand me?"

It took the angry blacksmith a moment before he said, "Yes Captain. I'm sorry. You won't have any more trouble from me." He knew he'd have to keep Escudero off his back until he could figure a way to sabotage the expedition.

"Get the hell about your business, then! Report for the midnight watch from now on!"

When Alfredo moved off, Luis said, "Keep your eye on him, Sergeant. He's a mighty sick man, who's going to ruin us if we turn our backs on him."

"Sick?" Lopez was puzzled. "He appears well enough to me."

"There are too many Alfredos," Luis said. "They're all sick men. They suffer from a disease that only the sight or possession of gold can cure. But it's even more than that. The Alfredos carry the disease of evil with them. Evil has its own smell, its own form. It's as alive as the people who carry it."

Lopez didn't understand what Luis was talking about—but sensed his deep philosophical nature for the first time.

Luis returned to the villa. Lopez walked to the corral and brushed the natives aside, when Diablo lashed out a mighty kick with both steel-shod hooves, narrowly missing a native boy who screamed and ran away.

Alfredo watched his comrades revel in the attention of Chichemetlan women. He gulped down a generous swallow of rum from his canteen, and nonchalantly sauntered to a small outbuilding in the compound where the gunpowder, falconet and other arms were stored. Looking furtively about, he ducked inside the building.

Ruminawi invited Luis, Sandoval and Kano to walk through town while he made arrangements for an evening feast. "Compare our village to those of your country. Have no fear of our people. They are peaceful." He smiled. "Perhaps that's why we're Aztec subjects!"

Luis, Sandoval and Kano strolled through town "What do you think?" Luis asked. "Have you ever seen a healthier or happier people?"

"I've been to many countries," Sandoval said, "but never one like this. It's clean and prosperous and I haven't seen a single deformity. They put Europeans to shame."

"How so?"

"Europeans are round shouldered, spindle shanked, crane necked, with padded breasts!"

"Thanks!" Luis grinned.

"Well, not us of course!" Sandoval grinned. "Look at their teeth when they smile. See that old man? He's got better teeth than our youngsters in Spain."

Kano spoke up. "I don't want to seem impertinent, gentlemen, but this place is much cleaner than your cities. I've never been to Europe but I've heard the streets are littered with garbage, human waste, buckets of urine and other offal cast into the streets to be scavenged by dogs or pigs. I've even heard that in the more modern cities herds of pigs are driven through the main thoroughfares nightly to do away with the waste, but only when the piles have grown so large pedestrians, carts and horses can no longer get by. The stench is unbearable. Is this true?"

Luis nodded affirmatively. "Though I hate to admit it, yes, it's very true."

The narrow main street between the buildings ended and broadened out into a very wide cobblestone road leading directly to the mysterious pyramid dead ahead. They stopped and stared. Luis shivered involuntarily. He had no idea why. He was filled with a strange foreboding he'd never experienced before, as he watched black smoke curling from a chimney protruding from a building atop the pyramid.

"Shall we go have a look?" Sandoval asked.

"Not today. Let's go back to the villa and get cleaned up for the feast this evening."

"All right," Sandoval agreed. "That pyramid is a most interesting structure. See how it's truncated? The main layer is the framework or foundation, and each layer above gets smaller as it grows skyward."

"I thought pyramids existed only in Egypt," Luis said.

"That's why this pyramid is so interesting. In every detail it's exactly like the earliest pyramids ever constructed in Egypt. Those pyramids were built to house their kings' remains. I have no idea what this pyramid is for."

"Let's find out," Luis responded. "Kano, ask that old fellow over there who built the pyramid."

The old gray Chichemetlan, with a heavy sack of maize on his back, stopped when Kano stepped in front of him. "Sir, can you tell who built that pyramid?"

"The ancient ones."

Kano turned to Luis. "He says the ancient ones built it."

"Who are the ancient ones?"

Kano asked the old man, who muttered something, and pointed his finger at Luis and Sandoval.

"He says they were men like you."

"Spaniards?"

"No sir, they were white men."

Luis and Sandoval stared at each other. Sandoval said, "They couldn't be Englishmen or Frenchmen if they're an ancient people."

Luis nodded. "Kano, ask him what's the purpose of the pyramid."

When Kano put the question to the old man, his face stiffened into a look of sheer terror. He stammered a few words before scurrying off, looking back over his shoulder, making sure he wasn't being followed.

"Well?" Luis asked.

"I'm not sure I understand exactly what the old man meant. Something to do with much evil. No one in the village is permitted to say anything about what goes on at the pyramid!"

15

"What do you think, Captain?" Sandoval asked, as Luis studied the map he'd drawn from Punta del Piedras, Cuba, to the Chichemetlan village.

"Excellent! You've not missed a detail!" Luis' words were quiet, the tone pleasant. "Just keep plotting our course as we move toward Tenochtitlan. Your map will be invaluable to Captain Cortez—if we live long enough to get it back to him."

Luis tapped his fingers on the table for a moment. "You know, Jorge, I'm glad things have happened as they have."

"How so?"

"Well, we've entered the Aztec empire without the loss of men or supplies. We're among a friendly people. We can gather a great deal of information about the Aztecs from Prince Ruminawi."

"Like what?"

"Where Tenochtitlan is located, what Aztec garrisons lie between here and there, and whether we'll find any gold and silver."

A knock came on the door and Kano stuck his head in. "Gentlemen, a couple of young ladies are here to escort us to a feast in the dining hall!"

The young women escorted Luis and his men to the large dining hall scented with exotic perfumes and incense, its walls adorned with sweet-scented herbs and flowers. Lamps hanging from silver chains lighted the room. Luis, Sandoval and Kano were seated at the head table, beside a huge gold and silver chair, while the men sat at long tables facing the head table.

Total silence came when Prince Ruminawi made his appearance, hardly recognizable as the same person who greeted the Spaniards at the mountain pass. Chichemetlan servants bowed low as he walked past them to the head table, using his golden staff for support. On his head was a splendid hat bedecked with gaudy feathers of red, green and blue; and over one shoulder a flowing robe of red cotton material hung loosely. Around his neck dangled a golden necklace. From his pierced ears hung golden earrings.

Luis and his men stood and snapped to attention. Ruminawi bowed, savoring the stunning effect his costume created among the Spaniards.

Ruminawi knew he'd have to speak simply and slowly, in short sentences, because the black interpreter did not use simultaneous interpretation. He waited until the speaker finished, then relayed a synopsis of what was said, the usual problem of all except the finest interpreters.

Ruminawi spoke slowly and Kano interpreted. "Welcome to our valley. We've prepared a feast, but before we dine, we have some gifts for you."

He clapped his hands and five elaborately costumed chiefs, attended by several women, filed into the dining hall, each carrying a gift. The soldiers gawked in total surprise as the first chief' placed a silver chalice with one hundred ounces of gold inside, on the floor in front of Luis. The next chief, followed by two women struggling with a silver vase so large a man couldn't circle it with his arms, set it next to the chalice. The two remaining chiefs, came in, side by side, one carrying a golden parrot, fashioned by craftsmanship so extraordinary its feathers appeared real, rather than fabricated from the precious metal. The other chief carried a golden fish with scales of alternating silver and gold.

The illiterate soldiers stared! Was this real, or some wild illusion? Nothing like this ever happened to rank and file foot-slogging soldiers. Never!

Luis stood. "Thank you, my Lord."

Ruminawi smiled and nodded toward the young women. "They are for your pleasure and amusement."

Luis walked around the table and picked up the gold-filled silver chalice and held it high. "Look comrades! Do you know what this is? It's gold!"

It was the perfect time to infect his men with the desire to push westward, appealing to their unquenchable desire for treasure—the hungry ones, like Esperanza, Taragona, San Estevan, Martinez and the others, who'd all go down to hell for a fistful of gold.

"You Martinez," he stepped up to the corporal. "Go on. Dip your finger in it. Feel it. Taste it if you like! Tell the lads what it is!"

Martinez scooped up a handful of gold dust and let it slip slowly through his fingers. "It's pure gold, Captain!" he said with disbelief in his voice.

Murmuring quickly spread among the men, stunned surprise showing on their faces. Luis continued. "This is nothing! Where we're going the houses are made of gold! There's piles of gold so high you can climb them and plunder the stars."

Ruminawi studied the effects his gifts produced among the Spaniards. He smiled with satisfaction and signaled his retainers to bring more.

The soldiers stared, completely dumbfounded, as a line of women walked in with ornaments, statuettes, collars, service of plate, all of pure gold. The heap of gold on the floor grew, shining under the torch light with a terrible liquid purity—treasure so rich there was no way to comprehend its value.

"Well, comrades," shouted Luis, "what say you? Shall we go see the emperor in his great palace?"

"Aye!" came the thundering response.

Luis bowed his head, as if inclining to their will. He turned to Ruminawi. "We humbly thank you for these precious gifts." He motioned Sergeant Lopez to fetch some trade goods which he placed on the table. The multicolored glass beads fascinated the Chichemetlan chiefs, but the small glass mirrors created a minor sensation as they studied their reflections, giggling with delight. Amused Spaniards watched these strange savages, with fabulous treasures of gold and silver, captivated by something as trivial as a mirror.

Ruminawi said, "Dinner is served." Servants filed in carrying platters of steaming food.

On the tables were plates of silver, cotton napkins and silver goblets of clear, cold mountain water. Then came turkey, a delicacy the Spaniards had never tasted. Vegetables and fruits of every delicious variety were arrayed along with delicate sauces and seasonings for flavoring meat and vegetables.

The men dug in with zesty appetites. Ruminawi leaned over and whispered something to Kano, then resumed eating.

"What did he say?" Luis asked.

"I don't think you really want to know, but I'll tell you anyway. He apologized for the food we're eating. He didn't have time to prepare a proper feast."

"What could be better than this?" Luis asked, munching, tearing dark meat from a turkey bone. "Normally they sacrifice a slave whose flesh is elaborately dressed and seasoned."

"Good God!" Luis gasped, fearing he'd been tricked into eating human flesh. "Are you sure you interpreted that correctly?"

"Yes, Captain."

Serving girls circulated around and gave each soldier a goblet of pulque.

"Holy Jesus Christ!" Lopez sputtered. "It's stronger than our rum, but it's damn good! What is it?"

Kano answered, "It's pulque, a beverage made from the leaves of the Mexican aloe tree. Juice from its leaves is fermented and made into a drink with the kick of a mule!"

🐾🐾🐾

Ruminawi stood, with Kano at his side. "We have an after dinner custom with which you are unfamiliar, but we'll teach you." He clapped his hands and several young women came into the hall, each carrying a small silver pipe. The prettiest woman, apparently a concubine of Ruminawi, handed him a pipe with smoke curling from its bowl. Fascinated, half drunk soldiers watched the Prince stick the pipe stem in his mouth, and take a long sucking drag. He compressed his nostrils with the fingers of his left hand, inhaled the smoke deep into his lungs, and blew it out. He repeated the performance several times. "We'll pass pipes to you so you may inhale the sweet smoke. It's most pleasing and relaxing to mind and body."

The women flitted about the tables demonstrating how to use the smoking pipes. After a bit of coughing the soldiers quickly mastered the art of smoking, dragging down into their lungs the smoke of the weed which did have magical, mind-altering qualities! Each man was overcome with a warm, relaxing euphoria; and their eyes followed the semi-nude women, erotically aroused as never before.

"Sergeant," Luis grinned. "I believe the men have finished dinner. Please dismiss them so they can become better acquainted with the young ladies!"

Lopez bellowed the order, and the hall emptied quickly!

Luis seized the opportunity to question Prince Ruminawi. "Please tell us about about your history."

Ruminawi settled himself comfortably, sucking his pipe, relishing the opportunity for after dinner conversation. "The Chichemetlans have lived in this valley a very long time—since the ancient ones went away." He spoke slowly, so Kano could translate. "The ancient ones were white men, like you."

He noted Luis and Sandoval's skeptical looks. "It's true, my friends. I have no reason to lie to you. They built cities and monuments all over this vast land, and they worshipped a strange and unusual God."

"What sort of God?" Luis asked.

"An invisible God. I've always thought that very strange, worshipping a God that can't be seen. Our Gods are carved of stone so we can see and touch them, Gods of substance."

"Where did the ancient ones come from?"

"Legends say they came from the eastern sea, just as you did. They were mighty warriors who claimed this land and lived here a long time before they disappeared. No one knows where they went. They ruled over the Chichemetlans and all other tribes."

"What can you tell us about the Aztecs?" Luis asked.

"They're a very fierce and cruel people, whom we hate. They've forced their vile religion and evil ways upon us. They're as numerous as grains of sand on the seashore, and they have a huge, unconquerable army."

Ruminawi took a long drag on his pipe. "Their emperor Montezuma is hated by all the tribes he's conquered. The Totonacs, our powerful neighbors and friends to the west, await the day when all the tribes can unite and destroy the Aztecs. Fifty years ago the Aztecs conquered this peaceful valley. Our ways were simple then. The Gods who send sunshine and rain were good enough for us. Now we have nothing but Aztec Gods. If we offer the slightest resistance the Aztecs carry off our young men for their army and our young women for their special sacrifices."

When Ruminawi leaned over to take a drink of pulque, Luis whispered to Sandoval, "Make a note of what the old man is telling us."

"I am. Right up here." Sandoval tapped his head. "I'll put it on parchment later."

"Anything else, Captain?" Ruminawi asked.

"How many warriors could the Totonacs muster to fight against the Aztecs."

"Oh, very many. They're a very powerful people with over thirty cities. They have at least fifty thousand warriors."

Luis nodded thoughtfully. Uniting the Mexican tribes under Spanish military leadership would be the key to defeating the Aztecs!

"This Aztec religion you mentioned. What do you mean they sacrifice people?"

"They murder men, women and children to satiate their Gods of war, love and fertility. We do not hold with killing innocent people. In the beginning the Aztecs used sacrifice sparingly, but each year sacrifices become more numerous, as though there's not enough blood and death in the entire world to placate their merciless Gods. Recently a new high priest in Tenochtitlan added a new dimension to the killing. The bodies of some of the sacrificial victims are eaten."

"How many bodies are we talking about?" Luis asked.

"Thousands! Often hundreds each day."

"The emperor permits this?" Luis drew a sharp breath. All three Spaniards came to the edge of their seats.

"I don't think he can stop it. His mad priests often initiate new innovations into their religious rites and the emperor is unaware of what they are doing."

"Do those innovations affect the Chichemetlan people?" Luis asked.

Ruminawi brought his shoulders tight around his neck, as if to shrug off a burden, seeming as though he'd rather not answer.

"I'm sorry, sir. I didn't mean to pry," Luis said.

"It's all right. It's difficult for me to talk about it. Several days ago warriors came from Papantla and took ten of our lovely young women."

"Why?"

"To be sacrificed to their blood-thirsty Gods. It's an impossible situation, but we do our best to survive."

"Can we help in any way?"

A slow, sad smile played across Ruminawi's wrinkled face. "Stay here with us, Captain. Pasture your stock in our green valley. We'll work together and you can teach us your ways."

"I wish we could," Luis responded sincerely. Never, in all my travels, have I seen a more desirable place. But we're on a mission for our king to visit the emperor in Tenochtitlan."

"I assumed as much. I hoped you might free us from the Aztecs…"

Suddenly, the reverberating booming of the huge drum atop the distant pyramid shattered the valley's peaceful silence.

Ruminawi's face paled. He dropped his pipe and jumped up. "Excuse me," he mumbled. "I must gather my chiefs!" He scurried from the dining hall, leaning on his gold staff.

"What's happening, Kano?" Luis eyes went wide, looking for any signs of danger. "The people have been summoned, sir."

"Summoned where?"

"I don't know. The Prince didn't say."

"We'd better find out, Captain!" Sandoval's voice was low and grim, "and pretty damned fast!"

Luis nodded. "Something strange is happening, Jorge. Go find Sergeant Lopez and have him round up the men. Then let's find out what the hell is going on!"

16

Dark brooding clouds hovered over the huge flat-topped pyramid, partially blotting out the full moon. The drum's ominous, reverberating rhythm grew louder and more menacing. Chichemetlans shuffled trance-like from their homes toward the pyramid. Their somber expressions troubled Luis. Why the change? It was as if they were walking to their own graves.

"Lieutenant, form up the men! Let's find out what's going on!"

Sandoval shouted the order and the men staggered into formation, still a bit tipsy from the strong pulque; but the cool night air quickly cleared their heads and they marched smartly behind their officers.

Several black-robed figures scurried about atop the truncated pyramid. Lieutenant Sandoval leaned over to Luis, and quietly murmured, "I've got a bad feeling about this place. There's going to be trouble!"

Before Luis could respond, they came face to face with Prince Ruminawi and his counselors at the base of the pyramid. "Please, my friends, understand this is not a Chichemetlan custom," Ruminawi apologized. "The Aztecs forced this horrible religion on us."

Sayri, Ruminawi's chief counselor glanced furtively about and whispered, "Keep your voice down, my prince. If the Aztecs hear you it'll go badly for all of us."

"I see no Aztecs," Luis said, peering into the darkness.

"Up there!" Ruminawi spat out, pointing to the pyramid's top. "There are your bloody Aztecs! They're not soldiers, but priests, and much more dangerous! However, their warriors are just a short march away at Papantla, so please be very careful! Don't offend them!"

At that moment a native in a black cloak stepped from the blackness. "Guatemotzin, master of the temple, sent me with a message."

"Let's hear it!" snapped Ruminawi.

"He's very angry with you for bringing these strangers here tonight. He said you should have gotten his permission."

"Who is Guatemotzin?" Luis asked.

Frightened, the messenger trembled when a huge black giant interpreted Luis' words. He stammered, "The rest of the message is for the leader of the foreign soldiers."

"Spit it out" Luis growled.

The messenger screwed up his courage. "Our Lord, Guatemotzin, invites you and your men to visit him atop the pyramid."

Luis nodded. "Very well! Take us to him."

"Your pardon, sir, but there is one further matter of business. "Cozu, first son of Sayri, has been selected to honor the great moon god tonight."

Sayri visibly trembled; his breath clogged and stopped in his throat, his eyes rolled, and he collapsed in Ruminawi's arms.

"What the hell is going on?" Luis asked. "What is this fool talking about?"

"Sir," Kano responded, "Cozu is that man's son." He pointed to Sayri.

Luis started to ask another question, but Sandoval grabbed his arm, and pointed to the top of the pyramid. "Good God almighty! Look up, Captain! Look at that."

High above, a dark-cloaked figure appeared, holding his arms skyward, looking like a huge bird of prey with wings spread for flight. He shouted something, and his guttural Aztec words echoed ominously off the great stone mound.

"Come up, white men! Come up!" A chill ran down Kano's spine as he relayed the words to the solders.

"Be very careful, Captain!" Ruminawi whispered a warning. "Guatemotzen is a madman. He's a sorcerer with many powers! He's perverted the Aztec religion to include many rites not yet found in Tenochtitlan, where the emperor resides. Montezuma has warned him several times to cease his perversions."

When Kano finished his translation, the Prince continued. "Whatever you do, don't look directly into his eyes. He and his priests have magical powers and can make you do things against your will!"

Luis scoffed, "I don't believe in any such nonsense!"

"Perhaps you will after you've met these evil Aztecs!"

The cadenced drum abruptly stopped. A deathly silence pervaded the valley.

Luis and the others craned their necks, looking up. Each checked his dagger and sword.

"Come, men of Spain, it's time to meet Guatemotzin!" Ruminawi motioned them to follow, and started a long slow climb up the steps to the top, leaning heavily on his golden staff.

Gaining the top they were met by met by four men, three dressed alike in black cloaks gaudily decorated with white triangles, circles and other geometric designs. Under their cloaks, the priests wore only thin loin cloths covering their thighs. Their long black hair was matted with dried blood, and their hands and bare torsos smeared with fresh blood. One bent, humpbacked priest, in a red cloak, sidled slowly toward them with a crab-like gait.

Fire danced from a large stone bowl, giving off an exotic incense fragrance which helped blot out the putrid stench coming from the Aztec priests. From a doorway the shadowy figure of a very tall, robust Aztec woman, walked majestically toward the group.

Her robe was black, and like the priests', open in front. Her dark beauty stunned the Spaniards. Her full, bare breasts bobbed as she moved, and her slim waist and delicately turned thighs, covered only by a thin loin cloth, exuded a bold sexual rhythm. She stood enticingly before them—her eyes flicked over the soldiers—bearded white men in metal suits. One in particular drew her immediate interest.

Older than the others, he wore a black patch over one eye. Smiling broadly, she locked eyes with his, and those dark sultry eyes burned into Sandoval's soul.

The red-robed priest spoke sharply to Ruminawi, "You know there's only one master in this valley, and it's not some ill-bred dog of a Chichemetlan! You know how I hate you to keep secrets from me. Why haven't you told me about the white men?"

Ruminawi blanched at the priest's words. "Sir, I..." Before he could finish the priest broke in, this time with a softer voice, but still just as deadly. "We'll meet later and discuss this in more detail!"

Guatemotzin turned his full attention on the Spaniards, whose leader was tall, lithe and well built. His strength did not give the impression of being locked up within himself as is the case with so many strong men. He moved with a flowing ease that advertised power more subtly than does mere muscle- bound hulk. And the strange black man was an oddity indeed! Guatemotzin had never seen a black man, nor a white one for that matter! The black man could speak and understand Nahuatl. Strange. Very strange indeed!

"I'm Guatemotzin, priest of the temple, and this is my priestess Techchupo, and the others are my assistants." Unexpectedly he emitted a high-pitched giggle, his oddly off-center head nodding and dipping. "Welcome to our valley! Who are you and from whence do you come?"

"We are soldiers from the country of Spain and I am Captain Luis Escudero."

"I know nothing of this country called Spain. But no matter, Captain, we'll talk of it later," Guatemotzin snorted. With an idiotic grin, the smelly, near-sighted Aztec sidled ever closer to Luis. The closer he came the more he exuded an unseen presence of pure, terrifying evil. When the deformed little man looked at you with those reddened eyes you couldn't look away—and you didn't want to! He reminded Luis of a sniffing dog, trying to discover if he were friend or foe. Evidently he found Luis of no immediate threat.

"Your visit comes at a most appropriate time. Most appropriate! Tonight we offer sacrifice to the moon god. Observe!" He raised his hand and the drum began to thump and shrill flute music wafted from the pyramid's darkened interior.

Techchupo tossed her cloak aside and began the sensuous Aztec dance of death, firelight casting her undulating shadow on the pyramid's bloody walls.

Roberto Esperanza and his companions stood hypnotically enthralled by the strange erotic dance unfolding before them. "Techchu..." He tried to pronounce her name, but couldn't get it out. Martinez whispered, "Isn't she beautiful?"

"Hell yes! She's a woman, isn't she?"

"Her face is too strong for me. But her eyes and hair are really something. And her figure, ah!" Martinez made a sinuous female shape in the air.

"Quiet!" Luis snapped.

Techchupo moved gracefully, keeping tempo with the strange, unearthly music. The drum picked up a faster beat while the shrill eagle wing flutes sounded out a haunting melodic piece. In the background priests began a low wailing chant. Techchupo's intricate steps and leaps were clearly part of an ancient ritual.

The soldiers had never heard such musical sounds. The rhythmic swaying of Techchupo's voluptuous body, its sinuous contortions glistening in the firelight, worked a sorcerer's spell, depriving the Spaniards of the will or power to move.

Techchupo's excitement grew more intense. Her dancing became wildly abandoned, building up to an eagerly awaited climax. Every eye focused intently on her. The priests' incessant chant rose ever louder which sounded like locktah! locktah! Kano had no idea what it meant.

Suddenly a new fire leaped from a stone basin in the center of the pyramid, and there spread eagled and naked, back down over a round shining jasper stone was Cozu. The seventeen year old was drugged; yet he seemed aware of his surroundings. His glazed eyes followed the shapely woman, dancing nearer and nearer!

Cozu grinned idiotically. "It's only a dream," his drugged mind told him, just a wild, funny nightmare! He sighed with pleasure at the clutch of Techchupo's soft fingers around his fully rigid, fully erect member. Their moving caress became more vigorous. His whole body tensed, his breath came in gasps as he tried to overcome the imminent spasm which he so greatly desired and yet wished to halt. Her mouth became an instrument of joy and torture to him. She became all searching fingers, all moist warm mouth, smooth skin, pressing against him, warm fingers manipulating his swollen erection. She dropped her loin cloth, straddled the helpless sacrifice, impaling herself and plunged wildly up and down. On her last might pump Cozu spent himself, groaning and gasping for breath as his release came.

Techchupo rested, caught her breath and slowly raised herself, donned her cape and prostrated herself at Guatemotzin's feet. Abruptly the music stopped. "My Lord, the gift for the moon god is ready."

Guatemotzin turned his face solemnly on the Spaniards. "Techchupo has received of his loins and body. Now the Moon God will receive his spirit. Come my dear!" He reached his hand out to Techchupo and together they walked to Cozu.

Dumbfounded, the Spaniards gaped at one another, each trying to find some frame of reference to help them understand what was happening. They visibly started when a maniacal laugh erupted from Guatemotzin, as Techchupo pulled a sharp obsidian knife from a colorful sheath in her hand, and presented it to the priest. Raising the sacrificial knife with both hands, high above his head, Guatemotzin plunged it deep into the boy's chest and cut a long incision.

Cozu screamed shrilly as his life ceased. Guatemotzin reached inside the jagged incision, deftly clutched the warm, bloody, still beating heart and held it aloft. Unexpectedly he then brought it to his mouth, tore a large bite from it, then placed it on a tray which Techchupo held.

Slowly and gracefully she turned toward Luis, held the tray out, and offered him the bloody heart.

He stared at the steaming organ in its moat of blood then into the bloodshot eyes of Guatemotzin, watching intently for Luis' reaction. To a man, the Spaniards' fire-lit, spell-bound eyes focused on their captain! Luis' throat felt its first constrictions of impending nausea. He knew he couldn't accept the proffered gift without vomiting, even though the lives of he and his men depended on it. But how could he avoid giving offense to this evil, mad priest?

17

Luis reverently took the platter, placed it carefully on the floor and beamed a look of sheer gratitude. He knelt in prayer, his hands clasped beneath his chin, his eyes closed. He began to rock back and forth, gabbling strange words, which he hoped conveyed a religious ritual not to be disturbed. The impromptu act produced the desire effect! Luis was conscious of a circle of brown faces, Guatemotzin, Techchupo and their helpers gazing in reverent awe. Luis' men gawked at each other, wondering if their captain had lost his mind!

Luis lifted his eyes heavenward, staring at the moon. Slowly and deliberately he dipped his finger in the blood, raised it to his forehead, made the sign of the cross and muttered, in nimine patris, et filii et spiritui sancti. It's all he could think of! He slowly picked up the tray and handed it back to Techchupo with a graceful smile and a slight inclination of his head. The Aztecs' full attention was riveted on him.

"Kano, tell the loco little bastard and his fornicating whore I and my men made a vow to our God to eat no human flesh until our journey to visit their emperor is successfully completed."

Kano's solemn interpretation brought broad, satisfied smiles from the Aztecs. Guatemotzin instructed his assistants to dispose of Cozu's corpse still tied to the sacrificial stone. They lifted the lifeless form, carried it to the edge of the pyramid and cast it down the steep side where it bounced to the multitude of Chichemetlans milling about below.

To the Spaniards the sacrifice was hideous and revolting, even though they'd steeled themselves to death in its various forms. It excited in several of them strange feelings they'd never experienced. Sandoval, especially, was greatly affected by the brutal, yet sensuous religious ceremony, and it showed in his troubled face.

"What's the matter?" Luis asked.

Sandoval didn't answer for a time, but closed his good eye, his facial muscles twitching. He drew in a long breath, and felt sick, not from the emotional pain of seeing Cozu murdered, but a spiritual fear buried deep in his soul.

"Sandoval," Luis asked sharply, "are you up to what faces us here in this place?"

"Ah, sir, I can handle a soldier's work—but this?" He spread his hands expansively. "Did you see what those cowardly buggerly bastards did to that poor lad?" His hand went to his sword hilt. "Just say the word, Captain, and I'll slit the priest's throat and run his mad bitch through!"

"Calm down!" Luis whispered. "This situation is not of our making. No matter what they do, we must learn everything we can about the Aztecs."

Luis' words put Sandoval a little more at ease; but the men fidgeted, edgy and nervous, hands on swords, peering into the temple's dark corners, as if expecting some great hideous beast to leap from the blackness and devour them, or worse.

"Sandoval, have Corporal Martinez take the men back to the villa," Luis ordered. "You, I and Kano will stay on for a bit. Tell Martinez to take Ruminawi with him and take care of him. I want no harm to come to him."

Sandoval relayed the order and Martinez saluted smartly, more than happy to comply. He and the men were anxious to be free of the reeking, bloody Aztecs and their foul practices.

Guatemotzin and Techchupo smiled relief when they saw Martinez and the others descend the steep stairway and march off. Now, if the officers could be eliminated, those soldiers would go back where they came from!

Guatemotzin giggled. "Were you pleased with the sacrifice, Captain?"

"I've never seen one to compare to it!" Luis answered honestly. Evidently his answer pleased the priest, for he smiled.

"Tell me sir, does this sort of thing happen often?" Luis asked.

"Oh my yes! We make sacrifice every day, to one god or another. But the sacrifice we offer to the moon god, when he shines in full glory is very special, as you witnessed here tonight. The one chosen for the sacrifice must be of royal blood, not just an ordinary person!" Guatemotzin's tone indicated he loved his work.

Techchupo's eyes never left Sandoval's face while Luis and Guatemotzin talked. Without intending to, he scanned her curvaceous naked body. Suddenly his head hammered with desire for her; her wide, dark eyes captured his gaze. He wanted to touch her burnished copper skin, to stroke his fingers around the shape of her face. He wanted to kiss her, to part her lips until her tongue met his. He wanted to feel those heavily nippled breasts, to explore that hairy triangle between her luscious thighs..."

"Sandoval!" Luis's voice jerked him back to reality. "Come, our host wants to show us about."

They followed Guatemotzin to a room lighted by torches, behind a small building, evidently some type of large sanctuary.

They studied gruesome instruments of death laid out on a table; and stared at grotesque statues lining its blood-splotched walls. Demons, dragons and oddly deformed gargoyles stared out from cold, stone eyes as if keeping watch over this unholy place. Large statues of men and women in every conceivable act of sexual perversion adorned the floor. None of them had ever seen anything so appalling.

"Techchupo, fetch pulque for our guests," Guatemotzin said, and within moments the priestess handed them each a goblet of the fiery Aztec liquor. Its warming, relaxing action eased tensions building in the Spaniards.

Luis, flanked by Kano and Sandoval, peered into the room's dark recesses, from which came a sickening stench. It oozed from the blood-stained walls in an almost visible miasma—a smell entrenched in the stone from centuries of bloody sacrifices, long before the Aztecs came to the Chichemetlan village. Luis wondered about the thousands of victims who had perished under demented holy men like Guatemotzin.

Suddenly all thought processes were overshadowed by an unshakable premonition screaming, danger! danger! Yet Luis saw nothing tangible posing any threat to him or his friends. Before he could come up with a course of action Guatemotzin clapped his hands and several nude young women were shoved before the startled Spaniards. Fully mature, each was delicately beautiful, well shaped, with long lustrous black hair.

"Take your pick, my friends. These Totonac maidens, captured just two moons ago are for your pleasure." Guatemotzin grabbed one of the women roughly and thrust her at Luis.

Standing before the white man, she was terrified.

Guatemotzin smiled evilly. "Here. Feel her skin and female softness. Is she not lovely?"

They could see the gooseflesh spring out on her naked body as the mad priest casually drew his finger between the cleft of her breasts, across the sensuous swell of her stomach and down through the dark springy mat of pubic hair, hooking his long finger suddenly inside her with a force that pulled her up on her toes and brought a sucking gasp of pain.

The Spaniards were stunned. Sandoval's hand went to his sword, but Luis put a hand on his arm.

"She and the others are lovely indeed," Luis agreed. "Perhaps another time. We'd like to see the rest of the building and learn more of your interesting religion."

Disappointment clouded Guatemotzin's face, though he tried to mask it. He shooed the women from the room.

Techchupo slowly edged closer to Sandoval, attracted by his aloofness and apparent revulsion of her. She knew it would challenge of her female charms to bring him under her power, as Guatemotzin had ordered. She studied him in the flickering torchlight, finally gathering courage to whisper in his ear.

He instantly recoiled from her touch and jerked away.

Kano grinned. "She wants to show you around, Lieutenant."

"I'll not go anyplace with the mad bitch," Sandoval growled. "My God, what kind of people are these? The stinking bastards make me want to puke!"

"Lieutenant, will you just go along with the woman?" Luis asked in exasperation. "Find out all you can about this place, and the Aztecs in general."

"But Captain, they're nothing but a bunch of goddamned animals."

Luis grinned. "But she's really very taken by you, can't you see that? You mustn't disappoint her."

Sandoval gave in, resigned to his fate. "Anything for king and country, eh? But God's blood, I'd sooner touch a rattlesnake!"

"It won't be for long," Luis said. "We'll leave soon. See if they have any gold or silver about. Watch what you're about and stay alive!"

With Luis' warning ringing in his ears, Sandoval reluctantly followed Techchupo to another part of the building.

Guatemotzin was pleased. "Your lieutenant will learn many things tonight, Captain."

The priest's most unusual eyes fascinated Luis and Kano and held them entranced They glowed red like embers, and in the dim light of the torches, expanded, growing until they were dark pits, ringed with fire, pits you fall into and drown.

They remembered Ruminawi's warning about looking into Guatemotzin's eyes, yet they were powerless to look away. They were bound to the mad priest by an invisible chain. Both felt odd, queasy inside. The pulque, the penetrating eyes—Luis fell to the floor. The next moment Kano slumped alongside him.

Guatemotzin gleefully rubbed his hands together, staring down at his helpless victims. "Now, if Techchupo can handle the one-eyed soldier!"

Techchupo led Sandoval from one room to another pointing out various weapons, statues and other strange oddities used in their religion and culture. Finally she led him into a woman's chamber, complete with a large bed and a pure silver mirror hanging on the wall.

He tried to shake the cobwebs from his brain as the drugged pulque began working on him. A fear he'd never experienced engulfed him. Techchupo was evil, perhaps even Satan himself in womanly disguise. From somewhere flute music filtered though the chamber. Techchupo's jaguar growled low in his throat and paced nervously back and forth, held by a length of golden chain about his neck.

The woman had no idea how a white man would respond to her advances—but a man was a man, regardless of color or country; so she practiced her craft on Sandoval, removing her cloak and striking a series of provocative nude poses. A low humming in her throat, a most unusually pleasant sound, almost a purr, came as she did a few dance steps, aware of his embarrassed fascination with her body.

Repulsed by the lewd display, Sandoval wanted to get away; but he couldn't move. Techchupo's wide, deep eyes held him enslaved. Sparkling light from those dark eyes penetrated his mind. Using every ounce of willpower he possessed he tried to turn his head away, but it wouldn't move. Her humming communicated something to him.

You want me, Spaniard. Is it not so?

"No, No, I do not!" he mumbled She smiled and her jaguar growled and stared at Sandoval through yellow obsidian eyes. Unceasing flute music echoed eerily through the room.

This was exceptionally pleasant! Techchupo was his friend. Perhaps she loved him. Yes, he was certain she loved him! He watched her as he would a deadly cobra, frightened yet fascinated.

Deliberately and sensuously she licked her moist glossy lips and anointed her body with a fragrant oil which glistened on her copper skin. Slowly she danced toward him, cupping her large breasts in her hands, making them bulge in ripe lusciousness; and Sandoval was completely washed over with a sexual desire he'd never known before. What was happening to him? He could see his wife's lovely face. Rosa was here with him! He embraced her passionately, feeling the warm, soft female body pressing against him. He whispered her name. "Oh, Rosa, it's been so long!" She helped him remove his armor and clothing. the scent of her was delicious. She was so beautiful—and the whole atmosphere of her, merged with his dreams and pent up desires, even the intense fantasy-like strangeness of his surrounding was so overpowering he didn't actually realize they were making love until her violent pelvic thrusts made him aware of the fact. Buried deep inside her, his pent up longing burst like a ruptured dam. It was over almost before it began, and it slowly dawned on his drugged mind what had happened.

Still dazed he raised up out of her, climbed slowly from the bed and stood naked, staring horrified as Techchupo rose like a specter from the bed and stepped toward him. What he saw in her face stopped his heart! She wore a thin smile, one that affected only the corners of her beautiful mouth. Her eyes were wide open, glazed, not with passion, but with hate! She was going to kill him! The jaguar growled viciously, lunged and tugged violently against his chain.

Now the Spaniard was all hers! She could do what she pleased with him! Slowly she embraced him and began fondling him again.

A spasm of fear engulfed him. "No, no," he gasped, as he struggled to free himself from her deadly clutches, away from those soft grasping fingers and her clinging, perfumed flesh. He fought with every ounce of strength in his body.

Growling rose from deep in Techchupo's throat, unearthly sounds, even more terrifying than those coming from the wild jaguar lunging against his chain.

She was strong, as strong as any man! Those soft fondling hands of moments ago were now hands of steel about his throat. The sight of this frenzied, naked female creature, a beautiful young woman moments before, triggered unknown energies in Sandoval. Using all his reserves of power he smashed his right fist into her face, and muttered, "You evil, devilish bitch!"

The blow staggered the maddened priestess. She stood swaying, blood running from her bruised nose, her eyes red. Little mewing, hacking sounds came from her throat, as she pitched forward at his feet.

His mind was muddled, but he knew he had to get away. Hastily he dressed, fastened his armor and went reeling like a drunken man down the long torch-lit corridor to find Luis and Kano.

Lying on a stone slab near the temple entrance he found Luis stretched out, and nearby, Kano lay crumpled in a heap. Stumbling to Luis, Sandoval felt his face to see if he was alive. Shaking him roughly he whispered, "Get up, Captain. Get up!" The rough shaking had its effect. Luis groaned. It took several moments before Sandoval finally got him to his feet, still very groggy.

"Help Kano," Luis muttered, trying to bring his vision into focus.

Sandoval reached down and lifted Kano's head, and he stared up with an idiotic grin. Sandoval slapped him across the cheek. "Wake up!"

"Help me, sir," Kano said.

Luis and Sandoval got Kano to his feet, slung his arms around their shoulders and hurried to the steps leading down to the street.

Guatemotzin finally located Techchupo, to help him dispose of Luis and Kano, when she staggered into the corridor, naked, dazed and battered. Blood streamed from her nose onto her bare breasts. She trembled with fear when she looked into Guatemotzin's wild red eyes. Madness lurked in those dark caverns, and she knew full will the penalty for failure. Perhaps, just this once, he'd forgive her?

"Did you kill the one-eyed man as I ordered?" he asked sternly.

"I tried, my Lord," she stammered, "by the gods, I tried, but he's no ordinary man."

"He did this to you?" Guatemotzin asked, his voice softening with concern, extending a bony hand to her chin, turning her head sideways so he could determine if her nose or jaw were broken; but he found them only badly bruised.

"Yes. And by all that's holy, he'll pay for what he's done," she hissed with hatred. "That's what I'd planned, but you failed me Techchupo," Guatemotzin reminded her. "I tried, my Lord," she repeated, avoiding his eyes.

"Dealing with these white men is going to be more difficult than we bargained for," Guatemotzin exclaimed as he watched her wipe the blood from her nose.

"I hate them all!" she sobbed.

"As do I, my dear," he responded sympathetically. "They must be destroyed. I know that for certain now. Did you note their curiosity about everything here? Their probing eyes missed nothing. They'll expose our sacred religion to the outside world. They must be destroyed!"

"I'll enjoy watching them die," she said, a slightly evil smile on her black and blue face. "Did you dispatch the runner to Papantla as I instructed?" Guatemotzin asked.

Smiling broadly, Techchupo answered, "Yes, my Lord. He left this morning. By tomorrow afternoon Teoamoxtli and his soldiers will be here! He will kill or capture all the Spaniards, and we shall have some worthy sacrifices!" She paused for a moment. "Am I forgiven?"

"You are, my dear! What's done is done! Let's speak of it no more!" He turned abruptly and walked down the hallway.

18

When morning came Sandoval sat off by himself in the courtyard away from the others, his head in his hands, full of self contempt, remembering his wife, longing for her, desiring her, wishing the expedition was over so they could be together, never to be separated again. God, he groaned inwardly, how could I have been so weak as to cavort with an Aztec whore?

Though it was a bright blue-sky day, Sandoval took no notice. He sensed only impeding doom. Maybe it was all a horrible dream! But Techchupo's naked native beauty filled his mind, that soft, responding female flesh...

"A couple of reales for your thoughts, Lieutenant," Luis said as he sauntered up.

"That Aztec bitch seduced me, Captain!" Sandoval grunted glumly. "I'd almost forgotten what a woman was like. And God curse me, I enjoyed it! Every minute of it!"

"So what's the problem?"

"Before I left Spain my wife and I vowed to be faithful to each other. I've broken my vow."

"Considering your occupation I'd say you made an impossible vow. You're only human. What happened with Techchupo wasn't your fault. She drugged the liquor and she and Guatemotzin put us under some kind of spell. They have devilish powers we don't understand."

Sandoval's brow knit with concentration. "Perhaps you're right. Yet I can't stop thinking about it. Why did I do it? I know better. What's wrong with me anyway?"

"Nothing's wrong with you, Jorge, nothing at all," Luis replied. "You're a man like the rest of us, with feelings and passions. You needed a woman and the Aztec priestess was handy."

"As simple as that, eh?" Sandoval smiled sadly. "Perhaps you're right. I don't know. I suppose we are sometimes confused by our hearts. You're not disappointed or ashamed of me?"

"Why hell no, man! You make too much of it. Put it out of your mind entirely. It's over and done with" Luis grinned. "There's nothing new in what you've done. It's been happening since the world began.

Just remember you're neither a priest nor a holy man. If your adventure at the Aztec temple continues to plague your mind, see a priest when we get back to Cuba."

Ruminawi and Kano walked up. "Kano told me what happened last night. I'm sorry. What you witnessed was never meant for outsiders' eyes. It was none of my doing I assure you. You're lucky you escaped from Guatemotzin alive!"

"Very lucky!" Luis agreed.

Ruminawi smiled. "If you need anything please let me know." He turned to walk away and took only a couple of steps when he remembered something. "Sometimes the Aztecs from Papantla drop by unexpectedly, and they always come through the pass, just as you did. If they catch you here they will kill you—or worse!"

🐜 🐜 🐜

Luis stationed sentries with care, posted the small falconet to command the entrance to the village and forbade soldiers to leave town. Yet for some unknown reason, he was still very uneasy. The pass troubled him—from there he was vulnerable to attack. He sent for Esperanza!

"Roberto, I want you to ride to the mouth of the pass and keep watch."

"Watch for what, Captain?"

"Aztecs! If they try to attack us they'll come through the pass just like we did. I'll send someone to relive you this afternoon."

Luis' order didn't make much sense to the scout. The Aztecs were a long ways off, and they didn't know the Spaniards were here. But orders were orders. Esperanza took a healthy swallow of pulque from his small flask, jumped on his horse and galloped the big bay gelding toward the pass.

Sergeant Lopez walked up, wiping his perspiring forehead with a dirty rag. "Sir, you'd better come with me, we've got a problem. Better bring Lieutenant Sandoval along too."

Luis motioned Sandoval and they followed Lopez to the building where their supplies were stored. Inside Lopez pointed to the four powder kegs. "Two of them are empty! Half our gunpowder is missing!"

"Are you sure?" Luis asked.

Lopez picked up an empty keg. "This one and that one." He kicked the other empty one. "We've got a traitor in our midst. Whoever it is stole the powder while we've been here. Probably last night. I double checked the supplies when we got here and everything was in tact."

"Do the men know about this?" Luis asked. "No, Captain. Only us."

"Keep it that way. We mustn't let them find out." Luis kicked the empty keg. "Damn it to hell!"

"Who could have done it?" Sandoval asked.

Luis thought it through and the pieces fell into place. "Governor Velasquez must have planted someone in our expedition to make sure we fail."

"But why?"

"So he can get the Aztec gold before we do."

"How can he do that?" Sandoval asked.

"I don't know, but I suspect there's more going on here than we're aware of."

"Who among us would do such a thing?" Lopez asked. "Do you want me to make some discreet inquiries among the men?"

"No, Sergeant. That would tip our hand. I have a better plan. We may just try a little trick of our own!"

MADRID, SPAIN, SPRING, 1518

Count Guy de Vey entered the king's chamber and bowed gracefully.

A few moments passed before the king became aware of his presence. His mind was preoccupied with a myriad of details, the most important being a concerted move by the Spanish Parliament to unseat him.

"You wish to see me, de Vey?" he asked sharply.

De Vey could see Carlos was tired and drawn, looking much older than he had just a few days ago. "Yes, your Majesty. I've got some good news for a change."

Carlos petulant expression changed, and a small smile appeared. "By God, I can certainly use some good news!"

"A dispatch just arrived from Captain Hernando Cortez. He advises that Escudero's expedition got away on time and should at this moment be somewhere in the Aztec empire."

"Excellent!" the king brightened, rubbing his hands together. "What else?"

"There were a couple of problems. The Catalan's captain was murdered in Punta del Piedras before the ship sailed. First Mate Juan Narvaez took command."

"Is that all?"

"No, sire. Governor Velasquez launched an expedition of his own. It sailed just hours after Escudero left Punta del Piedras."

Carlos's face darkened with rage. "What's the matter with Cortez? Why didn't he stop Velasquez? This changes everything!" His high pitched whine sounded like that of a spoiled child.

"The same question crossed my mind," de Vey replied. "As I thought it through, Cortez couldn't tip his hand. We've put him in a very awkward situation. Velasquez knows of our expedition and we know of his. Yet neither of us can risk an open confrontation. That's all Velasquez would need to take your throne."

That touched a sore spot with Carlos! "No one is going to take my throne, no one. I refuse to let Velasquez intimidate me!" He pounded the table. "I won't stand for it. I'm the king!"

"You needn't be concerned. Cortez has everything under control," de Vey said soothingly. "Oh?" Carlos caught his breath.

"Remember Kano? He speaks the Aztec tongue and is at Escudero's side as we speak, translating for him as they move deeper into the Aztec empire. Velasquez's expedition has no interpreter. I believe that gives us an edge!"

"Perhaps," Carlos replied thoughtfully. "What if those two expeditions run into each other?"

"Let's hope they don't!" de Vey replied. "I'm relying on Escudero's leadership ability to carry this thing off successfully. I think we chose wisely."

Carlos wasn't totally convinced. Nothing it seemed was certain. The Escudero expedition was a brilliant move and could save his throne; yet it was far from foolproof, he warned himself.

Like every other innovative idea now in the planning stage to save his throne he'd taken a big gamble on Escudero's expedition. Like a roulette wheel, the ball was in motion. Whether it would stop on the Carlos' lucky number remained to be seen!

19

Teoamoxtli led one hundred warriors at a steady-paced run toward the Chichemetlan village. Exceptionally tall for an Aztec, Papantla's military commander towered over six feet. He wore gold armor and a flowing feather cape. His warriors wore quilted tunics, two inches thick, which fit close to their bodies to protect their thighs and shoulders, and leather boots trimmed with gold. Their picturesque dress was surmounted by a fantastic headpiece made of wood and leather representing the head of some wild beast, displaying a formidable array of sharp teeth. These Aztecs were professionals!

Teoamoxtli knew there'd be no help from Guatemotzin. He was the most ill mannered, obnoxious human being he'd ever encountered. The very thought of the perverted madman was repulsive! He hated Guatemotzin and all Aztec priests who butchered innocent people by the hundreds of thousands to satisfy cold stone idols to which most Aztec warriors paid only mock tribute. Only battle, meeting a foe in single combat, brought a warrior honor and self respect!

🐾🐾🐾

Roberto Esperanza tethered his horse behind tall rocks where there were a few patches of tall grass. Lazily, the young soldier propped his back against a boulder. The warm sun, combined with a cool breeze blowing through the pass, lulled him into a peaceful reverie. In the distance he could see the sparkling blue waters of the Caribbean which reminded him of Spain. He wondered if he'd ever be able to return to his small village where nothing ever changed.

Immersed in daydreams, the young scout already loved this magnificent land with its jungles, mountains, rivers and oceans. It was difficult for the eyes of the mind to absorb its vast panorama stretched out as far as he could see. A lazy lizard skittering from stone to stone, and a few birds chirping were the only sounds.

Suddenly, Esperanza tingled with a strange premonition of danger nearby, though he'd not see or heard anything. Squinting toward the beach he caught the glint of sun reflecting off Teoamoxtli's golden armor as he rounded a bend in the jungle trail, into a clearing.

"Sweet Jesus!" he exclaimed out loud. His mind rapidly calculated his actions. He tried to steady his rapid breathing. How many are there; how fast are they moving; when will they be here? It wouldn't be long! Stretched out four abreast and running at an even clip the Aztecs were closing fast. They'd expertly used the jungle to escape detection.

Esperanza eased himself into a better position, careful to keep the boulder at his back, and studied them through his long glass. He estimated at least one hundred very well armed soldiers would hit the pass in a couple of hours. He jumped on his horse and galloped to the village to warn his captain.

🐾🐾🐾

When Teoamoxtli's small army emerged from the pass onto the flat plain north of the village, Luis and his men, in full battle armor, blocked the trail. Deployed in a v formation, the falconet commanded the center.

Luis touched Diablo's flank. He pranced forward under tightened rein, with a high, majestic step. Kano trailed behind, using Diablo for cover. The tactic confused Teoamoxtli.

Luis sat motionless. Only a yapping village dog broke the afternoon silence. Teoamoxtli studied the mounted knight on his huge black horse. He'd never seen a horse, though he'd seen Spaniards before. At the time of planting he'd done battle with a man called Ortega and drove him away from Papantla.

Teoamoxtli looked up into Luis' hard chiseled face, and detected no fear in those pale blue eyes. Though absolutely at ease, there was a coiled look to him, like the deadly serpent with rattles on its tail, poised to strike. This man would fight to the death!

Kano stepped up to the Teoamoxtli, towering over him, forcing the Aztec to look up to see his face. Kano smiled. "So we meet again! But this time we come in peace."

"Peace? You talk of peace?" Teoamoxtli snorted. "You and Ortega killed many of my warriors and now you expect me to believe you come in peace?"

"Yes I do! Captain Luis Escudero, here, has come in peace to meet your emperor. He commands you to take your men and return to Papantla so we may proceed on our journey."

A dark, humorless smile pulled at Teoamoxtli's lips as he folded his arms across his chest. He spoke loudly so all his men could hear. "You're on our land without permission, so we must take you to Papantla for judgment."

From the corner of his eye Luis watched an Aztec warrior lift his javelin and cock his arm to hurl it. It was a fatal mistake! Luis raised his left hand slightly. San Estevan's arquebus roared, shattering the quiet. The ball ripped into the warrior's chest killing him instantly.

Immediately came a low murmuring chant from the Aztecs working themselves up for the kill. Teoamoxtli shouted a command which quieted them for a moment. He wanted to capture the Spaniards, not kill them. Probing his mind for a solution, he watched fifty fully armed Chichemetlan warriors racing from the village to join the Spaniards.

Teoamoxtli hissed a warning. "You must surrender now or die! The choice is yours!"

"There's no need for this," Luis said as he tugged Diablo's reins and backed him slowly toward his men. His words fell on deaf ears.

The Aztecs let fly a volley of copper-tipped arrows which darkened the sun for a moment, like a passing cloud. Aztec archers fired three arrows at a time with deadly accuracy. Then came heavy stones hurled from their slings.

Luis' bugler sounded advance and the Spaniards and Chichemetlans advanced under the arrowy shower. They closed with the maddened Aztecs. Arrows glanced off their armor and stones falling from the sky crashed off their helmets. The Chichemetlans unleashed a flight of arrows which were deflected by Aztec shields.

Frenzied Aztecs ran in a massed charge toward the Spaniards. When within range of the falconet, loaded with metal balls, Luis shouted, "Fire!" The well aimed shot tore though the Aztecs mangling and killing a dozen warriors, who went down like wheat before a scythe. Alternating fire poured from the arquebusiers, causing chaos in Aztec ranks. Bullets couldn't find Teoamoxtli. He was everywhere, shouting encouragement to his men. But his efforts went unheeded. Terrified warriors milled about, uncertain what to do. He screamed for them to pull back and regroup. The Spaniards reloaded quickly, and waited for the next Aztec charge.

Here they came again, screaming hideous war cries which deafened the soldiers. It was like trying to stop an avalanche! The Spaniards and Chichemetlans fought desperately to break the Aztec charge, but were forced to give way. Luis charged Diablo into the oncoming horde, and hacked away with his sword. He shouted for his men to form up again. His voice was drowned out by screaming Aztecs.

They were all around him, wild faces, glaring eyes, gleaming coppery bodies leaping, twisting and falling. Their acrid smell smote him. He felt their soft bodies writhing under Diablo's hooves.

Right behind Luis came Sandoval, Lopez and Esperanza on their huge warhorses, smashing into the Aztecs. They swarmed around the horses, clinging to their bridles, manes and stirrups, trying to jerk riders out of the saddles. Luis shouted, "Break! Break!" His men tried to hack their way out of the human surge. It was hand to hand combat. The tide of battle was turning against the Spaniards.

Sensing impending victory, Teoamoxtli led his men forward with renewed energy, followed by his itztli fighters, shoulder to shoulder, in perfect order, each swinging a strange looking two-handed staff three and a half feet long. Along both its edges, inserted transversely, were long, razor sharp obsidian teeth. These formidable weapons, wielded with both hands like a broadsword, cut the unprotected Chichemetlans to pieces.

Spanish horsemen again drove their huge war horses, wedge-like, into the advancing column. One mighty warrior smashed his itztli into the neck of Esperanza's horse, and it crashed to earth.

Esperanza tried to jump clear but caught his leg in the stirrup and was pinned under the dying horse. The itztli fighter rushed in for the kill. Esperanza twisted as best he could, his sword ready. Being immobile, he was no match for the Aztec, who raised the itztli high above his head.

Corporal Martinez, bleeding from three wounds, his helmet gone, his buckler pockmarked by hundreds of blows, shouted a curse and limped toward the Aztec. Holding his huge, bloody, double edged broadsword in both hands, Martinez was unstoppable! The itztli fighter left Esperanza to face the huge bearded giant whose eyes bored into him with insane intensity. His wooden itztli was no match for the broadsword. Martinez made one mighty sweeping blow, which shattered the itztli and cut the Aztec cleanly in half.

Kano fought his way to Esperanza and grasped the dead horse's head with his huge hands. Grunting with a surge of power he twisted the heavy carcass enough for Esperanza to slip his leg free. From all sides panting, clutching, stabbing, sweating, wild eyed screaming Aztec warriors moved in, hungry for the kill.

"My God!" screamed a young Spaniard as an itztli buried its obsidian teeth deep into his sword arm. Blood spurted from the useless limb. The Aztec drew his weapon back to finish him off, but Ribera the ax man was on him before he knew what hit him. The bloody ax decapitated the Aztec.

Ribera, with his arching ax, back to back with Martinez and his broadsword, made a horribly frightening team. Aztecs circled them warily, trying to get past those deadly instruments, feinting with itztlis and javelins.

Sergeant Lopez worked his great warhorse close to the two men and scattered Aztecs in every direction, swearing loudly as he cut and hacked. "Hola, kinsman!" he shouted to Ribera. "Give 'em hell! And you, Martinez, off your lazy ass! Swing that sword so you don't have to back up to the paymaster next payday!" Martinez grinned broadly and raised the great broadsword in a mock salute. Lopez crashed his horse into another massed group of Aztecs.

Teoamoxtli knew he had to kill Escudero if he was to win. He and his men concentrated all efforts on Luis; but Sandoval came to the rescue. He spurred his huge horse directly into the massed warriors, and with magnificent swordsmanship, slashed and stabbed, and relieved pressure on Luis.

Luis shouted to his bugler, who blasted out recall, and the Spaniards fell back to regroup.

The cannoneers fought free of the mob and recharged the falconet. It spit fire, and the massed Aztecs were again slaughtered. Their very numbers increased their confusion. Taking advantage of that confusion, the three horsemen, followed by infantrymen, counterattacked. The Aztecs retreated!

At each sound of the Spanish bugle the Spaniards moved in unison as a single unit, their flanks protected by axes and swords. The arquebusiers poured heavy fire into the Aztecs.

A cheer erupted from the Spaniards when the Aztecs panicked and fled the field. Seventy five of Teoamoxtli's men lay dead, sprawled on the field. Above, black vultures circled lazily.

Miraculously, every Spaniard was still on his feet, many swaying from loss of blood, some dazed, but ready for whatever came next.

Teoamoxtli had never battled such ferocious fighters as the Spaniards. For an hour, under a blazing sun, they stood toe to toe with the Aztecs' finest warriors.

The armies, one hundred meters apart, glared at each other. Luis spurred Diablo forward, Kano trailing alongside, just as he did in the beginning.

Teoamoxtli limped forward and locked eyes with Luis, no hatred in either mans' eyes. Each had done his duty. Luis' use of firearms and tactics gave him the advantage. Added to this, the smashing effect of the huge warhorses frightened the Aztecs, many of whom were stomped and trampled into the dust.

"Teoamoxtli, this valley now belongs to the king of Spain," Luis warned. "Take your men back to Papantla and do not return."

The big Aztec nodded and conceded, "You won this battle, Captain. But I'll be back with more men."

"Surely you're smart enough to know I came here with more men than you see here. We're a small scouting party. My main army is on a ship only a couple of days away. They'll land tomorrow or the next day."

Teoamoxtli's face registered stunned surprise, and Luis knew his bluff had worked! However, it only sharpened rather than subdued the big Aztec's animosity. He burned for an opportunity to wipe out the stain of defeat. Without another word, he turned and walked back to his men. They began the gruesome task of gathering their dead.

Luis and his exhausted men limped back to the Chichemetlan village. Racing past them, the surviving Chichemetlan warriors ran screaming toward the distant pyramid to avenge themselves for the indignities perpetrated on their young men and women over the years by Guatemotzin and his evil followers.

Atop the pyramid, black-robed figures watched stoically as death raced toward them. Helplessly, they watched their last hope for life fade from sight—a single file of defeated Aztec soldiers marching toward the mountain pass.

🐜 🐜 🐜

Prince Ruminawi hurried as fast his old body would move and grabbed Luis in an embrazo hug. His eyes sparkled as he offered an enthusiastic, cheerful greeting. "Congratulations on defeating our hated enemies and your safe return! My, what a magnificent sight it was! Watching you and your men in battle was the most memorable experience of my life! Come my friend, bring your wounded men to my villa. My people will care for their wounds."

Five of Luis' men were so badly wounded and had lost so much blood he knew they'd not live to see morning. After he chatted with each of them he pulled Sergeant Lopez aside and instructed him to secretly bury them when they died. He wanted to maintain their reputation of invincibility—they couldn't be killed!

Ruminawi came to Luis' room and found Kano helping him and Sandoval remove their blood- spattered armor.

"What are your plans now, Captain? You can remain here with us as long as you like."

"I'd like nothing better, but we must be moving on. Tell me sir, this Aztec emperor you told us about. Do you know anything about him?"

"Montezuma? I've never met him personally, but I've heard many things about him."

"Good or bad?"

Ruminawi gave that thought. "Both—mostly good, if we forget he's responsible for uncounted human sacrifices. He's considered a very brilliant monarch for such a young man."

"How old is he?"

"About forty. He's tall and thin, though not ill made. He has a thin beard and short hair. He's paler than other copper-colored Aztecs. He's a good soldier as well as head priest."

"How might we gain Montezuma's favor?"

"The first thing he wants to know about anyone is whether they have royal blood. He'll not lower himself to associate with anyone not of royal birth. You must tell him you're closely related to the king of Spain. If you do, you'll be treated with princely courtesy."

"Thank you. That's most helpful." Luis nodded. "We're anxious to get to Tenochtitlan as quickly as possible. Do you know the way?"

Ruminawi smiled. "As easy as strolling along picking flowers, eh?" That's easier said than done, my friend. It's a long and dangerous road from here to the emperor's palace."

"Really? What are we up against?"

"It'll take you between seven and ten days, if it doesn't rain and Aztec warriors don't kill you!" He continued with a description of villages, mountain passes, rivers and streams they'd pass on the way to Tenochtitlan.

"Could you draw us a map?" Luis asked.

"I can provide something more helpful than a map!"

"Really? What might that be?"

"Urcos! He's scouted many times for the Aztec army and has been to Tenochtitlan many times."

"Would he scout for us?" Luis asked.

"Certainly."

"Excellent! That'll make our journey easier and much safer. How can we ever repay you?"

"Think nothing of it," Ruminawi brushed a hand through the air. "You freed us from Guatemotzin! It is we who are in your debt. I'll speak to Urcos and make necessary arrangements. In the meantime, why don't you and your men rest here for a couple of days? We'll gather provisions for you to take along."

"Thank you, sir! We'll do that!"

🐾🐾🐾

The hour was late. The moon slid down the sky over the quiet town, its reflection danced off the villa. Luis awoke from a heavy slumber sometime after midnight. When he rose on his elbow he could see the low, full moon hanging suspended from a totally cloudless sky.

The day's battle still pulsated in the back of his head. Standing, he grimaced, every muscle and joint aching. He threaded his way among his men sleeping in the courtyard. Three of his men were not there. They died earlier in the evening and lay buried in unmarked graves, far from home and family. Two others would be dead before sun up.

Luis was restless without knowing why. He walked to a nearby tree, urinated steamily on its roots. The cold night air on his skin made him shiver, but it braced him and he felt strong as he'd not felt strong since the start of the expedition.

Quietly he returned to his room, carefully stepping over the young woman sleeping on a mat on the floor—a gift from Ruminawi! He tried not to waken her, but his desire was too intense to ignore. He knelt down close to her. The warm musk of her body bathed him, and the fragrance of her faint flowered perfume enveloped him. His hand touched her gently, stroking her hair. She woke and smiled at him. Her breath sighed in and out of her nostrils, her bare breasts rose and fell as she reached up and felt his beard and explored his hairline. The beard fascinated her and she ran her fingers through it several times. Luis took her in his arms and kissed her lightly on the lips. She responded passionately, searching his mouth with her tongue.

After he made love to her, he drifted off into a deep, relaxed sleep.

20

YUCATAN PENINSULA, MAY, 1518

Pedro Armand tried to keep his footing on the Catalonia's rolling deck. Nervously he turned on his heels, surveying the low-lying jungle stretching south forever, then stared at the Santa Isabella, under full sail, trailing a quarter of a mile behind, transporting the horses and cannons.

He motioned Captain Alonzo Duero over. "I'm telling you again, Captain, this is not the Aztec empire! Where are the mountains?"

"What mountains?" Duero snapped.

"The Aztec empire is supposed to be in dry mountain country. Look! There and there! This land is table top flat!" Armand pointed to the heart of a jungle so dense it was impenetrable.

"By God, Armand, I am sick to death of arguing with you!" Duero growled and summoned Chief Navigator Miguel Escobar. "Armand tells me this isn't the Aztec empire. Have you navigated us to the wrong place?"

Escobar glared at Armand. "Are you blind? Haven't you noticed all the cities along the coast? Of course this is the Aztec empire! What else could it be? Who else could build such magnificent cities?"

Armand shook his head and replied firmly, "It's not the Aztec empire!"

"Are you calling me a liar?" Escobar's hand went to his dagger.

"Now, now, calm down, both of you!" Duero said soothingly, stepping between them.

"Damn it, Captain," Armand growled with frustration. "We're too far south and not far enough west. I demand you turn the Catalonia and Santa Isabella around, sail north and land us on Mexico's eastern coast!"

Duero was diplomatic. "I'm sorry, I can't do that. Governor Velasquez planned this voyage and instructed me where to put you ashore. He gave me the same instructions he gave Hector Ortega a couple of years ago when he sailed from Cuba."

"Yes, and Ortega was never heard from again!"

"Be that as it may, I take my orders from the governor. But just for your information, we have as much at stake in this venture as you do."

"In what way?" Armand asked skeptically.

"If you find any gold and silver we get ten percent of it."

"If? That's a mighty big if, Captain, especially if you dump us off here!" Duero scuffed his feet and didn't argue; neither did Navigator Escobar.

"Why won't you listen to reason?" Armand tried once again. "If the people in this area aren't Aztecs, we're in big trouble before our expedition gets started."

"Who else can they be?" snapped Duero.

Armand hissed, with a tongue that dripped vitriol, "I don't know! And I don't care!"

Duero just shook his head and shouted to the helmsman, "Head for that cove over there. Signal the Santa Isabella to follow us in!" He turned to Armand. "Alert your men. We'll off load them first, then get your horses and cannons off the Santa Isabella."

"And you'll pick us up in ninety days?" Armand asked, his face lined with worry. "Exactly ninety days—and you'd better be here!"

Damn! Armand thought. It'll probably take us at least that long just to find the Aztecs!

Captain Duero and Chief Navigator Escobar were dead wrong! Like most Spaniards of the day, they were unaware of two great empires, Aztec and Maya, existing side by side. Because of their ignorance, Armand and his soldiers were put ashore in the Mayan empire, on the western side of the Yucatan Peninsula, projecting northward into the Gulf of Mexico like a giant thumb, just a few leagues north of the slow rolling, serpentine river the Mayans called the Halech Uinic. It was the boundary dividing the two mighty empires. Armand's expedition was one hundred seventy five leagues southeast of the Chichemetlan town where Luis Escudero was preparing his expedition to march to Tenotchtitlan!

Armand's fifty troopers slowly hacked their way through the dense jungle, where oppressive humidity and biting insects made the going torturous, especially for the horses, nearly maddened by the huge biting flies and other jungle insects.

They were an unkempt lot! Several days at sea gave them the look of ruffians—mostly unwashed, untrimmed and unshaven. But they were in high spirits, and for two principal reasons; first, they'd encountered no opposition and suffered no casualties; second, from the numerous beautiful cities they'd seen along the coast, they knew the pickings would be good; and there'd be plenty of heathen women for sport!

For all their appalling lack of personal hygiene their weapons were honed bright, and their armor rust free and well oiled. Saddles and other leather gear were supple and shining; and every horse was in good condition after the long voyage.

Pleased as the soldiers were with the ease of the expedition thus far, they were even more pleased with their captain! Too often, in past campaigns, strict discipline made life a miserable hell. But Armand was easy going, relying on his foreign Portuguese sergeant, Magellan, to enforce discipline.

The men hated Magellan, a bully and degenerate of the lowest order. Some of them considered him quite mad. He'd rape, kill or steal without blinking an eye. But to a man, none could deny he was the toughest most ruthless man they'd ever soldiered with.

Armand ordered Magellan and two others to scout ahead and reconnoiter, and find a path out of the hot, stinking jungle.

The three scouts fanned out ahead of the column, following animal paths through a thicket, bending low over their horses' heads to keep from being scraped off by low hanging branches and vines.

All were battle hardened veterans. In the center rode Magellan, a silent man whose eyes, ears and nose missed nothing. On his right rode Juan Valdivia, a lancer and professional mercenary, almost fifty years old, stocky and pot-bellied. With an insatiable appetite for liquor and women, his constant complaints about aches and pains in his bones were endless. But nothing interfered with the old man's duty! He could stay in the saddle and day and night.

On Magellan's left rode Leon de Meza, also old for a soldier. His expertise lay in his ability to barter with natives and whites alike. At heart he was a trader and when this expedition was over he planned to return to Spain and open a shop of his own.

Four hours crisscrossing back and forth, following dead-end trails, they broke out of the jungle onto a flat, treeless plain. A roadway paved with white stone, as wide and level as any in Spain, led westward, parallel to the coast.

Magellan turned to de Meza. "Go back and bring the Captain up. Me and Juan will scout down the road a piece."

De Meza galloped back the way they'd come. Magellan and Valdivia rode cautiously along the road, senses alert to ambush, toward a walled town in the distance. The scouts thought it might be deserted; not a soul was in sight.

They dismounted to rest their horses and study the city more closely. Then leading their horses by the reins, they walked along side by side.

"It's too damned quiet, Juan." Magellan removed his helmet and wiped the sweat from his head and neck.

"I don't like it, Sergeant. Where are all the people?" Valdivia scanned the towering wall. A copper- tipped arrow clattered on the stone pavement near Magellan's feet. Instinctively they crouched behind their horses, glancing about to see where the arrow came from. There wasn't a sound. Even the raucous jungle birds were silent.

Another arrow swished over the horses and clattered harmlessly on the road. Advancing from the city gate, coming at the scouts, was a single warrior dressed in the most colorful gaudy feathered costume they'd ever seen. Strutting, weaving and dodging, almost dancing, he advanced a few yards at a time, his shield held before him.

The scouts jumped on their horses and warily eyed the unusual warrior. "Don't move, Juan!" Magellan hissed. "He's alone. Let's see what he's up to."

Chanting strange words, the warrior advanced, waving his bow to frighten the white men away.

Valdivia gave a wild yell, pulled his sword, spurred his horse and charged the hapless warrior. The Mayan had never seen anything move so fast, shaking the ground as it came. He saw the gleaming razor-sharp sword tip lower. It was the last thing he ever saw. Valdivia's sword struck him squarely in the heart knocking him violently backwards onto the road.

"Valdivia, you bloodthirsty bastard! Can't you ever obey orders?" Magellan screamed. "Ah, go to hell! The idiot wanted to fight, so I fought him."

Magellan gritted his teeth. "Well let's at least get him off the road," he growled disgustedly. They dragged the body off the roadway and rolled it down an embankment. Fearing to enter the city's open gateway they galloped back to join the others emerging from the jungle.

Armand was angry about the killing but there wasn't much he could do about it. He let Valdivia off with a slight reprimand.

Armand rode cautiously into the Mayan city of Uxamil, followed by his men, all amazed at the architectural design and layout of buildings spread out before them. Eight groups of white buildings surrounded some sort of house resting upon a high artificial mound of stone, covering three acres.

Three hundred feet wide and twenty five feet high it appeared to be the palace or residence of the city's ruler. A huge temple in a pyramidal shape loomed over all the other buildings.

At the base of the steps leading to the sanctuary above, on each side, was a polished stone phallus, fully twelve feet long, in gigantic splendor. The sight of the fully erect reproductive male organ, in such gigantic proportions, caused a minor sensation among the men.

Leaving several men to keep watch, Armand and the others climbed the steep stairway which led to the interior. There they found a life-sized effigy of an open-mouthed jaguar, painted mandarin red, standing guard over the temple. Further on were immense warrior colonnades, and motifs of marching jaguars and rampant eagles. On the floor near the jaguar was a prone stone figure, on its back, with a hideous face and a vacant, expressionless stare. Its clawed hands held a bloody stone dish on which rested a blackening heart.

"Probably that of an animal," Armand said to the men. He strolled about looking at the strange art decorating the white walls. Displayed were realistic perceptions with gesture, color and movement. One, nine feet high and twelve feet wide depicted every day life in Uxamil. Armand fingered the wall and felt the rough texture of cement over stone. The cement was the artists' canvas. Blue dominated through the frescoes with reds, yellows, browns and a lustrous black. Familiar with art of the period, Armand could appreciate the line and color and movement of the figures.

Several paintings were obscene, by Spanish standards, indicating phallus worship by the townspeople. In an adjoining room the entire floor was covered with beautifully polished stone phalli, each twelve inches high, resembling huge mushrooms.

Whatever the soldiers' thoughts were at the moment, they were interrupted by the sentry's shout, "People approaching!"

Valdivia fired his arquebus point blank at the leader of a Mayan delegation making its way up the temple steps.

That shot destroyed Armand's only chance to meet and negotiate with the Mayans. Before he could curse Valdivia, enraged temple guards, concealed behind various buildings screamed hideous war cries and attacked, firing volleys of arrows. But the guards were no match for the Spaniards.

Springing down the steps two at a time Armand shouted the old war cry, "Santiago, and at them!" The Spaniards charged into the Mayans, swords slashing and stabbing. Stunned by the fierceness of the attack, the Mayan sneak attack fell apart. Echos of cannon and arquebuses reverberated like thunder between the buildings. Smoke rolled in sulphurous volumes along the square, terrifying the Mayans. Like deadly apparitions, three Spaniards, astride huge warhorses, galloped out of the smoke. The Mayans threw down their weapons and ran!

21

Uluam, Ruler of Uxamil, concealed in shadows atop the temple, watched in horror as white strangers riding on huge animals murdered his people. He didn't understand their savagery. They gave no quarter and killed everyone in their path, men, women and children. Several of his people, ran for their lives and made it to the jungle's safety. Uluam dispatched a warrior to the garrison at Yahalum urgently requesting warriors to deal with these killers in metal suits.

Sergeant Magellan spotted a young woman in a body length cape of brilliant red and green feathers and a plumed headdress, running like a frightened deer, trying to reach the jungle's safety. He spurred his horse and cut her off. She quickly turned and ran the other way, but Valdivia and de Meza blocked her escape. Encircled by huge panting warhorses, she trembled, and stared at her captors like a frightened animal. She attempted to cover her nakedness with her cape. A shiny golden chain held a large medallion between her bare breasts.

Magellan laughed. "Well now, what have we here?" Leering down at the lovely young Mayan woman, he said, "Nothing to be afraid of, girl!" His foreign words terrified her.

Valdivia removed his helmet and ran his fingers through his sweat-matted gray black hair. "Goddamn, I want to get my hands on that!"

"Me too!" de Meza piped up. Both laughed, amused by the girl's terror.

The three men dismounted. Magellan growled, "If you have any prayers to say to your heathen gods, senorita, you'd better say them now! Here, let's have a closer look at you." His eyes ran up and down her shapely brown body. Small, scarcely over five feet, Cocoma was exquisitely graceful and beautifully formed. Her large, uptilted breasts gleamed in the sun's flat afternoon light, and the thin loincloth highlighted her slim legs and thighs.

Stunned with her dark beauty, the soldiers knew they'd captured a rare prize indeed! A great mass of black hair cascaded down her back, to her waist. The girl's delicate features made her more desirable than any Spanish woman. They were always buried under tons of petticoats to plow through! Although her cheekbones were high and her nostrils wide, she did have small ears and slender lips. Her copper-shade skin glowed with the lovely patina peculiar to primitive people. She visibly trembled, terrified by these uncouth, bearded men, wondering what they would do to her.

She somehow found enough courage to pull a small obsidian knife from its sheath at her waist. Holding it high, she ran straight at Magellan! He stepped back. "Holy Christ, boys, she's crazy!" He bellowed with laughter. The obsidian blade glanced off his metal breastplate. He grabbed her wrist, and with a quick twist forced her to drop the knife. Angered, Magellan ripped off her loin cloth.

Cocoma, Uluam's daughter, had never been so embarrassed and humiliated. She could no longer stand to look at them. They were too evil! She tried to cover herself with her hands. Her face wet with tears, she prayed, Oh great Vopol, be with me. Protect me. Comfort me!"

"Enough of this dallying. Let's get to it, boys! Bring her here!" Magellan indicated a grassy spot.

Valdivia and de Meza grabbed her. She fought and struggled to break away but they only hooted and laughed Valdivia pulled the bedroll from his saddle and pushed the girl down on it. de Meza knelt his weight on Cocoma's palms, holding her arms extended above her head. Valdivia crouched, locking his big hairy hands about her slim ankles, splaying her shapely legs wide, then tied them to saplings with a small rope. Kneeling between those legs, Magellan dropped his breeches. When Cocoma saw his huge erection, terror coursed through her body and she whimpered like a small child. She jerked again and again against the ropes binding her, trying to break free. She screamed as Magellan forced into her, enjoying her violent heaving efforts to escape. Twice he delayed the moment of ecstasy until, unable to constrain himself any longer, thrust mightily. Cocoma screamed as he deflowered her.

Spent, Magellan rose from her ravaged body, his place taken by Valdivia then de Meza. Cocoma lost count of the number of attacks. At one point she rallied and tried to bite de Meza. He viciously slapped and dizzied her and kept away from those teeth while he used her.

When de Meza was finished with her, Valdivia pulled the blanket from under her, and tied it behind his saddle.

"Did you hear the little bitch scream?" Magellan laughed, pulling up his pants. "God, my ears are still ringing. I think she enjoyed it. She was a maid and we've turned her into a woman.

Untie her, de Meza. We've had our sport with her."

The old Spaniard untied Cocoma, but she lay there, scarcely breathing, staring at the old man with those wide, brown eyes, which made him uncomfortable. She wished the soldiers had the decency to kill her, like they would a suffering animal. Suddenly she stiffened, groaned, convulsed and died.

The Spaniards stared at each other as it dawned on them they'd killed her. Uncertain what to do, they backed away. Killing her didn't bother them at all, it was their realization she was someone of importance that made them nervous. The exquisite golden medallion and feathered robe were symbols of her aristocratic rank.

Magellan's mind sought for a solution. Only one thing he could think of. Get rid of the body. Reaching down he ripped the golden necklace from the dead girl's neck and jammed it into his saddle bag.

"Juan, help me with her."

While de Meza held the horses, Magellan and Valdivia picked her up, and on the count of three, heaved her into the jungle underbrush.

"You'll say nothing of this to Captain Armand, understand?" Magellan growled. They nodded. "Good. Let's ride."

🐾 🐾 🐾

Uluam sobbed softly, tears flowed down his wrinkled cheeks as his mind tried to blot out the terrible scene now etched there forever. Sick to his stomach and completely helpless he watched the Spaniards ravish his daughter. Why would they do such a thing?

His heart was heavy, ready to break. Never in his memory had any woman of Uxamil been molested, and never had anyone entered the sacred temple except for religious ceremonies.

The Spaniards were out of control. Strong fermented liquor they'd found and the lure of gold and silver adorning the buildings turned them into maddened animals, fighting among themselves for every scrap of precious metal they could rip from the statues and idols lining the street.

Armand didn't know what to do! Finally he shouted, "Sergeant, stop those crazy fools."

"You want them stopped, you stop them, Captain. They're entitled to bit of fun as I see it!" Magellan smirked.

Angry and defeated, Armand swore under his breath and galloped off with Magellan's boisterous laughter ringing in his ears. Riding through the pillaged town, skirting around corpses littering the street, Armand remembered Governor Velasquez's warning about the Butcher; and wished he'd heeded his advice! It shocked him, an officer, that a mere sergeant would argue with every decision and every command. He was stuck with an insubordinate sergeant, and a group of over indulged mercenaries who considered themselves his equals and behaved as if it was his fault it was too hot or too cold or too wet, or there were no women!

He'd lost command and there was no way to gain it back! All he could do was hope the men would listen to reason—and not kill him. His only course of action now was to try to work out some sort of compromise with Magellan.

By the campfire that evening Armand tried to reason with Magellan. "Our orders are to get to the Aztec capitol and back here in ninety days. We'll need to bury the treasure we've found here so it won't slow us down. We can pick it up on the way back."

"Are you completely out of your mind, Captain?" Magellan growled. "Even if I agreed with you, the men won't give up any gold they've found. We'd have a mutiny on our hands."

"Oh? Are the men now in command?" Armand responded sarcastically.

"You know better than that! They risked their lives for those riches lying there." He pointed to the growing pile of gold and silver. "They're not going to march without it! Neither am I!"

Armand shook his head. Under his helmet's brim, his expression was invisible and his voice slightly choked. "You mean you'd sacrifice our mission for a little gold and silver?"

"You're damn right I would! Why? Do you disapprove?"

"Let me tell you something," Armand said stiffly. "The gold and silver in the Aztec empire would make this treasure look like drop in the bucket. Think of it, man, gold and silver and precious gems beyond your wildest dreams."

Magellan chuckled. "Hell, Captain, you know the old saying, a bird in the hand..."

"Are you saying you won't go?" Armand interrupted.

"Not at all. We'll go, but we're taking our treasure with us!"

"Damn it, Sergeant, it'll slow us down to a crawl."

"Why should I care?"

De Meza galloped up. "Captain, we've got trouble."

"For the love of Christ, what now?"

"Me and Valdivia spotted an army of savages approaching from the south."

"How many?"

"At least three hundred."

Magellan took over. "Are you sure?'

De Meza nodded.

"Sonofabitch!" Magellan growled abrasively. "Get the cannons ready!"

"Wait!" Armand held up a hand. "There's been enough killing. Let's work out a truce. They've got us outnumbered."

"So what?" Magellan spat out. "We're not afraid of a few savages. Either fight or stay out of the way!"

"But..."

"Bugler!" Magellan shouted. "Sound call to arms!"

The bugle's clear notes echoed across the town. The men donned their armor and checked their weapons. Cannoneers primed the cannons with grape shot and pointed them south. Huge warhorses pawed the ground, ready to charge.

🐾 🐾 🐾

The ground reverberated with the sound of sandaled feet padding the ground. Through the jungle veil came the flash of hundreds of copper tipped javelins. A muscular war chief trotted out front of his warriors. Behind the spearmen came the bowmen, stretched out in a seemingly endless line on the dusty stone road. They were here for blood and they came screaming like demons from the pits of hell—but they were no match for Armand's professional killers.

Sheer masses of screaming Mayan warriors jamming the narrow streets between the buildings proved to be a complete disaster. Cannons blasted grape shot into their ranks, cutting them down fifty and sixty at a time. Those the cannons didn't kill the axmen and swordsmen did! Within the hour the few remaining Mayan warriors fled in terror.

Ten of Armand's men were killed by Mayan bowmen, and they were quickly buried in a mass, unmarked grave so they'd never be found. Fearing a larger army might return, Armand called the men together and tried to reason with them.

"We'll all end up dead if we don't work together and get out of here. Some of you want to stay here and loot all the buildings. I say no! You already have enough treasure to make you wealthy men. But we can't lug it with us. You'll have to cache it—bury it around here someplace. We'll pick it up on our return."

"Leave the treasure?" Valdivia yelled.

"Shut up!" Magellan shouted. "Let's hear the Captain out, then we'll take a vote on what we want to do."

"Bullshit!" hollered Valdivia. "We're not leaving our treasure and we're sure as hell not taking any vote! Right men?"

"Aye!" came the thundering reply.

"Well, Captain, that's your answer!" Magellan said.

Armand's jaw was set! "Damn it, men! Are you fools enough to think we're safe—that we have no enemies? By now every Indian within five hundred miles knows we're here. Our orders are to get to the Aztec capitol and back here as quickly as possible."

"Orders?" Valdivia piped up. "We take our orders from Sergeant Magellan!" Armand gritted his teeth. "If you follow the sergeant you'll all end up dead!"

"You don't have much faith in my leadership abilities, do you Captain?" Magellan sneered.

Armand knew he'd lost the argument. Even so, he gave it one last try. "Sergeant, what the hell good is the treasure if you're all dead?"

Magellan thought on that for a moment; deep down he knew Armand was right. But he couldn't bring himself to sit right down on the notion of burying the gold! He'd been poor his entire lifetime, as had all the men. "We'll take our chances, Captain. If we're going to die, as you say, we might as well die rich!"

"Have it your way, Sergeant!" Armand said disgustedly. "Gather your treasures and let's ride at first light."

🐾 🐾 🐾

The expedition pulled out of Uxamil at daybreak, taking as much gold and silver as they and their horses could carry. Magellan, Valdivia and de Meza, scouting out ahead, didn't know where they were going only that they were slowly moving west, following the sun. No Spaniard had ever passed this way before.

A few leagues west of Uxamil, the expedition crossed a wide, shallow river which Magellan suspected was some sort of boundary line. People on the west side of the river were quite different from those of Uxamil—their features, their clothing, their villages, everything about them. They were fierce and hostile.

Pedro Armand and his men had crossed over into the Aztec empire!

Moving ever deeper into Mexico's southern jungle, Magellan made sure even the most inexperienced soldier became accustomed to the daily routines. Each morning the fire making detail rose first, at the first glow of dawn. The cook prepared breakfast. By dawn the entire company assembled ready for the day's march.

At noon they halted for three hours to rest under shady trees lining the trail, eating cold leftovers and napping. They resumed the march when the sun dropped below the trees.

Armand's biggest disadvantage, next to losing his command, was lack of an interpreter to question the natives about the lay of the land, how far it was to the Aztec capitol, if there were Aztec armies nearby. He was completely blind!

All he could do was keeping moving west as rapidly as possible and fight anyone who got in the way. Magellan would take care of that! The land stretched west toward the horizon, table top flat, the trees of uniform height, as if they'd been trimmed by giant scissors.

Ahead of them came the ominous booming signal drums alerting distant cities of the Spaniards unwanted, intruding presence.

🐜🐜🐜

When the last Spaniard disappeared around a bend in the road, Uluam came out of hiding and hurried as fast as his ancient body would permit to the temple of the warriors where he saw Yum Kaax bounding down the steps. The bent old man and twenty-year-old Yum Kaax hugged each other awhile tears flowed freely down their cheeks.

"Oh, my son, how happy I am the gods have spared you," Uluam sobbed. "Have you seen Cocoma?" the young man asked anxiously.

Uluam wasn't sure he wanted to tell him what happened to Cocoma. They had been promised to each other at infancy by their royal families, and were soon to be married.

"There is no easy way to tell you this, my son. Those vicious white men killed Cocoma. I need you to come and help me bury her deep in the earth."

Yum Kaax let out an anguished scream and sobbed as though his heart would break.

"Come, my boy." Uluam took his arm and guided him to the place where Magellan had discarded Cocoma's body, as if she were but a bit of trash.

Uluam and Kaax and several Mayan warriors buried her deep in the ground. By rank she was entitled to a stone tomb, but Uluam didn't want to take a chance that the rapacious white men might accidentally disturb her tomb looking for gold. No. Let her rest in the security and peace of mother earth.

Kaax's sobbed and his eyes filled with tears as he stared down at the grave wishing it were him lying there instead of Cocoma. Though heartbroken, his entire being was filled with cold, impotent rage and hatred for the white invaders. His beautiful Cocoma had been defiled and murdered and her murderers had marched away free. He silently swore on her grave he'd see them all dead, no matter what sacrifice he must make, nor how long it might take.

Uluam gently took Kaax's arm took his arm and guided him from the grave to his beautiful flower filled garden.

"Son, I have a very important assignment for you."

"I'm too numb for anything right now, Father."

"I share your grief. But I thought you might want to avenge Cocoma's death! We must take action against those brutal soldiers who killed her."

"What kind of action?" Kaax brightened, anxious to hear more.

Uluam smiled. "You're the champion runner in the Mayan empire, so I want you to take a message to my friend, the great Aztec Emperor Montezuma, in Tenochtitlan! Run like you've never run before!

Tell him what happened here. Leave nothing out. Warn him that those soldiers who murdered our people are on their way to Tenochtitlan."

"Oh yes my Lord Uluam! I will run day and night and never stop! Montezuma will certainly know how to deal with those evil men!"

Uluam gathered Kaax in his arms and hugged him close. "Be very careful, my son, you're all I have left in this world. May the Gods travel with you!"

22

CHICHEMETLAN VILLAGE, MAY, 1518

The weather changed in the high mountain country of the Chichemetlans where Luis and his men were preparing to get underway to Tenochtitlan. There had been high winds and rain squalls all night and most of the morning. Then the rain stopped, but the wind kept blowing.

Luis and Sandoval were completing an inventory of the gold and silver Prince Ruminawi had given them, then turned it over to Kano and

Sergeant Lopez who lugged it down to the secret vault under the Prince's villa.

"How much do you think this treasure is worth?" Luis asked Sandoval.

"Well, I'm no expert," Captain, "but I'm sure it's enough to buy us a small kingdom in Europe. It's a pity we can't take it right now, head back to the beach and wait for Narvaez to come pick us up."

Luis remained silent for a moment, then said, "Not a bad idea, but it would be a long wait, and we'd fail in our mission to gather information about the Aztec empire. We've got to get moving in the morning and make it to the Aztec capitol as quickly as we can."

Sandoval nodded. "What do you think of this fellow Urcos who will guide us there? Can we trust him?"

"Why don't you ask Kano?" Luis nodded toward the huge black man, grunting as he strained to lift a heavy golden object.

"What do you think, Kano?" Sandoval asked.

Kano was slow to answer, not sure if he should be so bold as to speak his mind. "I trust him, Lieutenant. Native people like Urcos and me do not lie. We value the truth."

Luis spoke up. "Are you willing to bet your life on Urcos?"

"Yes sir, I am," Kano said positively.

Sergeant Lopez wiped his sweaty face with a cloth and said, "I suppose we'll pick up this treasure when we come back from the Aztec capitol, and take it to the ship?"

"If the ship is there," Sandoval responded.

"It will be there, sir," Lopez said. "Have a little faith."

"Faith hell," Sandoval shook his head. "What we need is some luck and lots of it."

🐾🐾🐾

Luis and his men marched silently from the Chichemetlan village at sun up, and followed Urcos west toward Tenochtitlan.

Luis set the pace to conserve the animals; walk, trot, canter then walk again. At night they made dry camp without fire which would give them away to Aztec warriors.

When loud drums reverberated from valley to valley, Urcos said, "It is good talk. They say let the white men come."

"Kano," Luis said, "ask him why we're being permitted unmolested entry all the way to Tenochtitlan."

Kano talked to Urcos then turned to Luis, "He believes Montezuma must think you are Quetzalcoatl and does not want to anger you."

"The same Quetzalcoatl Prince Ruminawi told us about?"

"Yes sir."

Luis smiled. "I find this Quetzalcoatl legend and tales of an ancient white race hard to believe. "Do you think it's possible?"

"Perhaps," Kano responded. "Urcos tells me the Aztecs have many legends about a white race who spread their colossal architecture over this country long before the Aztecs got here. Another interesting thing, Captain. These Aztecs believe in the existence of a supreme creator who is lord of the universe. They address him in their prayers as the god by whom we live, omnipresent, that knoweth all thoughts and giveth all gifts." Here Kano grinned. "Those beliefs are similar to some of those in your Catholic faith, are they not?"

"They are," Luis replied, and gave that thought for a moment. "I wonder," he said, as if thinking out loud, "if white people actually were here long ago, would any of their posterity still be living in Mexico?"

Kano nodded affirmatively. "Urcos thinks so, though he's never seen any."

⁂

Early the third morning, Luis awoke fuzzily. Lying on his side, his eyes shut, his breathing deep and even. He heard a foot crunch gravel and someone clear his throat. He rolled over and grabbed for his dagger. Sergeant Lopez stood there.

"Next time you sneak up on a man announce yourself! I almost stabbed you."

"I'm sorry sir, but I have some bad news."

"So early in the morning?"

"Yes sir. One of our mules is gone. It disappeared during the night."

"What do you mean? Wandered off? Taken by the Aztecs? What?"

"I think the traitor amongst us drove the mule away. Shall I take a couple of men and go look for him?"

"No!" Luis said. "We've got to keep moving. We can't waste time." He slipped on his armor. "Do you think it was Alfredo?" Lopez asked.

"Yes," Luis nodded, motioned Sandoval over and explained the missing mule. "If it's the blacksmith, let's take care of the sonofabitch!" Sandoval snapped.

Lopez nodded agreement. "Say the word and I'll slit his throat."

"Do either of you have any solid proof it's him?" Luis asked.

"Begging the Captain's pardon," Lopez said. "Proof or no proof I think we should do away with the troublesome bastard!"

"No! Not yet! He has several good friends among the men which might cause them to turn against us. We've got to be very careful and catch Alfredo in the act. Keep your eyes and ears open and your mouths shut for the time being."

※※※

The fifth day, just on sunset, they climbed out of a lowland canyon. A gust of wind came along like a breath from an oven. Luis' bleak glance simmered on the boulder-covered mountains. He didn't see any sign of movement, but that didn't mean there was no hidden enemy. The great shoulders of these mountains could easily hide an army. He couldn't shake the feeling the Aztecs might try something to delay or destroy his expedition.

Sandoval crowded his horse up alongside Luis and said, "I've been thinking about Alfredo. If I was him I'd make my move tonight. We'll be in Tenochtitlan in two or three days and he won't be able to get at the supplies if we put them under lock and key."

Luis agreed. "Let's keep our eyes open tonight and catch him in the act." Sandoval's eyes widened. "Stay up all night?"

Luis laughed. "No. Not all night. Just until he makes his move!"

"Then what?"

"Let's catch him first."

Luis called a halt for the night.

※※※

Luis, exhausted like all the other men, stretched out on the grass for a few moments to relax and keep an eye on Alfredo. His eyes closed drowsily and he felt like he was lying on a raft in a whirlpool, and whirled off into oblivion.

Porfirio, a young sentry, quietly walked his post. All the men were sound asleep. He heard rather than saw someone rummaging through the supplies. Cautiously he worked his way close to the shadowy figure of a Spaniard leaning down, obviously looking for something.

"Hola, comrade, what are you doing?" Porfirio challenged.

Alfredo straightened, caught red handed. With no place to run, he turned and faced the sentry.

"Just stay calm, Porfirio," Alfredo said quietly. "There's no cause for alarm. I'm hungry. That's all. I was just looking for something to eat."

Alfredo's oily voice sent a shiver down the sentry's spine. Porfirio knew Alfredo was sly and extremely dangerous. He could snap a man in two as easily as cracking a twig.

Alfredo inched closer to Porfirio. His evil eyes glittered in the firelight. The viciousness and hate in Alfredo's battered face sent fear racing through the sentry. Alfredo flexed his huge hands, a lopsided smile making furrows in his bearded face. The man's gigantic shoulders hunched forward, while his right hand pulled the huge broadsword from its scabbard.

Porfirio stood his ground, ready to kill or die. His long, sharp lance near Alfredo's belly kept the huge blacksmith at bay preventing him from slashing out with his sword.

Luis suddenly woke to the sound of voices and realized he'd fallen asleep. Grabbing his sword he rushed to Porfirio's side.

Alfredo stared at Luis, then laughed, and that laughter had the cruel dry sound of leaves rattling in the autumn wind. "What's got your balls in an uproar, Captain?"

"You know what! You goddamned traitor! If I leave you alone for five minutes you find some stupid way to bring us to grief!"

Alfredo was shrewder than he looked! With an innocent but deadly undertone he said, "What are you talking about Captain? What have I done?"

"You've been trying to sabotage this expedition ever since we got to Mexico."

The men, awakened by the disturbance, clustered around, uncertain what was happening. They waited for an explanation before taking sides.

"Alfredo's a traitor!" Luis said, as Sandoval stepped up to his side. "He's been trying to sabotage our expedition ever since it began. He destroyed half our gunpowder and turned one of our mules loose."

"That's a goddamned lie!" Alfredo spat out. "He's lying men, don't believe him. You know me. We're friends. The Captain can't prove one word of what he's saying."

"I don't have to," Luis growled. "But I would like to know who paid you to betray your comrades."

"No one paid me to do anything!" Alfredo lied. "You'd better stop and think what you're doing! You're making a big mistake! You need me.

I'm a good blacksmith and I'm the toughest soldier in this camp!"

"That's true," Luis replied, "but we can get along without you! I'd rather have a rattlesnake in my pocket than have you behind me!"

Alfredo held onto his sword, nervously tapping it's blade on the ground, contemplating cutting his captain down. He thought better of it when he saw Taragona's cross bow trained on his heart.

Alfredo's face was deeply trenched by fear. Dark sweat-circles stained the armpits of his shirt. He stared at his comrades. "God, this is like a puking, rotten dream I'm never going to wake up from."

"I'm sure it is," Luis said. "My only regret is we didn't boot your ass down the road sooner."

Roberto Esperanza stepped forward. His eyes held on Alfredo, a man he trusted and considered friend. "Is Captain Escudero telling the truth?"

"No! It's a dirty lie!" Alfredo growled. "You and the others must help me!"

Lieutenant Sandoval said softly, "Roberto, lad, Captain Escudero tells the truth. Alfredo destroyed half our gunpowder. If we have to fight our way back to the coast, we may run out of powder and the Aztecs will have us! And you know the mule is gone."

"Don't listen to them, Roberto!" Alfredo pleaded. "Please help me! Ribera? Taragona?"

Roberto shook his head sadly, as did all the others. "We trusted you, Alfredo, and you betrayed us. It's too late now. Life is full of choices and you made the wrong one. We can't have a traitor in our midst. That's just the way it is!"

Luis turned to Sandoval. "What shall we do with him?"

"Stand him up against a rock and shoot him!" Sandoval said forcefully.

"That's way too merciful, Lieutenant," Luis said. "I have a better idea. You hired Alfredo. I think it's your duty to fire him."

"What?" Sandoval's eyes went wide. "What do you mean?"

"Simple," Luis said. "Dishonorably discharge him for his treason."

Sandoval smiled. "That's a fine idea. You're the captain. Why don't you do the honors and I'll be a witness."

Every eye went to Luis, who stepped in close to the blacksmith and said, "Alfredo Orlando, I hereby discharge you from the Army of Spain! You are hereby banished from this expedition!"

Alfredo's stunned expression betrayed his terror. He wasn't afraid to die. But banishment, alone, among millions of bloodthirsty savages, was incomprehensible.

Luis added, "Leave your weapons. We don't want you to return and use them against us." He turned to Sandoval. "Is there anything you'd like to add, Lieutenant?"

"Only this," Sandoval warned. "Don't ever come sneaking into our camp. Our sentries will kill you on sight!"

"On your way, Alfredo!" Luis ordered. "May god have mercy on your soul!"

"But sir," Alfredo begged, "at least give me a blanket. It gets cold in the mountains."

"Not if you keep moving fast, staying ahead of the Aztecs trying to kill you. You'll work up a good sweat!"

"But where can I go?"

"Anywhere you choose!"

All the men drove Alfredo, weaponless, from camp.

🐜 🐜 🐜

Dawn came slowly and turned into a glorious morning with snowy white cumulus clouds piled high above the horizon ahead. Urcos knew every roadway, trail and path and led the expedition along the shortest, safest route.

Signal drums reverberated from mountain tops to towns scattered throughout the valleys, all the way to Tenochtitlan. The Aztecs knew the Spaniards' exact location at all times.

With every step of their progress the woods became thinner; patches of cultivated land more frequent. Hamlets were seen in the green and sheltered nooks of the valleys.

Passing through those hamlets, the Spaniards were surprised to be received in such reverent awe by simple villagers who'd never seen white men. Aztec women decorated the necks of their horses and mules with great wreaths of multi-colored flowers and greeted the Spaniards with smiles, waves and food of all varieties. Men and women wore gold ornaments around their necks and golden rings in their pierced ears and noses. That gold did not go unnoticed by the Spaniards.

Everywhere they heard complaints from Aztec villagers about Montezuma, especially the unfeeling manner in which he carried off their young men for his armies and their young women for his harems or for sacrifices.

In the distance Luis studied a huge spectacular smoking volcano named Popocatepetl, which Urcos called Montezuma's throne. It sent an apprehensive shudder through Luis. Beyond that volcano lay Tenochtitlan and he had no idea what fate awaited them in that great city.

23

SOUTHERN MEXICO

Yum Kaax ran at a steady, measured pace on the Aztec highway to Tenochtitlan. For eight days and nights he ran through heat and rain. He paused only long enough for quick naps and a handful of maize. One thought kept him going—revenge. He'd do anything, even sacrifice his own life, to see Cocoma's murderers dead!

He prayed Montezuma would see him, though he doubted the Aztec god-king would lower himself to speak to a Mayan with no credentials, except for being the fastest runner in the Mayan empire.

He didn't like Aztecs, but he understood their culture and could speak and understand some of their coarse guttural language. They were very different from the gentle, more refined Maya people. Aztecs were barbarians interested only in war and bloody sacrifices to their many gods! Mayans were prudent in their use of sacrifice, resorting to it only as a last measure to gain favor of the gods of rain, sun and fertility.

Perhaps, Kaax reasoned, Aztecs' bloody sacrifices do appease their gods. Everywhere he looked, prosperity smiled on all—ample food, contented people and a mighty, unconquerable army!

Aztec warriors recognized him by his brilliantly plumed headdress, and allowed him unmolested passage and he waved as he passed. At the recent athletic contest between Maya and Aztec athletes, in the Mayan city of Jonuta, he'd beaten every Aztec runner.

Little love was lost between these two powerful native races, yet mutual respect had slowly developed over the centuries when battles to conquer each other proved fruitless.

On the ninth day from Uxamil, Yum Kaax, completely exhausted, stumbled through the front gate of Montezuma's palace in Tenochtitlan.

"State your business, Mayan dog, and be quick about it!" ordered the arrogant, elegantly uniformed Aztec captain of the palace guard.

"I'm here to see the Emperor Montezuma on a matter of grave importance."

The captain laughed. "The emperor? You fool! What makes you think our emperor wants his palace desecrated by a Mayan commoner?"

"He will see me!" Kaax replied calmly. "He is my friend!"

The captain's eyes widened. If this Mayan knew Montezuma it would be extremely wise to treat him with courtesy. "Take a seat over there!" He pointed to a stone bench in the palace foyer. "I'll inform the emperor you wish to see him."

Footsore, his lungs still burning, Kaax waited patiently in the foyer, happy for a few moments to catch his breath. He watched squads of elite Aztec warriors marching from one place to another while their commander called out cadence. Richly dressed courtiers passed to and fro discussing empire business.

He knew he'd never fully understand Aztec thought processes, and doubted he'd ever completely master their language—not that it was unduly complex. It was very down to earth, such as the old languages must have been before civilizations sprang up: languages that had to do with work, sickness, the essence of existence, sex, life and death. In ancient days, Kaax knew, when life consisted of killing to eat, killing or being killed, perhaps people didn't sit down to admire the landscape; they didn't pause breathless over the beauty of a flower; and they certainly didn't weep over the death agony of a sacrificial victim. Aztecs found it difficult to talk or reason in abstract terms. That's why Kaax felt superior to them. His people had long since mastered art, poetry, music and their priests had developed a calendar that went hundreds of years into the future. They could reason philosophically, could write and track all the major stars in the heavens.

Kaax jumped to attention when a middle-aged Aztec noble stepped up, followed by a dozen magnificently uniformed warriors. There was a gloss on the nobleman's copper skin and he walked with a swagger.

"Follow me, Mayan!" he growled, as though Kaax was beneath the dignity of such as he.

"The emperor has granted you an audience. Be quick now! Mind your manners! Speak only when you are spoken to!"

Kaax, tired and dirty, followed the nobleman into Montezuma's chambers, past muscular soldiers guarding the entrance.

Montezuma was stretched out, half reclining on colorful rugs spread on the polished stone floor. Kaax crawled into the Emperor's presence, since it was an offense to look into his face without permission. Several men and women sat in various places, talking and sipping from golden goblets. The Emperor rose to a sitting position. Instantly, absolute silence came, every person in the room froze into immobility.

Montezuma spoke. "I'm told you are Yum Kaax from Uxamil. We've heard of you! Your reputation as a runner has preceded you." There was not a sound except Montezuma's voice.

Motioning to Kaax, he said pleasantly, "Come closer. What brings you all the way from Uxamil to see me?"

Montezuma wasn't at all like Kaax expected, haughty, arrogant, a man who considered himself to be a god! He seemed like an ordinary man, kind, gracious and concerned. He waited for Kaax to speak.

A bit overwhelmed, Kaax kept his eyes lowered until he gradually built a little confidence. Then he described Uxamil's violent plunder by white foreigners. When he explained Cocoma's brutal rape his voice choked with emotion; but he quickly regained composure and completed his report.

"It is very sad to receive such bad news," Montezuma said sincerely. "I truly grieve for you and your people." A flat silence followed, a deep furrow pulled his brows together; and he sighed. A sadness lay heavily upon on him as Kaax's news sunk in.

He smiled and said with great gentleness, "I'll have my soldiers destroy the evil white men who killed your people. In the meantime I will send food and provisions to Uxamil. Will that will help?"

"Oh yes, my Lord!"

"Very well, then. Would you like to stay with us for a few days until my army is ready to move south to find these evil men? You could go with them."

Yum Kaax's tired, worn face came alive! "Oh yes, my Lord! That's the greatest desire of my heart—to see those men destroyed, as they destroyed my people."

"So be it!" Montezuma signaled his captain. "See that the Mayan is fed and provide anything he needs. Give him a room in the palace!"

Kaax backed from Montezuma's presence, eyes downcast and followed the captain.

Montezuma clapped his hands, ordered the room cleared and his counselors summoned. They came immediately and seated themselves in a semicircle around their emperor.

Montezuma advised them what happened in Uxamil. They all tried to speak at once. Montezuma held up his hand for silence. "Please hear me out. I've had the strangest dream for many moons now. It's always the same! Quetzalcoatl is coming back to reclaim his empire. This troubles me greatly. What does it mean? Tell me what you think."

The great Tezcucan King, Cacama, leader of the counsel spoke first. "It's not wise to put too much faith in dreams. What do your priests tell you? Have you talked to them""

"Yes. My priests and astrologers have read and studied the signs and all agree the coming of Quetzalcoatl is near at hand. Two groups of white bearded men now approach our city, one group from the east and one from the south. Perhaps the leader of one of these groups is Quetzalcoatl himself."

Naulinco, King of Tlacopan and commander of all Aztec military forces, never one to remain silent for long on matters of dreams and religious superstition, quickly interjected his thoughts.

"Sire, I rather doubt that. It's more likely these men are just soldiers from another land beyond our empire. We've heard from our Indian allies, the Caribes, white men live on the islands nearby and move about in huge sailing canoes." He paused, fearful of overstepping his bounds; but Montezuma nodded for him to continue.

"The white men approaching our city may not be at all like the ancient white men. Those men, followers of Quetzalcoatl, were a plague on the land then, and the ones you still hold in captivity could be again, if they ever escape. All white men create trouble and problems no matter where they come from. I say we must be extremely cautious in dealing with them."

Montezuma smiled at that. "Ah, Naulinco, had you but studied Quetzalcoatl's legend, you'd know he and his people were not a plague upon the land. He taught us many things. His people built the empire over which we now rule. You know, as well as I do, we do not possess the skills to build the mighty structures dotting our landscape."

Naulinco nodded slightly, knowing it was futile to argue with Montezuma when he'd made up his mind about anything! You couldn't tell him that the white god, Quetzalcoatl was merely a legend. He wouldn't believe you. What difference did it make anyhow? It was totally absurd trying to solve today's problems using a stone god from some ancient legend! How would an army ever win battles if it relied on priestcraft and legends? The only ancient ones Naulinco had ever seen or knew about were those caged in Montezuma's unique zoo. From what he witnessed there he couldn't believe that those white men and women had much more intelligence than jungle monkeys. Utterly repulsed by them, he couldn't understand the emperor's fascination with them, with their fishy white skin, light colored hair and blue eyes.

Cacamotzin, powerful Lord of Texcoco, patriarch of the entire group, and Montezuma's uncle, said, "Do you believe your astrologers, Montezuma? They've been wrong before. I, like Naulinco, put little faith in astrologers and priestcraft." The old man studied his nephew through red-rimmed eyes.

"My dear Uncle," Montezuma responded, "I have more than just their predictions. There have been many signs which my astrologers tell me cannot be ignored."

"What signs?" Naulinco challenged.

"Do you all remember the year I became emperor? The great Lake of Tezcuco for some unknown reason became violent, building with huge waves, like those on the sea. There was no visible cause. The lake overflowed its banks and poured rushing waters into this very city. Many of the buildings were swept away and thousands of our people drowned."

"That's true," Cacama nodded. "I lost one of my wives in that devastating flood."

Montezuma continued. "Only twelve moons later the turret of the great temple took fire, without any apparent cause. Although made of solid stone the temple burned for several days despite our attempts to put out the fire." Again the counsel members nodded in agreement. The leaping fire was indeed one of the strangest things any of them had ever seen—solid stone burning as though it were wood!

"Now, my friends, is it not strange or perhaps even an omen from Quetzalcoatl that three great comets have been seen trailing great tails of light over our city? But there is something even more startling.

Some interesting information just reached me early this morning from our outpost in Papantla." Naulinco interrupted. "That's where the white men entered our empire, is it not?"

"It is," answered Montezuma. "According to the runner, a strange light brightened the eastern sky. It was broad at its base on the horizon, and rose in a pyramidal form, tapering off near the top. It resembled a vast sheet of fire, transmitting sparkles that seemed like small stars. At the same time low voices were heard in the sky and wailings, as if to announce some strange calamity."

"Were the voices in the tongue of our people, Montezuma?' Cacamotzin asked, a curious, frightened look on his wizened old face.

"No, Uncle. The voices spoke the soft words of the white man's language."

Finished, Montezuma sat back moodily resting his chin on his hand, staring at his trusted counselors who helped him rule the empire. They remained silent, mulling over these strange events.

Naulinco broke the silence. "I see no reason to fear the white men, no matter how strong they are. No power can stand against our warriors. Have we not conquered all the tribes near and far?" Naulinco clenched his fists and pounded them against his chest with bravado.

Montezuma didn't respond, thinking, how like a child you are, Naulinco! Every problem can be solved with a spear or an arrow. You're like an immensely clever child; and you are, on occasion, as naive as a child. Yet your brilliant childishness is merciless; you have the cruelty of a child.

When necessary you slaughter with total abandon, yet I've seen you at times be as gentle as a woman with her baby. You're indeed a complete paradox. Montezuma couldn't find it in his heart to ridicule his military commander.

"I agree with what you say, Naulinco," Montezuma said, his somber countenance indicating the great concern he felt for making a correct decision on the matter before them. "But if I send you and your soldiers against the white men and you lose, they'll kill us all. On the other hand, if we permit them unopposed entry to our city, perhaps they'll visit with us and return to their own land."

"That's a good thought, nephew," Cacamotzin looked at Montezuma, "but the legend says they'll rule us. More and more white men will come. And they'll rule us. There's nothing we can do to thwart the plan of the gods."

Naulinco jumped to his feet shouting, "Legends, priests, astrologers, stone cold gods! They mean nothing! Are you all old women who fear a mere handful of ordinary soldiers?"

Immediately Naulinco knew he'd gone too far. Montezuma's glaring stare of distaste would have caused any other subject to be slain immediately. One of the magnificent Aztec warriors guarding the door raised his javelin, but the emperor waved him back to attention.

"Enough Naulinco!" Montezuma shouted. "I'll not listen to such talk! Do you understand me?"

"Yes, my Lord!" he answered humbly, bowing low, realizing how closely he'd flirted with death.

"It's time to decide which policy to pursue." Montezuma's voice had a note of finality to it. "Do we let the white men proceed unmolested or do we destroy them?" He nodded to Cacamotzin.

"Allow them unmolested entry, my Lord."

"Cacama?"

"Unmolested entry, my Lord."

"Naulinco? Never mind. We know where you stand." Naulinco said nothing.

Montezuma clapped for the royal messenger and said, "Take this decision forth to every village and town. Allow the white men coming from Papantla unmolested passage to Tenochtitlan. Treat them well! Any who hinder or harm them in any way will answer to me!"

Montezuma's eyes went around the circle of counselors and he said quietly, with great seriousness, "Now let's deal with the evil white men marching from Uxamil. Naulinco, send food and other provisions to Uluam and his people. Then quickly devise a plan to destroy the white men, except for their leader. Bring him to me for judgment. Do you understand?"

"It will be done, Montezuma!" Naulinco bowed and exhaled silently, thankful for the opportunity to redeem himself!

24

Pedro Armand thought it odd how the broad, stone roadway west several leagues from Uxamil suddenly narrowed and deteriorated into a muddy jungle trail. Somehow, they had veered off the Aztec highway's main fork. Heavy rains, flooding and landslides obscured normal landmarks.

The rain let up and the scorching sun created a jungle sweat bath. Armand's men griped and complained endlessly about a fate which had condemned them to this ungodly purgatory! Their progress was extremely slow. The horsemen loaded heavy sacks of treasure onto their horses. Plodding infantrymen took turns dragging heavy sacks of gold and silver they'd stolen from the Mayans.

Aztec women and girls in small villages satisfied the soldiers' sexual lust, but the women received no favors in return. Adding insult to injury, the Spaniards stole anything of value and killed those who offended them in any way. Aztec villagers kept track of the Spaniards, and took hope in a message from the talking drums, booming out a message: Montezuma's great general, Naulinco is on his way! Naulinco would have no trouble finding the Spaniards. Aztec villagers would happily lead him to their exact position!

Suddenly the drums went silent! It was too damned quiet for Armand. The jungle crackled with a sense of impending danger, but his three scouts out front, found no signs of Aztec warriors or any other cause for alarm.

Armand's utter ignorance about everything connected with this venture became more and more obvious and frustrating—landing in the wrong location, murdering friendly Mayans, trudging west to God only knew where!

One evening Magellan rode into camp tired, dirty and sweating. Armand asked him in jest, "Are you sure there's not an open canyon a thousand feet deep between us and the Aztec capitol?"

Irate, Magellan shouted, "You're the Captain. You tell me in which direction the capitol lies and I'll find it. If you're a better scout than me, get your ass out there! There are fifty different trails ahead of us. Which one should I follow?"

"Just do your best, Sergeant." Armand quickly backed off. "Face us in the right direction, so we don't end up on the far side of the world. Keep moving west and veer north if you find a suitable trail."

Magellan's continual assurances of no danger didn't ease Armand's heavy foreboding. He knew the natives were up to something, but what? Their unusual smiles, waves, bows, hand gestures to keep moving wasn't natural! Armand knew the natives hated him and his men.

Plodding along on their warhorses, out front of the column, Magellan said to Valdivia and de Meza, "To hell with that sonofabitchin' Armand!" He wiped sweat from his eyes. "He doesn't have any idea where we are. Let's do away with him, take our treasures and head back to the coast and wait for Captain Duero to come pick us up."

"That could be dangerous," Valdivia cautioned. "How would we explain the captain's absence?"

"Simple. He died of jungle fever. That would be the end of it," Magellan responded, and turned to de Meza. "What do you think?"

"I'll go along with whatever you want to do, Sergeant! We're sure as hell not getting anyplace the way we're going. If we go back, we could live like kings in that Mayan city "

Magellan nodded affirmatively. "Let me think this through. I'm sure the men will go along with me."

Then he laughed and changed the subject. "That was a hell of a filly I had last night. I fear I may be getting too old for these lusty young wenches!"

Valdivia chuckled. "They are indeed beautiful women! They must be trained in the art of love from the time they are babies."

"Santa Maria!" de Meza expressed mock disgust. "Is that all you old whoremasters ever think about? Do you have to gape at every skirt you see?"

"What skirts, de Meza? These women wear no skirts, or hadn't you noticed." Magellan roared with laughter.

They rode around a bend in the trail and Magellan threw up a hand. "Hold up, Men." The trail ended in a jungle opening covered with stone idols and a small, flat pyramid, evidently a place of pagan worship.

"Damn it to hell!" Magellan muttered. "We've lost the trail again. Let's go back and stop the others from coming this way." They wheeled their horses and galloped back to the main column.

"What's wrong, Sergeant?" Armand asked with alarm.

"The trail dead ended in a clearing with a pyramid and a bunch of heathen idols. We need to go that way." Magellan pointed straight ahead.

"Take the men and go on," Armand said. "I want to take a look at those idols. I'll catch up to you. Be careful and keep your eyes open."

"Good God, Captain," Magellan scowled, "I've been scouting for twenty years. You don't need to tell my duties!" He raised an arm. "Forward, men!"

Armand watched his men trudge slowly after Magellan, dragging their sacks of stolen Mayan and Aztec artifacts.

Damn, Armand thought, for a handful of gold, I'd turn this horse around and say to hell with the whole fouled up venture! But there was no place to go! He wheeled his horse and galloped down the dead end trail to take a look at the heathen idols.

🐾 🐾 🐾

Naulinco heard clopping Spanish warhorses coming closer. Perched high in a tree, his lips pulled back from his teeth in a snarl of pure pleasure, he gripped his jewel-studded itztli, ready to smash Spanish skulls! His trap was well planned. He waited confidently and watched the Spaniards coming closer.

Straggled out in a single line, they walked along casually, talking and occasionally laughing. Some walked backwards dragging heavy sacks.

Two hundred Aztec warriors lay concealed along both sides of the narrow trail. "Ready!" Naulinco hissed. He raised his itztli to give the signal to attack.

Magellan and his men walked into the cleverly-laid ambush as if they'd been a group of tired old women on a day's outing to gather flowers! Naulinco shook his head in disbelief that professional soldiers could behave in such a reckless, foolish manner. The muscular general clenched his teeth to keep from shouting out with the sheer excitement of the moment. Tensing his legs he leaped from the tree. "Attack!" he screamed waving his itztli over his head.

Magellan screamed, "Every man for himself!"

Aztecs dropped from the trees and came at them from the jungle. Magellan, Valdivia and de Meza pulled their swords and smashed their horses into the Aztecs. But it was too late! Cannons and arquebuses were useless. The attack came too fast. It was man against man, sword against javelin, arrows and itztilis at close quarters. The Spaniards were hopelessly outnumbered.

Magellan was everywhere he could maneuver his huge warhorse. "Give the bastards hell!" he shouted. Naulinco signaled his archers, and a volley of arrows cut Magellan down; he slid from the saddle, dead when he crashed to earth. Next Valdivia and de Meza were cut down.

Leaderless, the Spaniards fought ferociously, but one by one they fell. The Aztecs' short, deadly javelins quickly slaughtered all the horses. Within thirty minutes the battle was over and the troopers lay sprawled in various attitudes of death. Vultures circled overhead.

Naulinco left the Spaniards where they lay, many across their sacks of treasure. He motioned Yum Kaax. "My Mayan friend, I must be off now to capture the leader of these careless, stupid men." He pulled Kaax into a hasty embrace. "May what you see here bring peace to your soul. Have a safe journey back to Uxamil!"

Naulinco signaled his men. A squad formed up behind him and they ran at a fast pace to capture Armand.

Kaax cautiously approached Magellan's dead horse. He saw the big sergeant, lying dead, three arrows protruding from his throat. From the saddlebag he took a golden medallion which once hung about Cocoma's beautiful neck. He bounced the medal in his hand and smiled broadly as he studied the bloody battlefield. He knew beyond any doubt the gods had taken a hand in the white mens' destruction. It was a good day—a very wonderful day! Happily he began a steady-paced run to Uxamil to make his report to Uluam!

🐾 🐾 🐾

A few scattered natives passed Armand on the trail, but gave the lone white man a wide berth. Nothing stirred except creatures of the night, which couldn't tell night from day in the dark jungle. Enclosed in the hothouse of flower perfume, breathing the hotter incense of Mexico's southern jungle, Armand rode slowly to make sure he didn't lose the trail. That trail meandered between impenetrable walls of vines and jungle trees. Ferns brushed him as he rode along, and the tricky light splashed only here and there through the upper lacework of the branches. The quick rustle of small, unseen animals, the occasional plunging of a larger beast, the flutter of startled birds kept Armand totally alert, every sense keyed for danger. Behind him, out of sight, Aztec warriors carefully covered the trail with tree limbs and other foliage. It would be impossible to backtrack out of this place!

The path narrowed so much it forced Armand to dismount. Taking the horse's reins in his hand he walked forward, the horse sploshing after him, its hooves making sucking sounds in the mud.

Something was wrong! The jungle was too silent. Though Armand saw no one, he felt a thousand eyes were staring at him. He plodded on mechanically, hoping for a glimpse of the opening, and a way out of this morass of tangled vines.

In the rays of the waning sun he saw the path widen into a dark opening, which appeared to be a cleared field of some kind, it perimeters lined with mysterious stone statues. Standing at the entrance of this secret place, lightening flashes cut across the approaching vertical column of rain and brought out with momentary distinctness the hideous features of a great stone god looming over the alter.

Squatting, with fangs bared and glowing eyes, it had all the attributes of Satan gloating over a bowl of human blood left by his worshippers. The come and go light and darkness gave an effect of movement to the image. Armand, startled and engrossed in this jungle amphitheater, didn't notice the dark shapes moving stealthily from the darkness. His horse reared and neighed, jerked the reins loose from his hand ready to run to safety. Several Aztec javelins pierced the horse before it could whirl and gallop away. It was dead before its huge carcass hit the ground. Armand pulled his sword, warily eyeing the war-painted ring of Aztec warriors encircling him. He knew he had no chance. Archers covered him with stretched bows, with copper-tipped arrows.

Naulinco stepped forward and grabbed Armand's sword from his trembling hand.

25

Aztec Emperor Montezuma was a little worried and quite curious about the white men making their way toward Tenochtitlan from the Papantla area. Could their leader actually be the Aztec god of legend, Quetzalcoatl, returning to claim his throne? Montezuma's runners kept him informed daily of the white mens' progress.

Montezuma strolled leisurely in his exquisite flower garden when out-of-breath runner Itzocan stumbled in and prostrated himself before the emperor. Montezuma smiled and waited for Itzocan to catch his breath.

"What news do you bring me?" Montezuma asked pleasantly.

"The white men have reached Cholula, my Lord. They stopped to rest their animals and gather in a few provisions."

"Did you see them?"

"Yes, my Lord."

"Really?" Montezuma raised his eyebrows. "What were they like, big men, small men, what?"

"They were all soldiers, my Lord. Some are big, some are smaller. Their leader is a big, well-built man. He wears a metal suit around his body and he rides a huge black animal called a horse. Those soldiers have many weapons with which I am unfamiliar."

"Yes, yes," Montezuma said excitedly. "What else?"

Itzocan felt more at ease as he described the scene in Cholula. "The strangest thing I saw was a black man..."

"A black man?" Montezuma interrupted. "Do you mean he was black all over?"

"Yes, my Lord." Itzocan's voice was low. "He was the tallest man I've ever seen."

"How tall?"

"Half again as tall you, my Lord—and the strangest thing about him is, he speaks Nahuatl, our language."

"You actually heard him speak in Nahuatl? How can that be?"

"I don't know, my Lord," Itzocan answered. "Urcos, a Chichemetlan, is scouting for the white men.

He was telling the black man about Cholula and the black man was telling it in another language to the white leader."

"What did this Urcos tell them about Cholula?" Montezuma asked.

"He told them ancient white giants built the huge pyramid 180 feet into the sky to escape a great flood predicted by their prophets. Such arrogance angered the gods and they unleashed their fury on the pyramid, burning it and most of the workers. Those giant white men not killed disappeared and the great pyramid fell into ruin and decay."

"How did the white men react when they heard that?" Montezuma asked with interest.

"A white man with a black patch over his eye was most curious. He measured the pyramid's base by walking all the way around it. He told Urcos, through the black interpreter, that it had been the largest pyramid in the world, even larger than those in a place he called Egypt."

Montezuma nodded appreciatively. "If those white men do not delay in Cholula, they will be here within two or three days. I don't know why, but I'm rather anxious to meet them. Thank you for your excellent report Itzocan. Get yourself something to eat and rest up."

When Itzocan was gone Montezuma rubbed his slightly bearded chin, admiring the vast array of multicolored flowers in his garden, his thoughts pondering upon the white men who would be here at the palace in a matter of hours.

His mind wandered back to the time he'd first seen those heaps of unburned bricks in the ruins of the Cholula pyramid. He'd been a young man then, just an ordinary Aztec soldier.

When he returned to Tenochtitlan, from duty in Cholula, he was sweeping the stairs of the great temple. Messengers from the emperor approached and greeted him.

"What can I do for you?" Montezuma asked politely.

The groups' spokesman said, "Montezuma, we bring a message from the emperor. You are to be the next emperor."

Montezuma just stood there stunned, holding his broom while his mouth dropped open.

"No. Oh no," Montezuma said, shaking his head vigorously. "Oh no. You must have the wrong person. I'm unfit to become emperor. I'm just a common soldier."

The messenger laughed. "It's no mistake, my friend! He knew Montezuma was the nephew of the last emperor and grandson of a preceding monarch, and was now being chosen in preference to his brothers because of his superior qualifications, both as a soldier and a priest. As a youth he'd been a soldier in several wars throughout the empire.

Montezuma finally accepted the emperorship in the white man's year 1502, and governed as no other Aztec emperor in history. The Aztecs loved him. He was their advocate and he took care of them and protected them. He was the best and most intelligent emperor ever to ascend the throne. To make sure his people were never abused by unscrupulous politicians, priests or soldiers, he had the habit of patrolling Tenochtitlan's streets in disguise to ensure the peoples' rights were not violated!

Luis and his men reached Tenochtitlan's outskirts the evening of July 9, 1518, where they camped. With the first streak of dawn, July 10, 1518, Luis and his men polished their armor, looked to their weapons, curried the horses and mules, and marched smartly into the Aztec capitol.

Sacred flames leaped skyward on the alters of numberless teocallis, lighting the gray mists of morning, stretched as far as the eye could see. The rising sun slowly burned off low lying fog, lifting it like a veil. Luis marveled at the valley's spectacular beauty, surrounded by looming mountains.

Temple and pyramids dotted the entire landscape in every direction.

Luis, Sandoval and Lopez rode at the head of the column, on prancing horses, under tightened rein, followed by disciplined, veteran troopers.

A thriving population, thousands of houses, temples and principle buildings, covered with white stucco, glistened like enamel in the sun's slanting beams. Winding canals reminded Luis of Venice—canals darkened by swarms of brightly decorated canoes filled with Aztecs clambering up the sides of the causeways to gaze with astonishment for the first time at the white, bearded strangers.

Luis followed the main boulevard into the city's center. A group of Aztec nobles walked out to greet them. Behind them came a golden litter, carried on the shoulders of noblemen, moving at a slow measured pace. It was covered with a canopy of gaudy feather work, powdered with jewels and fringed with silver. When within a respectable distance of the Spaniards, the nobleman sat it carefully on the ground.

Luis reined Diablo to a stop and dismounted. Montezuma stepped from his litter and walked forward, leaning on the arms of Cacamotzin and Cacama. Slaves spread a cotton tapestry on the ground so the emperor's feet wouldn't be contaminated by the soil. Subjects lining his path lowered their eyes to the ground when he passed.

Luis and his soldiers gawked in fascinated wonder at the pomp and splendor. Montezuma wore a girdle and square cloak, made of the finest cotton, with embroidered ends gathered in a knot around his neck. His feet were encased in sandals with soles of gold and leather bindings embossed with the same metal. Both cloak and sandals were sprinkled with pearls and emeralds. His head was covered with plumes of royal green.

At forty, Montezuma was tall and slim. His black hair was short and straight and he sported a thin beard. He spoke first. "I am Montezuma, and I welcome you here." Kano translated softly in the background.

"We bring greetings from King Carlos of Spain," Luis said, and walked to Montezuma and hung a sparkling chain of colored crystal around his neck. He attempted to give the emperor an embrazo hug, but was immediately restrained by two noblemen, shocked anyone would dare lay a human hand on Montezuma's sacred person.

Embarrassed by the incident, Montezuma gave a half smile. He'd never considered himself more than a mortal man! He spoke softly, "My brother will see you to suitable quarters. We shall talk after you're settled." He turned away and made for his litter. Luis and his men followed Montezuma's brother through the city. "My God, Jorge!" Luis exclaimed, "Could you in your wildest dreams have imagined such a place?"

"Never!" Sandoval exclaimed. "I've been to Rome, Athens, Constantinople and other European cities and none even come close to this!"

They passed through the great square and its numerous marketplaces. Throngs of people swarmed in the streets. They filled every doorway and window, and clustered atop buildings. Dozens of canoes floated in the canals.

Montezuma's brother got them safely to his palatial estate, made them comfortable and gave them free run of the palace. It was low and spacious, consisting of one floor, except in the center, where it rose to an additional story. The apartments were of great size and afforded wonderful accommodations to Luis and Sandoval, as well as their men!

"This place makes me nervous!" Sandoval said. "Too many open doorways where the Aztecs can get at us."

Luis agreed. "Before we settle in, I'll have Sergeant Lopez take some men and look around."

Luis posted guards at four strategic locations and sent Lopez and four others searching for any secret doors or passageways from which Aztecs could surprise them.

Lopez discovered a basement level and studied an unusually large, hand carved door which seemed oddly out of place. He tested it—it was unlocked! Lifting a burning torch from its holder, Lopez motioned his comrades, "Let's take a look."

The door opened down into a sloping, mineshaft-looking tunnel. Lopez couldn't see beyond the torch light. "You two stay here, inside the door, and warn us if anyone comes."

Thirty feet beyond the door the tunnel opened out like coming from the neck of a bottle. Lopez's flickering torch only hinted at it cavernous dimensions.

Flanked by two of his men, Lopez crept cautiously, ever deeper into the gloom—and what the flickering torch revealed stunned him. He couldn't believe what his eyes were telling him! He felt his pulses stammer and stop. He stared at something completely beyond human comprehension—stacks of gold ingots, as tall as Lopez himself, covered the floor as far as he could see!

"Good God Almighty!" Lopez called out, between a shout and a whisper. "This has got to be Axayacatl's treasure. He's Montezuma's father!"

He moved along the stacks of gold, rubbing his hand on the cold shiny metal. "I didn't believe Urcos when he told us of Axayactl's fabled treasure. Neither did Captain Escudero or Lieutenant Sandoval! Who could have believed a wild tale like that?" Lopez walked a bit further and found stacks of silver and baskets filled with emeralds and rubies.

"Morales, go find Captain Escudero and bring him here—but be very careful. If the Aztecs discover us, we're all dead men!"

Morales returned within minutes, with Luis, Sandoval, Kano and Urcos in tow. "Is it Axayacatl's treasure, sir?" Lopez asked.

Luis glanced sideways at Urcos. "Is it?"

"It is indeed!"

Sandoval pointed beyond the gold to the silver and gems. "How much do you think this treasure's worth, Captain?"

"It'd take a banker or financier to estimate its exact value," Luis replied. "I'd say in the hundreds of millions, enough to buy all the kingdoms of Europe! It'll take hundreds of wagons to haul it to the coast and dozens of large galleons to get it all back to Spain."

Suddenly a death scream echoed through the tunnel as a Spanish sentry killed an Aztec warrior who'd stumbled onto the Spaniards. Ten of General Naulinco's best guards stepped over the sentry's body and advanced down the tunnel, backing the two Spanish sentries ahead of them. Luis glanced quickly around the room for an alternative escape route, but there was none. They were trapped!

"Slay them all!" growled the Aztec captain. "They've discovered the emperor's sacred treasure." The itztli-wielding Aztecs rushed the Spaniards, who whipped out their swords.

"Stay out of this, Kano," Luis warned. "We can't afford to lose you!"

Kano grinned, his short spear ready. He had no intention of staying out of a good fight!

The Aztec captain came at Luis, swinging his itztli. Luis' flashing sword met him. They fought back and forth along the stacks of gold, the Aztec swooshing his itztli like a scythe. Luis easily parried the blows, stepped in faster than a snake flicking its tongue, and ran him through.

Sandoval fought like a wild man, yet with all the skill of Spain's greatest swordsman. Lopez, beating his blade like a smith on an anvil, drove three Aztecs staggering before him. The force of his blows stunned the warriors. He knocked itztlis from two of them and instantly had them both, his massive arms locked about their necks, crushing them. The other Aztec raised his weapon to kill Lopez, but Kano's spear took the warrior squarely in the heart. Kano jumped into the fray. He dove under an Aztec, grabbed him as easily as a child picks up a doll, lifted him above his head and threw him crashing headlong into the wall.

Urcos grabbed an Aztec in a crushing bear hug until he went limp.

The fracas lasted ten minutes, but it seemed more like an hour, before the Aztecs were dead. Luis sat down on a basket of emeralds, suddenly aware of his quivering leg muscles. He sat there, his gory blade across his knees. Sandoval, breathing hard, leaned against a stack of gold ingots. Kano bent down, pulled his spear from the dead Aztec and wiped it clean. Sergeant Lopez walked among the bodies, bending over each, making sure they were dead.

"Drag them to the back of the cave and get them buried!" Luis ordered. "Do you think Montezuma planned this bit of treachery?" Sandoval asked.

"I doubt it," Luis answered. "If he wanted us dead we'd be dead at the snap of his fingers."

When Kano explained to Urcos what was going on, he said, "These are Naulinco's men. See the markings on their arms? He's the Aztec military commander. I've heard there's bad blood between him and Montezuma."

"What about this treasure?" Sandoval asked. "Are we going to take any of it?"

Luis nodded. "Take two ingots of gold, one of silver and some emeralds and rubies. Then inventory the gold and silver. Cortez will want a full report."

"What about this Naulinco Urcos mentioned? If he finds out we've been in here won't he try to kill us or at least report us to the emperor?"

"I don't think so," Luis answered. "We're under Montezuma's protection. Anyone who tries to harm us will answer to him. I doubt Naulinco wants to do that!"

🐾🐾🐾

Luis sat up into the night, alone, unable to sleep, unable to let his mind rest. He closed his eyes for a moment and tried to think clearly. He rose and gazed from his apartment at the huge pyramid in the city's center, highlighted by a full moon. It jutted heavenward, as if trying to reach the patron war god of the Aztecs to whom it was dedicated. Smoke curled skyward from its altar. He shuddered involuntarily, as he remembered Guatemotzin and Techchupo, and had a good idea what was going on.

So far I've carried out Cortez's orders. We penetrated the Aztec empire, made maps, learned about the Aztecs and most important of all found enough gold to warrant his expedition of conquest! But every hour we remain here weakens our position. How do we get out of here alive?

Next morning Sandoval said, "Captain, I've seen Aztec soldiers moving closer to the building. Something's going on—whether with the emperor's blessing or not, I have no idea."

"I've noticed! I think a little demonstration of our firepower might be just the thing to buy us a little time—maybe put the fear of God into the Aztecs."

Luis saw Lopez's brow contract. "You have a thought?"

"I do, Captain. "Using our cannon and arquebuses will undoubtedly scare hell out of the heathens. Our horses could also be used in such a demonstration. The Aztecs have never been around horses. They're frightened half to death of them."

Luis' eyes widened. "What do you have in mind?" Lopez explained a very simple plan to use the horses.

"Excellent! Let's keep our eyes open for an opportunity."

🐾🐾🐾

One of Montezuma's elite bodyguards strutted into the room unannounced and growled, "The mighty Emperor Montezuma wishes to see you. Immediately, if you please!"

Leaving Sergeant Lopez in command, Luis, Sandoval and Kano followed the guard.

26

"**W**elcome!" Montezuma said warmly. Sitting in his golden arm chair, surrounded by three counselors, he said, "Come, sit here by me so we may talk together." He waved them to chairs. Luis, Sandoval and Kano bowed respectfully and sat down.

"I'd like you to meet Cacama, leader of the council." The elderly Aztec smiled. "Next is my uncle, Cacamotzin." He inclined his head slightly. "And the warrior there is Naulinco, general of my army."

Luis glanced casually at Naulinco and met a scowl of hatred! Luis didn't know, or care, whether Naulinco liked him or not; but he got the distinct impression the man feared him—not in any physical way. It went much deeper than that.

"Did my brother get you comfortably situated?" Montezuma asked. "Yes sir!" Luis replied.

"Wonderful!" Montezuma rubbed his hands together. "We're most curious to learn more about you and where you're from. What manner of man is your king? How large is his kingdom?

Luis smiled and replied, "King Carlos is a very young man, sir, who rules a mighty empire called Spain. His subjects adore him, and his army has never been defeated in battle."

Hearing Kano's translation, Montezuma's eyes widened and he retorted immediately, "Do you think he could defeat my army? I have thousands of warriors."

Luis returned Montezuma's steady stare, and answered diplomatically, "Let's hope neither of us have shall ever have to find out. But let's talk of peace, not war. King Carlos wants to be your friend."

Montezuma managed a grin. "That is good. I would like to be his friend. Please tell us more about Spain where your king lives."

Luis explained details of Spanish culture which brought murmurs, smiles and incredulous stares from the Aztecs. Concepts of large ships with sails, wagons drawn by huge beasts called horses, in a land where they were unknown, along with other strange unbelievable details of European machinery and weapons were beyond the grasp of the simple Aztecs.

"And what of your religion?" Montezuma asked politely. "What gods do your people worship?"

It was a few moments before Luis answered, pondering the simplest way to explain Catholicism to men with no concept of God or his Son, Jesus Christ. Such abstruse doctrines as original sin, the Garden of Eden, temptation by Satan—the entire story would be completely incomprehensible—an invisible god divided into three separate entities, who teaches love, not hate or war—who is everywhere but nowhere, encompassing the universe, yet so small he can dwell in an individual heart. Luis did his best to explain his complicated religion, and Kano tried to interpret the explanation into concepts the Aztecs could understand.

Montezuma and his nobles listened with silent attention and respect until Luis concluded. Luis and Kano could tell by the Aztecs' expressions their explanation had fallen of deaf ears!

No! Montezuma decided silently. It's definitely not a religion for me or my people! Steeped in his country's superstitions and culture from earliest childhood, he was the empire's chief priest before becoming emperor. No! He would hold with his own religion!

He straightened his shoulders and smiled—a strange smile which made Luis uneasy. "Many of the things you say are good, yet our ways are good too. Many of them were handed down to us from an ancient white race who was led here by a very wise leader hundreds of moons ago. He gave us laws and ruled over us for a long time. When he felt we could govern ourselves he sailed away over the eastern sea."

"Did he teach you to sacrifice human beings?" Luis asked.

"Certainly not!" He stared at Luis for a second or so, then said softly, "I sense you believe human sacrifice is bad. But it's really not! Believe me! It's an integral part of our religion and so simple to understand. We propitiate the gods with blood and they make the sun to shine. That makes the crops grow, which sustains us. Our young men grow strong and become warriors."

Montezuma paused to see if the Spaniards comprehended his meaning. A note of pride crept into his voice as he continued, "My dear Uncle Ahuitzotl had the honor of starting multiple sacrifices. He sent his armies into Oaxaca's mountains to capture sacrificial victims. They abducted every male and female of proper age from the two main tribes. They were put in wooden cages, brought back to Tenochtitlan and sacrificed by the hundreds."

Montezuma's brow wrinkled, as though he didn't condone his Uncle's actions. "I really thought that was wasteful. Twenty had always been a good number up to that time. But Uncle Ahuitzotl, a most stubborn man, wouldn't tolerate any protests. He wanted to overwhelm the gods with his generosity. Endless lines of prisoners ascended the sacrificial alters and their hearts were taken. The bodies became so numerous they could no long be fed to dogs and people. We put their heads on long poles to dry in the sun so their skulls could adorn our skull racks."

Luis stared at Kano, his questioning eyes doubting a correct interpretation. Kano shrugged and nodded. It was an exact and literal interpretation! Luis and Sandoval had difficulty comprehending the enormity of Montezuma's matter-of-fact history of human sacrifice. Yet, they politely refrained from comment.

Montezuma continued. "At the eight temples of Tenochtitlan, the priests slashed and sweated and slashed. It was very hard work! Blood was everywhere, running down the temple steps and pouring over the plaza, and the skull rack was piled high. The people could eat no more flesh cut from arms and legs so our beasts in the royal zoo gorged on bone and muscle; still the bodies came tumbling down the temple's steep steps, creating heaps of limbs and blank faces until Uncle Ahuitzotl ordered the human carcasses to be thrown into the lake just be rid of them."

Montezuma paused to give Kano sufficient time for an accurate interpretation, then continued, "I argued vehemently with Uncle Ahuitzotl, and urged him to reduce the sacrifices to a more manageable number. But, being the strong-willed man he was, he wouldn't hear of it!"

Montezuma, shrewd judge of men that he was, could tell the Spaniards were horrified by the history he provided. In fact it left them speechless!

Stretching, he said, "I tire of talking about religion and sacrifices. I've given some thought to your religion, as you explained it. I'm convinced it would not do for us. It is a good religion, but ours is better, at least for us. We worship many gods and they all protect and prosper us. Let's talk of it no more." The inflection in his voice left no doubt the matter of religion, at least in a doctrinal sense, was closed.

"Tell me, Captain, are you and your men of the royal family?"

The unexpected question caught Luis off guard, and he knew he must answer wisely.

"Yes sir. That's why our king sent us directly from his court to see you. Kano, who interprets so ably, is from another land, but is highly favored of our king for his excellent translation skills."

Luis' answer satisfied Montezuma. He sat silent for a few moments, and studied the Spaniards covertly one at a time, measuring them before introducing a topic that might cause dissension in their relationship. Escudero: a dynamic leader, shrewd, diplomatic, practical and a dangerous foe.

Sandoval: Intelligent, level headed, a natural leader, and a very devoted subordinate to Escudero. Kano: a man unlike anyone Montezuma had ever met—he could easily be an Aztec. Intelligent, calculating and dangerous if crossed.

"Captain Escudero," Montezuma said quietly, "I have one further matter of business before we part company for the evening. Do you know a man from your country called Pedro Armand?"

Luis' face betrayed stunned surprise! "Yes, my Lord, I know him. But how would you know of Armand?"

Montezuma nodded to a guard who threw open the chamber doors. Four Aztec warriors roughly jerked a man, with a rope binding his wrists, into the room. His hair was short like a natives', and he wore a loose cloak and a filthy loincloth. Barefoot, unkempt and malnourished, his body was covered with whip welts.

The pathetic creature cast a terrified glance at Luis and his companions.

"Luis? Luis Escudero? Is it really you?" Armand gasped, scarcely able to believe his eyes. "Armand? Pedro Armand?" Luis stammered, gawking at the disheveled shell of a man.

"Silence!" Montezuma roared. "You may not speak to the prisoner!" The Aztec guard jerked the rope and Armand crashed to the floor.

Luis jumped to his feet, his hand on his sword—a vein in his forehead swollen and throbbing.

Montezuma hissed a deadly warning. "Don't do anything foolish, Captain! I want to tell you what this man has done and why he is my prisoner!"

Luis backed off, knowing Montezuma's elite royal guards would kill him before he could draw his sword.

"For God's sake, Luis, do something!" Armand screamed. The Aztec's golden-sandaled foot kicked Armand in the stomach. Jerking on the rope, he pulled the half dead Spaniard to his feet.

Montezuma said, "Armand and his men raided the Mayans' sacred city of Uxamil and stole its richest treasures. They raped helpless women and killed hundreds of men, women and children. I've pledged my word to Uluam, Ruler of Uxamil, a dear friend of mine, that Armand will pay for his crimes. He came uninvited to our land and butchered Mayans and Aztecs without quarter. Because he's a warrior, we've decided he'll make a suitable sacrifice to Huitzilopotchli, our great war god."

Montezuma's glittering, brown eyes remained unchanged as he pronounced a death sentence on Pedro Armand. Something else peered out as well, now and again, which Luis hadn't noticed before; something which smacked of dark, sinister evil and perhaps a bit of madness.

Pale and trembling, his quaking legs scarcely able to support his emaciated body, Armand stood dirty and tattered, with drops of cold fear oozing from every pore. "Help me, Luis. Oh God, please help me," he pleaded.

"Enough!" Montezuma shouted. "Return this scum to the prison, and see these men to their quarters!"

As the Spaniards reached the chamber doors, Montezuma called after them. "A moment, Captain Escudero..." his voice faltered as though he was trying to think of something to say to soothe over his curt dismissal of his guests. "Perhaps you'd like more servants? More girls for your men?"

"Thank you kindly, my Lord, but we have everything we need. You've been most generous. There is one thing I would like to ask. Can you release Armand to me? King Carlos will be angry if you sacrifice him."

Montezuma's tawny skin paled with anger, his eyes flashed and he replied harshly, "The subject is closed, Captain! Don't ever speak of it again in my presence." Then as quickly as the anger came it abruptly disappeared. "Tomorrow we should like to see how your weapons work." It seemed a command rather than a statement.

"Certainly, my Lord!" Luis responded, pleased with this turn of events. "We'll be pleased to entertain you and your counselors with a demonstration."

27

"**N**ow where the hell are you off to, Captain?" Sandoval demanded.

"To do a little spying. I've got to know what's going on in the jail where Armand is being kept before we try to break him out."

"You plan to help Armand escape?' Sandoval asked incredulously. "Are you out of your mind? We owe him nothing. He got himself into this mess, let him get himself out!"

"He's a countryman, Sandoval. We can't just leave him here to be slaughtered like a pig on a block"

"We'll I'm here to tell you I don't like it one damn bit! It's too risky! You'd actually place the entire expedition in jeopardy to save one man, and a thief and killer at that? I can't believe you'd make such a foolish move!"

"We've got to at least try."

"Damn, but you can be one obstinate bastard, begging your pardon sir!" Sandoval fumed, then with resignation said, "All right. Let's hear your plan."

"I don't have a plan until I check things out."

Sandoval managed a thin smile. "Please, whatever you do, don't get yourself killed!"

"I'm not planning on it. You take charge. I won't be gone long."

🐾 🐾 🐾

It was dark and a pale moon had come up over the horizon, a moon of muted blue. Luis disguised himself in an Aztec priest's cloak and slipped away to Montezuma's prison. He tip-toed past a sleeping guard to a lower level where prisoners were kept. Torches barely lighted the corridor.

Luis hissed softly, "Armand. Pedro Armand. Are you in here?"

"Who is it?" came a faint response.

"It's Luis." Through the barred door of Armand's cell the two men stared into each other's eyes. "Por Dios, Luis," Armand sighed, "Never have I seen a more welcome face." He extended his hand through the bars. He stood blinking, unkempt and haggard.

"We must talk quickly, Pedro, before the guard makes his rounds. Tell me, how did you get yourself into this mess? What are you doing here?"

Armand poured out his story while Luis kept a wary eye out for guards. Sometimes Armand was almost incoherent, but marshaled his straying wits enough to complete his amazing tale of working for Governor Velasquez.

"Is there any other way out of here?" Luis asked, as Armand went into a shivering spasm of jungle malaria.

"Yes, there are many passages leading to the outside."

Luis looked about but couldn't see beyond the nearest torch. "We're wasting time, Luis, let's go. Get me out of here!"

"Quiet! Let me think a moment. Perhaps we can take you with us when we leave." A plan was forming in Luis' mind. If he could arrange Armand's escape—once in the hills Armand could wait for Luis' men, rendezvous with them and return to civilization. The plan had possibilities. From what Luis had seen in Montezuma's court, anything could be bought or arranged for a price.

"We'll break you out Pedro, but not tonight. It's too risky."

Armand didn't believe him. Luis pulled up the hood on his robe and disappeared into the darkness. Staring through the bars like a pathetic, sick animal, Armand shivered with chills and fear. Panic-stricken he croaked out, "Luis? Oh my God, Luis, don't leave me here."

🐾 🐾 🐾

Montezuma arrived at his brother's palace, borne on his golden litter, followed by the empire's most powerful nobles. Most striking was dark, sullen war chief Naulinco in Aztec armor, with black leather bands around his mighty biceps. He had little use for the frills of soft living, and shunned wearing gold or jewelry. His haughty, contemptuous bearing, exuded hatred for the Spaniards, and it didn't go unnoticed by Luis.

The emperor and his retinue seated themselves in a semicircle in the courtyard. Luis turned his full attention to the Aztecs and spoke slowly and simply through Kano.

"We are greatly impressed with your magnificent city, more beautiful than any we've ever visited. We thank your for your kindness and hospitality." This brought smiles and nods of approval.

Pointing to the falconet, Luis explained, "This mighty weapon is called tepuzque in your language because it speaks like thunder from the sky. Tepuzque is our friend and will roar or kill upon our command. Observe."

A trooper with his back to the Aztecs appeared to talk to the elevated weapon. He touched a small, burning string to the fire hole. With a loud thunderous roar it exploded and sent the ball whistling harmlessly over the outbuildings. The roar, fire and sulphurous drifting smoke terrified the Aztecs—even the mighty Naulinco!

Luis threw up his hands. "Calm yourselves, my friends. Have no fear. Tepuzque speaks only to show his mighty power. He'll not harm you."

Montezuma sat impassive, trying to comprehend what he'd seen. His nobles buzzed with excitement, each with his own idea of what made tepuzque speak.

Instant silence came when Sandoval led Diablo by a halter rope before the curious Aztecs. Unsaddled, the huge warhorse's glistening coat, flowing main and tail greatly impressed them.

Luis stepped up to Diablo and patted his great, muscled neck. "This is Diablo. The gods made only one like him! He's fierce in battle and kills enemies when I tell him to."

Unseen by the Aztecs, Sergeant Lopez led his mare into an open-windowed building a short distance back of the attentive audience whose rapt attention was focused on Diablo.

He pawed the ground with steel-shod hooves. Sandoval played out plenty of rope, allowing Diablo to rear up on his hind legs and flay the air with kicking front hooves. Screaming shrilly, he wildly rolled the whites of his eyes.

Terrified, color drained from Aztec faces! Each looked frantically for a place of escape from the maddened beast.

Holding up his hands, palms forward, Luis called loudly, "Have no fear. I'll tell Diablo you are friends." He spoke softly to Diablo and the agitated horse immediately calmed. Sandoval led the horse away.

Naulinco, ashamed of his countrymen, himself included, jumped to his feet. "You show us your toys," he spat out sarcastically, "Without them you are nothing!"

Montezuma's head jerked up and his nobles gasped, surprised that Naulinco would be so bold as to insult the emperor's guests! Their faces turned to him, then back to Naulinco, then to Luis, waiting for his reaction.

It came swiftly! Luis leaned forward and slapped Naulinco smartly across the face. "For that you will die, Spaniard!"

"Do your best, my friend." Luis unhooked his armor and handed it to Kano.

Naulinco rushed Luis, who smashed his right fist into the base of his nose. That fist, delivered with Luis' full force behind it, threw Naulinco's head back. Luis stepped in quickly and drove his left fist into the Aztec's stomach—which felt like a tightly packed sack of flour! Luis' men cheered. To their surprise Aztec nobles cheered too—and began taking bets from each other!

Naulinco caught Luis' neck in the crook of his right arm and tried to grab his genitals with his left hand. With both hands free, Luis grabbed the groping fingers and twisted them backwards. But Naulinco's arm tightened intolerably around Luis' neck. His face was crushed against the Indian's bare chest, and was stifled by the animal reek of the man.

Luis tried to twist his head sideways so he could breathe, but Naulinco had him! A mighty cheer erupted from the nobles! Luis managed to jerk his right knee into Naulinco's groin and he gasped with pain. The choke hold loosened for an instant. Luis slipped free, keeping his chin sunk down around his neck so the Aztec couldn't catch him a second time. With his back to Naulinco, Luis locked his right arm over the man's elbow, fell to one knee and tried to toss him over his shoulder. Naulinco was too strong and heavy! He tried again to get Luis in a headlock.

Luis moved too fast. He weaved, dodged, stepped in and smashed a right fist to Naulinco's neck, where his jugular vein popped out. The Aztec threw his hands up to protect his face. Luis pounded him twice under the heart and danced back in time to avoid those long, muscular arms.

Naulinco staggered, hurt and dizzy. Blood streamed down his face. Luis kicked him in the groin with a jack-booted foot. Naulinco gasped loudly and doubled over. Luis smashed him twice again in the face with his full strength. The warrior's knees buckled and he toppled over on his back, staring up with sightless eyes, the lower part of his face a bloody sponge.

Luis sucked air in great gasping gulps that hurt him, and his quivering legs almost dropped him. But the fight was over.

He glanced at the Aztecs, every one of them stunned and terrified! Instantly he realized he'd committed a monumental error! Though the

Aztecs were used to scenes of violence, watching priests rip hearts from men, women and children and throwing them into altar fires, watching a man's face systematically beaten to a pulp with bare fists was completely beyond their comprehension or experience.

Luis acted quickly to turn the situation to his advantage. Throwing his arms about the nearest noble, he roared with laughter and shouted, "Did you see him fall? It was like a mighty tree struck by lightening. Smack, he hit the earth! Smack! Smack! Smack! Luis hit his fist against his palm. Kano laughed hilariously as he translated Luis' words.

Montezuma stared at Luis for a moment, then he began laughing! His nobles followed suit, laughing uproariously. Kano jumped in the air and twirled about, in a wild African dance, laughing all the while. Everyone was laughing, howling with delight. When the laughter petered out Luis gave a great bellow of mirth and it started up again.

Finally Luis held his hand up for silence. "Naulinco is a great warrior, stronger than any man I've ever fought. I now know why his is your top general!"

Aztecs smiled approval. They could understand man to man combat, winning and losing. Their general fought honorably, according to Aztec custom, as well as he could. That's all any Aztec warrior could do!

Satisfied he'd restored confidence and established his position, he walked to his men. Kano asked, "Are you all right, Captain?"

"A bit sore here and there. I wouldn't want to fight a man like that every day!"

Sandoval patted his back vigorously, and troopers clustered round, each congratulating him on his victory. They walked away talking and laughing.

Luis glanced back at Montezuma and saw the barest hint of a smile and a look of satisfaction as he stood there staring down at his military commander sprawled in the dirt.

🐜🐜🐜

Montezuma's messenger found Luis, Sandoval and Kano lounging in the palace flower garden sipping pulque. He spoke to Kano, saluted and left.

"You're not going to believe this, Captain, but we've been invited on a grand tour tomorrow, you, Lieutenant Sandoval, Sergeant Lopez and me, conducted by Montezuma himself!"

"A tour of his palace?" Luis asked.

"No sir. A tour of the main pyramid and temple!"

"Isn't that where they practice their abominable religion?"

"Yes sir. They butcher hundreds of innocent victims every day!"

28

Craning their necks skyward, Luis, Sandoval, Kano and Lopez stared up the long steep stone stairway leading to the top of the five-storied pyramid.

Montezuma led the way, with barely an occasional backward glance at the Spaniards. To him it was an easy, every-day climb, a nice bit of exercise. He hiked up those stairs at least three times a day; so he was patient with the huffing-puffing Spaniards lagging behind.

Gasping for breath, they finally reached the summit, Lopez blowing like a winded horse! "What do you think, my friends?" Montezuma exclaimed delightedly. "Isn't this a magnificent structure? Look at the view!" He made a sweeping gesture with his hand as he and his guests gazed out over the broad valley and down into Tenochtitlan's wide streets. The city stretched for miles, like a map of green and white, within the blue sheet of the lake, all they way to the distant rim of silver, snow-capped mountains.

Littered about the smooth stone floor were several large jasper blocks, used for stretching sacrificial victims, back down. The temple sanctuary, which rose three stories above the pyramid's summit, was, until today, forbidden to all but priests and priestesses.

"Please be seated." Montezuma motioned them to chairs facing a green, rounded jasper stone four feet high, its convex surface the length of a man's body. Beyond the sacrificial stone stood several stone statues covered in blood and human gore. Reluctantly, the Spaniards took seats, knowing human sacrifice would take place. They'd seen it a few days ago in the Chichemetlan village.

Warily they eyed the great stone statue looming above them, its terrible jeweled eyes glared down on the sacred fire which burned in the bowl on its lap. Several priests and priestesses, wearing only white capes and loincloths, their bodies dyed black, walked forward and bowed respectfully before Montezuma. Their long, blood-stiffened hair was bound up with leather thongs, their foreheads covered with tiny shields of colored paper. Their overwhelming stench in the warm morning sun was almost unbearable!

The Aztec chief high priest, called Topiltzin, walked majestically from the sanctuary. On his head tossed a crown of green and yellow plumes. Golden ornaments studded with emeralds dangled from his ears. His under lip sported a turquoise pendant. Dressed in a long red cloak and a loincloth, he took his place a few feet from his assistants, in a prayer-like trance, while they dragged the next sacrificial victim from the sanctuary.

A booming snake skin sacrificial drum announced another sacrifice taking place! Two priests walked with slow, cadenced footsteps, in rhythm with the drum. Between them, they supported a beautiful young Aztec woman who appeared drugged. Her nude body hung limp; but her eyes were open, and her mind tried to make sense of what was happening to her. The Topiltzin nodded. The priests stretched her back down over the jasper block. The morning sun, a vast splash of fire, filled the overhead sky, and blazed down on her voluptuous female form, tinting her smooth, bronzed body with liquid golden light.

The drum stopped abruptly. The Topiltzin chanted a reverent death prayer. An assistant handed him the sacred sacrificial stone knife.

The helpless, horrified victim stared hypnotically at the knife poised high above her chest; and watched in open-mouthed astonishment as it plunged downward. Her high-pitched, terrified scream was cut short when the Topiltzin jammed his hand into the butchered incision, jerked out her still throbbing heart and held it high for everyone to admire. The great drum boomed, announcing completion of another successful sacrifice to the gods. The Topiltzin turned to the idol and threw the heart into the fiery bowl in its lap; it hissed in the hot flames, spreading a burning stench through the air. Priests and priestesses sang, while the Topiltzin turned again to the gory corpse and dabbled his hands in blood flowing from its flanks to the floor. He anointed the huge fanged idol, and the sanctuary's cornices with blood. Three priests strolled about the platform swinging smoking braziers of perfume drifting up to purify the putrid air. Two others seized the girl's body, like a pair of butchers, and dragged it to a slab covered with knives and hatchets and chopped it apart. They carried the arms and legs to a large cauldron of water boiling inside the sanctuary. These cuts of meat would later be eaten by priests. The memberless trunk, now a travesty of a beautiful feminine body, which once rippled with zestful life, was cast into a bloody basket to be fed to the royal zoo's hungry beasts!

Pools of blood coagulated on the stone floor. Luis swallowed hard and gasped deep breaths to keep from vomiting. Sandoval breathed deeply several times to thwart impending nausea, and covered his mouth with the back of his hand. Kano shook his head, wondering what kind of gods demanded human hearts. Such practices were unknown amongst his people. Montezuma mistook the Spaniards' revulsion for sadness.

Softly he said, "Don't feel sad, my friends. This was her happy day, for which she was prepared. She was chosen of the gods, and her spirit now resides with them!"

Sergeant Lopez fought to turn his eyes away, and they narrowed when he watched the priests sever the girl's head from her torso. He brought his hand to his throat and whispered to Luis, "Oh Christ, sir, I'm going to be sick!" He started gagging, and with the agility of someone half his size, he ran to the edge of the pyramid and vomited.

Montezuma shook his head, absolutely puzzled, wondering how such a perfect sacrificial service, on such a magnificent day, could cause such an adverse reaction. He couldn't have performed it any better himself!

He turned to the Spaniards and said, "I must admit, in the beginning it's difficult for strangers to understand our ways. Perhaps as you see and learn more of our beautiful religion you'll come to understand and appreciate its truth and simplicity."

It was too much for Sandoval, still fighting bile rising in his throat from thick black smoke wafting from the bowl of burning hearts! He jumped up, his sword blade at low guard, ready to slash and kill the priests. Luis grabbed his arm, but he shook it off and lunged at the nearest priest. Sandoval's boots slipped on the blood-slickened floor. The priest darted into the sanctuary. Luis grabbed Sandoval with both hands and jerked him back.

Montezuma hissed a deadly warning. "You'd better keep your men under control or they'll not leave here alive. Do you understand me?"

"Yes, my Lord," Luis replied. "It won't happen again."

Montezuma accepted the apology, though still puzzled, wondering why these men were so shocked at a ceremony which had been part of his culture for hundreds of years, practiced in several cities throughout the empire!

Lopez, still green about the mouth, rejoined the group.

"Are you feeling better now?" Montezuma asked with concern. "Yes, my Lord," Lopez lied.

"Very well. Please follow me. No talking is permitted while we're in the sanctuary. It's a very sacred and holy place."

They followed him through the horrible open-mouthed Lord of the underworld, his huge, bloody stone fangs hanging down to devour souls. Inside was a brightly painted, barred cage, full of terrified men and women, sacrificial victims apprehensively awaiting their turn!

The Spaniards gawked helplessly at the pathetic creatures, then followed Montezuma into the steaming inferno beyond. Here too, were stone images of devils, demons and serpents, and in the center, another sacrificial altar. Darkness closed in about them. The patch of light around the altar contracted, flickering more and more wildly on the floor and walls as torch flames burned low, then leaped hungrily in the fetid, stench-filled air, sending tendrils of black smoke spiraling up into the blackness.

Several large pots bubbled over small fires, cooking flesh of the most recent victims. The Spaniards felt cold terror creeping up their spines, raising hair on the backs of their necks.

Panic settled so heavily on Lopez his eyes searched for unseen, lurking demons! Crowding close to Luis, he whispered, "Let's get out of this evil hell hole while we're still alive!"

"Quiet!" Montezuma growled and turned a dark look on Lopez.

"Allow me a moment, my Lord," Luis whispered. He pulled Lopez aside and said softly, "Do you want to go out and join the men? I have to stay and find out everything I can about these people. That's a direct order from Captain Cortez. We're not here because we enjoy seeing such things, Sergeant. I hope you realize that."

Lopez gave a low, agonized groan, wrenched up from deep inside him, and closed his eyes for a moment to shut out the grotesque sight of priests taking human flesh from the pots.

"Captain, when Captain Cortez comes, will he have priests with him?"

"He plans to bring three priests, if his expedition is approved."

"Oh thank the good Lord for that!" Lopez breathed a sigh of relief. "They will bring the word of Christ to these heathen bastards, and tear down their filthy monuments." He paused for a moment. "I'm sorry I lost control, sir. I'll not do it again!"

They rejoined the emperor and followed him from room to room and watched sweating priests stirring the contents of huge vats, with long wooden poles. Priestesses prepared various cuts of meat on trays to distribute to working priests throughout the vast structure. Lining the walls, between obscene idols of men and women, were wooden butchering blocks, each covered with obsidian knives and hatchets.

Montezuma's priests and priestesses weren't very old. Some of the priestesses, under their gory exteriors, were rather attractive. They came from royal families. Kano heard it rumored some of them eventually became the emperor's concubines.

Working in the sanctuary was very demanding, both for men and women—hot, bloody and smelly! But they were very well treated and had everything they needed; and above all, found status within the five levels of Aztec society.

"My Lord," Luis asked, "do the priests eat the entire body?"

"Oh no! They eat only the arms and legs and more delicate parts. The torsos we feed to our animals. You must see our beautiful animals!" He led them to a doorway at the far end of the room. Torches along the wall flickered like fireflies in the darkness as they followed the emperor up a flight of stairs to the next floor.

In the dim torchlight, they saw a long hallway of barred cages like those in a dungeon. Montezuma let out a blood-curdling scream. From the cages came the howl of wild animals and hissing snakes. The terrified Spaniards waited apprehensively for Satan himself to appear!

With a glottal shout from Montezuma the horrible noises ceased as quickly as they began. Luis could not prevent himself now from asking, "Did animals make those noises?" Montezuma nodded proudly. "Yes. This is my private zoo. Observe!"

Walking along a double row of cages the Spaniards saw wild animals pacing back and forth, jaguars, jackals, and smaller beasts they'd never seen before, and huge mastiff dogs. In a snake pit hundreds of snakes from throughout the empire, poisonous snakes as well as constrictors, crawled over the shapely torso of a headless female.

"What do you think?" Montezuma asked. "Have you ever seen a finer collection of wild animals?" Speaking truthfully, Luis replied, "No sir, never!"

"Good. Then follow me. One more floor and we'll be finished."

When they reached the sanctuary's top level, and stepped into clean fresh air, the Spaniards breathed a sigh of relief, thankful to be away from the kitchen sweat bath. After that bizarre experience, they knew nothing could ever shock them again!

29

A long, neatly aligned row of human skulls grinned from ledges above the room. Warriors armed with spears and shields, splendidly dressed in matching armor and quetzal feather headdresses, guarded the door. Just inside the entrance stood two intricately carved stone idols, a man and a woman. This level was a prison of sorts, with rows of dark, barred cages, used to house very special sacrificial victims.

Montezuma began to explain what the Spaniards were seeing. Suddenly he jumped in surprise, when one of his cackling jesters materialized from a dark doorway, jumping, dancing and clapping his hands.

Montezuma laughed happily. "Tepanec, you naughty boy! You almost made my heart stop! Go away! I'm conducting these visitors on a tour!" His voice had a light note in it.

Luis looked at Kano for an explanation.

"Montezuma often amuses himself with his jesters, just as monarchs in Europe do. He told me, whether in jest I don't know, that he gets more instruction and information from his jesters than he does from his wise men. They're all afraid to tell him the truth!"

"He has jesters?" Luis asked.

"Yes sir, many of them, along with jugglers and mummers and thousands of dancers. He is richer and more powerful than all the monarchs of Europe combined."

"Excuse the interruption, gentlemen," Montezuma apologized, as Tepanec skipped and hopped crazily down the hallway. Montezuma strolled along slowly. "As I was telling you, these special sacrificial offerings are..."

"Jesus Christ, Captain!" Sandoval grabbed Luis by the shoulder. "Are my eyes playing tricks on me? Do you see that?" He pointed.

Luis' head jerked up. His eyes went wide for a moment, then closed, then opened again. He couldn't believe what his eyes told him was there! Pacing back and forth, like a graceful, tawny cat, was the most magnificently formed white woman he'd ever seen. Clothed only in a green loincloth, her long, flowing blonde hair highlighted her dark green eyes. He guessed her to be about twenty.

Montezuma flashed a pleased smile, wondering how a mere woman could cause such a sensation among the Spaniards.

"My Lord," Luis asked in shocked surprise. "Is she a Spanish woman?"

Montezuma laughed. "Oh my goodness no! She's one of the ancient ones of whom we've spoken."

"You mean there are actually survivors?" Luis asked, completely dumbfounded, wondering how the ancient ones had survived murdering Aztecs, disease and wild beasts. "Yes. We've kept a few of them. Why? Do the ancient ones interest you?"

Luis didn't answer. He studied the woman, noting her defiant, resolute stride. "May I speak to her?"

"Certainly. But be brief. She's not worthy your time; hardly above the level of an animal!"

"Does she speak Nahuatl?"

"It's the only language she knows. Their own barbaric language was lost centuries ago." At that moment a red-robed priest at the end of the hall motioned Montezuma to join him.

"Damn these meddlesome priests! They couldn't make a decision if their life depended on it! Please excuse me for a moment."

Luis stepped up to the cage, uncertain what to say. The woman was full of excitement! Here was a white man, wearing silver metal around his chest and a long knife hanging at his side! Who was he? Why was he here? She stared at him. A strange man he was indeed, but strangely nice and disturbingly strange! It was his eyes, pale blue, eyes like she'd never seen before, which stared into her soul!

Her first words were, "I knew you'd come!"

"You did?"

"I know you! You're Quetzalcoatl! It's been prophesied for many generations you'd come back someday and rescue us from these brutes!" She pointed to Montezuma and his priest. She raked back her blonde locks with a quick nervous hand; her eyes shadowed with weariness and fear.

"Why are you a prisoner?" Luis asked.

"The high priest arguing with Montezuma is going to sacrifice me." She spoke quickly. Her eyes smoldered with hatred for the priest. "Can you help me escape from this evil place?"

"Do they allow you freedom of the temple?"

"No."

"If they caught you trying to escape, what would they do?"

"Kill me—but they plan to kill me anyway," she shuddered, "and soon, if that evil demon priest has his way." She chewed her bottom lip for a moment. "If you are the great god, Quetzalcoatl, you have the power to free me."

"I'm no god, just a soldier of Spain. My name is Luis Escudero."

"You're not...Quetzalcoatl?" She stammered with disappointment. "I'm afraid not," Luis grinned. "Won't I do?"

She felt color rising to her face, but said, "You'll do just fine!" She thrust a hand through the bars. "I'm Toloya." Her grip was firm and strong, that of a woman accustomed to working with her hands.

Holding that hand, looking into those sultry green eyes, Luis said, "Give me a little time and I'll see what I can work out with Montezuma."

Toloya was relieved when Kano translated Luis' words—but she cautioned, "Work fast, Luis, before they tie me to the altar!"

His bright thoughts of a rosy future with this beautiful woman were dampened by Montezuma's voice jerking him back to reality. "You actually find this creature pleasing?"

"I do indeed! The most beautifully intriguing woman I've ever met!"

Montezuma clasped Luis' shoulder. "I'd give her to you as a gift right now, my friend, but I'm in an awkward situation. The high priest is determined to sacrifice her to Jacapitla, at the next full moon, just days away. I forcefully explained to him my very serious reservations about sacrificing such a beautiful woman. She could certainly be put to more exotic pleasures."

Luis assumed Montezuma was helpless against his priests. It was through their power, more than his army, that he ruled his empire!

Sensing a very slight possibility Montezuma might find a way to overrule his high priest, Luis smiled and said casually, "It's of little matter, my Lord. I realize how difficult priests can be."

Relief flooded Montezuma's face. "Let me try again. Perhaps I can persuade him to give her to you as a token of our respect and friendship. Mind you now, I'm not promising anything, but I'll certainly work toward that end." With that, the emperor turned and led them from the temple. Luis glanced over his shoulder at Toloya, pacing back and forth, dead tired, but too terrified to sleep.

Three hours later an Aztec warrior strutted into Luis' room, where he, Sandoval and Kano were relaxing, drinking pulque.

"You!" the Aztec growled, pointing to Luis, "and the black man, follow me! The emperor wishes to talk to you!" He turned and made for Montezuma's reception room.

"Keep an eye on things, Sandoval, until we get back!" Luis called out.

🐾 🐾 🐾

Montezuma sat in his golden chair surrounded by five red-robed priests glaring sullenly at Luis. He waved Luis and Kano to chairs. Coming directly to the point he said, "I've finally persuaded my obstinate priests to parole Toloya to you for a few days to become better acquainted."

"Thank you, my Lord!"

"Save your thanks until you've heard the conditions of her parole. If she escapes, you must give us one of your men to replace her as a sacrifice."

"That's agreeable, sir. I'll make sure she doesn't escape."

"Wonderful! How would you like to travel to her village—see her people first hand?

It's only a short ways away in the hills, and Toloya could show you the way. Her mother, Sariah, is a very interesting woman! Seeing these white women close up may give you some second thoughts."

Luis stared in astonishment. "Toloya has people?"

Montezuma laughed. "We've kept a few of them for our amusement and for special sacrifices." He spoke as it was an insignificant matter.

Luis couldn't prevent himself from asking, "If I go to this strange village, what about my men? Will they be safe while I'm gone?"

Montezuma nodded. "You have my word on it. Having them here ensures you and Toloya will return!"

With a bit of worry in his voice, Luis asked, "What about Toloya? Will she be willing to take Kano and me to her village?"

"Let's ask her." Montezuma clapped his hands and a warrior shoved Toloya into the room. She walked gracefully to Montezuma and bowed respectfully, her heart contracting with dread. She dug her fingernails into her palms, waiting to hear the emperor pronounce her death sentence.

"Toloya," Montezuma said softly. "Tomorrow I want you to take Captain Escudero and Kano to your village to meet your mother and the other women. You must not try to escape. If you do, the captain will suffer for it! Will you promise to behave yourself?"

Toloya gave a startled gasp and as she did so she bit her lower lip to stop tears from flowing. "Oh yes, my Lord!"

"It's settled then. You'll leave first thing in the morning." He nodded to the warrior, who escorted Toloya out. The priests filed out behind them, one behind the other.

"My Lord," Luis said, "I'm most curious about these white people called the ancient ones. Will you tell me something about them?"

Montezuma settled himself comfortably in his huge chair, and began. "When the ancient ones ruled this land they were men of science and vision, but their ways were not our ways. They were farmers and landowners, while we were nomads and hunters, wandering the land from place to place following the game, killing wild animals for food.

The ancient ones had a major flaw—they had to rule! They tried to destroy us. After years of bloody warfare between our two peoples, we eventually prevailed and destroyed all but a handful of them."

"And Toloya is a survivor?"

"She is," Montezuma replied. "But what am I to do with the rest of them? I've given a great deal of thought to allowing a greater number of them to be produced so they can help us grow in learning and science. But my priests and army commanders don't support me in this at all. They feel that reintroducing these ancient ones into our society is dangerous. They'll scheme and devise ways to wrest our empire from us."

"Are you telling me there are male survivors?"

"A few we keep we keep for breeding purposes. They're a most rebellious lot, so we keep them imprisoned in a very secure, secret place, with many guards. We have no alternative. Without them we'd be unable to produce white women for sacrifice."

Montezuma eyes were hard on Luis now. "Why are you so curious about these people?"

"We've always believed a white man named Christopher Columbus, sailing for our king, just twenty six years ago, was the first white man to ever travel this area, which we call the new world. Now I find that may not be the case at all."

"Hm. That's very interesting," Montezuma nodded thoughtfully. "You have your explorers and we have our ancient ones. However, there's no correlation between the two. We don't know where the ancient ones came from. Perhaps they preceded the Toltecs—or maybe they were Toltecs."

"Who were they?"

"None of us really know. They knew agriculture, were workers of metal and invented the calendar we now call our own. They established their capital at Tula, north or here. Massive Toltec ruins cover that area."

"Did you learn human sacrifice from them?" Luis asked.

"Oh no! They never stained their altars with human blood. Perhaps they should have! Then the gods would have protected them as they have us. All the Toltecs left us were thousands of ruined temples and pyramids."

"Do you believe they were white men?"

"I've given that much thought, but I really don't know. It's a possibility."

🐾 🐾 🐾

"Well, Kano," Luis said as they strolled back to their quarters, "are you ready for a little adventure?"

"Yes sir! I can hardly wait for tomorrow!"

"Why so anxious?"

"I had the strangest premonition the very instant Montezuma told us about Toloya's village."

"Something bad?" Luis asked.

"No sir! That's why the premonition is so mysterious. Something good will happen to both of us."

"Like what?"

"I really don't know, sir! It's like a weird, wild dream—like I've traveled over the earth my entire lifetime to end up in that strange village, hidden away in the Mexican mountains!"

🐾 🐾 🐾

Luis tapped on Sandoval's door, stepped into his room, and found him lying down dozing. He gazed up sleepy-eyed at Luis. "What did Montezuma want?"

"He's letting me to take Toloya to her village so I can meet her people. Kano's going along to interpret for me. We're leaving at sun up in the morning."

That jerked Sandoval to his feet! "You're going to do what?"

"Just what I told you! While I'm gone work up a logistical plan to get us and our treasure out of here and back to the Caribbean. Have the men ready to march as soon as I get back."

Sandoval stared at Luis in astonishment. "Good God, man," he protested vehemently. "You're going on a fool's errand, can't you see that? It could be a clever trap to kill you and destroy our expedition!"

"I've carefully considered that, and you may be right," Luis replied, "but look at it this way, anything we find out about the Aztecs, their culture and their history will be invaluable to Captain Cortez when he brings his expedition of conquest to Mexico next year."

Sandoval didn't buy it! He smiled. "What's the real reason you're doing this? You're in love with Toloya, aren't you!"

"From the first instant I looked into those deep green eyes. She's going to be my wife one day!"

Sandoval grinned. "If you live that long!"

30

Sariah awoke this morning, just like every morning, filled with hopelessness and despair, thinking about Toloya, wondering if she was alive or butchered in some bizarre Aztec sacrificial ritual. A year ago Aztec warriors dragged her, kicking and screaming, to Tenochtitlan. That was the last time Sariah saw her.

There was a knock on the door. Xalapa stood there smiling. The young Aztec guard was assigned with others to guard the women and prevent their escape. But unlike his comrades, he'd developed empathy for the women imprisoned in this remote valley prison.

"Sariah, a runner just arrived from Tenochtitlan carrying a message directly from Emperor Montezuma concerning your daughter, Toloya."

There was a long pause; Sariah's heart filled with dread! Her voice was a thin whimper as she said, "Oh no, no! She's dead, isn't she?"

Xalapa laughed. "No, no, my lady. She's not dead!"

Sariah's mouth dropped open. "What? How do you know that? Are you making this up?" He shook his head vigorously. "No! She's on her way here to see you as we speak!"

The news shook Sariah! For a moment her mind was empty, thoughtless, as if all perceptions, all memories had fled into some dark void. It was almost impossible to believe Toloya was still alive! Not one word had ever been sent to Sariah about her daughter's fate.

"Are you all right?" Xalapa asked anxiously, as he studied Sariah's ashen face.

"Yes," she nodded. "Your message took my breath away for a moment. Are those bloody Aztec priests bringing her here?"

"No. She travels with a white man and a black man who is his interpreter. They should arrive this afternoon."

"A white man?" she stared in disbelief. "Who is he?"

"I don't know, my lady. He and his soldiers, called Spaniards, marched into Tenochtitlan a few days ago. We've been warned to treat them well, especially their leader, who brings Toloya to see you.

He's Montezuma's honored guest and travels under his protection."

A twinkle came into Sariah's eyes. "My daughter alive? A white man? This may be a day to remember!" She reached out and took Xalapa's hands in her own. "Thank you, my friend. Your news makes my heart sing. I'll never forget your kindness since you've been assigned here. The other guards treat us like animals."

"I know. But to me you're a very special woman, Sariah. I knew it the first moment I met you. I'll wave Toloya through as soon as she arrives, and make sure no one interferes with your reunion!" He bowed, turned and trotted off to the guard post at the valley's mouth.

Sariah stood in the door and watched him disappear. She considered herself and the other women fortunate to be surrounded by tall, rocky mountains which protectively enclosed their valley. Though she bitterly hated Montezuma, she was grateful he'd moved them far enough from Tenochtitlan to be out of sight of bloody Aztec priests. They visited the village only once a year to check on them and select a victim for their sacrificial altar.

She'd been a prisoner here since the powerful Tlascalan Lord Xicotencatl dumped her as a concubine. Montezuma gave her to his hated enemy to keep him and his fierce army from attacking Aztec outposts. Xicotencatl was the only man Montezuma truly hated and feared! The Tlascalan never ceased his efforts to overthrow the emperor!

Back then Sariah was high, now she was low! Had Xicotencatl not tired of her, she'd still be pampered with luscious dishes, served on glittering silver platters, beautiful clothing and a palatial estate.

Long lonely years here in the valley had changed Sariah. If one looked closely they'd see she'd once been exceptionally beautiful. Her features still retained a dignified, lovely cast which didn't show through a layer of accumulated dirt. She wore a long, dirty loose fitting robe which gave her a squat, shapeless appearance. Her unkempt blonde hair was bobbed on top of her head. Her total appearance was deliberately designed to repulse Aztec nobles who often bribed the guards to let them take their pick of village women to gratify their insatiable sexual lust.

But Sariah had survived long enough to know life's fortunes can change very quickly! An event splits the sky like lightning and the foreseen future, the expected continuation of the past, vanishes in a thunderclap! Just a few days ago white men marched into Tenochtitlan. Now one of them was coming here! She had no idea what that might mean for her and the other women; but she smiled broadly as she contemplated the possibilities!

🐾🐾🐾

Twenty village women gawked, open mouthed, staring at the strangers moving toward them. A metal man on a huge, black high-stepping beast, held up his hand in a sign of peace. He was a white man with a black beard. Someone was mounted behind him. A giant smiling black man walked alongside the beast. The beast stopped and the black man stepped up to Sariah, smiled and bowed. Toloya leaned out and peered around Luis. Sariah squinted her eyes, and slowly walked forward for a closer look; and her mouth dropped open!

"Oh my good God!" The words came out in a thin whisper as Sariah's eyes widened. "Is it really you, Toloya?"

Luis held Toloya's hand and let her gently down. The instant her feet touched the ground she ran into Sariah's outstretched arms. She hugged her daughter tightly while tears flowed freely down her cheeks. When she could speak again, she said, in a rush of words, "Where have you been? What's happened to you?" She took Toloya's arm and started to escort her to the house, the other women all chattering and asking questions at the same time.

Sariah held up a hand for silence, and shook her head in embarrassment, gazing up at Luis. "Forgive my manners, sir. I didn't mean to ignore you. It's just that I haven't seen my daughter..."

Kano waved her away. "Go! You two have much to talk about. We'll unsaddle Diablo, give him a drink, and wash up in that cool beautiful creek behind your house. Then we'll join you."

Sariah said, "I'll have some refreshments ready! All I have is pulque. I hope you that'll be satisfactory."

Kano's head went up and he laughed outright, saying, "Pulque will be just fine!" Luis dismounted and removed his helmet.

"Sariah, this is my Captain, Luis Escudero. He asks that you call him Luis." Luis bowed. Sariah nodded and smiled warmly. "Welcome to our valley, Luis."

🐾 🐾 🐾

Luis and Kano washed up in the creek, let Diablo drink his fill, then went to Sariah's house. Kano bent his head as he entered the adobe structure. The main room looked almost starkly bare. It was about twelve feet square, and one wall was almost entirely taken up by an open fireplace. There was a small wooden table and some chair in the middle of the room.

Beyond the main room were two bedrooms.

Sariah made no apology for the state of the dwelling, but said politely, "Please be seated."

She noticed Luis' manner was most formal, by which she gauged that he must have been brought up in cultured surroundings. She sat down on a wooden chair and watched Toloya bring two cups from the shelf, then pour each man full cup of pulque. Luis took a long sip and couldn't keep from choking and coughing and felt Kano's hand patting his back. He gasped, "I'm sorry. I can't seem to get used to this damn stuff!"

Sariah chuckled. "Pulque has been known to knock many a strong man flat on his back!" When Luis caught his breath he grinned. "I can believe that!"

Conversing with Luis seemed a bit difficult at first since Sariah had never used an interpreter before. But she found Kano's translation skills excellent, and the language barrier faded away. Kano had a way of smoothing the conversation to make everyone feel comfortable.

Toloya, sitting on a bench against the wall, drew her knees up, hugging them, lying her face down against them, relaxed, happier than she could remember. She was with her dear mother and the man she loved! "Oh Mother, it's so good to be home! Tell me I'm not dreaming!"

"It's no dream," Sariah said. Her voice was choked. "We're together—at least for now." She turned to Luis and said something to him. Kano interpreted.

"Sariah says Toloya has explained her captivity in Montezuma's prison and asks your purpose in bringing her here."

"It's two-fold," Luis answered. "I wanted to free her from those bloody Aztec priests and find out more about the Aztecs, especially their army."

Sariah nodded understanding. "Does your coming here give us any hope of being freed from the Aztecs?"

"Not right away. We're a scouting party for a large Spanish army coming next year to conquer the Aztecs. Captain Hernando Cortez will be in command."

Kano's eyes went wide. "Is it wise to disclose such information to this woman? We hardly know her. She could betray us."

"I doubt that. I think she hates the Aztecs more than Toloya does."

"Very well, sir." Kano explained their mission. Sariah smiled broadly. "Really? Next year? Your army is coming here?" There was relief in her voice. "Marvelous! How can I help you, Luis?"

"By telling me anything you can about the Aztecs, especially any weaknesses in their military forces we could exploit. Cortez's army will be much smaller than Aztec forces, so any information which will help him overcome that disadvantage will be extremely valuable."

"Let me think for a moment," Sariah said. There was a short pause. "The Aztecs are a strange, brutal lot, Luis, bitterly hated by several tribes in Mexico. Captain Cortez could consider forming an alliance of those hostile tribes. With them, fighting alongside his own army, he would be unstoppable!"

Luis' eyes were hard on her now. "You're sure that's achievable?"

"Positive! Montezuma is not a warrior or military commander. He's a priest, and as such, he lets his military captains decide military strategy. He gives his bloody, stinking priests freedom to do anything they desire. He's more interested in sacrifice than in running his empire! The object of war for him is as much to gather victims for sacrifices as to extend his empire. Hardly is an Aztec enemy slain in battle if there's the slightest chance of taking him alive so he can be given to Montezuma's priests to be sacrificed."

Sariah's face went grim when she issued a warning: "You should watch out for yourselves and your men, and tell Captain Cortez not to let any of his men fall into Aztec hands! A white man would be a most valuable sacrifice to Montezuma's evil stone gods!"

"How did you acquire such knowledge?" Luis asked.

"I've lived here all my life—and what a life it's been! When I was about Toloya's age, Montezuma gave me to Xicotencatl, his hated Tlascalan enemy, as a concubine, to keep him from attacking the Aztecs. Though I hated my new master, I learned many important things from him as he continually devised strategies to overthrow Montezuma."

Luis' head jerked up. "Who are the Tlascalans?"

"Very fierce, intelligent people living in the little republic of Tlascala, lying midway between Tenochtitlan and the coast. It's maintained its independence for two centuries against the Aztecs."

"Hmm," Luis mused, "such allies could go a long way in ensuring Captain Cortez's success. What about the Aztecs themselves? Is there any dissension among their rank and file?"

"Oh most certainly! Many Aztecs tire of the sacrificial bloodshed in Tenochtitlan, and especially abhor the cannibalism that goes along with the sacrifices, every day of the year! The Aztecs are not cannibals, in the true sense of the word. They feed on human flesh only in obedience to their religion. It's so degrading and so loathsome that the Aztecs will never improve their intellectual culture."

Luis nodded. "We've experienced Aztec rituals firsthand! Reports of such slaughter will shock the entire civilized world—if we're able to return to that world and report what we've discovered!"

Sariah turned away from Luis and poured herself a drink. She was silent for a time, then turned and stared at him." And what have you discovered?"

The unexpected question caught Luis off guard. "What we've talked about, Tlascalans, war between the tribes, human sacrifice."

"That's all?" Sariah studied him. "What about gold, silver and precious gems? That's what you're really here for, isn't it? To find out if the Aztecs have such treasure?"

Looking worried, Luis managed to nod in a grim way. "What makes you say that?"

Sariah smiled. "It doesn't take a brilliant mind to figure it out! And if I, a mere woman, can guess what you're up to, Montezuma will surely know for certain."

"I don't mind confessing it, since I trust you, Sariah. But it must go no further than this room."

She nodded her head in understanding. "You think it can be done? Conquer the Aztecs and take their gold?"

"After what we've seen here in Mexico, I'm not building my hopes too high. Optimism can be deadly."

"Montezuma can be deadly too, Luis!" Sariah warned. "You're in his lair, under his thumb. If you make one mistake you and your men will end up on the sacrificial altar in Tenochtitlan! Watch your back, and get out of Tenochtitlan as soon as you can!"

Toloya cut in now, putting a hand on Luis shoulder, saying, "Enough of this talk of war and killing. We'll only be here overnight. Let's talk of other things!"

The conversation turned purposely general until Luis inquired quietly, "Toloya, would you like to take a walk and show me about?"

"I'd love to!" she said pertly. "We'll leave Kano here to get better acquainted with my mother."

🐜🐜🐜

The late afternoon was sunny, the sky pure blue. Outside, holding Toloya's hand, Luis paused and stared at her. It was odd to be attracted to her, strange to want to make love to her, even if the act had begun out of a desire to learn more about Mexico, the Aztecs and Toloya's people. Though he'd not kissed her yet, he'd fallen madly in love for the first time in his life! But he couldn't express that to her personally because of the language barrier. He'd have to demonstrate that love, not talk about it!

31

Luis and Toloya left the house in late afternoon for a walk through the valley, Luis desperate to stretch his legs and get some exercise. They strolled alongside the cold, clear creek, their locked hands swinging between them. A gentle breeze, and the fading sun's strength, was weakened by gauzy clouds. Thickets of manzanita and dense brush covered the mountainsides. Shrill far-away cries of unseen birds echoed through the valley.

Toloya's yesterday sense of nightmare was gone, replaced by a joy that filled every fiber of her being. She was free—at least for now! She kneeled and bathed her wind burned face. Her nose and cheekbones felt afire and her lips were chapped. Being cooped up in Montezuma's cage in Tenochtitlan, she'd not been out in the sun for a long time. How she wished there was some way she could converse with Luis and explain the feelings in her heart.

They stopped to check on Diablo hobbled in a grassy knoll near the creek. His head came up, his ears pricked forward and he snorted loudly. Toloya jumped with fright, and scrambled into Luis' arms.

"I'm sorry," she apologized. "He startled me."

Luis didn't understand her words. From his saddlebag near Diablo he pulled out a handful of maize, handed it to her, and nodded toward the skittish horse.

She swallowed deeply and cautiously crept toward the huge animal, her handful of maize extended. Diablo shook his head back and forth, then stretched his neck forward and nuzzled the maize from her hand.

Luis nodded and smiled. "Good. You've made a friend of him."

She nodded happily; the fear was gone from her green eyes. They climbed a ways up the mountainside and walked along a rock shelf overlooking the valley through which the creek meandered. Luis studied the landscape in every direction—forage for horses and cattle, steep mountains to hold them in, water for them to drink—an ideal spot for a profitable cattle ranch! If he could return to Mexico with Cortez...

"Time to get back," Toloya said.

Luis didn't understand. She grinned and rubbed and patted her stomach. "Hungry!"

"Ah," his face brightened. "Me too!" She grabbed his hand and led him back to the village

"Are you ready for supper, Captain?" Kano called from the doorway. "Sariah and I cooked some turkey, maize and something with tomatoes."

"Good! Let's eat. I'm starved!"

"I also rounded up something good to drink besides pulque," Kano said. "It's called chocolatl. In Spanish we'd call it chocolate. It's very good—doesn't have alcohol like pulque!"

They sat down to supper, a very good one. Sariah's eyes sparkled as she visited with Luis and Kano. Toloya's eyes never left Luis' face. He felt a bit uncomfortable and embarrassed, and reached out and pushed his cup across the table toward her. She refilled it with chocolate.

Luis sat back in his chair. A faint quizzical expression softened the lean ridges of his face. "Kano, why is Toloya staring at me like that?"

Kano chuckled. "Because she worships you."

"But I'm not some god to be worshipped."

"To her you are!"

"She's a minority of one!" Luis grinned. "Where do we sleep tonight, outside by the creek?"

"You sleep in there." Kano pointed to Toloya's room.

Luis' head jerked up. "What will Sariah say?"

"She doesn't live by Spanish rules of morality, Captain. She says if a man and woman are in love they should do what comes naturally."

"How does Toloya feel about that?"

"I'll ask her."

To Luis' surprise, she got up, walked over and put her hand on his cheek. She surprised him still further by reaching down, taking his hand and pulling him toward her bedroom!

🐾🐾🐾

Toloya excused herself to freshen up. She returned beautifully clean and perfumed, her long, honey blonde hair brushed to a lustrous hue. A green loincloth with several strange symbols scattered over its entire surface covered her shapely thighs, and a golden necklace hung between her bare breasts. Luis gawked as though seeing her for the first time. He took her hand and turned her in a complete circle and sucked in his breath. "You're a goddess, Toloya," he whispered.

She didn't understand, but sensed his meaning. He took her lovingly in his arms and stroked her hair, threading his fingers through it luxuriance. Gradually she raised her face to his. All restraint melted from her, and she shuddered with pleasure as he kissed her for the first time!

That erotic kiss excited and stirred her blood as he gently pushed her onto the bed. His hands were dexterous and authoritative as he gently kneaded and caressed her breasts and stroked her tense shoulder muscles. She felt like a child in the care of a strong father. She shut her eyes as he removed her loin cloth, took off his uniform and lay beside her. He gently kissed her lips again, causing an unbearable sexual excitement.

She moaned and sighed with pleasure as Luis thrust deep into her warm, pulsating depths, while lacing his fingers through her long, blonde hair. "Oh My God!" He sighed. "Now I know why the Aztecs want to sacrifice you to their gods! You're enough woman to pleasure any god—and persuade him to grant any favor!" Though she didn't understand him, she knew she gave him pleasure.

Luis swelled ever bigger inside her, thrusting in and out, faster and faster and she met him thrust for thrust. Gasping and moaning she couldn't control the onset of a mighty, surging orgasm. the most pleasurable feeling she'd ever experienced. His hands gripped her buttocks and pulled her strongly into him. A convulsive shudder engulfed them at the same instant. Spent, they relaxed in each other's arms.

"Again? Please!" Toloya whispered in broken Castilian. Their lovemaking began again slowly and gently, as Luis kissed and fondled her curvaceous body, and whispered soft Castilian love words which she found enchanting. He kissed her breasts and buried his face in them while she shuddered and sighed and ran her fingers down his back. Their release came slowly, with even more ecstasy than the first time.

Reverberating thunder rumbled through the remote valley. Jagged lightening bolts lit the sky as a fierce rain squall settled in. Toloya pulled up a warm blanket and snuggled against Luis.

🐾 🐾 🐾

A while later, a flickering shadow on the wall startled Luis into a sitting position. He reached for his sword. Squinting, he made out Kano holding a torch, and behind him, Sariah.

"Don't be alarmed, Captain," Kano said softly, "Sariah has something she wants to say to you."

Toloya sat up and rubbed sleep from her eyes. Sariah dabbed her eyes with a handkerchief at tears blotting her vision. When she was able to see clearly she said, "I still can't believe you're here with me, Toloya, and I've never seen you looking so alive, so radiant." She stared at Luis. "Tell me, honestly, Captain, do you love her? I mean truly love her?"

"Yes Ma'am. More than you'll ever know." The tenderness in his voice reassured Sariah he spoke truth.

"Listen well, then, both of you, to what I have to say. Toloya, I wish with all my heart you could remain here to comfort me in my old age. But there's no future for us as long as Aztecs rule the land. You must go with Luis. To remain here is death, or worse. Your future is in Spain. With Luis you'll have a life of ease and comfort and give him fine sons who'll bring many honors to his house."

Toloya knew her mother was right. Still, the thought of never seeing her again tore at her heart. Tears filled her eyes "That means we'll never see each other again."

Sariah gave a warm smile. "Never is a long, long time, and none of us know what the future holds.

We must live each day as it comes. The Aztecs won't always rule this land. The Spaniards will take it from the Aztecs just as they took it from us. So I feel we'll meet again, under better circumstances, if God wills it so!"

Sariah stared at Toloya, then came to the bed and took her in her arms. "I love you child, with every fiber of my being." She turned to Luis and put a hand on his cheek. "I give Toloya to you, with my blessing, now and always! Take care of her, Luis!"

She took Kano by the hand. and led him from the room.

Outside the storm spent its violence and rain fell softly, purling in misty grayness over the mountain; wind fluted in the trees, gradually changing directions, then rushed in great puffs blowing down from the mountain tops.

🐾 🐾 🐾

Kano felt his heart jerk against his ribs when Sariah took his hand and led him to her room. Practiced in the art of arousing men, Sariah motioned Kano to a chair. He watched her slip out of her long, ill fitting robe and stand naked before him. She hummed as she brushed her blonde hair and painted her eyelashes. Utterly fascinated, Kano observed an enticing transformation, like watching a cocoon change into a beautiful butterfly. She came over and sat on his lap, wrapped her arms around his neck and kissed him.

"No!" He grunted, stiffened and tried to push her away. Startled, Sariah asked, "Have I offended you?"

"Oh no! I'm so sorry," he apologized. "Where I come from it's absolutely forbidden for a black man to speak to or touch a white woman. To be found in any kind of compromising position with a white woman brings beatings or death."

"Is that why you have these horrible scars on your back?"

He nodded. "It is." He told her about that experience. "I was carrying a heavy barrel of molasses on my shoulder and accidentally bumped into white female passenger, waiting to board a ship in St. Jago's harbor. She fell to the dock. Spanish soldiers instantly arrested me, stripped me, tied me to a post, and whipped me almost to death!"

"I assure you that won't happen here, Kano!" Sariah whispered softly and kissed him again. "Don't be frightened! Here, let's take this off." She stood, pulled him to his feet and removed his loin cloth.

He swallowed hard, helpless against her clutching fingers and moist, sensuous mouth. He closed his eyes and stood like a statue, greatly embarrassed by his huge erection. He picked her up and carried her to the bed.

Slowly he straddled her and eased himself into her. She moaned and sighed as his huge organ pried her open and penetrated her fiery depths. He moved languidly up and down at his own pace sharing her sheer sexual pleasure. They climaxed at the same moment, but didn't pull apart. They lay panting until Sariah felt the great organ come to life again and swell inside her.

After their lovemaking Kano sat up and whispered, "Sariah, I have something for you." He reached over to a small table and retrieved his leather pouch. From it he took a small jewel he'd carried all the from Africa. It wasn't a great jewel like the Aztecs wore, but a crystal clear gem which sparkled like fire—a gem from deep within a cave Kano found in the tangled African jungle near his home. The gem was attached to a simple string.

He tied the necklace about Sariah's neck and gently placed the glittering diamond between her bare breasts. The erotic gesture somehow stirred him more than anything he could ever remember, and he had no idea why. Perhaps it was his intense feelings for Sariah—a totally new, unknown sensation. In his lonely world of slavery, turmoil, fighting and death he'd never had time for any activity but trying to stay alive—and he'd never had a woman of his own!

Sariah was filled with wonderment that so much happiness could come at once. Tears filled her eyes. She held the diamond in her hand and stared down at it for several moments.

"Will you wear this gem as a token of my love and affection—a pact of devotion between us?"

Sariah's face bloomed. "I will! I'll wear it all the days of my life!" She closed her eyes trying to restrain her tears—then said, "Must you leave with Luis in the morning?"

"I have no choice. I'm a soldier and I must go." To soften the blow, he said, "but I'll be back with Captain Cortez, and when we've done away with the bloody Aztecs I'll race back to this valley, where I've found the greatest peace and happiness I've ever known."

"You promise?"

Kano laughed. "I have no choice! You've put me under some kind of spell that binds me to you like a chain."

🐾🐾🐾

Dawn came and the rain was gone. The sun was enormous as its first rays filtered over the mountains into the valley. Kano had Diablo saddled, ready to go. Luis took Toloya's arm and guided her to the waiting animal. Sariah walked alongside. "How will I know if you make it safely to the coast?"

Toloya took her mother's hand. "If Luis and I get away from Tenochtitlan alive I'll find some way to let you know."

Sariah nodded, pulled Toloya close and kissed her. "Always remember, I love you!" Luis mounted, reached down and pulled Toloya up behind him. "Ready, Kano?"

"Go ahead, Captain, I'll catch up."

Luis touched his heels to Diablo's flanks and headed for the valley entrance.

Kano reached out and took Sariah's hands in his own. He bent down and kissed her tenderly.

"Wait for me my love. I'll be back..." his voice choked and trailed away, and she smiled at him weakly.

"Oh please don't go, Kano," she pleaded. "Stay..."

Kano shook his head sadly, released her hands and ran after Luis.

Sariah's breath came in shallow gasps, and tears rolled down her cheeks. When Kano had almost disappeared he turned, waved and faded from sight.

🐾 🐾 🐾

Luis' heart sang as he nudged Diablo along the road to Tenochtitlan. Toloya's arms were wrapped tightly around his waist. Kano jogged up alongside, humming tunelessly.

"You seem in fine spirits this morning, my friend! Anything you'd like to tell me?"

"No, sir, nothing!" Kano grinned broadly.

"Well then, take a look down there! Have you ever seen more magnificent country?" Luis pointed to the broad green Mexico Valley stretching as far as the eye could see, all the way to Tenochtitlan.

"No sir!"

"Me either. It's a lovely land, a good place for a man to put down roots and raise a family.

And best of all, it'll soon belong to Spain! What say we come back here with Cortez—if the Aztecs don't kill us first? Do some ranching, raise horses maybe do some farming?"

"I'd like that, Captain! I'd like that a lot!"

32

Luis and Sandoval saddled their horses, rode from the palace and reconnoitered the main road leading into Tenochtitlan. On the outskirts of the huge city, surrounded by a lake, they stopped and studied the landscape.

"Do you have it all memorized, Jorge? Luis asked.

"I do. I'll put the finishing touches on my map this evening."

They rode on in silence for a ways before Sandoval asked, "What about that bastard Naulinco? Do you think he'll try to stop us?"

"Put yourself in his shoes. What would you do?"

"I don't know," Sandoval said. "Maybe try to kill us before we can leave the city?"

"I doubt that. The risk is too great. We're still under Montezuma's protection. I have a hunch he'll wait until we're a day or two out of the city, then ambush us."

Sandoval smiled. "The way it stands right now I wouldn't give one peso de oro for our chances of getting to the coast alive!"

"I'll worry about that. You just make sure your maps are completely accurate."

⁂

Toloya's world was bright with promise—yet there were so many things to learn! First and foremost she'd have to wear clothes! A loincloth wouldn't cover her nakedness—and modesty, she quickly learned, was a demanding European custom. Covering the female body from neck to toe was the fashion, though she didn't understand why, unless Spanish women were ashamed of their bodies! She dressed in soldiers' shirt and trousers, which, although baggy and unbecoming, covered her properly, so she could ride modestly on Diablo. She was learning Spanish under Luis and Kano's competent tutoring. Her quick wit and charm captivated the Spaniards! Her strong instinct for survival fit well with that of the steel hard, disciplined soldiers, who admired her for pulling her own weight, expecting no favors. With the best of intentions Sergeant Lopez tried to teach her the basic tenants of Catholicism.

When he explained the holy trinity, Toloya's forehead wrinkled, and he could see in her eyes it was completely beyond her understanding.

"It's very simple, Senorita," he said patiently. "They are three gods in one."

"Do they have bodies?" she asked.

"No. They are spirits."

"Where do they live?"

"Up there!" Lopez pointed to the sky. "Understand?"

She shook her head in a shamefaced way. "No, Sergeant. I don't understand at all."

Lopez was somewhat taken aback, and in exasperation said, "Kano, explain it to her will you?"

"I'm sorry, Sergeant. I'm no priest, and I don't understand your religion any more than Toloya does."

Lopez smiled kindly, realizing it would take a priest to explain Catholicism to both of them so they could grasp its soul saving graces. "Never mind, Kano. Thanks anyway. Perhaps another time." He walked away.

"What did he say, Kano?" Toloya asked.

Kano grinned. "He said it's too complicated to explain to the likes of heathens like you and me."

Toloya returned his grin. "Good! I've had enough of stone gods, spirit gods, nature gods—well all kinds of gods I guess. I'll stick to what I can see. Am I wrong?"

"Not at all, Senorita! That's what I do. It works for me!"

🐾 🐾 🐾

With little to do in her small apartment, Toloya brushed her hair, changed into a clean shirt and trousers and set off to explore the palace. When she turned a corner she came face to face with a tall, evil-looking Aztec warrior, who blocked the hallway. Stepping backward, she shook her head in fear. Naulinco grabbed her and jerked her roughly to his chest in a crushing embrace.

Fear quivered in her eyes. She broke free and backed into the wall; her hand went to her mouth. "Who are you?" It was a tiny whisper.

"I'm Naulinco!"

Toloya shook her head, mute. There was a thread of moisture on her upper lip. Her face, which had flooded with color in the beginning, had gone unnaturally pale. Her green eyes were very large. "What do you want?"

He laughed and cuffed her hard across the cheek. It rocked her head to one side and left red finger marks. She reached up with one hand to touch her cheek; she blinked and drew a ragged breath.

"I want you! After I kill Escudero I'll take you for my woman!"

"I'll tell Luis what you've done to me."

He grabbed her arm. "You do that!" Then he shoved her away.

The revolting thought of being Naulinco's woman turned her stomach; but she recognized his deliberate goad, intended to compel Luis to do something foolish, which would give Naulinco a valid reason to kill him before he could leave Tenochtitlan.

Distraught and sobbing, Toloya found Sergeant Lopez and tried to tell him what happened, but he couldn't understand her, except for the word Naulinco. He took her arm and escorted her back to her apartment. "I'll get Kano."

Kano was resting when Lopez rushed in. "I believe Toloya has been attacked by Naulinco! She tried to tell me about it, but I can't understand her."

The words jerked Kano to his feet. "I'll go to her. Keep this to yourself. Understand?" Lopez nodded.

It took Toloya a while to pull herself together and explain what happened. She was frightened and she was ashamed of herself for it. "Do you think we should tell Luis?"

"Yes I do! He just got back with Lieutenant Sandoval. I'll stay to translate. He'll be infuriated, and I may have to restrain him from going after Naulinco."

Luis' eyes burned like live coals when Toloya reported her run in with the Aztec general. He stood motionless for a moment, slowly fingering his Toledo sword. She'd never seen him so enraged.

"Damn him to hell! I'll find him and have his liver before the sun goes down!"

"That's exactly what he wants you to do!" Toloya said softly. "I'm all right. I've suffered worse things in my life. Forget him. No harm has been done."

Luis took a deep breath; then, with a slight smile on his face, said, "You're right. Now is not the time and certainly not the place. Senor Naulinco and I will meet again, I'm sure of it!"

Toloya put her arms about his waist. "Are we leaving soon? I can't wait to get away from this evil place."

"We'll be leaving in a couple of days. In the meantime please stay in your room away from the Aztecs!"

Luis turned to Kano. "Were you able to find some good men to help us break Pedro Armand out of Montezuma's prison?"

"Yes sir! I found five Totonac warriors—big strong men who hate the Aztecs like poison. They're hiding out and want to get back to Cempoalla, where they live, before the Aztecs discover them."

"Would they be willing to join us?"

"Yes sir. They'd jump at the chance."

"Good. I'll leave the details in your hands. But be careful. One mistake will be the death of us all."

🐾🐾🐾

Sandoval spread his map of Tenochtitlan and its outlying areas on the table for Luis and Sergeant Lopez.

"Well? "What do you think?"

"Excellent!" Luis said. "What do you think, Sergeant?"

"It's a damn good map, sir! It'll give Captain Cortez the lay of the land and guide him right here to the Aztec treasures."

There was a long pause before Luis said, "Yes it will—if we can get the map to him! We've got to wade through a hell of a lot of Aztecs between here and the coast."

"I'd say so," Sandoval agreed, "unless Montezuma guarantees us unmolested passage to the Caribbean."

"I doubt he can do that," Luis responded. "He can give lip service to our protection, but that's about all. I know for sure he won't give us any Aztec soldiers to accompany us to the coast."

"Are we going back to the coast the same way we got here?" Lopez asked.

Sandoval grinned. "I got to thinking about that while our good Captain was out rescuing damsels in distress and taking a vacation over in the land of beautiful women—without inviting me. Urcos and I put our heads together and came up with a faster route back to the coast. May I show you?"

Luis sat up straight in his chair and chuckled. "A vacation? Now that hurts! Show me what you've got!"

"Urcos wants to follow the Aztec highway southeast to here," Sandoval pointed to a spot on the map. "From there we'll turn and go straight east. Urcos anticipates no trouble, unless Naulinco tries to ambush us somewhere along the way."

"How much time do we save by going that way?"

"Two full days, if we don't encounter weather problems like heavy rain or mud."

Luis was relieved Sandoval had everything planned so well. "I have only one correction I'd like to make. How about we veer northeast, about here, so we can stop at the Chichemetlan village and pick up our gold. We'll use the horses and men to carry it through the pass, down to the sea."

"I see no problem with that, Captain," Sandoval said, "unless we run into Teoamoxtli. By the time we get to Prince Ruminawi's village we'll be out of gunpowder and totally helpless."

"I know. We're gambling with our lives. What do you think, Sergeant, are the men are up to it?"

"They have no choice if they want to stay alive."

Luis gave half a smile. "I wish we had a priest who could say a special mass for us."

Lopez grinned. "I'd settle for some extra gunpowder myself! I'll make sure no one fires a shot unless it's absolutely necessary. I'll try to scrounge up enough powder to charge the cannon one time. After that we'll have to abandon it."

"That's all we can do," Luis replied as he rolled up the map and handed it to Sandoval. "We'll follow your route, Jorge!"

🐜🐜🐜

The Spaniards used the remaining hours to visit the great slave market of Azcapozalco, not far from Tenochtitlan. Slaves were herded in from all corners of the empire and displayed on public auction blocks so Aztec noblemen and men of wealth could look them over before buying. Slaves, of both sexes, were instructed to sing, dance, and pose to enhance their purchase price.

Handsome young boys were greatly sought after by noblemen. Their strange and revolting practice of dressing boys as girls, and performing acts of sodomy, both in public and in private, disgusted the Spanish soldiers who totally abhorred this 'abominable sin,' preached against by the Mother Church.

Of all the sights the Spaniards observed during their short stay in the capitol none had such a mind-boggling impact as small children being borne through the streets of Tenochtitlan on open, golden litters—little boys and girls dressed in beautiful festal robes, their hair covered with colorful flowers. Their pathetic cries were drowned out by the chanting priests and cheers of people as the small ones were taken to the altar of the rain God, Tlaloc, to be sacrificed with pompous ceremony.

Luis glanced over at Sergeant Lopez who wept openly as a litter of small, bright eyed youngsters passed by the Spaniards and Lopez tried to touch their hands, hoping to give them the strength to withstand their horrible ordeal. Every soldier wanted to do something to save the children; but they were helpless, surrounded by thousands of hostile warriors who'd butcher them at a snap of the emperor's fingers.

In the marketplace they gazed at mounds of silver and lead from the mines at Tasco and copper from the mountains of Zacotallan, all on sale at the great square near the temple. Lieutenant Sandoval, with his knowledge of metals, noted Aztec smiths using an alloy of tin mixed with copper to make tools of bronze which could cut not only other metals, but also jasper stone used for sacrificial blocks, porphyry, amethysts and emeralds. In fact, emeralds so large they were valueless for jewelry, were fashioned into many curious and fantastic works of sculpture.

In contrast with the great architectural beauty of the city Luis and his companions were constantly reminded of death continually stalking its inhabitants. It was customary to preserve in each building skulls of victims sacrificed in that building. They observed skulls arranged to produce a gruesome and hideous effect on visitors. In one building they counted one hundred thirty six thousand skulls before giving up the task as hopeless. Lieutenant Sandoval and Sergeant Lopez were seized more keenly than the others by a remorse for the victims of brutal and obscene sacrificial rites. Those white skulls were all that remained of once vibrant, living human beings, until evil, foul smelling, devil- worshiping priests, holding the power of life and death over every subject in the empire, slaughtered them with impunity—and with the complete blessing of the head priest, the Emperor Montezuma himself!

Sergeant Lopez suddenly lurched outside the skull house to fresh air and a clean blue sky where his God resided. His eyes filled with tears and he stood swaying. Luis and Sandoval quickly followed him, shocked their stalwart sergeant was beginning to crack.

"Nombre de Dios!" Sergeant Lopez strangled, on the verge of retching. "Forgive me, amigos, that you should see me brought so low. I think I'm at the end of my rope."

"Nonsense, man!" Luis snapped, grabbing Sergeant Lopez roughly by the shoulders hoping to shake him out of this miserable condition. "Get hold of yourself, Sergeant! No man is low until he's disgraced himself and you've never done that!"

Sergeant Lopez blinked, as the statement penetrated his despair; he began to draw his heavy frame up taller, a vestige of his old pride beginning to flicker in his eyes.

Luis' tone softened. "You have our sympathies for what you've had to see and endure on this expedition, but here's no disgrace on you, man! Stand up and collect yourself and let's be about our business." He wanted to embrace Lopez, to share with him some of his strength and youth; but he couldn't do that with Lopez or any other man in his command.

Lopez lowered his head and smiled. "You're right of course, Captain. I'm sorry I let these damned Aztecs and their insufferable practices get to me. It won't happen again, I assure you!" He turned and walked briskly down the temple steps, followed by the others.

Sandoval, Lopez and the men were not the only ones suffering mental anguish over what they'd observed in the capitol. What Luis secretly witnessed last night, when the moon was full and bright over the clean, beautiful city of Tenochtitlan, silhouetted by the protruding volcano of Popocatepetl, with its wreaths of vapor floating skyward, would haunt his dreams the rest of his life! Devil- worshiping Aztec high priests in a long, single procession, shuffled, in step, trance- like, to a square, one story building in the center of the pyramids. It was time for a special Aztec ceremony which occurred every full moon. Twelve black-robed priests led the procession. Tethered on long chains, at each corner of the building to protect it from intruders, paced huge growling mastiff dogs.

Exactly at midnight, screams and strange growlings, unearthly laughter, women's cries and groans sent shivers down Luis's spine, which caused the hair on the back of his neck to stand on end! Were the priests meeting with their master who was not of this earth? Luis hoped he'd never have to find out!

Up to now, he'd controlled his hot temper, but the appalling Aztec practices had driven him to near distraction; and it was all he could do to keep from bloodying his sword on their miserable necks. The filthy, bloody priests and priestesses not only sacrificed innocent victims, but ran seminaries for the thousands of young boys and girls who would replace them as they grew older.

Luis crossed himself and silently prayed that Cortez and Catholic priests coming with him to Tenochtitlan next year might force an end to the human butchery.

33

Kano threw back his head and sniffed. "Damn Captain, something smells mighty good."

"It certainly does," Luis agreed. "Montezuma's chef is outdoing himself, preparing our last meal."

Kano grinned. "I hope you mean our last meal before we leave Tenochtitlan, and not our last meal before..." He drew his finger across his throat.

Luis laughed. "Don't worry. We'll be on our way in the morning. That's why Montezuma wants to talk with me privately this evening, without his counselors." He nodded his head toward two gaudily garbed royal bodyguards approaching. "I believe our escort has arrived."

Luis and Kano followed the warriors down a long hallway. The emperor's palace was the epitome of barbaric splendor as was everything else about him. Hundreds of lovely women filled his palace.

Montezuma provided them apartments and every luxury possible. Several naked women, not the least embarrassed by their nudity, frolicked in the baths scattered throughout the palace. Huge Aztec warriors guarded all entrances. Lighting torches made of resinous wood sent forth a fragrant odor that wafted through the building.

Behind a screen of richly carved wood, drawn around them to provide privacy, Montezuma, Luis and Kano seated themselves on cushions behind a low table covered with a delicate linen cloth. Serving women sat small bowls of water before them, to wash their hands before and after eating. The dishes were a service of gold, which would be given to the women after the dinner. The emperor never ate from the same dishes twice!

Women brought meat consisting of different types of game, turkey being the most conspicuous. These meats were seasoned with delicate sauces and spices, of which Montezuma seemed very fond.

Vegetables and fruits of every delicious variety covered the table. For delicious desserts, they munched fruit, and confections and pastry, made of maize flour and sugar.

Pipes were brought; and the three men smoked tobacco mixed with an intoxicating weed. They smoked and enjoyed watching women dancing sensuously and seductively to the solemn cadence of strange Aztec musical instruments.

"Did you enjoy your meal?" Montezuma asked, staring intently at his guests.

"A most excellent feast, my Lord," Luis responded. "I gorged myself. My compliments to the cook. His cooking style is poetry to the palate."

Montezuma's smile went from friendly to admiring. "He'll be pleased to hear it, Captain." Luis nodded, and settled back, enjoying his pipe. Kano belched loudly as was the custom of his people to show appreciation for an excellent meal. The emperor laughed delightedly at Kano's momentary embarrassment.

Quite suddenly the emperor's expression turned serious. "Tell me, Captain, where are you off to and what are your plans?"

Luis stared squarely into Montezuma's black eyes, knowing he must be extremely careful and politically correct in his choice of words if he hoped to pave the way for Captain Hernando Cortez's easy conquest of the Aztec empire. A slip of the tongue at this crucial point could cause Cortez's future expedition much difficulty, perhaps make it necessary to send Spain's entire army to conquer the Aztecs.

"Tomorrow, my Lord, we'll be on our way." Montezuma nodded. He'd expected as much.

"We'll return to the eastern sea, following the route by which we came, and our ship will pick us up near Papantla."

"Just a word of caution, then, Captain. Beware of Teoamoxtli. He's always been a thorn in my side! He's so far away he often rebels against my directives. Between Teoamoxtli and General Naulinco, I'm not sure which one is the biggest pain in the ass!" He hesitated momentarily, "But they're both excellent soldiers, I'll give them that."

Luis glanced questioningly at Kano. "Did you translate the emperor's words correctly?"

"Not exactly, sir. But I'm quite sure that's what he meant!"

Then came the question which Luis dreaded! "Do you plan to come back again?" The emperor asked. "We'd like to, with your permission, of course."

Montezuma's eyes registered an unexpected mixture of confusion and curiosity.

"Why? You've seen our cities, our people and our culture. Is there anything you wish to see that we've not shown you?"

"Oh no, my Lord Montezuma! You welcomed us with open arms. We could ask for nothing more. Your generosity has been truly overwhelming."

"Then why do you wish to return?" Montezuma persisted, an underlying fear gnawing at him. The next time the Spaniards came, it would be with overwhelming force and they'd take his empire from him!

Luis rapidly searched his mind for an appropriate answer. "When we return we'll bring medicines to cure the sick, horses and wagons to transport goods to distant parts of your empire, better weapons .... "

Montezuma interrupted, his eyes flashing hostility, "And what will you take in return? Our cities? Our treasures? Our religion?"

"We'd not do that, my Lord."

"Not you, perhaps, Captain. But when the white men come again you'll not be in command. I understand a soldier by the name of Cortez has been appointed. Is that not so?"

"That's true," Luis answered honestly, rather bewildered by Montezuma's astuteness. "What sort of man is this Cortez? Is he a man with whom we can deal peacefully?"

"I know Captain Cortez personally. He's an honorable man, and will come in peace if he's permitted unmolested entry into your empire."

"And if we refuse?"

"Captain Cortez can be a very forceful man, my Lord."

Montezuma studied Luis' face and detected no deceit. An uneasy silence settle over the two men as Montezuma digested the enormity of Luis's information. How can we fight what has been ordained of the gods? What if this Cortez is actually Quetzalcoatl in disguise? What good would it do to send my mighty army against him when he lands? Fate has already decreed the fall of my empire.

Luis watched Montezuma's tough facade dissolve, and in the torch light the young Spaniard suddenly saw the emperor as a tired, worn old man—a man burdened by centuries of old superstitions which would make the conquest of Mexico a relatively easy task for Cortez and a handful of Spanish soldiers and sailors.

"I suppose it had to happen someday," Montezuma lamented sadly. "I'm not fool enough to think our empire could last forever. But everything is happening so fast!" The voice seemed remote and far away as if the emperor was talking more to himself than to his guests.

Abruptly he said, "The audience is ended. I now wish to be alone. You've given me many things to think about."

Luis and Kano rose and bowed graciously to Montezuma, who said, "I fear we'll not see each other again, Captain. May I wish you a safe journey to your homeland? And you, my dear dear black friend, may the Gods be with you all the days of your life, wherever you might go." He touched Kano's muscular forearm. "You'll always be welcome here among us." Tears formed in Montezuma's eyes. "You know, Kano, we're very much alike, you and I—both lost in a world of white men who want to subdue and conquer us and make us their slaves."

Kano nodded and smiled, overwhelmed with intense admiration for this man who called himself emperor. Kano didn't interpret Montezuma's last words, though Luis looked askance at the tall black man. Bowing together, they quickly backed from the emperor's presence.

🐾 🐾 🐾

Within the hour Luis met with Sandoval and Roberto Esperanza. Luis sat at a long table. Sandoval leaned back in his high backed chair, his leg cocked up on the table, a glass of pulque in his hand. He wore his breastplate, and his sword stuck out across the floor.

"Are you ready, Roberto?" Luis asked.

"Yes sir! Those five Totonac warriors Kano gave me are big strong men. Kano explained everything they need to know to help me break Captain Armand out of prison."

"Very well," Luis said. "Be extremely careful, Roberto! Once you leave here you're on your own. If you get caught we can't help you."

"Don't worry about us, Captain! We can take care of ourselves!" Esperanza answered courteously, as always; but there was something about him—a gleam in his eyes, a kind of youthful arrogance that exuded confidence.

"I'll leave it in your hands, then. After Armand is free you and your Totonacs get him up into the hills quickly. We'll pick you up there in a couple of days."

Luis put his hand on Esperanza's shoulder. "Buena suerte, (good luck) Roberto!" Esperanza saluted the officers, turned and walked out.

Sandoval chuckled. "I like that young man, Captain. Kind of re-minds me of me when I was his age! He's got the right stuff in him. I always get on well with him. I cheat him a little now and then at dice, and he's never blinked an eyelid. That's what I call a gentleman."

Luis smiled at that. "I've done that a time or two myself! Roberto is smart—probably lets us win to stay on our good side!"

Sandoval turned serious. "I hope we're not making a mistake in trying to break Armand out of jail. If Roberto gets caught it's over for all of us. The Aztecs will..."

"Mistake or no, Sandoval," Luis interrupted. "We can't leave one of our countrymen in Montezuma's stinking prison, no matter what he's done."

"I suppose you're right," Sandoval grudgingly agreed. "Perhaps Armand's capture by the Aztecs is a blessing in disguise. We'd never have known about the Mayans otherwise. From the information I've gathered from the emperor and his noblemen it seems the two empires, side by side, are ten times bigger than Spain. Look, here on my map. I've pin-pointed the major cities and garrisons of both empires—and best of all, we've learned where most of their gold and silver mines are located That'll certainly interest King Carlos and Captain Cortez, don't you think?"

"I do indeed!"

Rolling up his map Sandoval cocked his head and squinted at Luis through his one good eye, feeling quite relaxed from the pulque. "By the Virgin, Captain. I still can't comprehend the riches we've discovered! It boggles a man's mind! Had I not seen it with my own eyes I'd never have believed it.

There's enough treasure here in Tenochtitlan alone to buy all the kingdoms in the known world."

Sandoval was referring to Axayacatl's gold, plus two circular plates Montezuma had given them when they complimented his metalsmiths' workmanship.

"Take them, my friends, if they please you," he said gracefully, as if giving away something as valueless as a couple of chickens. The plates were as large as carriage wheels, one of pure gold, the other of silver. It took thirty of Kano's huge palms to measure the circumference of each disc.

Sandoval estimated the golden disc's value at 20,000 pesos de oro and the silver one, weighing fifty marks, at half that.

"Have you inventoried the treasures Montezuma's given us?" Luis asked. "Yes sir! Sergeant Lopez and I have very carefully accounted for every item."

"What do we have?" Luis asked, so he could decide what to take with them.

"Let's see," Sandoval retrieved a parchment scroll from the table. "Two slave collars of gold and precious stones. A hundred ounces of gold dust from the mines at Xaltopa, just a small sample of the gold that is taken daily from that mine. Oh yes, there's a deer's head made of gold. It's so heavy it was all Kano and Sergeant Lopez could do to lift it. In addition to the two wheels of gold and silver, there's that large wheel of gold from the southern provinces—the one with figures of strange animals on it, with tufts of leaves worked in. It weighs in at three thousand eight hundred ounces. We also have one hundred bars of gold, and the same of silver."

"Too bad we can't take all of it with us," Luis responded "But it will still be here when Cortez comes next year. Montezuma assured me it's safe in his treasury!"

Sandoval got to his feet and stared at Luis. "It's not him that worries me—it's that sonofabitch Naulinco. I don't trust him."

"We'll deal with him when the time comes," Luis replied quietly. "Tell Lopez to be extremely careful not to overburden the mules when he packs samples of the treasure. Take just the small stuff. We've got to move fast through a lot of steep, rugged country."

Luis stretched and yawned. "I'm completely exhausted. Let's call it a day."

Sandoval turned to leave. Luis said, "Jorge, I hope and pray Narvaez and the Catalan will be at the rendezvous point when we get there!"

"I've been thinking the same thing. It's a mighty big ocean and lots of things could go wrong. But if Juan Narvaez can't get the job done, no one can. He'll be there!"

Luis nodded, a few worry lines above his eyebrows. "Have the men ready to march at first light."

"Yes sir! That won't be a problem! They're as anxious to get back to Cuba as we are!"

34

Close to midnight, Roberto Esperanza and the Totonacs peered around the corner of the temple, studying the building where Pedro Armand was imprisoned. Fires burned brightly above them on the temple summit, providing enough light to see there were no outside guards.

Leading the way, Esperanza, dressed as a Totonac, motioned the others to follow. Quickly and silently they crossed the vacant square and made it to the shadow of the prison. Stealthily they entered the corridor, backs pressed tightly to the wall. They stood frozen until a sentry disappeared down the long hallway.

Moving cautiously, they found Armand's cell. Esperanza could see him curled up on the stone floor asleep, his thin loin-cloth clad body shivering uncontrollably from the damp cold. Pulling back the outside locking bolt, Esperanza gently pushed against the door, listening apprehensively for Aztec guards. Pushing harder, the door opened with a rusty screech.

Terrified, Armand jerked awake and rolled over. He stared up at a warrior–with five Indians behind him! They'd come to kill him!

In Castilian, Esperanza whispered, "Good evening, Captain Armand. Would you like to go back to Spain with me?"

"Oh my God! You're a Spaniard?"

"I am, companero," Esperanza grinned. "Come. Let's get out of here! We've a long way to go." The Totonacs got Armand to his feet, cut the straps binding him, then their chief Hulado vigorously massaged his cramped limbs. When they released him he stood on weakened legs for a moment, then fell against Hulado, who crouched, slung Armand over his shoulder and followed Esperanza and the others from the building.

Outside two Totonacs cradled their arms and Hulado carefully lowered Armand; and the group scurried quickly through Tenochtitlan's darkened streets toward the eastern hills.

🐾 🐾 🐾

It was late in the night when Luis finished writing the last detail of their stay in Tenochtitlan. He blew out the lamp, and slipped quietly into the room where Toloya lay asleep on the bed. Leaning down, with his knees on the floor, he cupped her face in his hands, and memorized with his fingertips the tiny, miraculous convolutions of those ears he'd so often studied, those artfully sculptured ears which so often flamed with her embarrassments as she tried so hard to learn the Spaniards' strange ways.

She tossed and turned and trembled, perhaps dreaming of the cage where Luis found her. The nightmare came frequently, and often woke her screaming in the middle of the night.

She trembled in waves of intensity, causing such a tide of pity in Luis that tears burned his eyes and traced cool paths down both sides of his nose.

Toloya felt a teardrop fall on the bare skin of her arm—a teardrop, something she'd so little expected from this hard Spanish warrior that at first she didn't know what it was; then she understood, and was so moved by it she reached out and pulled him close.

"Luis," she whispered. "My Luis." He lay down by her, placing his cheek on her rising and falling bosom and her rapid heartbeat thudded against his right ear. The warm musk of her body bathed him now. She was now the center of his universe. He pulled her close, under the warmth of the blanket; they kissed and drifted off into an uneasy, exhausted sleep.

Two hours later Luis sat up, unable to sleep, unable to let his mind rest. He closed his eyes and tried to think clearly. The price to get here was high! Some of his men lay in unmarked graves near the Chichemetlan village. The mission was far from over. The most dangerous part, he knew, lay ahead of them, as they worked their way east to the coast. There wasn't enough gunpowder to fight more than one skirmish, then it would be swords against itztlis. He was outnumbered thousands to one. He'd reviewed Sandoval's map and done his calculations. He briefed Sandoval and Lopez and they briefed the men. What more could he do? Would Montezuma try to stop them? And where was Juan Narvaez? Was he enroute to rendezvous with Luis—if they reached the coast?

Toloya yawned and stretched and sat up. He thought there was something delightful in the movement. A quality that touched him. She reached for his hand and kissed the back of it. Then she put her arms around his neck and pulled him to her.

At daybreak, Montezuma and his counselors, dressed in their finest most colorful attire, stood silently on the palace balcony watching Luis and his men wind their way along the broad stone roadway leading from Tenochtitlan. Armed warriors lined the concourse on both sides to control thousands of noisy Aztecs who turned out to bid the Spaniards farewell.

With Toloya mounted behind him, Luis glanced up and touched fingers to his helmet in a farewell salute to Montezuma who bowed slightly.

Several Spanish soldiers turned their heads for a last look at the ominous pyramids and temples thrusting their heads above the early morning ground fog—and it sent a shudder down their spines! Within the hour chanting priests would begin their daily bloody sacrificial routine throughout the city.

Outraged, Naulinco watched the Spaniards disappear in the distance—taking Aztec secrets to the outside world! He watched Montezuma bow to Luis Escudero, like some lowly peasant just in from the fields, instead of emperor of the earth's mightiest kingdom.

Staring into the glorious blue sky Naulinco carefully opened small gates to let Escudero's haunting image flow into his mind—that smiling, bearded arrogant face as he beat Naulinco into unconsciousness—and Aztec noblemen laughing hilariously as he lay there, crumpled in the dirt!

The nightmare of that reality rubbed against Naulinco's brain like coarse grit, driving him to take the most desperate gamble of his career—defying Montezuma! He sent for his fastest messenger.

Within minutes, Tezchuco stood at attention before his general.

"I want you to take a verbal message to Teoamoxtili in Papantla. Use the secondary route so you're not seen by the Spaniards. Tell Teoamoxtli I'll try to kill the Spaniards somewhere between here and Papantla. If anything goes wrong and I should fail, Teoamoxtli is to kill every man of them. No prisoners are to be taken!"

Tezchuco's eyes widened. "Repeat the message back to me."

Tezchuco flawlessly repeated word for word the entire message.

"Be on your way now! And Tezchuco, make this the fastest run you've ever made."

🌺 🌺 🌺

It was done! The Spaniards would never reach the coast alive! Yet a nagging doubt played with Naulinco's mind. Both he and Teoamoxtli had underestimated Escudero once. They'd not do it again!

What angered and frustrated Naulinco most was Montezuma's silly superstitions! No power on earth could convince him the Spaniards posed a serious threat—he stubbornly refused to even discuss it!

Naulinco knew it was up to him to save the empire. Perhaps a prayer and a good sacrifice to the war god Huitzilopotchli would be in order?

No! He'd never believed in cold stone gods, especially Huitzilo-potchli, a cruel god, the patron god of the Aztecs. His stately temple rose above all others in Tenochtitlan, and its altars always reeked of human blood.

White fluffy clouds gathered low, floating over the mountains in the east. Naulinco gazed lovingly out over Tenochtitlan, where he was born. He was enveloped by a sadness he'd never felt before. But then, the empire had never been threatened before! He shrugged it off, fastened his dagger to his belt, adjusted his headdress and walked quickly to the garrison, assembled his special warriors and began his pursuit of the Spaniards.

The days of soft living began to tell on Luis and his men before they'd gone two leagues. Their feet and muscles protested with stiffness and pain until it was worked out by relentless marching. They ate their noon meal near a bubbling stream and followed it for some distance before veering off after Urcos, beginning their long climb over the mountains.

They came to a small village shortly before sundown. Hostile Aztecs stood defiantly in the road shouting and shaking their fists in the air. Urcos detoured them around the village and they made camp in an arroyo cut in the mountainside, where a cool mountain stream cascaded over the rocks.

Luis grunted. He eased himself out of the saddle and helped Toloya down. He took a long look around, turning slowly on the balls of his feet. He took the canteen off his saddle and dipped it into the stream. It bubbled and filled. He sat it on the ground long enough for debris and mud to settle to the bottom, then handed it to Toloya before he drank from it. The horses and mules guzzled thirstily from the stream.

"We'll camp here for the night," Luis said.

"We can make another league or two before dark," Sandoval replied.

Luis gave him a look of dulled anger. "I'm not about to get caught by those villagers sneaking up behind us in the dark, or Aztecs ahead maybe planning to ambush us in the dark."

"Damn, you're as grouchy as a stepped on rattlesnake!" Sandoval mumbled under his breath. "What was that?" Luis growled.

"I said we need to watch out for rattlesnakes."

Kano walked along the bank, upstream, until he saw several pebbles and rocks that had been kicked over. He knelt down and studied the stream bed, then went back to Luis.

"We'd better keep our eyes open Captain. A group of men is somewhere ahead of us or near us."

"How do you know?"

"They kicked over a few rocks and pebbles." He reached down into the water, up to his elbow and picked up a small stone. "Rough side up. It's been turned over recently, otherwise it would have been smooth and slimy like the other side."

Luis nodded. "Damn, Kano, I don't know what we'd do without you! I'll post double guards tonight, and every night from here on to the coast. I think trouble is coming. The drums are talking, and the Aztecs are all around us. It's just a matter of time now."

The exhausted men were finishing their supper when six Totonac Indians strode into camp, carrying Captain Pedro Armand on a makeshift stretcher. They put him in Luis' tent. Toloya scurried about like a mother hen making him comfortable. She cleansed his face and hands with a cool, damp cloth.

It took a few moments before the men recognized Roberto Esperanza! They patted him on the back, laughing and joking, and lifted his long loincloth to see if he wore anything beneath!

The Totonacs were a curious sight, with rings of gold, and bright blue gemstones in their ears and nostrils, and a delicately wrought gold leaf attached to their upper lip. Kano was unable to comprehend their strange language, but Hulado spoke Nahuatl which allowed them to converse normally.

Hulado looked older than his thirty five years. His pock marked face, though not handsome, was alive and animated. His eyes glowed as if they were burning the marrow out of him. He was taller than any of his men, with a great chest and thighs of a mountain warrior.

"Captain," Esperanza said. "These men carried Captain Armand all the way here without stopping once! I had a hell of a time keeping up with them, and I wasn't helping carry anyone!"

"Well done, Roberto! We were getting a little worried! Did you find out anything about them?"

"No sir. I can't understand a word they say, and they can't understand me."

Luis smiled and summoned Kano. "See what you can find out."

Hulado said, "We're from a small town near Cempoalla, our main city. Our people settled there many centuries ago, long before the Aztecs came from the north. They settled in peacefully among the ancient ones, who were white men like yourselves. When the Aztecs came they killed the whites, and subjugated us and all other tribes, under strict Aztec rule.

That's why we detest the Aztecs, as do most of the other powerful tribes. We'd all join together to fight them if we had someone to lead us!"

Luis listened attentively, learning first hand how Cortez could utilize the Indians' spirit of discontent to work them into a mighty and deadly coalition of Indian allies, which, added to his own army, could conquer the Aztecs.

"Are you getting this down, Sandoval?" Luis asked

Sandoval pointed to his head. "Yes sir. Right up here. Every word!"

35

A deadly premonition permeated Pedro Armand's entire being. Never a religious man, he was confused. Here he was in the new world, but couldn't shut out the old one, where he'd been born and raised until he was a grown man. He saw everything in two shapes at once, which baffled him as to what he should do. Fear surged incessantly below the surface of his mind. He thrust it down, but couldn't disperse it. Fairy tales from his boyhood of the Virgin Mary and her son Jesus and His sacrifice for mankind plagued his mind and wouldn't go away. What if the Jesus story was really true and not a fairy tale after all? The gold crucifix hanging here in Luis' tent, the symbol of his beliefs and strength, reminded Armand of his misdeeds of the past few years. He pulled the blanket up to his chin when the shivering fever caused his teeth to chatter. Every day in Montezuma's prison his condition grew worse, because there was no medicine, and the guards' inhumane treatment. Now, in company of Luis and his men, he felt he'd soon regain his health. But it was not to be. The black vomit, the headaches, the yellow skin, all the fault of this horrible country, drained his last ounce of strength.

He felt a hand gently wiping the sweat from his brow and looked up to see Luis staring down at him. Luis shooed Toloya from the tent so he and Armand could speak privately; and soon they were talking as old friends, like they'd been back in the days when they were green recruits in the barracks at Barcelona. Armand was an honorable, reliable comrade then. But something changed him over the years; what it was Luis never found out.

Both chuckled as Armand recalled a humorous incident. Suddenly Armand grew serious, hoping to free himself from the nagging guilt of his troubled conscience. He confessed to Luis he murdered Captain Julio Alvarez in Punta del Piedras to delay Luis' expedition. Until now Luis had absolutely no idea what happened to the Catalan's captain.

Armand continued. "I work for Governor Don Diego Velazquez, who wants all the Aztec treasures for himself." He chuckled. "I now believe I picked the wrong side!"

Suddenly Armand went into a violent spasm of coughing, and Luis detected a death rattle in that cough.

Armand asked weakly, "Luis, why did you risk your life to come to this savage land?"

"Very simple, Pedro. For wealth and glory. What about you?"

"About the same, mostly for wealth though."

Luis smiled. "Too damned bad we didn't get together in Cuba. We'd have made a hell of a team!"

Armand nodded weakly, wiped his mouth and managed a half smile. He seemed embarrassed when he asked in a very weak voice, "Do you have a priest with you?"

"No, I'm sorry."

"Never mind. It's not important. I haven't seen a priest since I was a small boy," Armand admitted.

Luis sensed Armand's soul was troubled, and asked, "Do you know Father Bernardino de Sahagun? He's a Franciscan priest in St. Jago."

"No," Armand whispered. "I've only heard his name."

"He's a personal friend of mine, a great scholar and a very kind and wonderful priest. When I get back to Cuba I'll ask him to pray for your immortal soul—with your permission, of course."

"You'd actually do that for me, Luis?" Armand asked, totally overwhelmed! "You have my permission, of course, and thank you from the bottom of my heart..." he gasped; and with a death- rattling sigh Pedro Armand died.

An hour later, in the campfire's flickering light, the Spaniards gathered, bareheaded around a makeshift grave, while Luis read Psalm 51, from his Bible: "Have mercy upon me, O God, according to thy loving kindness: according to the multitude of thy tender mercies blot out my transgressions." Luis' quiet smile that had always seemed to touch his face was gone. He stared down at the blanket-wrapped body of his former comrade, but it was as though he was looking far beyond this earth into heaven where the explanation of death and sorrow lay hidden. Too emotional to read the entire psalm, he skipped to verse 11. "Cast me not away from thy presence; and take not thy holy spirit from me." Luis' lips were still moving as the soldiers filled in the grave. It was skillfully concealed by rocks and unmarked.

Toloya watched in interested silence, never having seen a Christian burial. But she, as well as the soldiers, were thinking the same thought;

the unknown perils ahead were many, and before they reached the coast, where Narvaez's ship would pick them up, there'd be more graves!

Dawn came much too early for the Spaniards, exhausted from the fast-paced march eastward. Awakening to itchy mosquito bumps, bleeding fly bites and aching joints they dressed in the gray light beginning to dissolve the darkness; and soon they were again on the march.

The next evening Luis became suspicious of the cool reception they'd received at several villages along the way. That suspicion grew as he and Sandoval and the others listened to an unseen snake skin drum booming out their exact whereabouts to anyone within hearing distance.

Urcos explained to Luis that Aztec runners from Naulinco's army had alerted every village from Tenochtitlan to Papantla—the white men must be killed! Yet most villagers, still loyal to Montezuma, allowed the Spaniards safe passage. Urcos, however, had no idea which villages were friendly and which aligned themselves with Naulinco.

Without looking at the rocky hillside, Urcos said, "For the last hour I've noticed dark shapes near the far edge of our encampment. At first I thought they might be logs left behind by the villagers. But they seem to be increasing in numbers."

Luis carefully stared out into the fading light. He blinked his eyes, looked away and then looked back again. This time he made out the dark shapes his sharp-eyed scout was talking about.

"Are they logs or men?" Urcos asked in a quiet voice. Luis thought of sending one of his men to investigate, but if they were men, instead of logs, his man would be killed.

"We'll soon see what they are," he answered. "San Estevan, is your weapon primed?"

"Si, Capitan!"

"See that shape? There, off to the right?" Luis nodded his head rather than point to the Aztec warrior. "It's a bit far, but let's see what you can do."

San Estevan took careful aim at the form and slowly squeezed the trigger. There was a stunning crack as the burning rope touched the priming pan, and a flash of flame, immediately followed by a scream. The copper-skinned figure leaped up, staggered, and fell. For an instant there was absolute silence.

"Excellent, San Estevan, excellent," Luis shouted.

Suddenly the stillness was ripped apart by terrifying Aztec war cries! The entire mountainside came alive! A mass of Aztecs wearing black trimmings on their uniforms, Naulinco's colors, flooded down on the Spanish encampment. They came leaping and screaming, giving gasping groans to imitate the death rattle, stopping at intervals to hurl their light, deadly javelins.

"Bugler, sound hold fire," Luis shouted above the din as the warriors closed to fifty yards. The Spaniards waited. The gunners loaded the falconet with chain for close quarter fighting, and aimed it directly at the middle of the on rushing Aztec horde. There would be only one shot—there was no more gunpowder for the cannon! The arquebusiers waited for the order to fire.

The first wave of attackers penetrated the outer perimeter of the camp and loosed a solid rain of javelins and arrows.

Luis shouted, "Fire!" A huge crash shook the ground and a bright orange flash lit the semi darkness as the falconet spit fire and chain. The entire front row of Aztecs was mowed down in a bloody mass.

The arquebusiers opened up and poured round after round into the milling, confused Aztecs.

Luis spotted Naulinco, tall, handsomely dressed, leap into the fray, screaming, rallying his men for another attack

Luis shouted, "San Estevan, bring me your arquebus. Quickly man, quickly!"

The young man handed his gun to Luis. "Aim a little high, Captain, and that general is a dead man!"

Luis nodded. "That arrogant whoreson has tried my patience once too often! It's time to settle accounts."

Luis stepped into the open and shouted, "Naulinco!"

The Aztec general, twenty yards away, stepped out, a javelin in his right hand. His left hand held his decorated shield. He shouted something Luis didn't understand. Luis took quick aim, sighted half an inch above Naulinco's head and fired. Naulinco was slammed violently backwards, staggered two steps and crumpled, dead before he hit the ground. A triumphant shout erupted from the Spaniards as their attackers retreated, dragging Naulinco's body with them.

Luis handed the arquebus to San Estevan. "Good gun!"

San Estevan grinned. "Good shooter too! That was a hell of a shot, Captain. I couldn't have done any better myself."

"Coming from you, I consider that a compliment!"

The young soldier beamed, walked over and joined his comrades.

The ground bristled with spears and arrows. Luis realized the entire engagement hadn't taken more than a few minutes—but it seemed like hours! Miraculously, so far, none of the men were injured and the horses and mules escaped unharmed. The shadows were deep and sinister, the darkness all but total. It was possible to barely make out the darker outlines of trees overhead and clouds beyond. The men waited nervously; that waiting rubbed Luis' nerves.

"Urcos," he asked, "will they come again?"

"No, Captain, not with Naulinco dead."

"That's fortunate for us! We're out of gunpowder for the cannon. All we have now is what the men carry in their powder flasks."

"Perhaps this battle was favored of the Gods," Urcos said. "Word of your powerful weapons will now precede you. You won't have any more trouble with the Aztecs until we get closer to Papantla. It's there Teoamoxtli will try to annihilate all of you!"

🐾🐾🐾

Luis thanked and congratulated his men, then walked to his small tent to check on Toloya. She wasn't there! He asked the men if they'd seen her. No, they'd been too busy fighting attacking Aztecs.

The soldiers spread out and looked for her, but came up empty. Luis, Kano and Hulado tried to track her in the darkness. Hulado carried a makeshift torch which caused him to bend down to see the ground clearly. Toloya's abductors left sandal footprints in some of the softer ground, which headed toward the dark, looming mountain range.

"I'm sorry, Captain," Hulado said. "I can't follow these tracks. It's just too dark!" They reluctantly returned to the campfire.

"What do we do now?" Sandoval asked.

Luis quickly answered, "Get her back from the Aztecs!"

"Let's go then," Sergeant Lopez said, "before they get too far ahead of us."

"No," Luis replied. "It's suicide to go out there in the dark."

"But Captain" Lopez persisted, "by morning they'll be…"

Luis shook his head and held up his hand for silence, wrestling with the dilemma—if they stopped to search they'd miss meeting the Catalan and would be slaughtered by the Aztecs; if someone didn't go after Toloya the Aztecs would kill her or worse. That thought terrified him!

"Well, Captain?" Sandoval said impatiently. "What are your orders? Sergeant Lopez and I can take Urcos and Hulado and a few of the men go after her first thing in the morning."

Luis shook his head. "That's exactly what the Aztecs want us to do."

Sandoval's brow wrinkled and he glared at Luis through his one good eye. "Are you saying we're going to abandon her to the savages?"

"You know better than that!"

Luis motioned Kano and Hulado over. "Ask Hulado if he and his men will go after Toloya. They're expert trackers. If they can't find her, no one can."

Hulado smiled broadly when Kano put the question to him. "It would be an honor, sir! I never turn down an opportunity to hunt and kill Aztecs."

"Do you think she's still alive?"

"Oh certainly, though she won't have an easy time being an Aztec captive, Captain. You know what brutes they are. She's extremely valuable and her captors know it. Montezuma would pay a handsome sum to get her back again. Don't worry. If she's alive, we'll find her and bring her to you!"

🐾 🐾 🐾

Hulado and his men trailed the Aztecs for two days, and finally caught up with them. They froze and hit the ground. Inching forward on their bellies through the tall grass and bushes toward a clearing in the trees, they saw Toloya!

She was on her feet. Eight Aztec warriors encircled her, playing some kind of cruel game, pushing her from one warrior to the other. They were drunk on pulque and intended to take turns having her. The Aztec leader ripped Toloya's shirt open and kneaded her breasts brutally. He was going to take her roughly. Two others held her and lifted her off the ground as the warrior pulled off her trousers.

Completely naked, Toloya's screamed and fought them, but she was no match for the sinewy Aztec warrior who dropped his loincloth while his companions spread-eagled Toloya on the ground. The Aztecs' entire attention was riveted on the naked, helpless woman. The warrior waved his erection in Toloya's face before dropping to his knees between her thighs.

Hulado signaled his men, and they notched copper-tipped arrows to their bows. Hulado literally flew as he hurtled toward the closest Aztec warrior and plunged his knife all the way to the hilt in the man's back. The Aztec sprawled face forward to the ground.

Four bowstrings snapped at once, and four Aztecs fell with arrows protruding from their bodies. The others ran away so fast it caused Hulado to chuckle.

He pulled Toloya up and enfolded her in his arms. Uncontrollable sobbing racked her body. Hulado let her cry. Between sobs, she said, "Oh, Hulado, I've never been so glad to see anyone in my whole life."

"Are you all right?" he asked with concern. "I can see from here you have all the normal parts in all the usual places!" His usually stern countenance broke into a smile.

Toloya blushed and smiled through her tears. "I'm more frightened than hurt."

"Good. Here, put your clothes on and let's get out of here before those cowardly dogs gather up some friends and come back." He handed her the trousers and ripped shirt. Within minutes the small group moved out at a fast-paced trot to catch up with the Spaniards.

🐜🐜🐜

Hulado followed an old Totonac trail through the steep, rugged mountains, hoping to catch up with Luis before he reached the sea. These tough, hardy mountain warriors could run all day without a break. Hulado wasn't sure Toloya had stamina enough for the fast-paced mountain journey ahead. It would require every ounce of her strength!

36

AUGUST, 1518

Luis rode ahead of his men, under a blazing August sun. He kept Diablo climbing the steep trail until the big stallion clattered over loose rocks to the top. Luis could see the Chichemetlan Village across the valley, half a mile away. He recognized Prince Ruminawi's hacienda, now a burned out roofless shell. It stood at the end of the single street, which widened into a square. The entire town looked as if it had been bombarded by cannon fire—buildings burned, its main street littered with debris.

Dozens of vultures circle lazily overhead.

Sandoval pulled his horse alongside. "My God, Captain, what happened to the town? It's been completely destroyed!"

Luis shook his head. "Probably that sonofabitch, Teoamoxtli, taking revenge against Ruminawi for befriending us!"

Sandoval nodded, then leaned forward, squinting through his one eye. "Can you make out what that is in front of the village? Looks like some kind of fence made of tall sticks."

"Let's find out." Luis spurred Diablo, and his thirsty, exhausted men followed, ready to drop. Luis looked in every direction, hoping to catch sight of Toloya and five Totonac warriors! But there was not a living soul in the entire valley.

Kano, running alongside Diablo, kept his voice steady. "She's not here, Captain."

"I can see that!" Luis' words were sharp and held a touch of bitterness. But before Kano could make further comment, Luis said, "I'm sorry, my friend. I'm...all worked up and nervous. I hoped she might be here. I don't know why fate or perhaps God permitted me to free her, just to have her end up in Aztec hands again."

Kano, hardly puffing, said quietly, "I have a hunch your God will work things out. He usually does!" The comment surprised and astonished Luis, who smiled. "Where did that come from?"

"I've learned a few things about your God since we left Cuba! Sergeant Lopez and the others are good teachers!"

"Have they converted to Catholicism?" Kano laughed, "No sir! Not yet!"

Diablo suddenly threw his head violently from side to side, stopped, and planted all four feet in the dirt. A solid wall of Aztec spears, copper points down in the earth, blocked the road. Atop each shaft was a human head. Though the vultures had been at them Luis recognized Prince Ruminawi's wrinkled features and those of his counselor Sayri the father of Cozu, the first victim the Spaniards had seen sacrificed to Aztec Gods, as well as several other villagers.

Urcos let out a screaming wail and raced like a madman into his burned out village searching frantically in every direction for his wife and children.

The stench of decaying bodies permeated the air. Luis, Sandoval and Sergeant Lopez rode slowly down main street, fetlock deep in dusty ashes, which erupted in small, separate clouds under the horses hooves. Putrefying, headless bodies of men, women and children littered the ground.

Luis and his men had witnessed nearly every type of human brutality known to man; but the sight of so many mutilated bodies left every man fighting down the sour bile rising in his parched throat. Not a word was spoken as the men dragged themselves through the village. A terrible despair settled over them as they stepped over dead bodies.

"This is as bad as man's inhumanity gets!" Sandoval said sadly.

Luis nodded agreement. "There was no need for this. They were such a kind and gentle people."

The exhausted soldiers sprawled about Ruminawi's courtyard, too worn out to even curse the fate that damned them to this untenable situation!

Luis, Sandoval and Sergeant Lopez dismounted and let their horses drink from the pool.

"Sergeant," Luis said. "Take a couple of men and see if Ruminawi's secret vault is still intact and if our treasures are still there. If so, gather as much as the mules can carry. Divide the rest among the men. We'll move out as soon as you've got them loaded."

"But sir, the men need rest."

"I know. But not here, Sergeant. We've got to get away from this stink. They can rest when we get to the top of the pass."

When Lopez walked away, Roberto Esperanza stepped up, his face full of concern. "Captain, do you want me to ride back a ways and see if I can see any sign of Toloya and the Totonacs?"

Luis shook his head. "No, Roberto. We can't take a chance on losing you too! Some of Teoamoxtli's men may be lurking about."

"As you wish, sir. But the offer still holds!" He saluted and joined the others.

Luis walked a ways from the village for a breath of fresh air, hands clasped behind his back, thinking of a way to find out what happened to Toloya.

Sandoval strolled along with him, awaiting orders, and said nothing, He knew what Luis was thinking, and he had no advice to give.

Luis came to a standstill. "What am I to do, Jorge? I can't bear the thought of leaving here without knowing what happened to Toloya."

Sandoval's face was full of sympathy. "I hesitate to say this, my friend, but I fear she may be dead."

"Dead?" Luis gasped. "Do you really think so?"

Sandoval nodded. "Either that or the Aztecs captured her and took her back to Tenochtitlan. In either case there's nothing we can do for her now. We've got ourselves to think about. We'd better get our asses out of here, muy pronto, or we'll end up like the Chichemetlans."

Luis stared at him for a moment, frustrated and irritated. "Damn it, Jorge, you don't know she's dead!"

"You asked me. I told you!" Sandoval looked Luis steadily in the eyes and noticed the mistiness turn to tears. "What are your orders, sir?"

Luis' voice was low. "Ride to the top of the pass and see if Teoamoxtli and his warriors are waiting for us on the beach."

"Yes sir! But you know damn well they are!

🐾🐾🐾

Urcos walked into the courtyard leading a young woman by the hand. She was about sixteen, huskily built, with long black hair, steady unblinking dark eyes, and a firm determined set to her lips. Urcos slid his arm around her. "This woman is the only one who survived the Aztec massacre."

Luis motioned Kano over to interpret. "Can she tell us what happened?"

Urcos asked her. She nodded and began. "Teoamoxtli and his warriors came screaming into the village about noon." Abruptly she put her hands over her face and sobbed, recalling the fury of Teoamoxtli's attack and her terrifyingly long days after the raid, hiding from Aztecs bent on killing or raping everyone in the village. She regained her composure. "Our men were hideously tortured. Their wives and children were forced to watch. Then all the women and girls were raped repeatedly.

Those who didn't die were marched away to Papantla to be given to Aztec priests for their sacrifices."

"Where were you when this happened?" Luis asked.

"I was out beyond the village gathering firewood. I hid when I heard the screaming.

Her story caused Luis' being to ache for the loss of all her people. His lower jaw worked from side to side. "What will the two of you do now, Urcos?"

"We've decided to stay here, where we were born and raised. She's consented to be my woman. We'll see where it goes from there."

"Good!" Luis smiled. "When and if we get out of here and back to Cuba we'll come back next year. Would you be interested in scouting for us?"

Urcos' face broke into a wide grin. "Yes sir!"

🐜🐜🐜

Luis walked over to Lopez, tying treasure on one of the mules. "Finished?" he asked. "A few more items, Sir."

"I'll give you a hand."

The oppressive heat smothered them like a blanket. Luis' filthy shirt clung to him like the skin of a prune. In his way he had always been fastidious and the stink of himself offended him. When they secured the last sack on the mules Lopez said softly, "Sir, I'm so damn glad we're leaving this evil land. It's been a great adventure, but I'm not sure I'd want to do it again!"

Luis smiled and nodded. "I've thought about that a time or two, my friend! Which reminds me, I have something I want to tell you, and now is as good a time as any. Step over here in the shade of the building"

Lopez walked to the building, unbuttoned the top of his shirt and wiped away perspiration and dabbed at his face with his bandanna. Luis studied that broad, simple face. "Martin, I want you to know you've been an absolute God send to me on this expedition!" In a rare gesture, he patted Lopez's broad back. "You're a hell of a good man and there's no way we could have succeeded without you."

A restrained awe crept into Lopez's voice as he replied, "Capitan, it's truly been an honor serving with you. I do not yet understand how Lieutenant Sandoval and you picked a simple man like me to go along with you."

"Let me explain it then," Luis responded. "I don't know of any enlisted man in our entire army as widely and deeply respected as you are. You're reputation precedes you! Everyone knows you're a damned good soldier."

"But all the men make fun of me," Lopez shook his head dejectedly, "and I'm not brave. I know it. I'm frightened near to death all the time. That's not being a good soldier."

"Oh but it is!" Luis stated firmly. "They laugh and poke fun at you because it causes you embarrassment. But it's just friendly, well-meant joshing. It's done because the men respect you. You know, Martin, it's the highest degree of valor, that you recognize and accept your fears, then do your duty despite them. Soldiers who don't experience fear seldom live through their first battle, even Lieutenant Sandoval and myself!"

Lopez stood there, silent for a moment, pondering his young captain's words. Even officers experience fear and self doubt? Somehow such a thought had never entered his mind! For a moment he could only nod because of the lump in his throat and the tears in his eyes. When his voice returned he said quietly, "Thank you, sir."

Luis nodded. "Move them out, Sergeant! Lieutenant Sandoval is scouting ahead. He'll let us know what's up there. I'll catch up. I have something to attend to."

Energized as never before, Lopez shouted, "Up, up there, you lazy scum! What's the matter with you ladies? We're not on a picnic! Move it! Now before I put my boot up your asses! We'll camp at the pass tonight. By this time tomorrow evening, God willing, we'll be at sea, aboard the Catalan with food and wine in our bellies, on our way to Cuba." A mighty cheer rang out.

🐾 🐾 🐾

Luis walked to the tree marking the site where five of his men were buried. Kano trailed behind, leading Diablo by the reins. Luis crossed himself and touched his hand to his helmet in a farewell salute. Then he mounted Diablo. "Want to ride, Kano?"

"No sir," Kano grinned, "no horses for me. My big feet serve me just fine!"

Luis touched his heels to Diablo's flanks, and the great stallion broke into a gallop, Kano running effortlessly behind. Luis turned in the saddle for a final look at the burned out village. Urcos and the woman stood there, waving.

🐾 🐾 🐾

Luis was breaking up inside thinking of Toloya, doubting he'd ever see her again. Too much time had passed; and he figured Sandoval was probably right when he said she'd been killed or captured.

Darkness fell when Luis caught when up with Sergeant Lopez and the men. Even by starlight they were able to follow the broad, well-worn trail leading to the opening between the towering peaks.

Sandoval galloped up and motioned Luis over. He halted the column. In a low voice Sandoval said, "Just as you suspected, Captain. Teoamoxtli and his men are on the beach waiting for us."

"Are you sure it's him?"

"Who else could it be?"

"Goddamn him to hell," Luis cursed. "How does he know we're coming?"

"The drums. They've been talking ever since we left Tenochtitlan."

"How many men does he have?"

"At least two hundred."

Luis lifted his shoulders and shook his head dejectedly. "Please, tell me you saw the Catalan anchored in the bay!"

"I'd like to, Captain, I really would!" Sandoval grinned, "but the bay was empty."

"Do you have any brilliant ideas?" Luis asked.

"Not right at the moment," Sandoval said. "Let's assess our situation and maybe we can come up with something. Let's see, we're out of gunpowder, we're outnumbered at least twenty to one, we have no back up from the Catalan. It's too far to swim home! Hmm, if we were playing cards, I'd say we've dealt ourselves a losing hand. The only option I can think of is to get down on our knees and pray!"

Luis nodded. "You may be right! If we go back Montezuma's warriors are waiting for us. If we go forward Teoamoxtli is waiting for us. Well, you never know, Narvaez might show up. All we can do is head for the beach and trust to luck."

"Luck? Begging your pardon, sir, what luck? The only luck we're going to have is if the Lord Jesus Christ Himself miraculously shows up and rescues us from the jaws of death!"

It was Luis' turn to grin. "You know, Jorge, you're turning into a real pain in the ass pessimist! Why don't you look on the bright side once in a while?"

"Bright side?" Good God!" Sandoval rolled his one good eye!

Luis patted Diablo's neck. The horse answered immediately and trotted back to the men, all waiting anxiously to hear Sandoval's news.

"Well men," Luis shouted, "Lieutenant Sandoval reports the Aztecs are waiting for us. "Let's go to the top and take a look see, then we'll set up camp on this side of the pass so the Aztecs don't spot our campfires."

The men straggled as a group to the summit and gazed down on a calm moonlit sea shimmering endlessly eastward, each wishing there was a Spanish warship there to rescue them.

"Where the hell is Narvaez?" grumbled Corporal Martinez. "He's left us here to die!"

"That's enough, Martinez!" Sergeant Lopez growled. "We're not dead yet!"

"We will be in the morning!"

"Ah, horse shit! You men are all as scared as an old whore going to confession!" Lopez grinned. "Get those gloomy looks off your ugly faces! If we're going to fight those sneaky sonsabitches tomorrow let's do it on full stomachs. I'll even do the cooking. I brought along a few jugs of pulque I found in the village—it'll help take off the night chill and make all you scared old whores sleep like babies!"

⁂

Hulado held Toloya's hand and led her along the dark-shadowed edge of the trees. They walked for several more minutes, until she smelled wood smoke and saw horses picketed close to the camp, just inside the trees.

"Quien es?" came the sentry's loud challenge. The men grabbed their weapons. Six shadowy figures walked into the firelight.

Toloya raced into Luis' arms, trying to stammer something, tears streaming down her face. "Oh Luis, Luis!" she whispered breathlessly.

He couldn't speak. He just hugged her close while tears burned his eyes. When he regained his voice he said, "Thank God! You're safe!" He kissed her long and tenderly.

There was a buzz of excitement as the men crowded round, everyone talking at once, congratulating Toloya on her safe return.

"Here, you men. Be about your business," Lopez stammered, pulling his bandanna from his pocket, wiping his eyes and blowing his nose. When the commotion subsided, Luis turned to Hulado and his Totonac warriors, standing silently in the dim firelight.

In halting Nahuatl Luis said, "Thank you, my friend, for bringing a priceless gift to me. Now I want to give you a gift in return."

Before the startled chief could reply, Luis reached in his open trunk and pulled out a jeweled dagger and handed it to Hulado. "There is magic in this blade. It will protect you in times of danger, and always bring you good luck."

Hulado stared in awe at the jeweled handle and shining blade. "Thank you, Captain. I will treasure it always! When you come back to our land my people and I will fight at your side to destroy the Aztecs." Before emotion overcame him, he raised his arm abruptly, and he and his men disappeared into the blackness, heading to their homes in Cempoalla.

Sergeant Lopez brought Toloya a plate of food. She was starved and ate rapidly. She was nearly suffocated with embarrassment knowing all the soldiers were watching her.

When she was finished, Luis led Toloya to the privacy of his small tent motioned Kano to follow. "Ask her what happened after the Aztecs captured her."

Kano and Toloya talked for a few minutes, then Kano told Luis of her ordeal and rescue by Hulado and his men.

Luis smiled. "It's marvelous to have you back safely. I've been so worried." She nodded happily. "I'm very happy to be back!"

"Do you know what our situation is now?" Luis asked. "What do you mean?"

"Remember, I told you there would be a ship to pick us up and take us to Cuba?"

"Yes."

"There is no ship. The Aztecs are waiting for us on the beach. We plan to fight them in the morning, and it's no place for a woman. I want you to stay here."

Reaching for her hand, Luis continued, "Will you do that for me?"

Her mouth fell open. "Why must you fight the Aztecs? We could flee into the mountains..."

"No," Luis interrupted. "We can't run away. We have to fight. There's no alternative."

She resisted his outstretched hand. "What if you don't come back? What would I do? No! Whatever happens to you happens to me."

"I can order you to stay," Luis replied.

"Oh please"—her voice was soft—and tears began, "don't do that. Let me go with you!"

"Please don't cry! If you've got your mind set—I just hope you know what you're doing." He put his arms around her and held her tight. After a moment he pressed her head upward and said softly, "From that first day I saw you locked up in that terrible cage I knew there had to be a reason. I found the woman I'd been searching for all my life. I can't leave you here alone. From now on, no matter what the odds, we'll face life together!"

"You'll never be sorry, Luis! I'll be with you always." She put her arms around his neck and kissed him passionately. When their lips parted, Luis glanced over at Kano. "Are you still here?"

"Yes sir," Kano grinned. "I'm comfortable. And you may need me to keep interpreting for you. I have no other duties at the moment."

"Get!" Luis gave a half smile and pointed to the tent flaps. "If you insist! I'll make sure you're not disturbed, Captain!"

Luis kissed her again. He was caring and gentle, and Toloya responded to him as never had before. They lost consciousness of time, of everything except their love and mutual desire for each other.

Toloya relaxed, thrilled with Luis' tenderness, after her brutal handling by the Aztecs. She snuggled close, perfectly fulfilled and secure.

Toward morning Toloya dreamed she was being chased by three evil Aztec priests. They slavered with bloodlust, their eyes fiery red, their voices and evil laughter echoing in her head. They waved their bloody sacrificial knives at her. She was running, with her hands over her ears, trying to shut out the sound, thinking she would die of terror. She stumbled, pitched forward and a red-robed Aztec priest grabbed her by the ankle. The other priests flipped her over on her back and held her. Red Robe Priest raised his bloody obsidian knife in both hands. She was helpless! The knife came plunging down!

"Wake up!" Luis said. "It's only a dream you're having. Wake up!

Sobbing and moaning, she fought clear of the nightmare into the gray half light. "Where are the Aztec priests?"

"The only Aztecs around here are the ones waiting for us down on the beach. No harm done. Get up now." Luis yawned and scratched his chest. Dawn was now a hint of grayness in the eastern sky. He pushed the blanket aside and climbed to his feet.

Toloya watched like a full fed cat as he picked up his tunic lying in a crumpled heap near by and pulled it right side out. She smiled and stared, with her head on one side. He smiled back.

"What?"

"I never realized you looked so good like that."

He blinked down at his nakedness then laughed. "You've seen me like this before."

"Yes, but this is the first time I've really seen you."

He bent down to kiss her and she pushed him away. "There'll be time for that later!"

He handed her clothes to her and they hurriedly dressed. She helped him on with his armor, and he buckled on his sword. Together they walked hand in hand to Diablo, all saddled, shaking his head, pawing the dirt, ready for battle.

Luis found Sandoval saddling his horse. He looked drawn and weary. "Ready, Jorge?" Luis asked.

He nodded. "Yes sir. Sergeant Lopez woke the men a while ago."

"What's their mood?"

"The same as ours," Sandoval said. "They've resolved themselves to fight this last battle with every ounce of strength they have left!"

The well-worn trail went up through the pass. Luis led the way followed by Sandoval and Sergeant Lopez, the men tramping behind. The wind came up with the sun. They had to lean into it, as if pushing against an invisible but overpowering force.

Diablo started down the other side, slipping and sliding on the loose shale rock. Toloya held onto Luis' waist, fearing they might both go headlong over the horse's head.

"Are you afraid, Luis?" she asked.

He shook his head. "I was last night, but I'm not any more. I'm ready!"

She whispered, "Don't let the Aztecs take me alive, Luis. Promise me."

Her words hit him like a blow. He turned his head and looked into her eyes. "I don't think I can do what you ask."

She stared at him, her eyes wide, and said quietly, "You know what they will do to me." She saw tears in his eyes.

"All right, my love."

From somewhere, far off, came the echoing boom of Aztec drums. Sandoval called out, "Teoamoxtli has seen us, Captain!"

37

The entrance to the isolated Mexican bay was guarded by a formidable line of surf, so Narvaez carefully maneuvered the Catalan in along the south shore. A couple of times she passed so close to shore it would have been almost possible for a sailor to leap onto the land without wetting his feet. Once past the bar the water deepened. Under mizzenmast sail only, the Catalan glided slowly and gracefully around the point. Just ahead, lay the only open stretch of sandy beach. Everywhere else the jungle came down to the water's edge. Huge trees with great twisted masses of roots like long fingers formed a wall. Behind them showed the feathery green fronds of towering palms. As the caravel slipped silently past, squawking flocks of birds took to the air. What frightened them? The ship was too far out to disturb them. For at least the fiftieth time Narvaez glassed the beach, hoping to see some sign of Luis and his men. Suddenly he stopped, straining at the long glass for a better look at a mass of Indian warriors flooding onto the beach.

"Indians, by God!" Narvaez growled to first mate Leon Camargo. "We're too late! They've killed Luis and his men, and they're probably waiting for us to go aground!"

"Well, sir, " Camargo replied dejectedly, "we did the best we could. We don't control the weather or the tides. Storms come and go. We're just damned lucky we got here at all!"

Narvaez only nodded, and shouted irritably up to the lookout, "Why are those Indians massing on the beach?"

"They seem to be forming up for some kind of skirmish, sir!" came the lookout's shouted reply.

"What the hell for?" Narvaez asked, more to himself than anyone else. "There's no one there for them to fight. Surely they don't plan to fight us?"

"It looks like that's exactly what they're planning to do!" Camargo replied. Narvaez started to close his glass.

"Captain," shouted the lookout excitedly, pointing. "Horsemen, off to starboard. There, just coming out of the jungle."

Narvaez again opened and trained his glass on the beach. "God be praised. It's Escudero. He's made it!" Narvaez shouted enthusiastically.

"Captain, the Indians are moving toward our men!" the lookout warned.

"The pivot gun, Camargo!" Narvaez shouted. "Put a shot into those heathen bastards to hold them off until we can bring the big guns to bear! Elevate the gun as high as you can and fire when ready!"

"Yes sir!" Camargo ran forward, tore off the canvas cover and jerked out the tampion.

The gun crew quickly loaded the gun. Narvaez shouted to the helmsman, without turning his head.

238

"Keep her steady!"

"Si! Steady as she goes!"

All hands divided their attention between the gun and the Aztecs advancing on Luis and his men.

Camargo crouched behind the gun and sighted along the barrel, his beard hanging over the small cannon's breach. He stepped back and touched the burning match to the fire hole. There was a flash, a puff of smoke, a sharp report and a brief wait until the shell exploded amidst the milling Aztecs, killing several warriors.

"Well done, Leon!" Narvaez shouted excitedly "That'll slow those whoresons down long enough for Escudero to form up his men! Prepare the big guns for a broadside, and no shooting until I give the order—we've got a tricky situation here. Let's not hit our own men."

Steering the ship and aiming the big guns had to be perfectly co-ordinated. The Catalan must be kept exactly parallel with the beach, her guns brought to bear, fired, and the ship heeled about for another run in the opposite direction, all in a matter of minutes.

Narvaez crossed himself and said a silent prayer. "Camargo, lower the longboats and signal Escudero we're coming to pick him up. He must destroy his horses and mules."

Sailors scurried in every direction. Camargo and twenty seamen lowered two long boats. Gunners loaded the big cannons. Narvaez con-trolled the ship's direction, carefully watching for the gun captain's hand signals.

As if by some prearrangement from the hand of providence the caravel hauled wind. She lay in the trough of the swells heaving up and down like a great piece of driftwood, while the two long boats slipped into the sea.

"Out oars!" Camargo shouted. "Pull you sonsofbitches! There'll be prize money for all of us if we can get Captain Escudero out of there! Bend those oars! Put your backs into it, men!" The men raised a great shout and the two long boats raced to rescue the Spanish soldiers just straggling onto the beach.

Luis' gunpowder was gone. He and his men fought with swords, lances and daggers defending themselves against wild, screaming Aztecs. Four soldiers dragged heavy sacks of treasure to the water's edge.

"Stop that, you damn fools and fight!" Luis shouted. He ordered Martinez to slit the animals' throats so their bodies could be used for cover from Aztec arrows and spears. He forced Toloya down behind a dead mule. Then he formed his men in a group, ready for the Aztecs' final onslaught. His heart pounded, and his face was flushed. From the corner of his eye he caught sight of the longboats slicing toward the beach. The sailors opened fire on the Aztecs. The noise of the arquebuses was deafening, mixed with the angry whistle of lead, yelling warriors and shouts of seamen anxious for some action.

A seaman screamed and fell out of one of the longboats when a copper-tipped arrow smashed into his chest. On the thwarts of the other boat a sailor doubled over with an Aztec javelin protruding from his stomach. Sailors swung their guns as clubs to beat off the Aztecs, others sliced and jabbed the Aztecs with swords and cutlasses.

Luis knew Narvaez couldn't fire a broadside into this confused mass without killing Spaniards. He grabbed Kano by the shoulder and shouted something in his ear. Then he ordered his bugler, "Sound your trumpet! Loudly man! Loudly!"

Above the din and scream of battle, the clear loud notes of a Spanish bugle startled Spaniard and Aztec alike. Each man paused momentarily from his killing. From that dead silence came Kano's deep, booming voice floating across the beach, mouthing Aztec words that stunned every warrior within hearing distance.

"Where is the great war chief of the Aztecs? Where is the mighty Teoamoxtli, butcherer of women and children? Is he in hiding fearing the might of the Spanish soldiers? Our Captain offers him single combat, if he's not afraid! Where is that coward?"

The Aztec's set up a mighty howl. To be called a coward was the greatest of all insults to an Aztec warrior. But Luis' strategy worked.

The Aztec ranks opened. Teoamoxtli proudly strutted forward, in full regalia, his feathered headdress and gaudy, gold uniform glistening in the bright sunshine. He motioned his warriors back to give him some fighting room. With his long, sharp itztli in his right hand, he smiled, and with his left hand motioned Luis to come on.

Luis, sword in hand, stepped forward. Behind Teoamoxtli stood his warriors, a great breathing mass of gleaming brown faces, greased skins, their loincloths decorated with brilliant colors. Some wore golden bands about their muscular biceps and others displayed gold nose rings and earrings. They glared at Luis with intense eyes and impassive faces as the two leaders sized each other up.

Luis took a deep breath and inhaled the odor of the huge body of Aztecs—that pleasant, sweet, smoky musty smell so evocative of his past few days among the Indians. His eyes flickered over their faces as he took a couple of practice swings with his sword.

Luis handed his helmet to Kano while Teoamoxtli removed his headdress. Luis motioned his men back several times, creating a very distinct break between the two groups.

Narvaez tried to figure out what was going on—all he knew was that he must act rapidly while the savages were massed together. He shouted to the gun captain, "Prepare to fire on my order!"

Luis took his eyes off Teoamoxtli for a split second to see what the Catalan was doing. Only Toloya's scream saved his life! Teoamoxtli was nearly on top of him, viciously swinging the golden handled itztli with both hands like a broadsword.

Luis quickly side-stepped, parrying the mighty blow, smashing his sword against the itztli, shattering one of its obsidian razors.

Sandoval unobtrusively backed away, using the wall of Spanish soldiers and sailors for cover. He grabbed Toloya's hand and pulled her toward a longboat. He grabbed her around the waist lifted her into the boat. "Stay down!" He pushed her head down and quickly returned for the treasure. He motioned Kano, Sergeant Lopez and some of the sailors and they dragged heavy sacks of gold and silver to the longboats. Frenzied shouting from both groups, their complete attention riveted on the fight, provided the cover Sandoval needed. Within moments a longboat sliced through the sea toward the Catalan.

The wind stirred Toloya's hair and a chill ran through her body. She shivered and put one hand to her heart. She'd never seen a ship before and the sight of the big wooden vessel towering above them frightened her.

"Narvaez," Sandoval shouted. "Get the woman aboard first, then take these sacks. Quickly man, so I can go back and get the rest of the men."

The makeshift slings hoisted Toloya and the treasure safely aboard, amid the commotion on deck. Sailors primed the cannon with chain for a broadside into the Aztecs.

Narvaez stared wide-eyed and dumbfounded at the beautiful woman in soldier's clothing. "Are you Captain Narvaez'?" Toloya asked in heavily accented Castilian.

"Si, senorita," he responded.

"Please hurry, Captain! We must get Luis and the others away from the Aztecs." Narvaez shouted at the helmsman, "Bring her in closer. Steady! Steady!"

The ship cut diagonally toward the beach. Narvaez knew it was terribly risky. If the Catalan grounded in the sand, it was all over for the Spaniards! Teoamoxtli pressed his attack! Luis tried to check that mighty, swooshing hardwood sword. Luis stepped in fast, feinting and slashing. His sword thrust in and out quicker than a lizard's flicking tongue. He drew first blood as his sword tip sliced a gash across Teoamoxtli's stomach. The big Aztec grunted with surprise. Sweat dripped into his eyes.

Enraged, he made a mighty swinging blow to kill his hated enemy. Luis jumped aside and ducked, and with a lunge quicker than the eye could follow, ran Teoamoxtli clean through. The Aztec slumped forward on his knees in the sand, his hands clutching his stomach. Absolute silence came as Spaniard and Aztec alike watched Teoamoxtli pitch face forward onto the sand.

The shrill high-pitched twitter of a bosun's pipe floated across the water. Sailors on the ship let out a mighty cheer which was answered by soldiers on the beach, who instantly dove, belly down into the sand.

The little caravel shuddered and heeled as the recoil from her cannons, loaded with chain, shook her entire frame. The Aztecs were instantly changed into a bloody mass of dead and tangled bodies sprawled along the entire length of the beach.

Leaderless, confused Aztecs, still alive, milled about for a few moments trying to regroup. Terrified, they saw the great canoe with sails turn gracefully and come about, the long smoking black tubes which spit fire and death again staring straight at them! They'd had enough! Leaving their dead on the beach, they scattered madly in head-long retreat, to the jungle's protecting cover, before the big fire sticks could find them again.

Sailors pulled at the oars, heading the longboats back to the Catalan, Narvaez kept a wary eye on the beach, covering Luis' withdrawal with his cannons. Through his telescope he watched hundreds of Aztec reinforcements converging from the jungle at a dozen different points onto the beach, evidently reinforcements.

The longboats bumped against the Catalan and were hoisted aboard, amid frustrated hideous war whoops coming from spear-waving

Aztecs running to and fro on the beach, unable to prevent the Spaniards' escape.

Narvaez was shocked by the appearance of Luis and his men, unshaven and dirty, their clothes tattered and filthy. He instructed Old Barba to fetch wine for the weary soldiers and prepare them a good meal.

Luis grabbed Toloya in his arms and gave her a big hug. Then he winked at Narvaez. "Let's head for home, my friend!"

🐾 🐾 🐾

Within moments the ship was underway, keeled over under full sail, slicing its way toward Punta del Piedras. There was little talk among the soldiers as they watched Mexico's mountains recede into haziness.

Corporal Martinez, still bleeding from a few wounds, stood alone at the rail. Nearby Esperanza, Taragona, San Estevan and Ribera stood silently, each immersed in his own thoughts. Ribera's great bloody war axe dangled from his wrist.

Old Barba served up a round of drinks, the first Spanish wine the soldiers had tasted in many days; and it was received with reverent awe! They raised and touched their cups in a toast when Luis said, "To God, our king and to us. Oh yes, and to Captain Narvaez!"

The sight of so many good humored-faces, the feel of a solid Spanish ship underfoot, and above all, the friendly camaraderie of the rescuers was a charming contrast to the dark, bloody sojourn in the Aztecs' forbidding empire. The soldiers sipped their wine slowly and lovingly, savoring its wonderful bouquet; and totally relaxed for the first time in many days.

Narvaez and Lieutenant Sandoval, relaxing on the poop deck, watched Luis and Toloya stroll, hand- in-hand, to the bow.

"What was it like, Jorge?" Narvaez asked. "I wish I could have been with you."

"No you don't!" Sandoval replied mildly. He launched into what happened to the expedition after Narvaez dropped them off on the beach two months ago. When he described Aztec rituals of ripping hearts from victims of all ages and sexes, Narvaez's eyes went wide.

"They did what?"

Sandoval replied, "Exactly what I described!"

"And that woman?" Narvaez pointed to Toloya. "Where did she come from?"

Sandoval explained the ancient white race from which Toloya descended, but from Narvaez's stunned expression, he could tell the man didn't believe him!

Sandoval couldn't think of anything he'd forgotten. "Come along, Juan, and let me show you what we brought back! Now that's something that's really hard to believe!"

The two officers walked to the sacks of treasure stacked on the deck. Sailors quickly gathered from all over the ship to see the mysterious treasure the soldiers brought back from the Aztec empire.

Sandoval motioned them forward with both hands. "Gather in closer gentlemen and see something white men have never seen before!" Dropping to one knee, he slowly opened one of the sacks. "Look!"

Along with incredulous stares, a huge, collective gasp erupted from the sailors, as Sandoval picked up Aztec gold and silver and precious stones and handed them out to curious dumbfounded sailors.

"Go ahead! Feel them. Taste them. Look at the exquisite workmanship! There's tons and tons more just like this, waiting for us to come back and pick it up! Are there any among you who want to come back with Captain Cortez to pick up the rest of the goods!"

"Aye!" came the thundering response of every man.

🐜 🐜 🐜

Luis and Toloya stood together at the bow of the ship, each thinking their own thoughts. Luis had no idea what the future held for Mexico. Even if he could have guessed how this wild, savage country would be transformed in another decade it would have mattered little at the moment. For now it was enough to know he'd successfully completed his mission. He'd proved there was enough gold and silver in Mexico to make Spain the richest nation on earth. Next year Captain Hernando Cortez would come, conquer the Aztecs and send galleon loads of treasure back to King Carlos.

"Look, Toloya!" Luis pointed toward the sky. "Here comes the moon. Ah, by the Holy Virgin, isn't that a beautiful sight! And look, down there," he said, pointing to the reflection of the moon touching the calm, shimmering waters of the Caribbean. "Isn't it a pleasant sight to see, the moon washing itself?

Many a night when I've been at sea I've watched her riding alongside, skipping over the waves." His voice dropped to a soft whisper as he squeezed Toloya's hand. "I want to remember this very special moment always, you and me together, the breeze in our faces, free...sailing to our destiny." She didn't understand all of his words, but it didn't matter, as he took her in his arms and continued.

"The new world I'm taking you too will seem strange and a bit frightening, but together we'll find it more enchanting than you can imagine!"

"Oh Luis!" she sighed contentedly, in broken accented Castilian. "I'll never be frightened by anything ever again as long as I have you to protect me!" She paused and smiled. "I still think I must be dreaming! I've never known such happiness and contentment."

For a long time they stood there in the moonlight listening to the wind puffing the sails and the sea lapping against the keel. She broke the silence, "Will we ever come back to this land? Will I ever see my mother again?"

"Oh yes, my darling. Next year! Our future is here!"

She went up on tiptoes and kissed him. "Thank you, Luis," she whispered softly.

EPILOGUE

OCTOBER 15, 1518

Hernando Cortez, in his best drss uniform, and Luis Escudero stood on St. Jago's pier, waiting impatiently for the ship from Spain to tie up.

"Why are they so damn slow?" Cortez demanded irritably when a couple of sailors finally placed the gangplank from the pier to the ship. Luis only shrugged, understanding Cortez's anxiety. Today he'd find out if his plan to invade Mexico and take its gold and silver would be approved!

Count Guy de Vey was the first passenger to descend the gangplank. Cortez and Luis rushed forward and welcomed him to Cuba. De Vey's eyes searched the pier for Governor Don Diego Velasquez who should also be on hand to greet him. Cortez conveniently forgot to tell Velasquez de Vey was coming to Cuba!

Cortez said pleasantly, "After such a long voyage you'll probably want to freshen up and rest, then we can discuss business."

"Nothing of the sort! I'm sure you know what's been on my mind, all the way from Spain!"

"Gold and silver?" Cortez cocked an eyebrow.

"You're damned right, gold and silver!" de Vey exclaimed enthusiastically. "How about it, Luis? Did you find anything of value in Mexico?"

"A few odds and ends, sir."

"What the hell kind of an answer is that? Did you find anything of real value? Was there any gold and silver?"

Cortez jumped in, rubbed his hands together with a melodramatic flair, and said, "Would you like to take a look at what Luis brought back?"

"You're damn right I would!"

"It's safe under lock and key in Punta del Piedras. Come." Cortez motioned de Vey and Luis to the waiting coach.

Before the coach cleared the pier de Vey said impatiently, "Well

Luis? I didn't travel all the way from Spain to sit here in silence. Tell me about your adventures in Mexico!"

"Go ahead, Luis. Tell him that wild tale you told me. I'm still not sure I believe half of what you described. Were it anyone but you, I'd call him a damned liar!"

Luis plunged headlong into his strange narrative describing at length the sights, sounds and smells he encountered in Mexico.

For some reason, de Vey was not as shocked as Cortez had been. It was as though he somehow knew or at least guessed what it must have been like. The middle-aged Flemish warrior listened wide-eyed, stopping Luis from time to time, to clarify a point or ask a question. It took a long time to tell it all, and time passed quickly as the coach rumbled northward toward Punta del Piedras.

"An absolutely incredible story, Luis!" de Vey said spiritedly. "The king will be most pleased with what you've accomplished!" He patted Luis on the shoulder. "And you married the white woman you found among Montezuma's captives?"

"The very moment we got back to Cuba!"

"My congratulations to the two of you. I'm most anxious to meet her."

De Vey halted the coach to relieve himself alongside the road then climbed back aboard. "Damned bladder. It's hell to grow old! But back to business. This Pedro Armand episode puzzles me greatly. What the hell was Velasquez thinking? He should have known better than to try a stunt like that. Of course you've let him know what happened to Armand?

Grinning broadly Cortez answered, "Why hell no, Count, we never tell the damn fool anything; and I believe it's beginning to drive him a bit mad! He knows Luis is back, but for the life of him he can't figure out what happened to his man Armand. Of course he has too much pride to ask the likes of us lowly peasants if we know anything about Armand. He was absolutely furious when he learned through his spies in Madrid that King Carlos was going to appoint me to lead an army to conquer Mexico." Cortez stopped and chuckled. "We didn't even have the decency or courtesy to tell him you were coming to Cuba. That's why he wasn't on the dock to greet you."

"Really?" de Vey grinned. "You must have a very unusual degree of self control, Hernando. I'd have told him what happened in Mexico and rubbed his face in it; but perhaps it's best you didn't. I've been instructed to meet with Governor Velasquez before I return to Spain, so my visit will come as quite surprise for him. Somewhere in our conversation I think I'll just casually mention the Pedro Armand debacle to him, with your permission of course."

Cortez nodded affirmatively. "Sounds like a damned good idea to me. But knowing Velasquez I wouldn't put it past him organize another expedition before I can get mine underway. After all, he's still governor. Perhaps you can suggest how I should deal with him, if he tries it?"

"Don't worry yourself about it. I'll take care of Velasquez. When I'm through with him I think he'll be more than willing to behave like a principled man—otherwise Cuba may have a new governor! Rest assured, my friend, Velasquez is through sending expeditions to Mexico, or anywhere else!"

"Perhaps, Count," Cortez responded in a wry voice. "Don't underestimate our dear governor. He's not one to give up easily. I'll give him that. You can bet he'll do everything he can to thwart our plans."

"He'd better not try it!" de Vey warned.

Cortez nodded his agreement, but his long experience in the Spanish army taught him tranquility was an illusion. He knew conditions in Cuba, yes even in Spain, were unstable and it was likely there'd be political trouble, but he didn't wish to worry de Vey unnecessarily.

"Are you ready to depart for Mexico?" de Vey asked.

"Completely organized and ready to sail. All I need is official word from the king."

"You've got it! Carlos empowered me to grant you captain-generalcy of the expedition and get you on your way—that is if Luis' expedition proved successful."

Sentries guarding the southern road into Punta del Piedras stood at rigid attention, presenting arms, as Cortez's coach rattled by; and through the dust spiraling behind the coach they watched it go directly to Cortez's large villa high on a bluff overlooking the sea.

Though Luis had described Toloya, his description didn't do her justice in de Vey's estimation. The woman who greeted him at the front door was far and away the most beautiful woman he'd ever seen. She was slender and lively with a fair complexion and a mass of long blonde hair cascading down about her shoulders.

"Count, this is my wife Toloya."

"Welcome to Punta del Piedras, your grace," Toloya exclaimed in charmingly accented Castilian. She curtsied gracefully, her low cut European gown revealing her ample bosom, and stretched forth her hand.

"My dear," he responded, bowing and kissing her hand.

"Come along," she said, and taking de Vey's hand, led him and the others to the study where Lieutenant Sandoval and Kano stood at attention, waiting nervously to meet Spain's second most powerful man!

De Vey gasped when he looked up into Kano's smiling face. He'd never seen such a tall man, yet he didn't hesitate to grab the big man's hand and shake it vigorously; then did the same with Sandoval. Toloya excused herself to see to the dinner preparations, leaving the men to discuss business.

"Sandoval, is the treasure ready for the Count's inspection?" Cortez asked. "Yes sir!"

"Very well, let's not keep him waiting—after all he's traveled thousands of miles to see what you brought back from Mexico. Follow me."

The men descended to the basement where Cortez unlocked a huge, solid wooden door and entered the treasure room.

Awe-struck de Vey gazed upon gold and silver objects, emeralds and other precious stones, scarcely able to believe what he was seeing. His eyes widened in astonishment.

"My God!" was all he could say as he picked up a silver chalice full to the brim with emeralds. Moving slowly about the room, as if in a trance, he drank in the sight of enough treasure to absolutely convince the Cortes, Spain's parliament, there's enough gold in Mexico to make Spain the richest nation on earth. de Vey's face glowed in the light of the lamps, and everyone in the room became a blur. His couldn't pull his eyes from the treasure for several minutes. Finally he spoke. "How I wish young Carlos could see this! With these treasures, and those you'll bring back next year, Hernando, Carlos' kingdom is secure."

"Hear, hear!" Cortez shouted, diplomatically shooing de Vey and the others from of the treasure room. He locked the door and ushered them upstairs into the dining room where a feast awaited.

As they dined de Vey turned to Luis and said, "You exercised great personal bravery and loyalty in bringing the treasure back, returning your men safely home and gathering vital information. I daresay m'boy you may have saved the kingdom itself."

Luis blushed, trying to think of a suitable reply. "You'll find me ever ready to serve."

"I know that and so does King Carlos.That's why I'd like invite you and Toloya to return with me to the court in Madrid. We'll find you a key post in our new government. Your lovely wife would be an absolutely stunning sensation in that otherwise drab court. What say you?"

Toloya blushed at the compliment as Luis squeezed her hand.

"Thank you, Count, for your consideration, but we've all decided to return to Mexico with Captain Cortez. It's truly the land of the future and we have some unfinished business there. Toloya's people are still being held prisoners by the Aztecs. And I think our experience will prove invaluable on this new expedition. Another time, perhaps?"

"King Carlos will be disappointed, but the offer still stands, Luis, anytime you decide to take advantage of it." De Vey knew how extremely valuable these experienced men would be to Cortez. Were he a bit younger he'd be sorely tempted to go on the expedition himself just to get away from the Spanish court's political environment!

Turning his full attention to Lieutenant Jorge Sandoval, de Vey smiled warmly. "You know, Lieutenant, one of the greatest pleasures life affords me is rewarding loyal subjects for various deeds of valor and courage for king and country. Therefore, Captain Sandoval, accept our sincere thanks for a job well done. Hernando and Luis explained your extraordinary contributions to Luis' expedition."

Stunned, Sandoval stammered, "Captain..."

"That's right. You've regained your captaincy, and, I might add, a key military role in the Hernando's forthcoming expedition, should you care to accept it."

"Aye Count, I accept, and most willingly!"

Cortez grabbed Sandoval's hand. "Congratulations and welcome aboard, Jorge." But Sandoval scarcely heard his new commanding officer. His mind was racing—he could send for his wife to join him in Cuba—and perhaps they could rebuild their lives and their marriage here in the new world.

"And you, my good man," de Vey turned to Kano. "Without you and your invaluable interpretive skills it's quite doubtful Captain Escudero could have succeeded. The king will be made aware of your talents and your courage. I assure you, your future holds great promise. I daresay you'll probably end up being one of the richest men in the Spanish empire."

Bewildered, Kano could do little more than mumble, "Thank you, your grace." His eyes blurred. He'd never had more than a few reales to his name. Never enough money to buy anything of value. Now he'd be financially secure for life. But that wasn't the uppermost thought in his mind—there was an exciting new world to explore; and Sariah was waiting in Mexico to explore it with him. And, black man that he was, he was now an equal of the Spaniards. He'd won their admiration and respect!

Clearing his throat, de Vey continued. "Luis, there's one other little matter which has certainly aroused my curiosity. This Mayan empire of which Pedro Armand spoke—you say it's of immense size, covered with large cities?"

"Yes, sir."

De Vey nodded. "Hmm." Two rich empires existing side by side, neither claimed by France or England! "We'll have to look into that opportunity."

Smiling at Toloya the count said, "My dear, would you be so kind as to pour us all a drink?" She poured rum into the glasses.

De Vey raised his glass and said, "Damn, if it hadn't been for Luis' expedition King Carlos and I would be kicking horse turds down the road, looking for new jobs! Join me in a well-deserved toast to Luis and his men!" All raised their glasses.

De Vey lowered his glass, yawning sleepily "If you'll excuse me, please, it's been a very long and tremendously exciting day, and I have a big day ahead of me tomorrow. I'll be meeting with that jackass of a governor to convey a message directly from King Carlos—basically explaining exactly how Governor Don Diego Velasquez is to govern Cuba while King Carlos sits the throne of Spain!

HISTORICAL NOTE

NOVEMBER 18, 1518

Governor Don Diego Velasquez waited patiently for months for a letter from King Carlos granting him authority to organize the expedition to conquer the Aztec empire. But it never came!

Velasquez was on the verge of a nervous breakdown as he watched Hernando Cortez and his men loading ships with food, armaments, grain for horses and mules and other necessities—right in St. Jago's harbor, within sight of the governor's mansion! They'd set sail within ninety days! The governor could only grind his teeth, swear and try to devise a plan to stop Captain-General Cortez who was always at least two steps ahead him!

During the night of November 18, 1518, Hernando Cortez secretly sailed his fleet from St. Jago Bay, and anchored a safe distance from Velasquez's soldiers whom the governor secretly planned to use in the conquest of Mexico. The following morning the governor, upon hearing the news, dressed quickly, jumped on his horse and galloped madly to the pier, followed by his entire staff! Cortez, in a small boat, came within speaking distance of the livid governor.

"And is it thus you depart from me?" Velasquez shouted hotly, "A courteous way of taking leave, truly!"

"Pardon me, Excellency. Time presses and there are many things I need to do. Has your Excellency any commands?" Cortez waited patiently. But the mortified governor had no commands to give; and Cortez politely waving his hand, returned to his vessels and the little fleet sailed for the port of Macaca about fifteen leagues distant.

Velasquez rode back to his mansion to digest his chagrin, as well he might; satisfied he'd probably made at least two blunders; one in trying to match wits with Hernando Cortez and the other in attempting to go against the new Flemish regime in Madrid.

In the following three months Hernando Cortez assembled and outfitted his expedition in his own port almost under the nose of Governor

Velasquez. The day before sailing for the Aztec empire Cortez gathered his soldiers and in essence said, "We are entering a noble enterprise which will make your names famous to all ages hereafter. We are going to a land more opulent than any ever before visited by Europeans. Why you go I do not know. But as for me I go for the renown, the noblest resource of man. But if any of you covet riches be true to me and I will be true to you and will make you masters of such wealth as our countrymen never dreamed of."

Mass was then celebrated with great solemnity, and the fleet placed under the immediate protection of St. Peter, the patron saint of Cortez.

On February 10, 1519, the little squadron of eleven vessels, under command of thirty-three year old Captain General Hernando Cortez, got under way. The ship in which Cortez traveled was 100 tons, three others were 70 and 80 tons. The remainder were caravels and brigantines. Navigation for the entire squadron was under direction of Antonio de Alaminos, Chief Pilot, a veteran navigator who had acted as pilot to Columbus on his last voyage.

The force with which Hernando Cortez conquered the mighty Aztec empire consisted of: 110 sailors, 533 soldiers, including 32 crossbowmen and 13 arquebusiers; 200 Indians and some Indian women; 10 heavy guns and 4 lighter pieces called falconetas and 16 horses (which Cortez credited as being the decisive factor in his successful conquest of Mexico).

www.ingramcontent.com/pod-product-compliance
Lightning Source LLC
Chambersburg PA
CBHW031943010726
47493CB00007B/2062